THE TORCH BEARERS

By Alexander Fullerton

SURFACE!
BURY THE PAST
OLD MOKE
NO MAN'S MISTRESS
A WREN CALLED SMITH
THE WHITE MEN SANG
THE YELLOW FORD
SOLDIER FROM THE SEA
THE WAITING GAME
THE THUNDER AND THE FLAME
LIONHEART
CHIEF EXECUTIVE
THE PUBLISHER
STORE
THE ESCAPISTS
OTHER MEN'S WIVES
PIPER'S LEAVE
REGENESIS
THE APHRODITE CARGO
JOHNSON'S BIRD
BLOODY SUNSET
LOOK TO THE WOLVES
LOVE FOR AN ENEMY
NOT THINKING OF DEATH
BAND OF BROTHERS
FINAL DIVE
WAVE CRY
THE FLOATING MADHOUSE

The Everard series of naval novels

THE BLOODING OF THE GUNS
SIXTY MINUTES FOR ST GEORGE
PATROL TO THE GOLDEN HORN
STORM FORCE TO NARVIK
LAST LIFT FROM CRETE
ALL THE DROWNING SEAS
A SHARE OF HONOUR
THE TORCH BEARERS
THE GATECRASHERS

The SBS Trilogy

SPECIAL DELIVERANCE
SPECIAL DYNAMIC
SPECIAL DECEPTION

The SOE Trilogy

INTO THE FIRE
RETURN TO THE FIELD
IN AT THE KILL

THE TORCH BEARERS

Alexander Fullerton

LITTLE, BROWN AND COMPANY

A *Little, Brown* Book

First published in Great Britain in 1983
by Michael Joseph Ltd
This edition published in 2001
by Little, Brown and Company

The author is obliged to BBC Written Archives for permission
to quote from the morning news bulletin of 8 November 1942.

A CIP catalogue record for this book
is available from the British Library.

ISBN 0 316 85296 1

Typeset in Palatino by Palimpsest Book Production Ltd,
Polmont, Stirlingshire

Printed and bound in Great Britain by
Omnia Books Limited, Glasgow

Little, Brown and Company (UK)
Brettenham House
Lancaster Place
London WC2E 7EN

'In war you don't have to be nice.
You only have to be right.'

Sir Winston Churchill

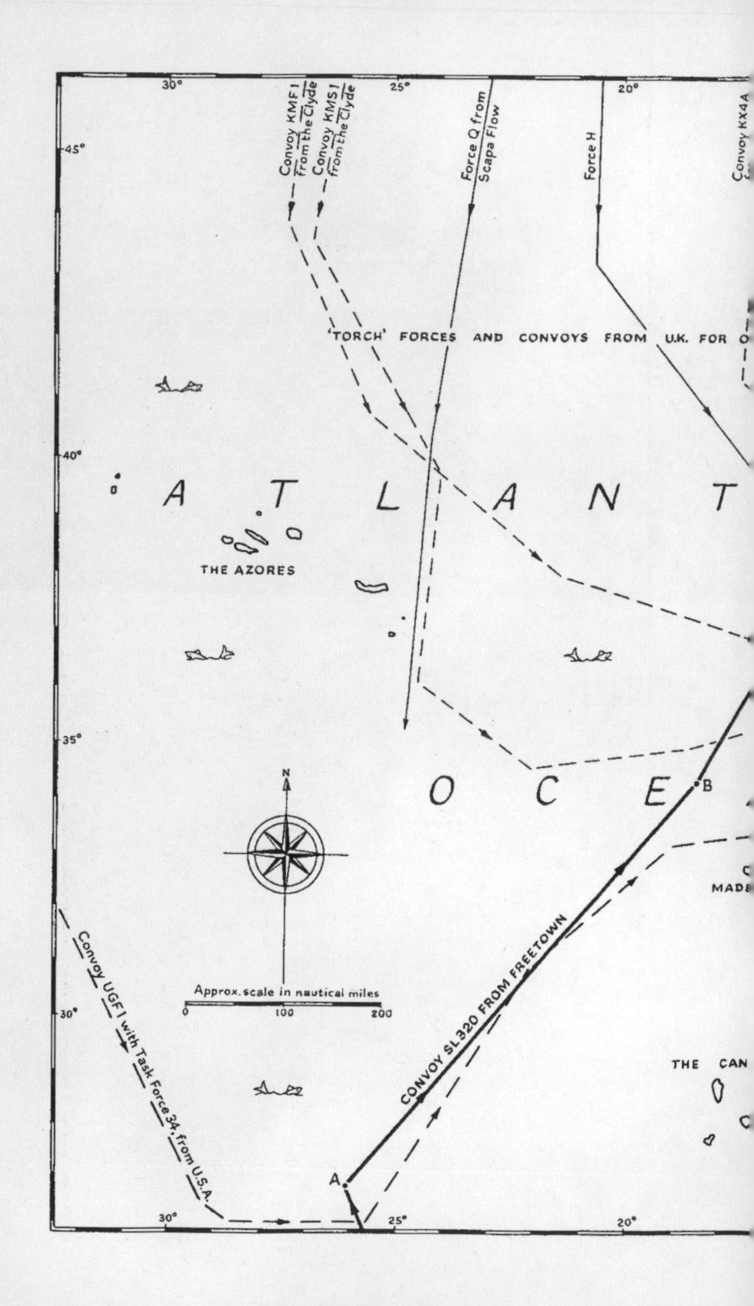

Convoy KMF1 from the Clyde
Convoy KMS1 from the Clyde
Force Q from Scapa Flow
Force H
'TORCH' FORCES AND CONVOYS FROM U.K. FOR
THE AZORES
A T L A N T
O C E
B
Approx. scale in nautical miles
0
100
200
Convoy UGF1 with Task Force 34, from U.S.A.
CONVOY SL320 FROM FREETOWN
A
THE
45°
40°
35°
30°
30°
25°
20°

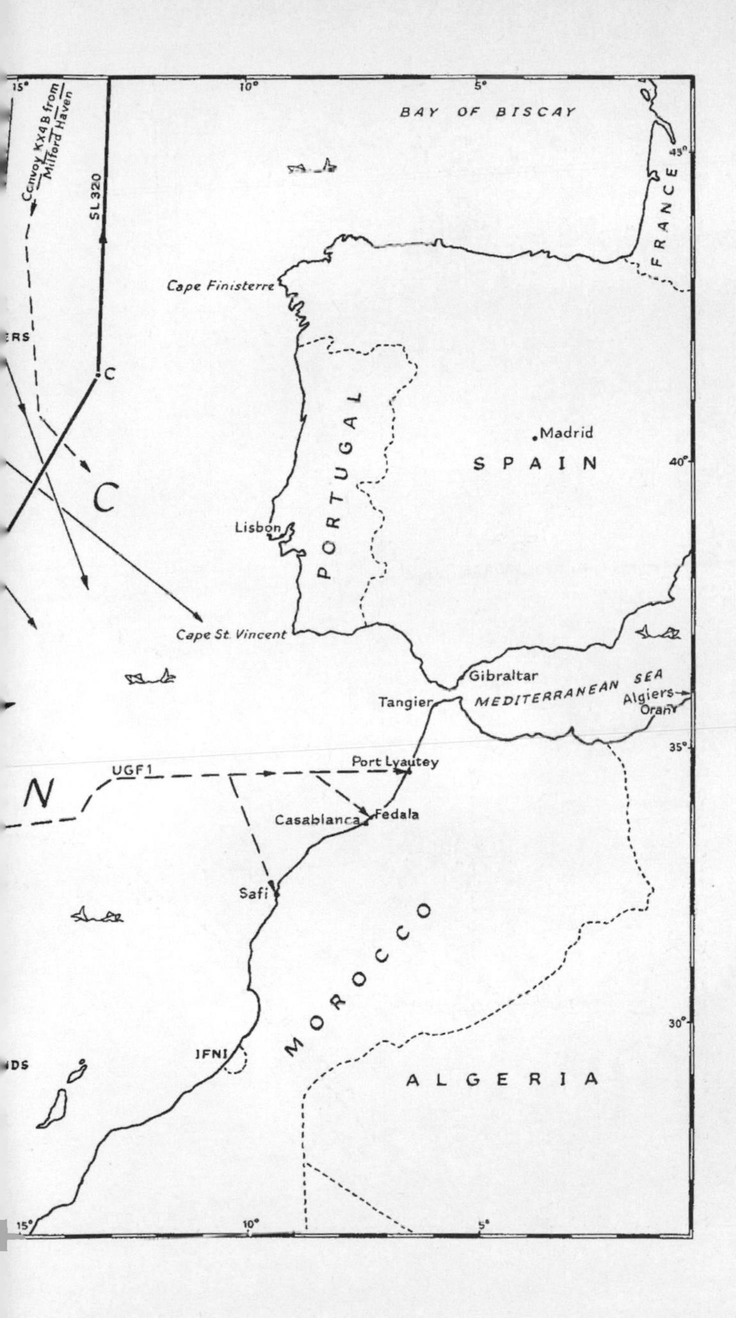

BAY OF BISCAY
FRANCE
Convoy KX4B from Milford Haven
SL 320
Cape Finisterre
PORTUGAL
SPAIN
Madrid
Lisbon
Cape St. Vincent
Gibraltar
Tangier
MEDITERRANEAN SEA
Algiers
Oran
Port Lyautey
UGF 1
Casablanca
Fedala
Safi
MOROCCO
IFNI
ALGERIA
C
N

Chapter 1

5 September 1942: Winston Churchill to President Roosevelt: We agree . . . We have plenty of troops highly trained for landings. If convenient they can wear your uniform. They will be proud to do so. Shipping will be all right . . .
President Roosevelt to Prime Minister Churchill, same day: Hurrah!
6 September: Winston Churchill to President Roosevelt: OK, full blast.

But meanwhile, here in mid-Atlantic *this* was the war – even if plans were being made elsewhere to change it drastically . . . *Harbinger* fighting like a game fish as she lurched round to starboard across howling wind and whitened sea, her stem pointing at black night sky as she climbed, screws deep and thrusting, her frames jolting, loud with a thousand rattles and the creak of straining high-tension steel: steadying on the new course, she was on a crest, poised for a long moment over the abyss and then abruptly committed to the downward plunge, bow digging into black sea to scoop up a few tons of it and toss it back on to the heads of the men in her bridge. Nick Everard heard the yell of 'Course one-three-five, sir!' and at the same time a ring of the bell from the HF/DF office: through the voice-pipe he took Gritten's report, 'Three of 'em out there now, sir – one-three-five, one-six-oh, one-seven-eight!'

Three U-boats – talking their heads off, and Petty Officer Telegraphist Archie Gritten listening to every word. Which was what HF/DF was for. The letters stood for high-frequency direction-finding: and an expert operator like Gritten could distinguish one U-boat from another, could deduce all sorts of things from the bursts of dots and dashes . . . *Bruce* – a destroyer Nick was ordering out to starboard with him – had been stationed on the convoy's port quarter; *Watchful* had already started out from her position on the bow, when she'd been the first to detect a U-boat surfaced and in contact. One had been shadowing all day, and there were at least four out there now, all in touch with the convoy and talking about it, arranging their tactics for the night's assault and probably also calling others, homing them in on this fat, slow-moving target. CPO Bearcroft had finished passing the order to *Bruce* – over the radio-telephone system known as TBS, talk-between-ships – but Nick guessed that *Bruce* would already have been moving in this direction across the convoy's rear, coming over towards the centre to cover the area that *Harbinger* had left unguarded. Only a minimal amount of signalling was necessary between captains who'd sailed together long enough to know without having to be told what was expected of them in this or that circumstance. Like a football team of forwards and halfbacks, the four destroyers as forwards and the six corvettes as a close defensive screen. Destroyers had to be the strikers, since they had the speed which the tubby, hard-rolling corvettes lacked.

Siren – a banshee wailing out of the blackness to leeward: it was the convoy commodore ordering an emergency turn to port. Swinging his mass of ships – a rectangular formation five miles wide and a mile and a half deep – forty degrees away from the threat on this side. There were thirty-seven ships now: three had been lost last night and one the night before. One Norwegian, two British, one Dutch. Things were hotting up again; after a comparatively quiet summer the U-boats were back in mid-Atlantic. Tonight and tomorrow night, Nick guessed, would be the worst: after that the convoy would be nosing into range of air patrols from UK bases.

'Anything near us?'

'*Iris*, three thousand yards abeam to port, sir. *Watchful*'s well clear on the bow.'

Iris was number two in the starboard-side screen: she'd be turning to port now with the convoy. The convoy would be on the RDF screen too, of course – part of it would – only young Carlish, *Harbinger*'s junior sub-lieutenant, hadn't bothered to mention it. He had an eye-piece slot, like the peep-hole of a 'what-the-butler-saw' machine except it looked directly downwards, above the radar (still called RDF) and the navigational plotting table. The hope and intention now was to locate the lurking enemies and get out at them before they could put in their attacks: at the least you'd force them to dive, put them down where they were blind and slow-moving, while the convoy lumbered away out of danger. This was the object of the strikers – to break up an assault before it could develop, and ideally of course to draw blood in the process.

And this group had proved it *could* draw blood . . .

Radio telephone crackling: it was bringing in a report from *Watchful*: 'In contact, attacking!'

'RDF contact bearing one-three-one, range four thousand three hundred.'

'Come to one-three-one, Sub!'

You had to scream, pitch the voice right up over wind, sea and ship noise. Four thousand, three hundred yards was only a little over two miles, very short range at which to have picked up an enemy: he'd be trimmed right down, hiding in the waves . . . But in *this* sea? Nick heard Chubb, the Australian sub-lieutenant whose action duty was to conn the ship under his – Nick's – orders, yelling down to the wheelhouse for that small change of course. And Tony Graves, his first lieutenant and asdic expert, speaking on the telephone to the depth-charge crew aft, ordering them to put on shallow depth settings and stand by. You'd want the charges to explode close to the surface, because *Harbinger* was charging her target now, flinging herself like a lance across angry, resistant sea: the U-boat would dive, or would *be diving*, when she reached it, but it wouldn't have got far under.

'B gun with starshell, load, load, load!'

Matt Warrimer, gunnery officer: he was an RNVR lieutenant, formerly in insurance. Using B gun because A, the one down on the foc'sl, wasn't workable in this weather: men would have been swept away, drowned . . . Even on B gun's raised deck the gun's crew would be soaked and in constant danger of being flung overboard. Besides which, gunnery wasn't likely to be effective in such weather, particularly as *Harbinger* had no director-sight or fire-control system other than that telephone to the sight-setters. Nick heard Warrimer warning the crew of the point-five machine-guns to stand by. Nick with his binoculars up, his body jammed for stability into the port forward corner of the bridge, between the corner and his long-legged wooden seat: attempting the impossible, namely to search the black wilderness ahead and simultaneously keep the front lenses of the glasses dry . . . 'Range and bearing now?'

'Three thousand two hundred, one-two-six, sir!'

'Come to one-two-oh degrees, pilot.'

The change in the U-boat's bearing indicated that it was moving quite fast towards the convoy, across *Harbinger*'s bow from right to left, a mile and a half distant through that wet darkness . . . Muffled booming of far-off explosions would be depthcharges from *Watchful*: and they might put *Harbinger*'s U-boat down too, if its captain frightened easily. Once he was down, he'd be safe, because asdics wouldn't be worth a damn in these conditions. In any case the primary object would have been achieved, in that the immediate threat from this quarter would have been blocked: a killing would be jam on the bread-and-butter but you wouldn't hang about out here, having forced the bastards down you'd nip back to guard the convoy and counter other threats as they developed. And if *Bruce* didn't pipe up with an RDF contact soon, Nick decided, he'd send her back into station too: following the convoy's emergency alteration to port, the two HF/DF contacts on those after bearings would have been left pretty well astern.

'Course one-two-oh, sir.'

Steve Chubb had his arms wrapped round the binnacle, clinging to it as the ship flung over . . .

'Bearing one-two-four, range two thousand one hundred, sir.'

One mile now was all that separated them from the U-boat. And it was still on the surface, cool enough or determined enough not to have been deterred by the charges *Watchful* had dropped. The surface in this weather would be a decidedly uncomfortable place for a U-boat, Nick guessed; and if he had the slightest chance, he'd make it a lot *more* uncomfortable for this one. He decided he'd let *Bruce* carry on a bit longer, make certain the other pair had dived . . . 'Range and bearing?'

'One thousand six hundred yards, bearing one-two-two, sir.'

CPO Bearcroft was acknowledging a message from *Watchful*: she was returning to her station on the convoy.

'Try a starshell, sir?'

Warrimer, beside Nick in the pandemonium of wind, sea, and bucking, gyrating ship. Tall, stooping, oilskins gleaming wet, long arms and legs spread spiderlike for support . . . Nick told him no, not yet. One good thing about this rough sea was that the U-boat might not see the destroyer approaching until she was really very close: the Germans did *not* have RDF in their submarines . . . He yelled at the departing Warrimer, 'Load X gun with SAP!' He'd been drying the front lenses of his glasses: he put them up again now, calling for another range and bearing.

'One thousand yards, bears one-two-one, sir.'

'Steer one-one-eight . . .'

Warrimer was on the telephone to X gun, the one on the raised deck aft. There was no Y gun: that quarterdeck mounting had been removed to make way for a bigger outfit of depthcharges. X gun wouldn't bear, of course, couldn't be brought into action until *Harbinger* had run over her target and turned. Graves was telling the team aft, over the depth-charge telephone, 'Half a mile to go. On your toes, all of you!' They'd need to be: seas were breaking right over the iron deck, the ship's low midships section, and thundering aft in floods that would have swept any unwary sailor away to watery oblivion. The old seamen's phrase 'one hand for the ship and one for yourself' had to be the rule, in a sea like this, and often enough you needed *both* hands for yourself.

'Right ahead, seven hundred yards, sir!'

But still invisible . . .

'Starshell, fire!'

'Fire!'

The harsh cracking explosion of it, just down below the bridge's forefront, whipped back on the wind with a familiar whiff of cordite. Warrimer squawking like an old crow into the telephone, 'With SAP, load, load, load!' SAP stood for semi-armour-piercing. He added, talking to the sightsetter who'd be wearing headphones and yelling it all to the gunlayer and trainer in there against the shield, 'Target will be right ahead, about six hundred yards!' Nick took the glasses away from his eyes, waited for the shell to burst: as it did, *now*, a spark like the splutter of a match and then the brilliant, magnesium-white flare hanging under black wind-driven cloud.

And *there* – as she hung on a crest, bow beginning to fall away under their feet . . .

'B gun target!'

'Open fire!'

A gleam of black, the shape of a coming-tower and the shiny silver of a U-boat's long fore-casing jutting as it pitched across white piling sea: the gun had fired, and then there was nothing to see but water, wave-slopes, as *Harbinger* drove down into the trough. Shaking herself free, bow coming up, listing to starboard as she climbed, Nick yelling to Chubb to come five degrees to port: the gun had fired again in that instant but the flare was sinking seaward and he'd lost sight of the U-boat . . . then he had it again, the conning-tower's upper edge tipping forward as the German dived, two hundred yards ahead and fine to starboard. B gun let rip again, but there was no hope at all of spotting the fall of shot to correct the aim, and in any case with so much motion on her it was hit or miss and a hundred to one against a hit . . . There'd been a call on the TBS: Bearcroft was answering it, getting a rapid, crackly gabble inaudible from this side in so much racket. Warrimer was ordering B gun to cease fire, since his target had now vanished – with about a hundred yards still between them. That TBS call might be *Bruce* turning back to rejoin the convoy, Nick guessed.

'Come three degrees to port.'

For more aim-off, to allow for the time that would elapse between dropping the charges and their pistols filling to explode them. In that interval the U-boat would still be travelling left, he guessed, because attempting to alter course in the act of diving would slow him, virtually halt him in one patch of water, and his dive would as likely as not be hampered anyway by the amount of turbulence near the surface. It was a reasonable bet he'd maintain his present course, and just concentrate on getting under.

'Stand by.'

Graves – talking to his depthcharge team again, a group presided over by Barty Timberlake, the torpedo gunner. *Harbinger* in imminent danger of breaking her back as she crashed her bow down into another yawning trough . . . A destroyer's long, slim hull wasn't designed for this kind of work: the corvettes were slow and cramped and they rolled like hell but they were a good shape for the Atlantic, they'd buck around and stand on their ears but they'd always finish the right way up – which, in the case of a herring-gutted destroyer, in this kind of weather, didn't always look so certain.

Coming up to the spot where the U-boat had disappeared. *Now*.

Graves pressed the depthcharge buzzer, and at the same time ordered over the intercom, 'Fire one!' Sending the first charges rolling out of the stern chutes: 750lb cannisters of high-explosive . . . Graves shouting, 'Fire two . . . Fire three!' The cannisters would be splashing out from the quarterdeck chutes while others were flung from the throwers, lobbing high on each side of the ship and projected forward by the impetus of her forward motion, Timberlake seeing to it that the throwers fired at a moment when she was on an even keel. Between the savage rolls, there were such moments, *en passant*. Then another pair of charges would roll out of the chutes to sink midway between the two from the throwers, making the centre of the diamond-shaped pattern: and finally there'd be a last one to complete it. *Harbinger* thrashing on . . .

Astern, the sea lifted in muffled thunder. Set shallow, the surface upheaval from these charges was bigger than it would be from deep ones. Deep-set charges produced only mounds of sea, but these were like great trees of foam towering white in the dark astern, spray pluming and scattering like heavy rain. Somewhere down there, under a lot of water, the crashes of the explosions would be deafening, terrifying: but you needed to place a depth charge within twenty feet of the U-boat's hull to be sure of killing.

'Port twenty!'

Nick had his glasses up, looking aft. So had quite a few others: a lookout on each side, and Graves, Chubb, Warrimer – all of them braced hard against solid fittings or the bridge's side, to stay upright and yet have hands free . . . Nick told Carlish, 'Watch the PPI, Sub.' The letters stood for Plan Position Indicator and referred to the new type of RDF screen, which resembled a large poached egg – orange centre, white surround . . . If the U-boat surfaced – either by being blown to the surface, or so damaged that it might have no other choice – you might get it on the RDF screen before you saw it, in this weather and the darkness. *Harbinger*, under helm and flinging herself around, a motion more erratic than any roller-coaster in a fairground, was swinging her stern across the direction of wind and sea, and the men working back aft would need to watch out for her being 'pooped' – for a big one overtaking, swamping over from astern . . .

'Captain, sir!'

'Hang on, Chief . . . Sub, what were we steering?'

'One-one-five, sir.'

'Steer three-oh-oh degrees.' He turned his streaming face

back to the dark shape that was his chief yeoman of signals. 'Yes, Chief?'

'*Goshawk* reported RDF contact on oh-oh-five, sir, and she was going after it.'

He remembered he'd heard some report coming in, a few minutes ago when he'd been preoccupied. *Goshawk* was the destroyer on the convoy's port bow. So there were more of the bastards out on that side too. It wasn't anything to be surprised about; HF/DF transmissions during the past forty-eight hours, plus signals from the Admiralty tracking room, had indicated that as many as ten or twelve U-boats had been converging on this convoy, called in by shadowers. When you heard a shadower giving tongue you tried to get at him quickly, silence him and put him down so he'd lose touch; but it wasn't always possible, and in daylight there were aircraft snoopers too . . . The asdic set was pinging away but you couldn't hope for results from it with the sea as lively as it was tonight, and with *Goshawk* off on a hunt now, the convoy was being guarded only by the six corvettes – plus *Watchful* thrashing back towards her station – and it was time to order *Bruce* back to where she belonged. He told Bearcroft in a yell across the gale, '*Bruce* rejoin convoy if he has no confirmed contact.'

'Aye aye, sir . . .'

Asdic pings throbbing out into deep-churned sea were getting nothing back. It was needle-in-haystack stuff tonight. And nothing had shown up from that pattern of charges.

'Course to resume station, Sub?'

Carlish would get it from Mike Scarr, the navigator, who was down in the plot with the RDF display at hand to help him, as well as an automatic plotting table. Nick lowered his glasses, to clean them for the umpteenth time. That U-boat might have been damaged, would surely have been shaken, but it had not been destroyed: and it was always a matter of fine judgement – in fact often dilemma, a toss-up – how long to stay out in the deep field and hunt, how soon to break off a search and get back. You wanted to kill U-boats, you longed to kill them and from time to time you managed it, but the golden objective remained – as laid down so emphatically in WACIs, Western Approaches Convoy Instructions, the escort vessels' bible – *Safe and timely arrival of the convoy.*

Of convoy after convoy. Month after month, year in and year out. More of it in foul weather than in the other kind. A brutal, interminable struggle, straining men and ships through the limits of endurance. The Atlantic was the artery of continuance, survival and eventual victory, the constant fighting-through of convoys its pumping heart.

There'd been depthcharge explosions out to port, heard on asdics but inaudible over the surrounding racket and at such range; but *Goshawk* had drawn a blank too, and had reported that she was resuming station. *Harbinger* was back again, near the convoy's starboard rear corner, *Bruce* a few miles abeam to port. The stern position was the best at night, Nick thought, for an escort commander. You had the whole field out there in front of you, you had only to crack on some extra power to get to wherever trouble might be starting.

The commodore had swung his ships back to the original course, shortly after *Goshawk* had gone to investigate that contact. Nick was on his bridge seat, hunched with binoculars at his eyes. All escorts were back in station, waiting for the next interruption to the convoy's steady progress: it could start with a bell ringing, or a buzzer, or a call over the radio telephone, or the heart-stopping thud of a torpedo crashing home . . . Gritten had reported two U-boats talking to each other five or six miles astern: it was quite possible they'd been the ones out to starboard who'd been forced to dive and had now surfaced again to call their friends, reporting the convoy's last observed position, course and speed, letting colleagues up ahead know it was up to them now . . . The pair astern would have their work cut out to get back into attacking positions, at any rate during this night, because although they were technically capable of seventeen knots – as opposed to the convoy's seven and the corvettes' maximum of fifteen – they wouldn't manage anything like full speed in present sea conditions.

Touch wood, they'd be out of the action for a while, at least. This was truly lousy weather for submarine operations, and it would be tempting for any U-boat to dive to sixty or a hundred feet where they'd be quiet, level, warm and dry. And safe . . . But Admiral Dönitz's centralised control of them would make that impossible: and there'd be others deployed ahead still, and perhaps out on the beams as well, keeping pace, guided by 'homing' signals, virtually on strings from that U-boat HQ . . .

It had been a fairly easy task, protecting Atlantic convoys during the spring and summer of 1942, mostly because since America's entry into the war at the end of 1941 the U-boats had been concentrating on the US east coast, enjoying their second 'happy time'. The first had been in 1939 and early '40 when the Royal Navy had been desperately short of escorts: but ignoring British experience and advice, the Americans experimented with everything *except* convoys. In March the rate of sinkings had risen to average nine ships a day, and most of them had gone down within sight of the US coast. More than half a million tons a month . . . The hard lesson had been learnt, eventually, and by the end of May the 'happy time' had been over; by July the U-boats had shifted their main effort to the mid-Atlantic air gap, the area out of reach of air patrols from either side. There were a lot of U-boats at sea, too, by this time, they'd been coming off the slips faster than the Royal and Canadian navies had so far been able to destroy them; the packs were concentrating in mid-Atlantic, and off Freetown in Sierra Leone, and all down the African west coast, the Middle East convoy route round the Cape. Middle *and* Far East route. Which, for personal reasons, was something Nick Everard would have preferred not to think about.

Because Kate, whom he'd married in Australia at the end of March, had decided about a month ago to come to England. She was pregnant, and she'd told him in her letter, *I want to be near you when I have it. I hadn't thought about this when I promised I'd stay out here . . .*

He'd wanted her to stay with her family, where she'd be safe and where in any case she'd have plenty to do, since she was an Army nurse and the battle for the South Pacific would be keeping all the Australian military hospitals busy. But Kate's father, old Ted Farquharson, had written soon after she had, saying: *There's no checking her, I'm afraid. Remember I told you you were marrying a headstrong female? And you certainly didn't improve matters in this area when you changed her from Kate Farquharson to Lady Everard. I warned you about that in the vestry, didn't I? But someone over there, High Commissioner or similar, has promised her employment in her own line of work, and she's bending other ears in one place and another, and the end result is I gather she may be on her bicycle pretty soon now. I'm sorry I haven't been able to talk her out of it – I've tried, believe me . . .*

In a lot of ways it would be marvellous – fantastic, really a daydream just to contemplate it – to have her within reach, to go home to for occasional short leaves. But the idea now of Kate afloat anywhere on this ocean was enough to scare him awake at night . . . Marriage to Kate was the foot of the rainbow: she was so right, so perfect for him, so complete and miraculous an answer to a personal life which had not, up to that point, been at all satisfying or successful. Captain Sir Nicholas Everard Bart., DSO** DSC* RN might to some people look like a man who had everything, but since he'd had Kate for a wife he'd come to realise how little he'd ever had before.

Remembering that line of Kipling's: *I'd rather fight with the bachelor, and be nursed by the married man . . .*

Radio telephone noisy suddenly: it was *Goshawk* calling. It woke him – or at least switched his mind back into the present . . . But he did feel he'd been dozing, or half-dozing . . . Which, on the gale-battered bridge of a ship that was throwing herself about as violently as this one was, might have been deemed impossible but was in fact a necessary accomplishment, since catnaps, being as much as you could hope to get over considerable stretches of time on this job, were necessary as compensation for a lack of *real* sleep.

Contact on bearing oh-seven-one. Investigating. Out.

Nick looked round towards where he knew Graves would be. 'Here we go again.'

'I *thought* they couldn't 've all gone home yet.'

One thirty-five. A lot of dark hours yet to come.

'Kye, sir?'

'Thank you, Wragge.' He accepted the mug of cocoa. Wragge was a bridge messenger, trained in the art of kye-making by bosun's mates who believed in only the highest standards of excellence. Nick was enjoying his first scalding sip when the sound of a torpedo-hit came as a hard thump in his left ear: then a shout from the asdic cabinet like an echo of it, 'Someone got fished, sir!'

Sound and percussion had been all. No flames, and no alarm rockets. By convoy law a torpedoed ship was supposed to send up two white rockets, but it was probably the last thing you'd think of . . . A call on TBS now: *Aquilegia*, second corvette on the convoy's port side, reporting number thirteen torpedoed and falling back. The number thirteen meant it was the third ship in the first – left-hand – column; and the attack could have come from bow, beam or quarter . . . *Aquilegia* came up again, confirming that the torpedoed number thirteen was the *Verumi*, a Polish freighter, and that she was stopped and sinking by the stern. Nick told the corvette to stand by her, and *Bruce* to carry out an A/S sweep to the north of them. He told Chubb, 'Port fifteen. Come to oh-four-oh.'

Moving over towards the centre of the convoy's rear, to make up for *Bruce* being absent for a while. He ordered a few knots extra speed to cater for the diversion. *Bruce* wasn't likely to locate the U-boat responsible for that attack, but her activity out there would help to screen *Aquilegia* when she stopped to pick up the Pole's survivors. The radio telephone started up again: it was *Goshawk* announcing, 'Close surface contact, attacking . . .'

Might be the one that hit the *Verumi*? But just as easily it might not be. And he still did want to have *Bruce* out there covering the rescue operation.

'Course oh-four-oh, sir!'

Wind and sea on the quarter now: *Harbinger* giving a demonstration of her corkscrew motion, the combined pitch and roll that was guaranteed to induce nausea in anyone who hadn't been thoroughly Atlantic-hardened. It wouldn't have been an easy job reloading the depth-charge throwers, back aft. The 750lb cannisters had to be hoisted on tackles slung from the derricks, and a swinging weight of that size, controlled in pitch darkness by men working up to their knees or even waists in water, was a dangerous beast indeed. Nick could imagine the kind of language that would have been flowing out of Mr Timberlake and his torpedo men . . . The radio squawked again: *Gilliflower*, the corvette in the centre-van position, was reporting a surface contact on bearing 105. As that message cut off, *Watchful* came up with another: contact on 089, attacking . . .

'Tell *Gilliflower* to remain in station.'

It would be the same target, the bearings different only because the ships were widely separated. And it meant there were two U-boats ahead of the convoy now, because *Goshawk* was already chasing out after one on the other bow.

'Sub – where's *Viola*?'

Carlish bent to the viewing slot . . . 'Oh-nine-eight, three thousand two hundred yards, sir.'

'And *Aquilegia*?'

'Two-six-oh, five thousand three hundred—'

'Come to mean course oh-nine-oh, zigzag thirty degrees each side.'

Aquilegia was on TBS now: her report, delivered in a Scottish accent, was that the Polish ship had sunk and she was picking up survivors. Underwater concussions from some distance ahead could only be depth-charges: the sound seemed to come from the southeast, and Nick guessed it would be *Watchful* plastering her target. *Goshawk* spoke up then: she'd lost the contact and was resuming station. On the heels of that, which had come in a tone of flat disappointment, there was a suddenly loud and excited call from *Gilliflower: U-boat sufaced astern of Watchful, attacking!*

So those *had* been *Watchful*'s charges, and they'd brought results . . .

Aquilegia reported that she had forty-seven survivors inboard and was returning to her station.

Nick thought of recalling *Bruce*, now the rescue had been completed. But *Goshawk* had lost contact with a U-boat out on the port bow, and if that one should come up again for a snap shot from the beam it might be handy to have a destroyer out there and off the leash. For the moment, therefore, he'd leave *Bruce* to sniff around.

More depthcharges: a long rumble of them from roughly the same direction. It could be the attack *Gilliflower* had promised, if that one had got down under again. But the TBS call coming in now was from *Daphne*, front-runner of the two starboard-side corvettes: she had a surface contact bearing one-three-seven, range five miles. Then *Gilliflower* was calling and Nick recognised her captain's voice, the north-country accent of Lieutenant-Commander Dick Horsman RNR, informing him, *U-boat attacked with shallow pattern as he went down, and I reckon we got him. He pushed up again stern-first, went near vertical and slid under with a lot of bubbles. Look for survivors and stuff, may I?*

'Reply negative, maintain station. Then tell *Watchful* to investigate *Daphne*'s contact southeastward.'

It would be satisfactory to have confirmation of a kill, but not satisfactory enough to risk exposing the convoy to unnecessary danger by removing *Gilliflower* from her close-screen position in the van. It could have led to confusion anyway, since the convoy's front rank was very close on the corvette's heels. If that had been a kill, which it probably had, it would be a bird shared between *Watchful*, who'd put in the first attack, and *Gilliflower* who'd completed the job: and since it was unlikely there'd be two attackers approaching from the same quarter within minutes of each other it should be safe enough, he thought, to send *Watchful* out to starboard now. It was what the destroyers were for, anyway, in Nick's intentions and in the way he disposed his ships: every escort commander had his own ideas, and these were his and they seemed to answer the problems as well as any other schemes he'd heard of. The two really basic requisites were to have enough ships and to have them trained, used to working as a team, and remaining together as one permanent and increasingly efficient unit . . . A 'snowflake' – the illuminatory rocket that ships in convoy were equipped with – had burst high over the starboard columns: he saw black hulls, swaying masts, then *Harbinger* was pretending to be a submarine again, diving with stunning impact into another trough, leaving only the encircling wave tops visible, and way up, the edge of that weird brilliance seeping over. Someone may have suspected the presence of a U-boat between the columns, or become suddenly scared of collision: with big ships densely packed as they were in this convoy, and on a night as dark as this, masters and officers of the watch needed cool nerves as well as brains and judgement. *Harbinger* was standing on her nose as she swung under helm, Chubb at the binnacle and CPO Elphick, the coxswain, down in the wheelhouse, maintaining an irregular zigzag to and fro across the convoy's stern. A huge, white-topped mound of sea rose swelling across her stubby bow, rolling back clear over the top of A gun-mounting and swirling around the feet of B gun's crew before cascading over her sides . . . Shaking herself free now, steadying on a new course, a mountainous slope of sea looming ahead and the bow coming up slowly, *too* damn slowly: you found yourself leaning forward, urging her with your own puny movements, as if encouraging a horse with a steep jump ahead . . . A bell rang from the W/T office: the messenger, Wragge, clawed his way to that voice-pipe and bawled, 'Bridge!' He was listening with his ear down to it: then straightening, yelling 'Signal from the commodore, sir – ships in starboard column report passing through wreckage and floating bodies!'

'Very good.'

In fact it was very, *very* good. It could, of course, have been co-incidental, wreckage from another sinking, but on the whole it seemed reasonable to accept it at face value. He told

Bearcroft to call *Gilliflower* and *Watchful* and confirm the kill. Then *Bruce*, in order to send her back to her station. Chubb didn't need telling to take *Harbinger* over to starboard, to let *Bruce* in. Time now – two-forty. So there were still some hours to go, to be passed through, to try to keep ships afloat and men alive through . . . He heard Chubb telling Elphick down the voice-pipe in that strongly-accented Aussie voice of his, '*Watchful* and *Gilliflower* just got one of the bastards, cox'n!' It was warming news on a cold, black and dangerous night: the old slogan about the only good ones being dead ones was indisputably correct, here in mid-Atlantic in 1942.

And young Chubb, irrepressibly optimistic, was the sort of man to latch on to good news when he saw any around.

Thick darkness again, up ahead. *Harbinger* ploughing over to starboard, her port-side gun'ls under water as she rolled . . . He wondered where Kate might be at this moment. He'd heard nothing since that letter, and then her father's . . .

He'd said goodbye to her the last time in Sydney, New South Wales, in May, when he'd been leaving for Panama in command of *Defiant*, the light cruiser he'd brought out of the Java Sea under the snouts of the all-conquering Japanese earlier in the year. He would have taken *Defiant* to the Battle of the Coral Sea, in company with two Australian cruisers attached to the American Rear-Admiral Fletcher's striking force, if the old ship hadn't chosen that moment to develop yet another spasm of engine breakdowns. *Defiant* was not only old, she'd been worked half to death through three solid years in which there'd never been enough cruisers for the work that needed doing. They'd docked her in Sydney for temporary repairs, and he'd missed taking part in that Coral Sea battle which on paper had been a draw but effectively had put an end to Japanese expansion. He'd taken her over to the States for a complete refit, left her and travelled to St Johns, Newfoundland, to take command of an east-bound convoy escort: which was how he'd landed back in small ships, no longer a cruiser captain, and with nothing to show for that Java Sea fracas except a scar from cheek-bone to mouth on the left side of his face.

Which he could have done without. Not that he'd ever been exactly a thing of beauty.

He was sorry, in many ways, to have left *Defiant*. To command a cruiser wasn't far from being the ideal job, from several points of view, and it was a sought-after appointment. On the other hand, he was a destroyer man at heart; and this Atlantic convoy work was as crucial as anything could be. If the U-boats won, Britain would starve: and equally, if the Royal Navy did not defeat the U-boats, then the huge build-up of forces and material that was essential for an invasion of the European mainland couldn't possibly be achieved.

He'd dozed again: woke leaning dangerously hard a-port as his ship flung over. But it was the bell from the HF/DF office that had woken him. Checking the time – getting towards three-thirty . . . He answered the huffduff voice-pipe himself, and through the cigarette stink in the tube Gritten told him, 'Two U-boats transmitting, sir, bearings one-oh-oh and one-one-oh, eight to nine miles.'

Gritten sounded as if he'd been asleep too; he'd have been alerted by the junior telegraphist on watch with him. In that fug-hole, anyone would drop off – anyone who was in it nearly twenty-four hours a day . . . The convoy's course was now 106 degrees: so those Germans were right on its line of advance, even though they might not know it yet. Gritten added, 'These are two new ones, sir.'

He knew them all. He had pet names for some of them.

Weather might have eased slightly, Nick thought. It was still rough, still unmistakably North Atlantic, but the gusts were less savage and there was less white streaming from the high, tumbling crests. He guessed the trough of low pressure was passing over and might soon leave them: in which case a shift to calmer weather could come suddenly, even as soon as dawn. And if those two U-boats, roughly one hour ahead of the seven-knot convoy, didn't know how well placed they were, there certainly wouldn't be any sense in alerting them to their good fortune by using radio. Not even TBS, at only eight miles.

He slid off his seat, and moved to the binnacle. Mike Scarr, the young RN lieutenant who was *Harbinger*'s and group navigator, was there in place of Chubb now.

'I'll take her, pilot. Keep an eye on the PPI, will you?' The RDF screen, that meant. Checking the softly-lit gyro repeater . . . 'Starboard ten. What are the revs, pilot?'

He conned her out to starboard and up that side of the convoy, *Harbinger* lengthening her stride and overtaking effortlessly, despite an increase in the amount of sea that came inboard. A blue-shaded Aldis lamp stuttered morse, first at *Bruce* that she was being left to look after the rear of the convoy, alone except for *Viola* closer in, then at *Iris* and *Daphne* so they'd know who this was, as he moved up past them to the convoy's front. Wind and sea *were* easing: you had to put your mind back to how it had been a couple of hours ago, to realise it . . . He called over to Wolstenholm, the killick signalman, 'Make to *Watchful*, "I am coming up to starboard of you."' Then from that southeast corner, cutting speed again so as to hold her in station, he called the commodore – the leading ship of column four – and flashed 'Two U-boats eight miles ahead. Suggest emergency turn starboard to pass clear.'

Three fifty-five . . . The commodore acknowledged: then his siren blared, and the turn of forty degrees put *Harbinger* in the lead, with *Watchful* and *Daphne* on her quarters, the whole spread of ships, convoy and escort, now in a rough arrow-head formation. Nick thought those U-boats probably did have a fairly good idea of the convoy's present position: they'd surely have had reports from their friends who'd been in contact earlier in the night. But two hours, say, on this diversionary course ought to by-pass them: they couldn't know they'd given away their own positions.

'Want me to take over again, sir!'

Scarr, at his elbow . . . Nick asked him, 'Had any sleep yet?'

He had. Down in the plot, before he'd come up to relieve Chubb. Graves was snoozing down there now.

'All right. Mean course one-four-six.' The D/F bell rang:

with a sense of foreboding he moved to the voice-pipe. 'What is it, Gritten?'

'More transmissions on one-one-oh, sir. And there was another, new bloke again, on one-five-oh – right ahead now, sir.'

'Very good.'

But thinking, *Damn* . . .

There could be a whole patrol line, not just an odd pair but a pack, right across the convoy's front. It had been a toss-up, which way to turn, and it seemed he'd chosen badly. He glanced over at the hunched, dark figure of the signalman: 'Wolstenholm – blue light to the commodore . . .'

Four forty-two. Graves had taken over at the binnacle from Scarr. Dawn was a hint in the eastern sky. Convoy course 066, forty degrees to port of the planned route at this stage of the crossing, and *Harbinger* was on the starboard bow of the solid mass of laden ships forging northeastward into improving weather. For four days they'd endured nothing less than gale force, and an easing of the sea-state would be welcome now – even if it did make things easier for the U-boats too . . . Nick was sipping another mug of kye when the deep *crump* of an explosion jarred ears and nerves, bruised minds . . .

Twin white rockets soared. Then snowflakes, from more than one ship. He had his glasses up, looking back over the quarter and waiting for a TBS report probably from *Iris* or *Viola*: his glasses were focused on exactly the right spot when the second torpedo hit – this time with a leap of flame, then a whole blossoming, lighting sea and sky back there. He knew instantly, sickeningly, that it would be the tanker, *Rio Pride*. Yellow flames spreading, other ships black in silhouette against them: it was the sight, the horror, that you most dreaded – an oiler in flames, the knowledge of men in her and in the burning sea. Your hate flared with it like a long-smouldering glow suddenly fanned: loathing of the foul, murderous, lurking enemy . . . The tanker had been in column eight, with only one other column outside her to starboard, but on this adjusted course, steering forty degrees to port, the shape of the formation had changed so that there'd been no ship actually on her beam. She'd been fourth from the front: number eighty-four . . .

'Starboard fifteen.' He thumbed the alarm button, sending all hands back to their action stations and waking those who'd been sleeping around the guns. They'd been in the second degree of readiness, a partial relaxation. Graves reported, 'Fifteen of starboard wheel on, sir!'

'I'll take her.'

Leaving Graves to look after the asdics and the depthcharges. *Harbinger* flinging herself round – heeling hard a-port, and pitching to the head sea – but her motion wasn't nearly as stiff and violent as it had been earlier in the night. *Iris* came up on TBS, at last, reporting that the first ship that had been hit, the *Dogger Prince*, was stopped and sinking. She was one of the tiddlers of this collection, only about two thousand tons: she'd been in column nine and on the *Rio Pride*'s bow, so it was obvious the two hits had come from one salvo of torpedoes – from somewhere on the beam, since they must have passed astern of *Daphne*. The *Rio Pride* gushing flame and falling back: the corvette in silhouette against that inferno would be *Iris*.

'Steer one-four-oh.' Asdics pinging . . . He could see the *Dogger Prince*: ironically, she'd been designated a rescue ship, detailed as a picker-up of survivors if called upon to perform that task – and she'd started out at the rear of that column, had been moved up in some re-shuffle a couple of days ago. Lying at a steep bow-down angle now, on the edge of the circle of flickering orange light surrounding the burning tanker. Flames spreading across the water too, as burning oil spilled out of ruptured tanks. He'd seen it before, seen swimmers not only chased by it and caught but also ambushed by pockets of oil that rose to the surface from below and immediately burst into flame ahead of the swimmers or among them: onlookers seeing it from a distance, incapable of helping . . . *Iris* would be nosing in as close as she dared, to get to any survivors that could be reached. The group of casualties and rescuers was well astern of the rest of the stolidly advancing convoy, and there was a second corvette there – he saw it suddenly – which must be *Daphne*. He told Bearcroft, 'Call *Daphne* – tell her resume station forthwith.' 'Forthwith' meant 'jump to it', and implied criticism. '*Iris* collect swimmers from the *Rio Pride* then embark survivors from the *Dogger Prince*. *Bruce* to cover *Iris*.' Because *Iris* was in danger: it wasn't beyond the capacity of U-boats to torpedo ships engaged in rescue work. He dipped to the wheelhouse voice-pipe: 'Port ten. Three hundred revolutions.'

340 would be the maximum. But it was still too big a sea for that flat-out speed, unless there was some positive reason for taking the risk of knocking the ship to pieces. Like the sight of a surfaced U-boat and a chance of getting at it. He was going to make a cast out on the convoy's quarter now, in the faint, long-odds hope of catching that bastard still on the surface, perhaps keeping pace with the convoy so as to get in another attack by and by. You never knew your luck: instinct plus a few disjointed pieces of evidence told him that this most likely *was* the northern end of the U-boat line, so that any attackers would be on this side of the convoy . . . 'Steer one-eight-oh.'

One mile on this course. The picture – theoretical, and his scheme for dealing with it – was in his mind like an imagined PPI screen. Casting south now: then he'd come round to port and return towards the convoy on a wide curve so that if there should be a U-boat shadowing or encroaching on this flank he'd be approaching it from the direction its captain would least expect.

If . . .

But the German or Germans in its bridge would have that burning tanker in sight in the northwest, as well as the convoy ahead.

Two and a half minutes on 180. Then edging round to port: to 090 first, due east, which would still be a divergence, widening the gap between *Harbinger* and the convoy.

'Course oh-nine-oh, sir . . .'

The tanker was a distant glow now, a long way out on

the port quarter, a yellow glow and a long shine on the sea – which was lower, more regular, an ocean gradually becoming tame. The asdic set was pinging away steadily, and there'd be some point in it now, with conditions so much easier. 'Port ten. Steer oh-seven-oh.'

'Port ten, sir—'

'Surface contact oh-eight-three range one thousand eight hundred, sir!'

His mind, jolted: in astonishment, then acceptance . . . 'Steady on oh-eight-three, Cox'n!' And it was necessary now to get this *right* . . . 'All quarters alert. B gun load with SAP. Depthcharges shallow settings – stand by . . .' Eighteen hundred yards was less than one sea mile: he guessed the U-boat must have just surfaced – in which case he'd be closing on it fast. He called into the pipe 'Steer oh-eight-oh!' Then binoculars again, straining his eyes into the faint beginnings of dawn light. *Harbinger* would be coming at the U-boat out of the dark sector and she'd have it well placed against the lighter section of the sky.

'B gun ready, sir.' Warrimer was alerting the point-fives now, the quadruple machine-gun mounting in its circular nest between the funnels. A rather unsatisfactory weapon, better than nothing but please God to be replaced before long by a two-pounder pompom. He warned, 'Searchlight stand by!'

'Standing by, sir—'

'U-boat fine on the port bow, sir, stern-on!'

Bearcroft had spotted it . . .

'Open fire, sir?'

'Wait.'

He was close enough to stand a good change of ramming. But ramming, although in these circumstances it was about the simplest and surest way to make sure the bastard didn't slip away, invariably caused damage to one's own ship, sometimes very serious damage: and there was still a long haul ahead, a convoy to be nursed home . . .

Range would be roughly fourteen hundred yards now. Maybe twelve-fifty . . .

'B gun open fire! Steer – oh-seven-five . . .'

Warrimer had passed the order: the gun barked, recoiled, you heard the crash of the brass shellcase hitting the steel deck. Graves on the intercom, readying his team aft. The U-boat seemed hardly to be moving, it almost certainly *had* just surfaced and hadn't got its diesels going very quickly: you'd guess the roughness of the sea had deafened its hydrophones to *Harbinger*'s propeller-noise. It was sheer luck to have happened on it at just this moment: but then, some small proportion of gambles *did* pay off – else bookmakers would have had no customers . . . Nick had the burning tanker in the back of his mind and cold hatred as an overlay to the picture, plus a determination not to waste this chance, not to make any mistake that could waste the opportunity. The gun had fired a second time, and the first spout had gone up short, a white plume that lifted, hung with the wind blowing its top away, quickly subsided. Warrimer wasn't correcting the range-setting because *Harbinger*'s fast approach was shortening it anyway. And – hit! A flash of orange and a blossom of black smoke instantly disintegrating on the wind, from the back of the U-boat's conning-tower: it had probably been his first intimation of the destroyer's presence, and a fairly abrupt way of getting the news, at that . . . Warrimer had bellowed 'Down one hundred, shoot!' while Nick sighted over the repeater's bearing-ring and adjusted course ten degrees to port. He saw the plumes of spray which were the tell-tale signs of the enemy diving, vents opening in the tops of his ballast tanks: that shot had missed, badly aimed and out of line, raising a white splash to the left of the German as he nuzzled down into the waves.

Another small course adjustment . . .

'All yours now, Number One!'

Graves' spray-wet face nodding: he knew damn well the rest of it was in his lap. Five hundred yards – four hundred . . . Warrimer had passed the order 'Check, check, check!' to B gun. *Harbinger* plunging and rearing, charging with the silvering dawn in her eyes, Nick aiming her at the froth of sea where the U-boat had slipped down: they'd be passing over from astern, on the same track, and Graves had to judge his moment, pick the spot on which to centre his pattern of explosive. He was about as good an A/S officer as there was anywhere: he'd done reservist's time at the A/S school at Portland before the war – and a refresher, updating course since – but he had an instinct for it that no-one could have taught him, and two solid years' Atlantic experience. He was Nick's second-in-command but also Group A/S Officer, responsible for the performance of nine ships besides this one. Before the war, he'd been a miller: actually an assistant miller . . .

Instinct? Or experience that had come to *feel* like instinct? Either way, it was a concentration so intense that it became a kind of transference, put his mind virtually inside that U-boat – over which *Harbinger* would be passing about – *now* . . .

'Fire one!' Counting, and with his eyes on the sea . . . 'Fire two!' There went the charges from the throwers, and just enough light now to see the dark shapes lobbing out on either side . . . 'Fire three!'

You could visualise the frantic haste to reload, back aft. Mr Timberlake dancing around like a foul-mouthed, crazy ape. Fifteen seconds was the drill-book interval for reloading, but on a wet and heaving deck it took some doing.

'Deep settings now!'

Staring aft . . .

With luck, at least no *bad* luck, having caught the German with his pants down, this first pattern – coming on top of a direct hit with a four-inch shell – might do the trick. If it didn't, you could bet he'd be down deep by the time you threw the second lot at him.

The sea astern erupted. Geysers of sea lifting . . .

'Port twenty!'

Warrimer had all his weapons ready, and he was itching to use them: weapons and searchlight, all the crews just as eager. This was the moment you waited for, the seconds that justified the months of foul weather, cold, acute discomfort

. . . *Harbinger* leaning to the turn as her rudder gripped and hauled her round.

'U-boat surfacing, sir!'

Wragge yelled it: Wolstenholm, the leading signalman, whooping an echo to the shout. Warrimer snapped, 'Searchlight *on*! Open fire!'

X gun crashed: the point-fives opened up: the twenty-inch searchlight from its platform aft had the target brilliantly illuminated. It had come up at a steep bow-up angle. All guns scoring hits . . . 'One-eight-oh revolutions. Midships the wheel.' Keeping her at a distance from which all guns could reach, could depress enough to score. Smoke poured black across the searchlight's beam: a man had appeared in the conning-tower and gone over the edge in a sprawling dive, shells bursting and tracer lashing all around. Then another – several – a group piling over as if trying to get to their gun – and another hit . . . Nick had taken his eyes off them for a moment while he steadied *Harbinger* on an adjusted course, and when he looked again that group of Germans had scattered or taken to the sea: a newcomer in the U-boat's bridge was waving a white cloth.

'Stop firing!'

It was a few more seconds and a few more shots before the order took effect. He told Warrimer, 'Keep all guns trained and loaded, and keep the searchlight on them.' Into the voice-pipe: 'One hundred revolutions.' And port helm again, to circle the enemy, which was still hanging in that up-angled position, he guessed with stern compartments flooded. Seas were rolling right over its afterpart and seething high around the conning-tower: there'd be a certain amount of flooding through the hatch, even, and you could be sure it wouldn't last long, at that rate. Men were flocking up, diving over – expecting a greater element of mercy, Nick thought, than the *Rio Pride*'s men had met with. He'd reduced speed but he was keeping her moving, circling, for the time being, because there could, conceivably, be another of them hanging around. Asdics pinging, searching, probing into deep, cold water . . . He'd glanced over his shoulder towards Graves, about to say something about asdics and improving conditions, and Graves asked him, 'Scrambling net, sir?'

He nodded. He certainly wasn't going to put a boat into this sea, risk his own men's lives for those creatures.

'Port side, please.' He told Chubb, who was wearing a fixed and savage Australian grin, 'Go down and see to it, Sub. Keep 'em all on the iron deck. And I don't want anyone risking his neck for 'em. Nobody's to go down on the net – right?' Chubb nodded, understanding and agreeing too. Nick said, 'Make it quick. I'll allow two minutes.'

He kept her circling. Cutting speed again, but still moving round them, letting them sweat a little . . . Not that 'sweat' would be the word for it, in that stuff . . . But also waiting for them to collect, bunch together, so that the picking-up could be effected swiftly and all in one place. The U-boat was slipping down by the stern now: after the tower went under, it took only seconds.

'Searchlight on the swimmers.'

'The net's rigged, sir.'

He slowed her to a crawl, edged in closer, then finally stopped the engines, and had the twenty-inch aimed downwards at the ship's side where the netting waited for Germans to grab it and climb up it. There was still quite a sea running: stopped, and broadside to the weather so as to give the floundering men a lee, *Harbinger* rolled drunkenly from one beam to the other . . . Down on the iron deck, sailors were tossing lines to swimmers, hauling them in to the destroyer's side.

The U-boat's captain was a stockily-built man of about thirty, dark-haired and blunt-featured. He was a lieutenant, and his name was Neumann. Nick had sent for him, and then kept him waiting – at the after end of the bridge, bare-footed and shrouded in a blanket, guarded by the heavyweight Gunner's Mate, PO Hacket. Nick settled *Harbinger* on course to rejoin the convoy at twenty-five knots, and then came aft to question his prisoner.

'Was it a salvo from you that hit the tanker?'

Neumann scowled. 'You have taken me by surprise. From astern, I was not expecting—'

'Where did you learn such good English?'

A slight, involuntary smile . . . A nod. 'In England. Before the war.'

'Was it you who hit the tanker?'

A jerk of the head. 'Good fire, huh?'

'*Your* torpedoes?'

'*Nein*. My friend Max Looff, I think. He likes to see the – what you call it – fireworks?'

'Looff . . . That's U 187, or—'

'U 122.' Later, after the shock had passed, Neumann would realise he'd blabbed too much. Now, he wagged his close-cropped head. 'Max is an ace, you will not catch *him*. I was his second in command, I learn from him, but—'

'Likes to see them burn, you say.'

The German shrugged.

'Did you learn to enjoy it, too?'

Silence: the disdain, Nick guessed, was not of Looff but of the question. He asked him, 'Are you glad I stopped to pick you up?'

'Naturally. As is only correct, however.'

'Do *you* stop for survivors?'

'How would it be possible?'

It was a perfectly good question. But the stare and the arrogance were something else. Nick told Hacket, 'Put him in with the other officers.' He'd intended to allow him the use of his own day cabin aft, but in the last minute he'd thought better of it. There were only two other officers surviving, an engineer and a lieutenant, and one small cabin with two bunks in it would do for the three of them.

He thought, making a mental note of it for later inclusion in his Report of Proceedings, *Max Looff – U 122 – an 'ace', likes to see ships burn . . .*

Chapter 2

> *Prime Minister Winston Churchill to President Roosevelt:*
> Delay due to change already extends three weeks. Free French have got inkling and are leaky. Every day saved is precious . . .

The convoy had altered course again, swung to a track to compensate for the northward detour. The new course of 120 degrees would return them to the route as planned. Overhauling the mass of ships now, seeing masts and upperworks etched black against the flush of sunrise, Nick called *Iris* on the TBS and asked for details of survivors from the *Rio Pride* and the *Dogger Prince*.

Tony Graves had the watch. The crew had fallen out from action stations, and there was a general impression that the immediate danger of attack had passed. It was satisfying to have sunk that U-boat; this, plus the ending of a night that might have been a lot worse, was giving them all a feeling of well-being. He felt it himself, and saw it in others: in stubbled, strained faces materialising again as the half-light crept over sea and ships: you could detect it in their voices too, the tones of tired but contented men looking forward to their breakfasts.

It was partly reaction to strain. He understood this, having experienced it hundreds of times before, but it still provoked a twinge of guilt, to be cheerfully anticipating a meal and a sleep when only about ninety minutes ago a number of men had died, some very unpleasantly and all of them people who'd sailed in his, Nick Everard's, protection.

Iris came through with her report. She had eleven

survivors from the tanker, of whom two were unlikely to live much longer. Three who'd been picked up had already died of their burns. From the little *Dogger Prince* she had twenty-seven.

He frowned into the dawn. Overlaying the prosaic report, the figures, were other recent memories he'd sooner have forgotten. Sights, and sounds. He'd seen a lot of battle, in other ships and other seas, but here in the Atlantic the more or less constant strain, monotony of convoy routine and unrelieved discomfort made for a drably grim background that seemed endless: months, years of it, punctuated by moments of starker horror.

He glanced at Tony Graves, who had his glasses up and was sweeping the still-dark surface to port. Graves was a stocky, wide-shouldered man in his mid-thirties; he had a roundish face fringed at the moment with ginger beard. Nick asked him, 'What induces anyone to go to sea in tankers?'

'Often wondered that myself, sir.' He added, 'They're well paid, of course.'

'I'd bloody well hope so!'

Harbinger was closing in on the convoy's rear, and dawn had become a silver brightness streaking up to the loosely-hanging underside of pinkish cloud. He wondered whether there'd be rain coming now, and guessed there might well be. It felt like it. Wind still dropping, down to about force four now, and the ship's motion had become more regular – after four days and nights of being flung from end to end and beam to beam. The messdecks, he knew, would be in a filthy state; a destroyer's living spaces always were after a bout of really bad weather. In other words, on most convoy trips, for at least half the year in these latitudes. There'd be water sloshing to and fro, rubbish and vomit in it, wet clothes in heaps as malodorous as dead cats. And the wardroom wouldn't be all that much better.

TBS – a call from *Goshawk* . . . It was the voice of Jock Audsley, her captain, asking, *Did we hear bumps in the night? Over*.

Audsley, a lieutenant-commander RN, was the group's senior CO after Nick.

'Reply, "Affirmative. Score is now two-seven. Your turn next, please."'

Congratulations began to crackle in from all of them. And it *was* a heartening achievement. It sounded like an uneven score, that 2–7, but when you appreciated that the enemy had only about two hundred operational submarines at this time, so that last night their overall strength had been reduced by one percent, it wasn't at all bad.

The sea ahead was grey now instead of black. He could make out the stern-on shape of *Iris* just off the convoy's starboard quarter, and on the other bow *Viola* zigzagging astern of the central columns. *Bruce* was broader on the bow, visible mostly by the churned foam under her pitching counter as she moved away to make room for *Harbinger*. Daylight coming, weather improving, and so far as anyone knew, no U-boats around.

'Just as well we fuelled yesterday, sir.'

Graves had his glasses on the convoy, and he was referring to the fact that there was no oilder in it now. All four destroyers had replenished from the *Rio Pride* in the past twenty-four hours; the corvettes, who burnt less oil, would last out with what they had in their tanks. The more you had to dash about, the more fuel you burnt, so an interval of peace and quiet now would be doubly welcome.

He yawned, added, 'And by tomorrow evening we should have air cover.'

Theoretically, they might have had it some time later today. Long-range cover by Liberators could reach up to 750 or even 800 miles from land bases. But Coastal Command had only one squadron of Liberators, and the normal range of Atlantic air patrols was about 450 miles. The U-boats' technique was to locate their targets, shadow them until they were entering the aircraft-free zone, then close in and attack until they were about to leave it.

Mike Scarr came up, stared morosely at the sky, shook his head. There were no stars visible, so he'd get no dawn fix from them. Nick said, 'You can get it down again, pilot.'

'Yes.' The navigator turned to him. 'May I make a suggestion, sir?'

'If it's a good one.'

'For the sake of convoy morale – parade the prisoners through the columns? Put 'em on the foc'sl, and steam up through the convoy?'

'I'll – think about it.'

'Sir.' Scarr left the bridge; and Nick found two reasons for disliking the idea. One was that it was the sort of thing a German might do. The other was that it might be making too much out of the destruction of one U-boat. It would be much better if such successes were to be accepted as routine, part of an escort vessel's daily work. In fact it would have to become so, if this battle was to be won.

'I don't think I'll parade our prisoners.'

Graves said, 'Must say, I thought it was a lousy idea, sir.' Graves lowered his binoculars. 'We're about in station now.'

'And I'll leave you to it.' Nick told him, 'That was a very well-placed pattern, incidentally.'

A laugh: 'Have to get lucky sometimes. Thank you, sir.'

Modest old former cornflake manufacturer. He was *too* modest, Nick thought, sometimes, too content to stay in the background . . . But now, breakfast. Then some sleep. Just as he was about to leave the bridge, the bell rang from the W/T office, and Signalman Bloom jumped to the voice-pipe: 'Bridge!'

Cocking his ear to it. Bloom was about twenty: pink-cheeked, with dark stubble blue-black on his jaw. An HO – Hostilities Only – rating, he'd worked in his father's grocery business until he'd been called up. He turned from the pipe and told Nick, 'From Admiralty, sir, "D/F bearings on four-nine-nine-five KCs indicate U-boat west of convoy was reporting your position at oh-six-oh-one stroke A," sir.'

0601/A meant 0501 by ship's time. Convoy and escort were keeping Greenwich Mean Time – Zone Z, not A. The Admiralty tracking room's information therefore was that a U-boat astern of the convoy had been transmitting a report of it just twenty minutes ago. At that time the convoy had already settled on the present course of 120 degrees: so if that U-boat's observations had been accurate, others at sea and also Admiral Dönitz's submarine headquarters in France would know where it was now and have a good idea of where it might be tonight.

On the other hand there might not be any U-boats to the east and southeast – except a few on passage to or from patrol, which might not be easily re-deployed now. Nor was there any certainty that if there were some they'd be ordered to do anything about it. This wasn't the only convoy at sea in the North Atlantic; the enemy had made a strong attack on it last night and lost two of their number in the process, and there wasn't so much of the air gap left to traverse. They might easily decide to concentrate their attentions elsewhere, perhaps against some less well defended convoy.

They were like rats: they liked *easy* pickings.

Graves was looking at him quizzically.

'Think they're still after us, sir?'

'I wouldn't be surprised.' He nodded to the signalman. 'Put it on the log when it comes up.' He told Graves, 'I'll be in my hutch. Send word to Foster I'd like some breakfast, will you?'

A kind of skinless sausage called a Soya Link, with fried bacon and fried bread: bread and marmalade: coffee . . . The aroma of the coffee was so good it made him smile.

'Thank you, Foster.'

PO Steward Charley Foster nodded. 'Not a bad night's work, sir, was it?'

'There've been worse . . . What's it like aft?'

'We're getting ourselves to rights now, sir.'

'Are the Hun officers behaving themselves?'

Foster snorted: he was a short man with a leathery seaman's face; you wouldn't have taken him for a steward. He said, 'GM 'll see they do *that*, sir.' GM stood for gunner's mate, and meant PO Hacket. 'They was complaining there wasn't room enough for 'em in there. He told 'em they could belt up or they'd get a couple more blokes in with 'em – their choice, like.'

'Good.'

Foster touched the tray. 'I'll leave this till later, sir, shall I? Dare say you'll be gettin' your 'ead down.'

He'd have it down in about three minutes flat: just as soon as he'd gulped down this food . . . He pulled off the jacket of his purloined RAF flying suit, and kicked off his seaboots. The strip of towelling he'd wrapped round his neck was soaking wet, and so were the shooting mittens which had already been taken away by Foster. There were dry spares in here. Sitting down to eat breakfast, he was wearing the flying suit's trousers and a white submarine sweater and oiled-wool seaboot stockings, all over silk pyjamas which when he'd bought them had been called p*a*jamas – three months ago, in New York. Under them he had on a string vest and long johns. There was no point in being colder or wetter than you had to be, when whole nights had to be spent on a bucking, sea-swept bridge: it was in the best interests of the ship and the convoys she escorted that he should not be.

This sea-cabin, below the bridge and adjoining the plot, was about the size of a large cupboard, most of its space occupied by the narrow, high-sided bunk with drawers under it. There was a small corner washbasin and a table that flapped up on hinges from the bulkhead. Over the head of the bunk was a voice-pipe to the bridge, a telephone to the plot and the RDF office, and an illuminated repeater from the gyro compass.

He'd eaten all the food and drunk the coffee. To hell with shaving: U-boats permitting, there'd be time for it later. He climbed on to the bunk, over the high lee-board which was there to stop him being flung out of it in weather such as they'd had in the past few days. Now, the motion was so regular that it would be soporific. And the most pleasant way he knew of falling asleep was to think about Kate. Not of the worry, of Kate at sea at this moment, but of Kate in England, the daydream of going on leave and having her with him . . .

Asdics pinging: he could hear it all the time, that constant pulsing, high-pitched probe, keening into the ocean depths. Even in his sleep, if it found a contact and an echo came back, it would bring him instantly awake. There were other background sounds as well: from time to time the voice-pipe funnelled down a helm order, and more distantly there'd be thc quartermaster's response as the ship kept up her irregular zig-zag across the convoy's rear. If he'd opened his eyes he'd have seen the lubber's line shifting around the glowing face of the gyro repeater, two feet above his pillow; but there was no need to look, you felt the turning motion anyway, and the list as the wheel went over.

Nearly a thousand miles southeast and two hours later – Big Ben, visible from the window of his office rising above a mist lifting from the quiet Thames, showed London's time as 0849 – a tall, slightly stooped man, white-haired and dressed in the uniform of a captain RNVR, leant forward to slide a sheet of paper across a desk.

'We've narrowed it to a choice of three, sir.'

'Quick work, Cruance. Excellent.'

'It's been a matter not only of the individuals' experience and suitability, but also – rather complicatedly – of the present location of the various groups, which of them might be split up at this short notice and still get down there in time – and so forth . . .'

'Yes.'

Aubrey Wishart, rear-admiral, looked as if he'd been at his desk all night. He certainly hadn't shaved. He blinked, tired eyes scanning the typed summary. They sharpened as he came to the third name on the list.

'Everard? Nick Everard's commanding an escort group now?'

'Yes. Destroyer called – *Harbinger*.'

'Sit down. I wonder how the devil—'

'Here's some detail of his recent appointments.' Cruance selected it from other papers in his file. 'Do I gather you know him, sir?'

'Extremely well. Since – believe it or not – 1918, in the Dardanelles. But I *last* saw him in Alexandria, in—' Wishart passed a hand over his eyes – 'well, only months ago.' He read the notes: Cruance sitting back, watching, noticing three stained cups-and-saucers on the desk and a heaped ashtray, guessing that Wishart *had* been here most of the night. The admiral said, 'Everard's our man. If anyone alive could make a success of that job . . .'

'Would he be – well, *intended* to – er – achieve success, sir?'

The blue eyes lifted. Tired, but also grim.

'What do you mean?'

Cruance showed surprise . . . 'Only that – that this *is* intended to deceive the enemy, and must surely incur exceptionally high losses – at least, if they take the bait—'

Wishart said thinly, 'The point is that if anyone *could* – pull it off, with minimal losses of ships and lives – and incidentally also come out of it alive himself—'

'Quite.'

Wishart mimicked him: '*Quite* . . .' Cruance's eyes steady, thought behind them: they were the eyes of a man accustomed to listening while his brain selected and interpreted . . . Wishart asked him, 'Is that how you used to look down at the poor sods from the bench, or whatever—'

A twitch of the lips . . . 'I do assure you, admiral—'

'Everard's a personal friend of mine, don't you understand?'

'Well, of course—'

'He's also so plainly the man for this job that it would be wrong of me to pick either of the others *because* of that friendship. What counts is the success of the main effort – the biggest and most complex operation ever mounted yet, and the most vital, with many thousands of lives at risk – not just a few – and aimed at changing the whole course of the war—'

'I know. I do understand. Of *course* . . .'

'Well, fix it, will you? Everard, and forget those others. You'll need to get on to Derby House in Liverpool, C-in-C

Western Approaches.' Cruance was half way to the door when Wishart spoke again. 'Are you free for lunch today?'

'Why, yes—'

'All things being equal, twelve forty-five? My club? I'd like to tell you some stories about Nick Everard . . .'

'Captain, sir?'

A bridge messenger – Holloway – was in the doorway of the sea-cabin, cold air driving in. Waking, Nick realised there was still less motion on her now, that conditions tonight would be entirely different for both attackers and defenders.

This was the second time he'd woken. The first had been after only about thirty minutes, when he'd come-to as sluggishly as a corpse to be told through the voice-pipe that *Prunella* had reported an asdic contact. It had turned out to be a school of fish.

Blinking at the messenger. This wouldn't be urgent: urgent calls came through the pipe.

'What is it, Holloway?'

'Lieutenant Scarr's compliments, sir, and we have a Focke-Wulf in company.'

'Damn.'

'Yessir.'

Nodding, from the doorway. Holloway had been starting in the building trade: apprentice bricklayer, something of that sort.

'I'll come up.'

'Aye aye, sir.'

The door clicked shut. Time, eleven-twenty. Course, 145 degrees – southeast, the starboard leg of the zigzag. He needed a pee and a shave, but the shave would have to wait. As he arrived in the bridge, Scarr pointed: 'There it is, sir.'

A familiar and thoroughly unwelcome sight. Like a limping, damaged moth, out of range and close to the horizon, circling. But if only there *was* some way to damage it . . . There would be, if one new idea that had been mentioned recently became reality. It was a scheme to fit merchant ships with launching gear for a single Hurricane. If this convoy had one with it now, the fighter could be fired off to drive away or shoot down the Focke-Wulf, after which it would ditch near one of the escorts and its pilot would be picked up, to fly another Hurricane another day. He'd need to be tolerant of cold water, of course. But it was a very good idea, because there'd never be enough escort carriers to go round: and here and now all you could do was watch the thing circling the convoy, its crew as safe as houses while they sent out a stream of information: position, course and speed, size of the convoy, number and disposition of its escorts . . .

'Frustrating, sir, isn't it.'

Mike Scarr, his navigator, scowling at it. He was a tall, bony young man with a shy manner and apparently an unfailing supply of attractive girlfriends. Graves had expressed the view – standing with Nick in a corner of *Harbinger*'s wardroom during a drinks party they'd given in Liverpool, watching young Scarr effortlessly monopolising the best-looking of several pretty Wrens – that he thought the navigator aroused maternal instincts in them. But there'd been nothing in the least motherly about *that* girl . . . Graves was jealous, of course. Nick had met Mrs Graves, and he wasn't at all surprised. He took the signal log from Wolstenholm, and leafed through a few routine messages that had been added to it during the forenoon. There was only one that was of interest, another from the Admiralty tracking room, with time-of-origin 1025/A, reading, *Bearings on 4995 KCs* at 0950/A indicate U-boats gathering eastward of you.

The Focke-Wulf was passing round astern now. Distant and inaudible, giving the impression it had nothing to do with the plodding convoy. But its radio man's morse key would be tapping, tapping . . .

'Why wasn't I shown this one?'

Scarr moved over to peer at the sheet of signal pad with that message in a telegraphist's blue-pencil scrawl.

'We did consider it, sir. That was in Chubb's watch. But

you'd only just turned in again, and he didn't think you'd want to be shaken for it. He asked me – the first lieutenant had his head down too – and I agreed with him. I'm sorry, if—'

'No. You were right, I suppose.'

Because if he'd been shown it, he still wouldn't have done anything about it. It was rather a borderline case though, and it was very important that they shouldn't hesitate to rout him out if there was the slightest chance he'd need to know and act on such a signal. Scarr added diffidently, 'It seemed to me that as it gave no distance, also that "eastward" might be quite vague, and our mean course now being nearer southeast than east anyway—'

'You were right.' He handed the log back to the signalman, lifted his binoculars again and focused them on the Focke-Wulf now dawdling up the starboard side – safely out of gun-range . . . 'Do we know where we are?'

'There's a reasonably good fix on the chart, sir, by D/F, and I've run on from it for the noon position.' He glanced up at heavy, lowering cloud. 'No hope of anything much better, I'm afraid.'

No chance of using his sextant, he meant, no sight of sun, stars or moon in prospect. Rain still held off, but plainly threatened. The sea was lower, smoother, and conditions tonight would be easier for the U-boats than they had been lately. They'd have preferred some moonlight, though: for the surface ships, who were fitted with RDF, there was more advantage in darkness.

Nick checked the time: because at noon every ship in convoy hoisted flags giving that ship's own estimate of the position in latitude and longitude. The signals were supposed to be hoisted simultaneously, like a sudden showing of cards face-up, and there was an element of rivalry in it . . . Scarr had seen him glance at his watch; he confirmed, thought-reading, 'Signal's already bent on, sir.'

And the Focke-Wulf seemed to be departing. Having seen all there was to see, and relayed the information to its clients.

'Captain, sir?'

Bruce Hawkey, *Harbinger's* engineer officer, was at his elbow. Hawkey was a lieutenant (E) RN, a graduate of the naval engineering college at Keyham. He was in white overalls, and offering Nick a sheet of signal pad with figures pencilled on it.

'Fuel state, sir.'

It was routine, a report of oil-fuel remaining at midday. Similar reports would be flashed from all the other escorts.

'All well down there, Chief?'

'Except for the usual problems, sir. Nothing a month in dock wouldn't solve.'

'In about a month's time, we might get ten days. If we're very lucky.'

There were still not nearly enough ships for the work. Even when there was nothing out of the ordinary going on, every destroyer, sloop and corvette that was three-quarters fit was needed at sea. When something big was happening – like a Murmansk convoy, that deadly delivery-run that was keeping the Russians in the war – Atlantic resources were invariably stretched beyond the limits of effective coverage. Hence the difficulties of getting a group like this one together and keeping it together. The looming danger was that the U-boats might get the upper hand before this situation could be improved: U-boats were being churned out like sausages from the German shipyards, and they were getting new weapons too – new types of torpedo, for instance, and new evasive devices, and there were even new, deeper-diving types of U-boat. Some recent Intelligence summaries didn't make cheerful reading.

Hawkey, leaning against the side of the bridge, lit a cigarette. A hooked nose matched his surname: strangers tended to assume it was a nickname. He murmured, gazing skyward, 'Rain about, would you say?'

Scarr grunted as he checked a bearing. Hawkey asked him, 'Did I hear we had a visitor?'

The Focke-Wulf, he meant. It had left them now. And at this stage the convoy wasn't in a position where any evasive change of course could be large enough to be useful. For one thing, nobody knew exactly where the threat was – as Scarr had pointed out, 'eastward' could be a vague indication – and for another, even if the convoy did alter course now, the odds were that in a few hours they'd be found by another airborne snooper who'd update its predecessor's reports.

The engineer muttered, 'I suppose that means we're in for another night of it.'

Matt Warrimer, with young Carlish as his assistant OOW, came up while the position flags were still flying and took over from Scarr for the afternoon watch. Warrimer towering over the shrimp-sized sublieutenant. Carlish had only recently been promoted from midshipman, and would need a lot more experience before he'd qualify for a watchkeeping certificate and be entitled to stand watches on his own. Then there was a visit from Mackenzie, the doctor, reporting on the condition of two German prisoners who'd been hit and wounded in that brief flurry of gunfire. And presently Tony Graves came up, accompanied by Mr Timberlake, the torpedo gunner, who had an account of depthcharges expended and remaining. Timberlake was twitchy with anxiety.

Nick studied the figures. 'Looks all right to me.'

The gunner's eyes bulged. 'Sir – you say *all right*, but—'

'Guns, it's one of your idiosyncracies, whether or not you're aware of it, that as soon as we've fired one pattern you start worrying about not having enough left.'

Warrimer muttered from the binnacle, 'Like an old blackbird counting its bloody eggs.'

Carlish sniggered, and CPO Bearcroft turned away to hide his grin. Timberlake did look like some kind of bird. Graves growled, 'Enough from you, Matt.'

'Sorry.' Stooping to the voice-pipe. 'Midships.' Nick told the Warrant officer, 'We'll get by with what we have, Guns, don't worry. Tonight ought to be the last busy one, for this trip.'

An Admiralty signal during the afternoon told them: *Aircraft was reporting and homing U-boats towards convoy at 1245/A.* It wasn't news, but it might have been if the Focke-Wulf hadn't been so plainly visible. In fact, visibility now had begun to deteriorate; a light, cold drizzle was falling, blurring the horizon and making binocular work more difficult. Drizzle had thickened into rain by the time the next warning arrived, in the first dog watch: *D/F bearings on 4995 KCs* indicate U-boats establishing patrol line approximately 40 miles ahead of you.

Scarr murmured as he plotted it on the chart, 'Have to admit they're hot stuff, sir, those characters in the tracking room.'

No-one could have denied it: the Admiralty's tracking room had been supplying accurate and useful information to the convoys for a long time now. The fly in the ointment was a suspicion that the enemy might be intercepting and decoding at least some of the signals, possibly all of them. Three years ago the Germans had had all the British naval codes and cyphers – until the Admiralty had woken up to it, and changed them – and there were signs they might have made a fresh breakthrough.

Leaving the chart-room, Nick thought about this new assembly of U-boats. Forty miles ahead meant just under six hours' steaming for the convoy. The signal had originated at 1650 ship's time, so taking the information at its face value you might expect to be in U-boat territory at about 2230. On the other hand there was no reason to suppose the reported patrol-line would be static: it would more likely be advancing towards the convoy. And suppose some German staff officer in U-boat headquarters had a transcription of this Admiralty message on his desk right at this moment: wouldn't he order his pack to start moving west?

It was a distinct possibility. So, cut the interval by a couple of hours – and sunset might be the time. As the light went, it could start.

In the bridge again, Nick climbed into his tall seat, thumbed tobacco into a pipe Kate had given him, pondering meanwhile on the changed conditions that would apply tonight. This low, smooth swell, for instance, and rain that was not only heavy now but looked to be set in for the night. Who'd profit most from lousy visibility? Well, whoever foresaw it, laid plans to take advantage of it . . .

And *there* was a thought!

In the act of lighting his pipe, crouching for shelter from the rain while the match flared in wet, cupped hands, he'd stopped, forgetting what he was doing, the match fizzling out while cold dampness seeped down below his neck-towel and one thought triggered another and what had started as a vague idea began to harden into a line of action, into orders he'd have to transmit between now and sunset.

Dusk wasn't far away. There'd been no signals or new developments since he'd re-deployed his destroyers, explained his ideas to the commodore and alerted the corvettes to the action he required of them. The convoy was now steering a mean course of 100 degrees.

Harbinger was three miles ahead of the central columns. Another three miles ahead was *Goshawk*, with *Bruce* four thousand yards to port of her and *Watchful* the same distance to starboard. Daylight was fading: there was no horizon to be seen now, only the surrounding curtain of rain.

HF/DF had been silent. If the U-boats were out there – and you could bet on it – they weren't talking to each other. They'd probably done whatever chatting was necessary earlier in the day, when the Admiralty had heard them; they'd be dived now, Nick guessed, listening for the sounds of approaching ships. If they heard what they were expecting to hear, just as the light went altogether and gave them the cover they'd need for surface action, they'd imagine they had it cut-and-dried.

All this was guesswork, of course. And in a new kind of war, or at any rate a kind of warfare in which weapons and systems were constantly evolving, new tactics had to be tried before you could assess their worth. This ploy tonight, for instance, was full of risks. For example – if the U-boats were not all out there ahead: if there were some converging from the beams, while he had three of his four destroyers deployed six miles ahead . . .

Asdics weren't all that reliable, either. Dived U-boats could slip under, dipping deeper to pass under a destroyer screen, rising again astern of it with the slow-moving, bulky merchantmen at their mercy.

Chubb was conning the ship, Graves loitering in the doorway of the asdic cabinet. Graves wasn't happy with this plan: he'd argued, quietly and sensibly, and when Nick had countered his arguments he'd surrendered, though still (Nick thought) unconvinced. Scarr, on the other hand, had been very much in favour of it. Nick would have been happier if it had been the other way about: young Scarr was an efficient navigator and a good destroyer officer, but his comparative immaturity would tend to make his judgements less sound than Graves'.

Not that it made the slightest difference. It was your own judgement you had to go by. He'd only opened the idea to general discussion to see if any of them might come up with some point he hadn't thought of. It was good for them, anyway, to know what was being done and why.

He thought, with his glasses up and sweeping slowly, carefully across the bow, passing over the very small stern-on shapes of the other three destroyers – they were already as indistinct as thumbprints on a dirty window – *It probably wouldn't work a second time . . .*

The question was, would it work *this* time?

Because this was no kind of game. The stakes were lives, ships and cargoes . . . Too late now to pull back. He'd set it up, the lives were at risk, the ships were targets, and if he'd been right the action might start at any minute. A change of mind now could be the worst thing of all: if you faltered, tried to re-deploy at this stage, you could get *really* caught . . .

But if it failed? If tonight saw half the convoy lost?

He lowered the glasses, to dry their front lenses yet again. Aware of Chubb's quiet helm orders behind him, but not really hearing. *Harbinger* listing as she turned to a new leg of the zigzag. Asdics pinging, RDF aerial on the foremast turning steadily, the set's narrow white beam sweeping around the poached egg down below, painting-on dark blips for the three ships ahead and for *Gilliflower* close to the convoy's mass astern. Here in the bridge half a dozen pairs of binoculars probed the darkening, streaming surroundings for the dark loom of an enemy or the white feather of a periscope . . .

The rain enclosed and quietened a stretch of ocean that seemed empty.

Perhaps he'd tried to be too clever, and complicated what might really be a simple, straightforward situation. If he'd accepted that Admiralty signal without drawing further conclusions of his own, accepted that the encounter would take place at about 10.30 pm . . . Perhaps he should have: and perhaps he *should* pull those three ships back, put all four destroyers back in station around the convoy?

He'd dried the glasses again, and he was pushing back a wet sleeve to check the time, when the TBS burst into sudden, loud excitement. *Goshawk* – reporting from her position three miles ahead, *Surface contact bearing one-two-four, six and a half thousand yards, attacking* . . .

He hadn't got as far as seeing what time it was. It didn't matter a damn now either. He had his glasses up again: *Goshawk* would be cracking on speed, readying her guns and depth-charges. And thank God, the enemy was here, where he'd expected him!

TBS again: *Bruce*, now – reporting urgently, *Surface contact one-one-five, seven thousand yards, attacking!*

Those had been divergent bearings, clearly two separate targets. It looked very much like the real thing . . . He told Chubb, keeping his tone even and unexcited, allowing himself the deceit of letting them all think he'd had no doubts at all, 'Come to one-two-oh degrees. Two hundred revolutions. All quarters alert.' Two hundred revs would give about nineteen knots. At any higher speed, asdics wouldn't have been any use.

Those U-boats had to be put down, and plastered with

depth charges: kept down, kept busy and deaf, confused. Ideally, of course, destroyed: but the priority was to get the convoy past them – intact, over this last hurdle . . .

TBS again, as *Harbinger* surged ahead: it was *Watchful* reporting, *U-boat dived on bearing one-one-oh range seventeen hundred yards: attacking* . . .

Baxendale must have got that one on his RDF screen suddenly at close range: he'd have been in the process of turning to attack before he'd had time to think about reporting it. It might have just surfaced – then seen the spot it was in and pulled the plug again . . . But all destroyers up there had targets now, and *Harbinger* was moving up to support them. It wouldn't matter if there were several more, so long as they were all forced down, blinded, deafened by racing screws and exploding charges. He had his glasses up, sweeping the milky-dark surface ahead: it wouldn't be any surprise to find one surfacing, thinking it had passed under the screen and was inside now, with the convoy exposed to its torpedoes. Gunfire out on the starboard wing, *Watchful*'s bearing: everything was happening at once, and in a closely concentrated field of action – the U-boats had been taken by surprise, as the convoy might so easily have been.

Almost time for the main event, now. Give it – oh, say five minutes, just to make certain—

Asdic bell: and Garment's high shout of 'Contact, contact!'

Graves called, 'Red two-four, sir, range fifteen hundred!'

'Port ten.' He slid off his seat. 'I'll take her, Sub.'

'Confirmed submarine contact, sir. Moving left to right.'

'Midships.' He was at the binnacle, displacing Chubb. 'Depth-charge settings one hundred and fifty feet.' Because this German would have gone deepish, but probably not all that deep: he'd have been intending to come up again soon for a shot at the convoy . . . 'Steady as you go.'

'Bearing oh-eight-four, range thirteen hundred!'

'Steer oh-eight-oh. One-sixty revolutions.'

More gunfire eastward. Then a deeper rumble: depthcharges . . . There'd be no TBS chat from the corvettes, except in emergency: if there were U-boats on the surface in listening range, there'd be nothing for them to pick up, except the brief exchanges between the destroyers, and those wouldn't lead them to the convoy. Besides which, any surfaced U-boats would be blinded too, before much longer.

'Chief Yeoman – by light to the commodore, "Starboard now please" . . . Number One, I'll turn up this bugger's wake.'

'Target course three-four-oh, sir!'

He heard the clack-clacking of the eight-inch Aldis as Wolstenholm passed that pre-arranged signal to the commodore. Nick had left it open, whether it would be to port or starboard, but either way it would be a double emergency turn, two successive swerves of forty degrees each time. The convoy would end up steering due south. *Daphne* and *Iris* would be in the lead, *Gilliflower* and *Prunella* to port, *Viola* and *Aquilegia* to starboard: *Daphne*'s captain, Lieutenant-Commander Charles Rose RNVR, would be commanding the six corvettes.

'Message passed, sir!'

'Very good.' *Harbinger* rocking smoothly across the swell. Back aft, on the quarterdeck, Timberlake would be fretting over the imminent loss of yet more depthcharges.

'Bearing oh-four-one, range one thousand and fifty yards!'

The turning circle under fifteen degrees of rudder was eight ship's lengths . . . Depthcharges a long way off to starboard were a muted thunder. He bent to the rim of the voicepipe: 'Port fifteen.'

'Port fifteen, sir!'

'Bearing oh-oh-three—'

He heard the wail of the commodore's siren, and told Bearcroft, 'Make on TBS to the close screen, "Comply with previous orders".'

'Fifteen of port wheel on, sir . . .'

But the turn was going to be too sharp: she'd end up inside the U-boat's track – or where he guessed that track would be . . . He told Elphick, 'Ease to ten.'

'Ease to ten, sir!'

Reducing the angle of rudder, so the turn would be less

tight. *Harbinger* still leaning hard to starboard as she swung – and more depthcharges exploding, somewhere out there in the night.

'Bearing three-four-three, range four hundred, target moving left to right!'

'Midships and meet her.'

The U-boat had altered course, in the last half-minute . . .

'Meet her, sir . . .'

Reversing the wheel, that meant, to take the swing off her . . . 'Carlish – tell the engine room to stand by to make white smoke.' He'd warned Hawkey, and the other destroyers too. Corvettes, which lacked the equipment for making white smoke, had been told to have smoke-floats ready on their sterns. Nick ducked to the pipe again: 'Steady!'

'Three-five-five, sir—'

'Steer three-six-oh.'

'Target bears three-five-four, range two-fifty yards . . . *Lost target*, sir!'

'Change depth settings to two hundred and fifty feet—'

More underwater explosions rumbled distantly. And from the other direction a new howling from the commodore's siren was the order to his lumbering consorts to begin the second stage of that evasive turn. At this moment, as they turned, each of the corvettes would be dropping a second smoke-float in its own wake. The first would have been dropped as they made the first turn: the end-result would be a large area of sea dotted with floating cannisters emitting a grey-white, surface-hugging fog . . . And the reason for deepening the depthcharge settings at this last minute in the attack was that losing the target at 250 yards indicated it was almost certainly deeper than 150 feet. The asdic beam in vertical cross-section was elliptical in shape, and couldn't be raised or lowered, so as you ran towards a contact you lost it when it passed out of the lower limit of the beam.

'Two-fifty feet set, sir!'

'Stand by . . . Fire one!' As chancy, he thought, as a coconut shy. Couldn't be helped. The closer the better, and ideally right on top of the bastard, but the main thing was to shake him, scare him, keep him down and too busy to wonder where the convoy might be . . . 'Fire two! Fire three!' To have a reasonable chance of success you needed two ships on the job, so that one could stand off and maintain the asdic contact while the other ran in to drop depth-charges; then they'd swap places, one reloading while the other attacked, contact being maintained by one or other all the time: until the U-boat was finally brought to the surface, or until you heard the underwater crash that would be its hull imploding . . . Nick ordered, 'Tell the engine room, start making smoke . . . Chief Yeoman – TBS to destroyers, "Make smoke".' Astern, the charges exploded, deep ringing blasts impacting on the ship's hull, and the sea lifting in humps in her wake and on the quarters – where in a minute there'd be smoke drifting, adding fog to rain, reducing visibility to just about nil. The other three would be adding their quota to it while they continued to hunt and bomb their targets: and the U-boats' ears would be filled by four lots of churning screws as well as by intermittent explosions of depthcharge patterns. And the smoke might hide a convoy, or might not: over a widening area no periscope view or glimpse from a daringly-surfaced U-boat would tell its captain anything at all: none of them would have any way of knowing that the convoy of thirty-five surviving merchantmen was slipping away southward, hidden in the smoke-thickened deluge and with the sounds of their propellers getting fainter every minute.

'Starboard fifteen.'

Please God, may there be no others down south there, to make this whole exercise a waste of time . . .

The last of that pattern had exploded, its echoes reverberating away through fifteen hundred fathoms of black water. Binoculars were sweeping the surface as the turbulence subsided. Distantly, another destroyer's charges sounded like a roll of muffled drums.

'Fifteen of starboard wheel on, sir . . .'

'Contact, contact! Bearing two-five-five—'

'Midships.' *Damn* it . . . 'Port twenty.'

The German must have reversed his turn, swung sharply to port just after they'd lost contact. So that pattern had gone wide, and he'd be thinking he was clever . . .

'Bearing two-five-two, range eight-fifty yards—'

Watchful reported over TBS that she'd lost her target. Nick snapped, 'Tell him to join *Goshawk* . . . Midships.'

Throbbing asdic pings were being reflected back very clearly, the sharp, hard echoes that come unmistakably from a U-boat's hull. Down there in the black water, a steel eggshell casing at the very tips of the hunters' fingers: you needed to grasp it, crush it . . .

'Bearing two-five-nine, range nine hundred . . . Moving left to right now . . .'

Wriggling like some kind of snake . . . 'Set charges to three hundred feet. Steer two-eight-oh. Tell the engine room to stop making smoke. Chief Yeoman, pass that order to the others. One-eight-oh revolutions.'

After the fourth run, asdics couldn't regain contact. A wider cast, a curving track designed to cross the U-boat's escape route at some point no matter which way it might be steering, still failed to produce results.

Frustrating: but not unusual . . .

'Had the sense not to hold to a straight course, obviously.'

Graves muttered, 'Can't win 'em all, sir.'

The main achievement was that the U-boats had been held off, that there'd been no shouts for help from the convoy. Nick thought, *Touch wood: plenty of time yet* . . . The whole scheme could fall to ruin so easily and suddenly, and he had to be ready for that too – for the worst, which would be sudden slaughter, loss of ships and lives for which he, Nick Everard, was directly and personally responsible – losses he would actually have caused, through trying to pull a fast one.

Bruce lost her contact only a few minutes later. Nick called down to the plot, where Mike Scarr was at work with two assistants, and elicited that *Goshawk* and *Watchful* were seven miles southeast. *Bruce* was four miles away on 080 degrees.

'What's my course to join *Goshawk*?'

'One-three-oh, sir.'

Scarr had had the answer ready, anticipating the requirement. More depthcharges rumbled, shivering *Harbinger*'s steel: so those two were still on their target.

'Chief – TBS to *Bruce*, "Join me. My course one-three-oh, speed fifteen."' He told Chubb to take over the conning of the ship and bring her round to that course. Hoping to God the convoy was in the clear, with no U-boats trailing it, no separate concentrations lying in wait ahead of it. The corvettes would only use TBS in emergency or when an enemy was already in contact with them, so continuing silence on the air was a reassurance. He reminded himself again – it would only take one second for the sudden shattering of that silence . . .

'*Bruce* acknowledged, sir.'

'Very good.'

Chubb reported, 'Course one-three-oh, sir.' *Harbinger* see-sawing at half speed across low, rolling ridges glistening pock-marked under the lash of rain.

At 2230 – the time at which they might have expected the convoy on its original course to run into the U-boat pack – *Goshawk* and *Watchful* made their kill.

Harbinger and *Bruce* had kept clear of the hunt, had spent the past hour patrolling a wide circumference around it, like circling an arena in which two matadors alternately played their bull. If the U-boat had broken away from them there'd have been a good chance of picking it up again here in the deep field; in fact it might have been difficult for the German captain to know which way to run, when he had two hunters on top of him and two guards widely separated on the perimeter and constantly moving round. Nick hadn't evolved this tactic in any deliberate way, it had simply arisen from the circumstances, but it wasn't a bad scheme at all, in a situation where you had the ships to spare. *Harbinger* and *Bruce* were protecting the hunters too, against interference by any stray U-boat that might have been in the vicinity and tempted to come to its friend's assistance. A destroyer moving slowly on a steady course, or even stopped, holding a U-boat in its asdic beam, would make an easy target for another.

Nick had relaxed his crew to the second degree of readiness, although officers and key ratings were still closed up. Nick on his tall seat, hunched against the rain, watching the contest in the centre. *Watchful* had made a pass, dropped a pattern with deep settings, at twenty minutes past the hour. You knew they'd been deep ones by the sound of the explosions and the amount of disturbance on the surface: and he was watching the time because of the arrangements he'd made with the convoy's commodore . . . *Goshawk*'s captain had told him over TBS when *Harbinger* and *Bruce* had first arrived, 'I think Fritz is in trouble. He's slowed down, and we've heard some funny noises.' Then there'd been some minutes of alarm when the U-boat had given its tormentors a false target, an SBT – submarine bubble target, known to the Germans as a *Pillenwerfer*. It was a kind of underwater bomb which a submarine could eject to explode chemically in the sea, fizzing strongly enough to provide an asdic echo very much like the real McCoy. If the operator on the surface let himself be fooled by it long enough, the U-boat had a chance to creep away. But *Goshawk*'s man had caught on quickly, swept around and picked up his real target again.

You could imagine – if you cared to think about it – how sickening that must have been for the Germans.

After *Watchful*'s last deep pattern had burst, there were sounds of the enemy's pumps running and tanks blowing. Searchlights from both hunting ships swept the surface, with guns' crews standing ready, weapons loaded. But nothing appeared, asdics still held the contact, and Nick, watching through wet binoculars, hearing his own asdic's regular, penetrating pulses and Chubb's low Australian tones as he kept her circling, saw *Goshawk* gathering way, the white plume of bow-wave lifting as she picked up speed, running in for a fresh attack.

He'd thought, crossing his fingers, *This one, now . . .*

Imagining those people down there, you could almost feel sorry for them. If you could think of them as just ordinary human beings.

Deep thunder: then the surface quivered, lifting in patches that heaved and boiled. *Harbinger* felt the kicks of them in her steel belly: and then another—

'Submerged explosion, sir!'

That shout had come from the HSD – Higher Submarine Detector – Leading Seaman Garment. Tony Graves, who'd been with him in the tiny A/S cabinet, was backing out, pulling earphones off his head. 'That was *it*, sir. Not a doubt.'

Searchlight beams swung, criss-crossing. *Goshawk* slowing, heeling under a lot of rudder. Calling now on TBS: Bearcroft answered, and the message came as, *U-boat believed destroyed. Searching for evidence.*

Circling on: waiting, and believing it, everyone in *Harbinger*'s bridge *knowing* it – there'd been cheers, and there was some chatter now . . . but you did need evidence, and the only real proof would be the grisly kind. A U-boat could try to persuade its tormentors to consider it dead, and leave it, by spilling oil and firing wreckage and clothes out of a torpedo tube: so you needed more than that.

Goshawk spoke up again, *Surface is thick with oil fuel. Other stuff as well. I'm lowering a boat.*

You could smell the oil. *Goshawk* was lying stopped, *Watchful* circling her, and out here *Harbinger* and *Bruce* circling both of them, all four ships with their asdics and RDF active. *Bruce* was the only one, Nick realised, that had not participated in the destruction of a U-boat on this trip. *Watchful* had taken part in two successful hunts. Polishing off three of them wasn't at all bad, particularly if there were no more losses from the convoy . . . But Peter Instance, Bruce's lieutenant-in-command, would be feeling a bit out of it.

He'd have to look forward to better luck next time, that was all. *Bruce* just hadn't had the luck to be in the right place at the right moment. Instance and his A/S team were just as competent as any of the others: and the four together, backed by the six corvettes, were getting better at it with every trip they made . . . He heard Chubb's voice, into the wheel-house voice-pipe: 'Port five . . .'

Then the TBS again: Jock Audsley's voice, *My whaler has recovered one complete body and a number of – er – assorted spare parts. Also gear and papers. Seems it was U 102.*

For a moment Nick had the numbers confused, and linked that one with the so-called 'ace', Max Looff . . . Then he remembered that Neumann had said Looff's boat was U 122, not 102 . . . But something else in his mind: it was that flippant *assorted spare parts* . . . Audsley, *Goshawk*'s captain, was a very civilised, thoughtful man: the questionable humour was self-protective, a product of this endless nightmare of a battle, the need to make a joke of horror.

He swung round to Carlish. 'Sub, ask the pilot for a course to rejoin the convoy, at twenty-five knots. Then go aft, shake Lieutenant Neumann and inform him with my compliments that we have just destroyed U 102.'

He thought, *We're all bastards* . . .

By dawn the rain was finished and the cloud-cover was breaking up, giving a very pretty sunrise – shades of pink deepening into scarlet over blueish, low-lying haze. If you'd been imaginative enough you might have seen that brilliant hoop of colour as a triumphal arch into which convoy and escort were streaming as they left the Greenland air gap behind them.

The course was due east. The convoy had steamed south for three hours, as Nick and the commodore had agreed it would, then altered to east. He'd brought his destroyers down at twenty-five knots on 170 degrees and made the rendezvous before midnight. During the run south they'd listened to HF/DF transmissions astern, and Nick had guessed at bewildered U-boat captains surfacing and wondering what had hit them, where they were, where the hell the convoy might be, where was the vanished U 102 . . .

Goshawk and *Watchful* were flying the signal *U-boat sunk*.

The convoy hadn't been molested at all. The commodore

had signalled thanks and congratulations, and Nick wondered how many of the merchant captains might realise how lucky they'd been, how easily the scheme could have ended in disaster. He guessed the commodore, who was a retired vice-admiral of about the same vintage as Nick's old uncle Hugh, would have a shrewd idea of it, would be drawing his own sighs of relief as he looked around at his surviving company of thirty-four valuable ships, crews and war cargoes plugging east into the lurid dawn, on course for Malin Head and, with air patrols likely to be around from about this point on, comparatively secure.

Until next time . . . And meanwhile there was no discomfort in the knowledge that if he had *not* backed his hunch, some of those freighters would now have been under nine thousand feet of water, in the ocean-bed silt with dead men inside them: men who instead, in just a few days' time, would be in the arms of wives, parents, lovers, children. It was an enormous, really frightening privilege to have been in a position to influence an outcome of such huge importance: for the rest of one's own life, he guessed, one would remember it and feel humbled by it in a way that would be very difficult to explain.

Except perhaps to Kate.

The colours of the dawn were fading, becoming nondescript, more typically Atlantic shades above the still fiery curve of the horizon. Thinking of Kate now, not ships: of the hope there'd be a letter waiting – even a letter she might have posted in England.

Chapter 3

Prime Minister Winston Churchill to Premier Stalin:
We shall attack in Egypt towards the end of this month, and 'Torch' will begin early in November . . . 'Torch' will be a heavy operation in which, in addition to the US Navy, 240 British warships will be engaged . . . Naval protection [to convoys to North Russia] will be impossible until our impending operations are completed. As the escorts are withdrawn from 'Torch' they can again be made available in northern waters.

The convoy had split up into its various sections according to ports of destination, and the six corvettes were continuing into the North Channel, where they'd hand over to local escorts. *Harbinger, Goshawk, Watchful* and *Bruce* had separated from the rest and diverged to turn in around Inishowen Head and enter Lough Foyle. They'd be stopping to take in fuel from the oiler that was anchored in the lough just off Moville, then continue on to Londonderry, twenty miles inland.

It was a grey day with a southwest wind and low, fast-moving cloud. Greenish water with a lop on it, reflecting the green of the surrounding land. He put *Harbinger* alongside the oiler, and *Goshawk* secured opposite her; they'd fuel simultaneously while the other two lay off to await their turn.

'Looks like our old friend *Passenham* approaching, sir.'

Mike Scarr had his binoculars focused on the bow-on ship. It was a high, graceful stem, when you saw it in profile. *Passenham* was an old yacht that had been re-equipped for service as a local tender.

'Squad of pongoes in her waist.' Scarr still had his glasses on her. 'Coming for the prisoners perhaps, sir.'

'Pongo' was naval slang for 'soldier'. How the word had come into general use wasn't certain; one dictionary defined it as, *a large African anthropoid of singularly repulsive habits*, but the term wasn't used in a derogatory sense: rather to the contrary . . . It seemed unlikely, Nick was thinking, that they'd have sent the old yacht all this way just to collect the U-boat prisoners, when *Harbinger* would have been delivering them at the base in a couple of hours' time.

He was in his day cabin down aft, visiting it for the first time in eleven days, when Tony Graves tapped on the door and told him, '*Passenham*'s alongside, sir, and Lieutenant Boustead would like a word, if it's convenient.'

'Has he come for the Germans?'

Graves nodded. 'But he's also brought a few sacks of mail – it's being sorted now, sir – and orders, he says. I don't think they want us up at Derry, for some reason.'

Nick wondered what the hell he was talking about. But he was also thinking about the mail being sorted – wondering whether it would include one letter in particular. He told Graves, 'Wheel him in.' He pressed the bell to his pantry, and told Foster to make some coffee.

If *Harbinger* and the other destroyers were being turned round here, not allowed to stay for even one night's rest when they'd come this close to it, having been at sea in lousy conditions for the past fortnight and now in need of provisions, fresh water and other important items, either some staff officer had gone nuts or there must be a major flap on.

Boustead knocked, and entered, removing his cap and pushing it under his left arm. He was a man of about forty – in fact he looked the same age as Nick, which would have made him forty-six, but he'd left the Navy in 1928 when he'd been a lieutenant aged twenty-five. Which made him thirty-nine now. As Nick had also been on the beach between the wars, they had a certain amount in common.

The smile on Boustead's reddish face was accompanied by a few moments' silence. He wasn't exactly a chatterer.

He mumbled, 'Congratulations are due, I'm told. Three U-boats – sir?'

'We were lucky . . . What's this about orders, and not going on to the base?'

'Ah.'

A long brown envelope, with OHMS in large letters and BY HAND OF OFFICER in smaller ones. There was also a slip of paper for Nick to sign . . . 'Very sorry we're not to have the pleasure of your company this time, sir.'

'Sit down.' He ripped the envelope open. 'Coffee's coming.'

He was to 'proceed forthwith, on completion of fuelling': he was to take *Goshawk, Watchful* and *Bruce* with him to the Clyde, from where they would escort the cruisers *Nottingham* and *Rhodesia* to Gibraltar. All victualling and ammunitioning would be done on arrival at Tail o' the Bank: ships were to signal their requirements ahead to Greenock immediately.

Re-reading the order with its complicated address – it was repeated for information to a whole crowd of other authorities – it sank in that this escort group, which had begun to settle down very well and make itself really quite useful, was being broken up. The six corvettes under Charles Rose would be arriving in Lough Foyle some time tonight or tomorrow morning, by which time he'd have his four destroyers anchored in the Clyde.

Boustead grunted, watching his face as he read, 'Not good?'

Foster had arrived with a tray of coffee. Nick shook his head. 'I'd say bloody awful.'

Whatever the reason for it, splitting the group could be good news only for the U-boats. It had been agreed at high levels, in recent months, that the principle henceforth would be to keep groups intact, as permanent teams, so far as could possibly be managed.

He nodded to his PO steward. 'Thank you, Foster.'

'I was told to give you a private message.' Boustead looked round, to see the pantry door shut. 'To the effect that the division of your group into two sections is only temporary. Also regretted, but *force majeure,* etcetera.'

'Was any reason given?'

'All I have to go on is that message. Which suggests they're sending you off somewhere . . . Murmansk run?'

He thought it was more likely to be a Malta convoy.

'Rough trip, was it?'

He nodded. 'We got bumped around a bit.'

'Seven losses?'

News travelled on the winds. He nodded again. Boustead finished his coffee and stood up. 'Darned good getting three of 'em, anyway . . . But I'd better push along. Many thanks for the coffee. Sir.' Boustead made a point of slipping in a 'sir' now and then. He added, 'I hope we see you back pretty soon.'

'Thanks, Andrew.'

He preceded his visitor out of the day-cabin, through the flat past curtained entrances to other officers' cabins and the door of the wardroom, then up the steel ladder and out through the port-side screen door . . . There was a puddle of oil on the iron deck – the middle part of the ship, where the torpedo-tubes were – and a stoker was standing by the valve of the fuelling connection. The Chief Stoker, Podmore, would be overseeing the operation: he was on the oiler's flat, pipe-ribbed deck, talking to a fat man in green overalls. Nick turned away, crossed to his ship's starboard side where the old yacht was secured – temporarily, with men standing by her lines, ready to cast off.

Boustead saluted vaguely. 'Good luck – sir . . . Whatever it turns out to be.' Graves told him, 'Prisoners are all on board.'

'Your mail, sir.'

Carlish – proffering a batch of envelopes.

'Thank you, Sub.' It was an inch-thick wad of letters enclosed in a rubber band. He pushed it into a pocket of his reefer jacket, kept a hand on it while he watched *Passenham* casting off and then sliding away stern-first. Tony Graves asked him quietly, 'May I know where we're going, sir?'

'To start with, the Clyde . . . Send Hawkey along, will you? And check with Mr Timberlake, and Warrimer – we're to signal our requirements to Greenock right away. It'll be a fast turn-round there, and we'll be escorting some cruisers down to Gib. So list all requirements . . . Then come down to my cabin.' He looked past Graves. 'Sub – nip over to *Goshawk*—' he pointed across the tanker – 'and ask Lieutenant-Commander Audsley to spare me a few minutes. Bring him down to my cabin . . . Oh, Number One—' Graves stopped, came back – 'The quack's stores list too.' Medical stores, from Ian Mackenzie, surgeon-lieutenant. 'And send someone to find Scarr, tell him I want to see him . . . Bosun's Mate!'

Able Seaman Webb sprang out of the steel shelter where the Tannoy broadcast system was housed. 'Yessir?'

'Webb, get hold of the Chief Yeoman, and tell him I want him right away.'

To draft a signal to *Watchful* and *Bruce*, the two who were lying-off astern, and then compile the longer ones to Greenock. And this was only just the start of it: he'd have his four ships out of the lough and on their way, he guessed, before he'd have time to read Kate's letter.

Ideally, she'd have written from somewhere in England, have arrived already.

Waiting, making notes of things to be seen to in this or that department either now or when they got to the Clyde, he wondered again what kind of operation this could be if it was *not* a Malta convoy. Something sizeable, obviously; if it had been only a matter of transferring two cruisers from the Home Fleet to Force H there'd have been no need for this upheaval. And it *might* be another Russian convoy: if the cruisers had simultaneously to be taken south for some purpose, and an Arctic convoy operation was about to draw off all available fleet destroyers?

Malta was the likely thing. The last convoy, 'Pedestal', hadn't got much through, and the island would be desperately short of everything by now. With Rommel's Afrika Korps within striking distance of Cairo and the Canal, the island's value as a base for operations against the Axis supply lines was even greater than before. It would be Malta, he thought – probably . . .

'Lieutenant-Commander Audsley, sir.'

More than an hour passed before he had a quiet moment, to check on the contents of his personal mail. And when the moment came, he immediately wished it hadn't. There was no letter from her. Disappointment added to impatience while he waited for *Watchful* and *Bruce* to finish oiling. Worry, as well as disappointment: the only reason for her not to have written would be if she was actually on her way.

He got away, at last, and by cutting some corners he found himself leading the other three destroyers into the naval anchorage off Greenock only a few minutes after sunset. The signal station had flashed the numbers of their berths to them, and it was just as well they'd arrived while there was still some daylight: the anchorage was packed, fuller than he'd ever known it. There was too much here, he saw at once, for just another Malta run.

The firth was grey and bleak, as well as crowded. A cold wind had followed the flotilla in, and it was freshening, getting back to normal for this area and the time of year. He heard Graves mutter under his breath, with his glasses up too, 'Well, bloody hell . . .'

'Are you making sense of it, pilot?'

Negotiating this anchorage when it was even reasonably full could, to a newcomer, be rather like getting through the Hampton Court maze. He wanted to let Scarr sort it out on his own, if possible.

'Well, sir.' The navigator lowered his binoculars, and pointed. 'If we clear that starboard-hand buoy, then pass round astern of those sweepers . . .'

At the side of the bridge CPO Bearcroft was using his signal telescope and showing off to Leading Signalman Wolstenholm. 'That's *Jamaica* – and the little 'un ahead of her's the old *Delhi*, bless her heart—'

Wolstenholm's mutter: 'Carriers, beyond.'

'Escort carriers, lad. But look over *there*, now. See that lot? Them's the big boys – *Formidable*, and *Victorious*, and—'

'Chief Yeoman, can we have some quiet, please?'

'Sorry, sir!'

He'd been getting carried away, at the sight of so many old friends, and his voice had been getting louder without his realising it. Nick bent to the voice-pipe: 'Starboard ten . . .'

Bearcroft's ship-recognition was not at fault, anyway, and if those and others were congregating here for one single purpose – well, it would have to be something very big indeed.

'Midships.'

'Midships, sir!'

Some large-scale landing operation? And if the jumping-off place was Gibraltar, where might the assault be going? Sicily? South of France?

When *Harbinger* slid into her billet and anchored, the other three dropping their hooks simultaneously astern of her – each into exactly the correct square of water – there was a motorboat lying-off near and obviously waiting for her. It had brass dolphins on its sides and a snotty at the wheel, and so was clearly a big ship's boat. It came alongside as soon as they had a gangway down, and it was from the cruiser *Nottingham*. Its midshipman had brought a message to the effect that Rear-Admiral Freelling requested Captain Everard's immediate presence on board his flagship; the boat would wait for him now and also bring him back to *Harbinger* later on.

Twenty-four hours later the four destroyers and two cruisers were in the Irish Sea with Holyhead well back on the quarter. They'd weighed anchor in mid-forenoon and slipped down the Firth of Clyde past Arran and Ailsa Craig with the sea green and sparkling, a southwest wind whipping spray off the crests, the ships' bow-waves curling high, ensigns crackling . . .

His visit to the flagship had been brief. He'd had one glass of gin with the admiral, and then a briefing from his staff – route, screening dispositions, tactics in the event of submarine or aircraft attack, zigzags, wireless wavelengths . . . Nick had tried a slightly different question when he'd been taking his leave: 'After we reach Gib, sir, shall I be staying with you?'

Freelling had looked surprised, and said he hadn't the least idea. Asked later by Tony Graves what this admiral was like, Nick's answer was, 'He's a gunnery specialist.'

'Oh . . .'

A high proportion of flag officers came from the gunnery branch. They were the parade-ground specialists too, but the gun was God and they were its apostles. In effect, they were the antithesis of the Nick Everard type, which was basically a maverick. None of this made Freelling inadequate, incompetent or unpleasant: it only meant that one was serving under a man with whom one would have very little in common.

But 'maverick' was right, and he knew it. It was why he'd left the Navy between the wars, and why in days gone by he'd incurred the displeasure of more than one senior of the Freelling kind.

Midnight saw Ushant well back on the quarter. They were steaming at eighteen knots, which allowing for the zigzag gave a speed of advance of about fifteen. Air cover was sporadic: and they were crossing Biscay now, where the Ju 88s were sometimes to be encountered. They were two-thirds of the way across, just after 0800 next morning, when *Bruce* picked up an asdic contact. As Nick reached the bridge she was heading westward with the flag signal, 'contact confirmed', sliding down and a new one, 'attacking with depthcharges', shooting up to the yardarm in its place. Flags for the information of the admiral: Peter Instance, *Bruce*'s young captain, was on the TBS to *Harbinger*, as usual.

It had been made clear on board *Nottingham* that no lengthy A/S hunts would be permitted. Freelling wanted to keep his screen intact. *Bruce* would be allowed to make about one pass at this U-boat now, mainly to keep it deep and harmless while the squadron swept on southward.

Charges burst, back on the quarter and three miles away.

Nick saw the geysers lift and heard the rumbling thuds of them. Instance would have lost his target now: if he regained contact quickly he might be allowed one more run over, but no more than that: if he was allowed off the leash for too long there'd be a terse signal from the flagship. Freelling was the sort of admiral who'd have suitable reprimands poised permanently on the tip of an Aldis lamp . . . The zigzag bell rang down in the wheelhouse: Warrimer, who was officer of the watch, checked the ship's head by gyro as the quartermaster brought her round. The quartermaster had the zigzag manual open at the selected diagram, beside him at the wheel, and there was no need for orders from the bridge. But the alteration left *Bruce* almost right astern now, and the U-boat would be astern too, where it no longer presented any danger to the cruisers.

Carlish took a new TBS message from *Bruce*: it was Peter Instance's voice, reporting he'd lost contact and requesting permission to continue searching. Nick's answer had to be, 'Negative. Resume station.' As Instance would have known, before he'd sent the message . . . Nick's sense of discomfort wasn't only from having a U-boat within reach and being forced to leave it: nor was it only from the fact that what was left of his breakfast would be cold by this time. Behind the immediate irritations was the fact that an escort group was an independent command: you ran your own show, carried heavy responsibility, took your own decisions and stood ready to be judged by the results: whereas here and now, commanding four slightly antique destroyers and under another man's orders – well, it was a chore, and a dull one, and hardly suitable employment for a four-stripe captain. Jock Audsley of *Goshawk*, for instance, could have handled it perfectly well.

He climbed on to his seat, took out a pipe and began to fill it. The zigzag bell rang again: and the swing to starboard that was coming now would make it easy for *Bruce* to get back into her station on that wing. If Instance had his wits about him this morning, he'd have anticipated it. He'd be grinding his teeth, too, frustrated at being recalled so quickly

. . . Nick put his glasses up, to check where *Bruce* had got to: the pipe was between his teeth, filled but as yet unlit . . . There – in sight now on the quarter as the squadron altered course: obviously young Peter Instance *had* been ready for this turn, and had been steering so as to cut the corner. Nick was about to lower the binoculars and get his pipe going, when *Bruce* blew up.

Initially, a vertical leap of what looked like smoke but would have been spray: then steam gushing, and with that the sound arrived, the deep knocking crash of the torpedo. A streak of jet black lined the dirt-coloured cloud for a few seconds, and then the muck was expanding, thinning, dissipating, swirling away on the wind. Within seconds – certainly less than half a minute – where a few blinks of the eye ago there'd been a ship with a hundred and sixty men in her, there was nothing.

Except a splash: a piece of funnel or a locker, some large object landing in the sea. A scattering of others, smaller . . .

'Starboard twenty-five, three-four-oh revolutions. Action stations . . . Sub, pass to *Goshawk* and *Watchful* "Take station on the cruisers' bows".' Graves had his thumb on the alarm buzzer, *Harbinger* heeling to port as full rudder came on and her screws speeded to increase the power behind the turn. Nick and others with their glasses up were searching the area of sea where *Bruce* had disintegrated. The torpedo had hit her somewhere amidships, and that would have been one of her boilers bursting – that steam . . . Speed mounting, *Harbinger* lying almost on her side as she turned. 'Midships!' Nick had taken over at the binnacle: Scarr was on his way down to the plot and Chubb was standing back out of the way, joining in the binocular search. 'Steer three-six-oh!'

Graves at his elbow: 'Sir, at these revs we won't—'

'I'll come down in a minute.' Practicalities, action, held the sense of horror partially, temporally, at bay. Come down in revs, he'd meant: Graves's reminder being that at this speed asdics weren't operable. But the need was to get there, find any survivors there might be: although he doubted, in the circumstances as he'd seen them, that there could be any. *Harbinger* pounding, hurling her narrow length crashing across the undulating green, smashing through it, spray from her forefoot and blunt stem sheeting white in flying wings and an intermittent canopy whipping overhead as she tore northward. Poor little *Bruce*: conceived 1928, born 1930, along with – oh, the family's names were *Brilliant, Boreas, Bulldog, Beagle, Blanche: Blanche* had gone in the second month of the war . . . Ducking to the voice-pipe: 'Two hundred revolutions.' Up again: 'Anything to be seen yet?'

Asdics pinging as the speed fell off. Familiar sound: and the sick feeling, sense of inerradicable loss and waste was also familiar now, joining an already semi-digested residue in the dark corners of memory . . . And there'd been no U-boat here: the bastard would have sneaked away out of it, and he could have fired that shot or salvo from any direction at all. *Bruce* had been on her own: the torpedo had been meant for her, not for the cruisers who'd been out of range and had their sterns pointing in this direction. Nick cut the revs again, slowing her to about eight knots. He had his own glasses at his eyes now, as did everyone else who possessed a pair, intently examining the rumpled Biscay surface, rolling white-streaked green. There was enough white in the green for no-one in *Bruce* to have seen the white feather of a periscope when that bastard had poked it up.

'Object red three-oh, about three cables' lengths, sir!'

Chubb had been the first to spot it. Nick swung his glasses that way, and found it at once. A hump in the water: black, sea-washed, dark in the white swirl where the green broke open around and over it. He knew at first glance what it was: everyone knew, because the sight was not unfamiliar. Closer in, one saw detail: that the body was supported by its inflated lifebelt, slumped in the waves and rocking to their motion, the edging of broken water seething to and fro as the arched hump lifted and subsided.

'Port fifteen.'

'Port fifteen, sir . . . Fifteen of port wheel—'

'Captain, sir.' Warrimer was on his right. Nick looked

at him, and Warrimer said quietly, 'That body's headless, sir.'

'Slow together. Midships.'

It was half a minute before anyone else saw it as Warrimer had just for an instant. But Nick had verified it for himself now: the body was enclosed in a black-looking, sodden duffel-coat, and pinkish blood was seeping into the water from its jaggedly severed neck.

There was nothing else here.

'Signalman – by light to the flagship.' He interrupted himself, to call down to the wheelhouse: 'Three-four-oh revolutions. Port twenty.' Straightening, putting his glasses on the cruisers which were several miles away now: he dictated, 'No survivors. Am resuming station.'

At least Freelling had left him to get on with it, not bothered him with signals.

Coming up to midday: and Cape Finisterre lay about a hundred and fifty miles on the port bow. *Harbinger* was the tip of an arrow-head formation, with *Goshawk* on her starboard quarter and *Watchful* to port, and the two cruisers still in line abreast astern of them. Revs for eighteen knots, maintaining the zigzag, and asdics pinging, pinging, a banshee keening into the hidden depths. Nobody talking much, but everyone's thoughts would be much the same: the three destroyers were ships in mourning, ships feeling each others' company more closely in the aftermath of *Bruce*'s loss.

Freelling had flashed a message of sympathy, and Nick had thanked him for it. Those signals were on the log, as was one to Admiralty reporting the loss with all hands. And on Bearcroft's TBS log was Nick's last message to *Bruce, Negative. Resume station.*

HF/DF had heard nothing, and the only blips on the RDF screen were those of the ships astern. A Liberator had made a few wide circles around the squadron earlier in the forenoon, but that was the only aircraft they'd seen. The U-boat had most likely been on passage across Biscay, either going out on patrol or returning to its French base, because current Intelligence reports indicated that U-boat concentrations in the southern area were to be expected mainly in the Canaries-Madeira-Azores vicinity, and from there southwards to Freetown, a disposition aimed at taking advantage of the Azores air gap, and at convoys between the UK and the Cape of Good Hope.

Or from the Cape northward, homebound. A convoy such as Kate might be taking passage in . . .

He scowled, catching himself at it again – fretting, worrying like an old woman . . . As if he was the only man in the ship with a wife, for God's sake – which he most certainly was not. Matt Warrimer, for instance – Warrimer, still at the binnacle but nearing the end of his forenoon watch, was married. He was a Londoner, he'd been in some broking business for a few months between coming down from Oxford and the watershed of September 1939; he'd married his wife in London during the blitz of 1941. He'd gone directly from his honeymoon to sea in the Atlantic, while his wife stayed on in London where she had some hush-hush Military Intelligence job. He'd admitted, 'It wasn't an easy time.' And Tony Graves, with his rather stout, staid wife who lived in Liverpool, which had also been subjected to the fury of the Luftwaffe: Graves, who was an exceptionally good asdic man, simply got on with it, and wrote to his wife at such length and so frequently that his letters must have been like instalments from some endless serial – which wouldn't have found much of a readership, as there was so little of interest that could be sent through the post, even when you censored your own letters . . . Bearcroft was from Liverpool too, and he had two small daughters as well as a wife: he carried family snapshots in his paybook, and tended to thrust them under people's noses. Mr Timberlake was married, too – to a woman who bore some resemblance to Popeye's girlfriend Olive Oyle: but quite a few of the older men in the ship, those in or near their thirties, say, had anxieties far removed from the ship herself. All of which made him ask himself what right *he* had to be fussing.

The answer was, he'd had the luck – and in wartime it

was good luck, by and large – not to have any really deep, vital involvements. Until now. At least, he'd never felt for anyone as he did for Kate. You lived and learnt, and old dogs *could* learn new tricks.

'Pipe hands to dinner, sir?'

'Yes, please.'

It would be a quieter mealtime than usual, on the mess-decks. The Harbingers had had a lot of friends in *Bruce*.

The next day's pipe of 'Hands to dinner' came when they were passing the latitude of Lisbon; and at the end of the afternoon watch the flagship signalled for an alteration of course to port, to cut the corner as they rounded Cape St Vincent. At sunset the cape was distantly abeam, and Nick heard Graves quoting Robert Browning's verse to Mike Scarr:

Nobly, nobly, Cape St Vincent to the northwest died away;
Sunset ran, one glorious blood-red reeking into Cadiz Bay;
Bluish mid the burning water, full in face Trafalgar lay;
In the dimmest northwest distance dawned Gibraltar grand and grey . . .

Scarr had been taking evening stars. Still cradling his sextant he remarked to Chubb, who had the watch, 'Aren't we lucky to have such an erudite first lieutenant?'

'You can say *that* again.' Chubb frowned. 'Erudite? What's—'

'Don't you have schools in Australia?'

'Plenty, for those who need 'em. Me, I'm—'

The zigzag bell had rung. Graves finished the sentence as Chubb paused, watching to see the turn was being made in the right direction. Graves suggested, 'Ignorant?'

'Too right.' Watching the swing, Chubb nodded. 'And happy.' He asked him, 'Let's hear that piece again? *Who*'s sneaking into Cadiz Bay?'

Gloom was lifting, largely because an effort was being made to counter it. The awareness of loss was still there, but although the destruction of one of your own group and the death of friends was a blow that staggered you when it came, by this stage men had learnt to weather the shocks quickly – at any rate more quickly than they could have done a year or two years ago. As initial shock faded you thought *There but for the grace of God* – and then tried to put it out of mind.

Gibraltar, grand and grey, grew out of a dawn mist next morning. Speed had been reduced to twelve knots at 0400, when Cadiz had been less than sixty miles northeast; the Rock loomed massive against sunrise as the cruisers formed into line for the approach to harbour.

Chapter 4

Prime Minister to Secretary of State for Foreign Affairs:
We shall have to watch . . . Spanish reactions to preparations for 'Torch' which will become evident at Gibraltar . . . How much of these preparations would exceed the normal for a big Malta convoy?'

Captain Cruance, RNVR, was a tall man with white hair and a stoop, and he lived in a hole in a rock. That was how he'd describe him to Kate, Nick thought: some day, some place, when they'd be together and all this would be finished, would be in the early stages of being digested into history. The notion matched a feeling that history might well be in the making, here and now; and behind that was the puzzle of what his own part in it might be. Cruance stooping, as he shook his hand, as if he'd lived his whole life with the weight of the Rock bearing down on him; and he was as pale as if he'd just slid out of some crevice in it, would slither in again when his visitor left.

'I'm delighted to meet you, at last, Everard. Heard a great deal about you, from a mutual friend.'

He didn't have to ask the friend's name. Cruance glanced at the young paymaster lieutenant who'd brought Nick to the tunnel. 'Thank you, Hobday. I'll give you a call when we've finished.'

'Right, sir.' Neither Hobday nor Cruance spoke or looked as if they belonged in the Navy. Cruance turned to Nick, as the door shut. 'Please sit down, my dear fellow . . . I'd offer you coffee or something, but we're not *quite* that well-organised, as yet.'

'Just moved in?'

'I'm what they rather quaintly refer to as the "advance party".' He sat down, facing Nick across a littered desk. 'I have to see to it that it all does become organised by the time Sir Andrew Cunningham gets here—'

'A B Cunningham?'

'His very self.' That quirky smile again. 'Although my boss so far has been Admiral Wishart.'

Hobday had mentioned Wishart, in the car on the way to this subterranean headquarters. *Harbinger* had only just secured at the oiling berth when he'd arrived. There'd been a signal allotting berths to which *Harbinger, Goshawk* and *Watchful* were to move when they'd completed fuelling, and the one to *Harbinger* had added that orders would be arriving 'by hand of officer'. The officer turned out to be a tubby, freckle-faced 'paybob', but he'd brought no orders, only a message.

'Captain Cruance's compliments, sir—'

'Who's Captain Cruance?'

'Staff Officer (Operations), sir . . . He'd be grateful if you could find time to call in at his office, at your convenience. He has all the details there, and he'd like the opportunity to – well, discuss certain plans which involve you, sir.'

'You say he's Staff Officer (Operations). Whose staff?'

'It's – a very new set-up sir. I think he'd prefer to explain it to you himself.'

Mysterious, and distinctly irregular. Hobday had added, pointing towards the end of the jetty beyond the oiling installation, 'I have transport here, sir, if you were free to come at once. Otherwise if you'd name a convenient time after you've shifted berth, I could come whenever—'

'I'll come now.' Tony Graves could take her into the other basin: it would be good for him to get in some ship-handling practice. And the sooner one could find some answers to current questions, the better . . . He asked Hobday, who was driving the car himself despite the fact it had roundels painted on its doors and evidently belonged to the RAF, 'Who did you say this Captain Cruance is SO(O) to?'

The paymaster had hesitated before he answered.

'I was rather simplifying, sir, with that SO(O) answer. His immediate boss is actually Admiral Wishart.'

'Rear Admiral Aubrey Wishart?'

A nod . . . 'But it's for Captain Cruance to explain, sir.' He'd added diffidently, 'If you don't mind?'

If Aubrey Wishart – Nick had thought then, and continued thinking now as Cruance mentioned him – if Wishart was behind this, or involved, there had to be some sense in it. Wishart was a very old friend, about the oldest and best he had in the Navy. He'd been on Admiral Cunningham's staff in the Eastern Mediterranean, when Nick had been commanding a destroyer flotilla there, and one had heard since that they'd moved him to some desk job in the Admiralty when Cunningham had transferred, six or seven months ago, to become the Royal Navy's representative on the Combined Chiefs of Staff Committee in Washington.

He asked Cruance, 'Is Admiral Wishart coming here?'

'No.' The white head wagged. 'He's holding the fort in London. But Admiral Cunningham will be on his way quite soon, and I've so much to do before he gets here that frankly it's nightmarish. We're sharing this tunnel with the RAF, which puts space at a premium – quite apart from its being so frightfully damp and airless. I *hope* I may be able to get some improvement made, somehow . . . But as well as ourselves and the Air Force, the offices on the other side of the tunnel are all reserved for Americans. Notably a General Dwight D Eisenhower.'

'I don't think I've heard of him.'

'Well, the only ones any of us have heard of so far are in the Pacific area, aren't they. But you'll hear plenty of this chap, if things go right.' He blinked, as the corollary struck him. 'Or for that matter, if they go wrong!'

'Combined Op, is it?'

'What makes you think so?'

'A Yank general isn't coming for the fishing. And I was at Tail o' the Bank in the Clyde a few days ago. Packed with all sorts of stuff – including LSTs. Also carriers.'

Cruance nodded. 'The enemy's noticed some of that, too.'

'I'm not surprised.' It would have been difficult for an alert enemy *not* to have discovered such a concentration of ships. But the only discernible expression on Cruance's face was one of mild satisfaction. Nick asked him, 'Doesn't it worry anyone?'

'If our guess is right – and it's an *informed* guess – they'll be divided in their opinions as to whether we're mounting a very large Malta convoy or an assault on Dakar.'

'Why should they think Dakar?'

'Perhaps they've reason for it. They could have been fed some clues that point to it?'

'I see.'

'It's rather my line of country, actually. I'm basically NID, Naval Intelligence, but my speciality is deception. Of course here and now I'm a Jack of all trades – including furniture removals, interior decoration—'

'Where will the landing be?'

'Ah . . . Well, Sir Nicholas, at risk of boring you by stating what must be self-evident, I must say that all this is Top Secret: indeed, it's Hush Most Secret, in the newer vernacular. I'm sorry, but I'm obliged to make the point . . . And the only reason I'm about to impart a certain amount of this secret information is that you're cast for a rather special role in the operation, and you'll need to have the broad picture in mind. But it is very, very important that we maintain the strictest possible security. We're going to considerable lengths to do so. For instance, only about three people now on the Rock know that ABC is coming here. He's taking passage in a cruiser, from Plymouth, and the impression is being given that after a call here he'll be continuing in her to the United States. It's a much bigger and more important operation than you can yet have guessed, and I'm bound to emphasise that in the area of security *nothing* should be risked. For instance, and with all respect, I'd suggest that nobody in your ship, other than yourself, should know anything at all about it. You could be sunk, men picked up—'

'If nobody else knew what to do, and I dropped dead of a heart-attack?'

'We'll just say prayers for your continuing robust health.'

'I'd suggest that *Goshawk*'s captain, Lieutenant-Commander Audsley—'

'You won't have either *Goshawk* or *Watchful* with you on this job.'

Nick stared at him. Cruance explained, 'You'd have taken *Bruce* with you, from here. I'm – *very* sorry about *Bruce*, by the way. I should have said so at the beginning . . . But the other two have a more humdrum task ahead of them, you see, as part of a screening force, and those are plans I can't even dream of interfering with . . . You must know as well as anyone how short of destroyers we are – at the best of times, which this certainly is *not*, with demands soaking up everything we've got!'

'Hence the disbanding of my group. Just as we were beginning to amount to something.'

Cruance caught the tone, and the feeling behind it.

'I know . . . We heard, moreover, that you sank three U-boats during your last eastbound convoy. Most impressive. And an extremely regretable necessity – I mean this temporary disbanding.'

'Can we be sure it's temporary?'

'We can be sure that's the intention . . . But incidentally, Admiral Wishart – and I understand Admiral Cunningham too – was surprised to hear you were back in small ships. You had a cruiser – *Defiant* – which you succeeded in extracting from the Java Sea débâcle?'

He nodded.

'Admiral Wishart has been somewhat out of touch in recent months, deeply involved in planning some peripheral elements of this operation, and he was surprised because he'd been under the impression that you'd have remained a cruiser captain, after such an achievement – or even gone on to – higher things . . .' Cruance had shot him a quick glance: assessing the results of that little hint. He wouldn't have seen any reaction at all. Nick recognised – and dismissed immediately – the carrot that was being held out, and which in effect was meaningless, coming from this character . . . And in other respects he was baffled – some enormous landing operation in which he'd have some highly individual role, so individual that he'd be carrying it out – apparently – with a command consisting of just one destroyer?

Cruance said, after a few seconds' finger-drumming on the desk, 'I think the best way to approach this is to start by describing the broad essentials of the operation. Then when I come down to detail of your own sideshow, you'll see it's of very considerable importance.'

Nick thinking, *Sideshow* . . . Cruance getting to his feet. 'I've a chart in the safe here. Excuse me . . .'

But he'd forgotten his keys. He came back for them, muttering self-critically. Then he was at the safe again, mumbling as he tried one key after another, 'You'll see the whole shooting-match at a glance, from this . . .'

He was more of an absent-minded professor than a naval officer. Nick asked him, 'Do I gather this is something I take *Harbinger* to do on her own?'

'Not – exactly . . .' He'd hit on the right key, at last. 'No. You'll be sailing from here on your own, but you'll be joining – taking command of – a large number of . . . er . . . others. But—' he had a rolled chart in his hand, and he was swinging the heavy door shut – 'let me give you the outline picture first.'

He sat down. Glanced round, at the closed door of the office: turned back to Nick, and spoke in a lower tone.

'The code-name for the operation is "Torch". It's a joint British and American invasion of French North Africa. We're going into Morocco and Algeria – not a raid, a full-scale invasion. The Commander-in-Chief is General Eisenhower, and the Allied Naval Commander is Admiral Sir Andrew Cunningham. There'll be more than 70,000 assault troops storming Casablanca, Algiers and Oran. Then of course a lot more follow-up, after beachheads have been secured. You'll appreciate the size of this task – the weight of manpower, equipment and supplies and the distances we have to bring them before they can be put down on those beaches?'

The problems would be staggering: the risks enormous. That much was obvious at a glance.

'Oran and Casablanca, all American. Algiers is an invasion-point only on British insistence – the Yanks didn't want to go in as far east as that. Algiers will be a joint Anglo-American assault, but it'll be the British First Army pushing on through the bridgehead. Whereas the Casablanca landings – actually they'll be at three places, north and south of Casablanca itself – are coming direct from the United States. All other convoys are from the UK. Now, let me show you . . .'

Unrolling the chart. Nick thinking how remarkable it was that an undertaking so huge in concept could be outlined to him in no more than a minute. The movement of 70,000 men across oceans and on to enemy-held coastlines. If the French did regard themselves as enemies . . . Cruance murmured, 'I should have mentioned, in case it's not obvious, that the object is to drive the Germans and Italians out of North Africa, thus opening the Mediterranean and also providing opportunities for the invasion of southern Europe. As far as North Africa is concerned, don't forget we have an army poised at the Egyptian end as well, eh?'

The desert army now on the El Alamein line, he meant. Generals Alexander and Montgomery. Rommel's drive on Egypt had stopped in late August, early September, when Montgomery had defeated him at the battle of Alam el Halfa, and since then the two sides had faced each other virtually on the Egyptian frontier. But – *poised*? If the Eighth Army had been reinforced and re-supplied to the extent that it could now be described as poised – ready to attack, roll westward across Libya as the 'Torch' invasion forces advanced eastward into Tunisia – you could see the point, all right!

'As you'll have gathered, the assaults are to be almost entirely American. The entire operation will be represented as American – although all the naval side of it inside the

Mediterranean will be ours, and the Algiers invasion too. It's considered, rightly or wrongly, that the French are less likely to oppose landings by Americans than by ourselves. Resentment lingering, supposedly, over Oran, Dakar, you know . . . But now . . .' Cruance touched the chart with a long, bony finger. 'The red-ink routes here are the tracks of convoys and naval squadrons. Nearly all, as you see, from the UK and terminating, as I've shown them here, where they converge to pass in through the Straits of Gibraltar. But that southernmost one is Assault Convoy UGF 1, direct from US ports and covered by Task Force 34. It comprises thirty-eight ships in convoy, and fifty-six escorts, with a covering force that includes three battleships, five aircraft carriers, seven cruisers – all US Navy . . .'

Red-ink convoy tracks fanned out into the Atlantic from Britain and curved southward, forming a crescent of interlocking paths over a thousand miles of sea. The American force, UGF 1 and Task Force 34, had much farther to come, right from the US east coast. That track dipped southward to the latitude of the Canaries, then turned up to loop around Madeira for the last part of its approach to the Moroccan coast.

Cruance had given him time to absorb the general pattern of it. He began to lecture again now, pointing at individual red tracks.

'Six British advance convoys, all prefixed KX. Whereas British *assault* convoys are either KMS or KMF – the S standing for slow, F for fast, as usual. Also, you'll see that four of them have an "A" or an "O" in brackets after that prefix, indicating either Algiers or Oran as destination. So we have this convoy here, for instance, in all forty-seven ships and eighteen escorts, coming from the Clyde and Loch Ewe, sailing October twenty-second and due to pass through here on November fifth and sixth. Two dates, you see, because it's in two sections, KMS(A)1 and KMS(O)1. Ditto with this fast lot – eleven and a half knots, actually – KMF(A)1 and KMF(O)1, sailing from the Clyde October twenty-sixth. In both cases the Algerian and Oran components separate west of Gibraltar and enter the Med as separate forces. Then here we have KMS2 and KMF2 . . . See the system of it?'

He nodded. It was clear enough on paper. When you tried to imagine the reality of it, it was a hell of an operation.

'This is only the first stage.' Cruance pointed out, 'There'll be an enormous amount of follow-up convoys to bring in, and they'll all need protecting. Just for the assault stage we've had to strip other convoy routes almost bare of escorts. It imposes great risks, of course, but there's no option, you see.'

Nick thought the risks to convoys elsewhere might be fairly small. Every U-boat the enemy possessed would surely be deployed against these convoys. And the result could be devastating: with so many eggs packed into so few baskets and exposed to attack over such distances . . .

'What about disruption by U-boats?'

'Ah.' Cruance nodded. 'This has been a major anxiety. To an extent, it still is.'

He pointed at the red-ink tracks. 'Apart from the fact they'll do their utmost to make a meal of it, what about sighting reports? There are bound to be some – from U-boats and aircraft – with this volume of shipping on the move. So they'll know we're coming, and even if the French don't fight wouldn't the Germans have time to send troops west through Tunisia?'

'Yes.' Cruance nodded. 'And it's where you'll be playing *your* part.' He leant over the chart. 'Possible interference by U-boats – and measures to avoid it . . . Well, to start with, we have a few red herrings laid out here and there – *and* some still to come – and I'm fairly confident we can keep the enemy confused about our intentions. So if this or that convoy or squadron did get reported by a U-boat or an aircraft, it wouldn't tell them much. They'd connect it with what they already believe – Dakar or Malta, for instance . . . Second, the routing of these convoys has been planned carefully. The slow ones are all within reach of our own shore-based air patrols – which will be intensified – and the fast ones, routed right out here as far as twenty-six degrees west, will have air cover from carriers accompanying them. For convoy defence, incidentally, we've managed to rake up about a hundred escort vessels.'

He looked as if he thought he'd proved something. But – Nick thought – if enough U-boats were deployed, and pressed their attacks home determinedly, a hundred escorts spread across this amount of shipping wouldn't cut much ice. There had to be some angle he'd missed. That, or some fairly staggering risks were being accepted.

Cruance told him, 'There's one convoy not marked here. Yours. We'll put it on now – by sleight of hand, you may say.' His voice changed, to an assumed Cockney accent. 'The quickness of the 'and deceives the eye. Now you sees it, now you don't . . .' He was unfolding a sheet of transparent paper: his narrow, long-fingered hands spread it on the chart, adjusting it so that its latitude and longitude co-ordinates fitted those on the chart. He added in his own natural voice, 'Or rather, now you *will*.'

The red tracks were still visible through the transparent paper, but a new one, green instead of red, had been superimposed on them. It started south of the Canaries and slanted up west of Madeira, crossing all the red convoy routes where they converged towards Gibraltar.

'What you're looking at, Everard, is the route of convoy SL 320. Nearly forty ships assembling now at Freetown, Sierra Leone, for convoy to UK ports. By the time you get down there the assembly will be complete and they'll be under starter's orders. You'll go there in your *Harbinger* and assume command of the convoy escort. You'll sail from Freetown on October twenty-third, and follow this route precisely. No diversions will be allowed under any circumstances.'

The green track crossed ahead of all the advance assault convoys. So if there were U-boats waiting on the assault convoy routes or anywhere near them, SL 320 from Freetown would lure them away northward – leaving safe waters for the 'Torch' convoys.

While SL 320 would be slowly shredded.

'My convoy's to act as bait?'

In a macabre way, it wasn't a bad idea. If the ends justified the means. And as this was a war not for gain but for survival, they *would* . . . Cruance protested mildly, 'I believe I'd baulk at the word "bait" . . .'

'Slow convoy, is it?'

'Well—'

Cruance hesitated . . . Nick nodded, seeing *all* the answers. He'd have put money on it here and now – slow convoy, and weak escort . . . He said, watching Cruance, 'I'm to bring a large, slow convoy right through a U-boat patrol line. Maybe more than one line? And they'll flock to the easy pickings. I'll have escorts who haven't worked together before – right? Perhaps not many of them, either? And if I'm not allowed to divert, the U-boats should find it easy to stay with me – drawing blood all the way?'

Cruance said, into a silence and while Nick was taking another look at the chart and the green-ink route, 'Bait, in normal usage of the term, implies that the material is expendable. That's not the case here. You'll be escort commander, and as usual your task will be to get the convoy through with as few losses as possible.'

'What ships will I have in my escort force?'

'I believe – some corvettes . . .'

'How many?'

'. . . and A/S trawlers . . . Numbers depend on the situation prevailing down there. Normally they have a substantial escort force, which might be drawn on, but with "Torch" in the offing . . .'

Trawlers. Through the middle of a U-boat pack, and no evasive action permitted. A weak escort would ensure that the U-boat commanders saw what a splendid chance they were being offered, and stayed with it. He had an analogy of it in his mind as he stared at Cruance – Cruance finding it difficult, evidently, to meet that stare – an image of ships like wounded swimmers leaving a trail of blood for the sharks to follow.

* * *

Taking *Harbinger* out of Gibraltar next morning, later exchanges with the white-haired RNVR captain still trickled through his memory. For instance, asked whether Aubrey Wishart had personally approved the scheme, Cruance had affirmed, 'Of course he did . . . Are you wondering how the choice happened to fall on you?'

'Obviously it was his decision. But *why*—'

'To start with it was a question of who might be available, which escort groups were already committed to "Torch" as entities and which could be split up, and so on. How to get enough escorts together and still leave a modicum of protection elsewhere has been quite a problem on its own, you see.'

Anger came in waves. He'd spent the night half sleeping and half waking, his mind struggling with the problems that lay ahead. It was pointless to seek solutions of any definitive kind before he reached Freetown and knew what ships they'd be giving him, but his brain churned independently, ignoring his attempts to stop it.

Cruance had told him, 'We produced a short-list, and as soon as Admiral Wishart saw your name on it he said "That's the man I want!"'

Would he have, Nick wondered, if he'd realised Kate might be a passenger in that convoy?

Her image had been part of the incoherent, night-long battle. And he had to take control of it now, he knew, before it led to a thousand other nightmares. This thing was bad enough without inventing far worse angles to it . . . Meanwhile, snatches of his conversation with Cruance ran intermittently through his mind: for instance, asking him – in the context of Wishart having picked him for the job – 'That snap decision was enough to break up my escort group?'

'You could put it like that, I suppose—'

'I'll put it like *this*. That it was bloody silly, extremely wasteful and quite pointless. He could have taken anyone at all—'

'Nobody *wanted* to see your group disbanded.' Cruance making heavy weather of it. 'But Admiral Wishart has a very high opinion of your abilities, and – well, obviously there'd be no point in disguising the fact that this is an undertaking which could well turn out to be exceptionally – er – *demanding* . . .'

It had been midday when he'd got back on board *Harbinger* at the berth to which Graves had shifted her – without scrapes or dents, it was a relief to find. Graves was at the gangway to meet him as he crossed it from the jetty. Nick told him, as the squeal of the bosun's call died away, 'We'll be sailing at oh-nine-hundred tomorrow. Special Sea Dutymen, and single up, oh-eight-forty-five. You can give leave to one watch.'

'Are we escorting the cruisers again, sir?'

'Only ourselves.'

'Us and *Goshawk* and—'

'*Harbinger* alone.'

He'd joined his officers in the wardroom for a drink before lunch. Mike Scarr had asked, 'May I know where we're going, sir?'

'After we've shoved off, you may.'

'I was just wondering about charts, sir.'

That old dodge. All eyes wide, all ears flapping. Nick asked the navigator, 'Is your Med folio up to date?'

Scarr said yes, it was. Nick was aware of glances being exchanged, sharp interest in the prospect of heading east. He waited a few moments, and then asked, 'And West African charts, down as far as the Cape?'

'Well, yes, that's—'

'We'll be all right, then.' He winked at Graves. Men would be going ashore this evening, and Gib was said to be thick with spies. He could have sailed that night, in darkness, but a run ashore for half the ship's company and a night's rest for the others wouldn't do them any harm.

All those huge 'Torch' convoys, of course, would be passing through these Straits during the hours of darkness.

Mr Timberlake took a glass of pink gin from the steward's silver tray. He raised it towards Nick, who'd ordered it for him. 'Your good 'ealth, sir.'

'And yours, Guns.' Timberlake was very partial to pink gin. Nick asked him, 'How many heavies did they give us at Greenock?'

The new 'heavy' depthcharges could be set to explode as deep as eight hundred feet. They were a counter to the deep-diving capability of the latest U-boats. Timberlake's facial muscles twitched, betraying sharp anxiety: he said, 'Didn't 'ave any, sir. All we got is Mark VIIs. They'd been cleared out, they said – well, all them ships there . . . I did report this, sir.'

'I remember now. But you were going to try here?'

'More 'n just *tried*, sir. I been down on my bloody knees!'

'Well. Long as we've got all the Mark VIIs we can carry . . .'

Ian Mackenzie, the doctor, enquired, 'Are we likely to be coming back here, sir?'

Nick looked at him. Mackenzie was a short, curly-headed man in his mid-twenties, and he came from Edinburgh.

'Why d'you ask?'

'Wardroom's low on sherry, sir. I wouldn't bother if we were coming back, but this is the place to get it, of course, so—'

'Better stock up. While you're at it, add two cases of Tio Pepe for my private account, would you?'

The Gibraltar Straits were well astern now, and Nick handed over the conning of the ship to Warrimer. *Harbinger* was already zigzagging, with mean course due west, revs for eighteen knots. Graves and Scarr were both in the bridge, thirsting for information – which they could have, now, to a limited extent . . . Thinking about the part he would *not* tell them, meanwhile – what it was going to be like to hold to those orders, a fixed, unvariable course no matter what losses were being inflicted: Nick glanced astern, deciding they'd come far enough to have ceased to be of interest to Nazi ship-watchers on the Spanish coast. He turned to Scarr.

'Give me a course to pass two hundred miles west of Palma in the Canaries. That'll be a run of a little more than two days. From west of Palma we'll steer for Freetown, which will take another four.'

Six and a half days' steaming altogether. Then one day in Freetown: a convoy conference and a meeting with the captains of whatever other escorts were allotted to him. The day after that would be the prescribed sailing day for SL 320.

The Tio Pepe was safely stowed in his private store now. Such a triviality to have bothered with in these circumstances, he'd thought when he was writing the cheque to Messrs Saccone and Speed last evening. Across the flat from his cabin the wardroom loudspeaker had been pumping out the familiar, slightly cloying strains of *Your's* . . . Vera Lynn, the 'Sweetheart of the Forces', featuring as prominently as always in the programme called *Forces' Favourites*: the mess-decks would have been booming to it too . . . Graves asked him, 'What happens after Freetown, sir?'

'It's as far as we go. We'll be picking up a convoy there and taking it home with us.'

Scarr looked puzzled as he moved away, heading for his chartroom to lay off those courses. Graves murmured, 'All that way on our own, just for *that*?'

Nick stared at him. Graves frowned. 'Sorry, sir.' He was embarrassed. 'Only it seems so – well—'

'I know how it seems.'

He'd asked Cruance yesterday, pressing a question that had gone unanswered earlier, 'How many corvettes am I likely to get?'

'Depends what's available. There's a Freetown-based escort force which at full strength is quite large, but – as I've said already, demands on available resources are exceptionally heavy. And incidentally, a fast homebound convoy from the Cape will have veered off westward – heading for Trinidad, actually – just ahead of you.'

'Homebound from the Cape *via Trinidad*?'

Cruance had nodded. 'Yours will be the last SL convoy northbound for quite a long time. We have to keep this area as uncongested as possible, to allow for a steady flow of follow-up convoys into the North African ports, so Cape shipping will be routed across and up through the American coastal system, then home across the North Atlantic. It's a long way round, certainly, but once we have the Med open there won't be nearly as much Cape traffic anyway.'

They had it all worked out, cut and dried. Nick commented, 'You say *when* the Mediterranean's open, not *if*. As if it's a certainty.'

'But it is! As long as "Torch" is a success – which with the help of your convoy it will be.'

'Are you sure there'll be any corvettes at all down there?'

Cruance had left his chair and begun to pace up and down. Stooping, with his hands clasped behind his back. Muttering, 'Everard – now, listen . . . You seem to me to be over-dramatising this. You appear to assume you'll suffer heavy losses. It isn't necessarily so, however. Your function – I make this point with all deference to you as an experienced and accomplished seaman – will, as always, be to protect your ships, to ensure their – what's the phrase – safe and timely arrival . . . Now, the possibility that you may attract the attentions of any U-boats who in twelve to fifteen days' time may happen to be on your convoy's route is obviously a real one. But for heaven's sake, a large proportion of convoys today do still have escorts who haven't trained together! And the long-distance slow convoys do tend to have coal-burning trawlers among their escorts. It's advantageous, isn't it, from the point of view of their endurance, over those long hauls? But here's another point I'd like to make. Every man who puts to sea in wartime knows the risks he's running. *Whatever* kind of ship or convoy he's in . . . What it amounts to, surely, is that while the routing and timing of convoy SL 320 may well contribute substantially to the success of "Torch", the risks and chances will be the same that any other convoy runs!'

'Were you a barrister, in civvy street?'

Cruance had stared at Nick in surprise. Then he smiled, and bowed. 'My eloquence has betrayed me?'

'No. Not your eloquence.'

* * *

By midnight on the second day out of Gibraltar, Madeira was fifty miles to starboard and Palma in the Canaries two hundred on the port bow. It seemed more likely that any U-boats in the area now would be on the far side of Madeira, in the four hundred mile gap between it and the Azores. But that was only a guess. *Harbinger*'s anti-submarine zigzag was being scrupulously maintained, RDF and HF/DF and asdics working twenty-four hours a day, and bridge lookouts were being harried to keep on their toes.

Nick had asked Cruance, 'What happens to your Freetown convoy if my ship gets sunk before we get there?'

'The convoy would sail with whatever escorts were available, under whichever CO might be the senior officer.'

'You mean senior trawlerman.'

Cruance had ignored that. Rightly, in a way, since there were plenty of very good men in the escort trawlers. But they didn't have the speed or the armament to do more than supplement the long-haul convoys. Not, Nick thought, that Cruance would know much about it: he was a desk man, he'd probably never even seen a trawler. He assured Nick, 'You'll get there, all right – there and back. Admiral Wishart has great faith in your powers of survival.'

It was pointless to argue. They'd been over the same ground half a dozen times already. He asked instead, 'Do we happen to know who the commodore will be?'

'A former Cunard master, name of Sandover. He's settling himself into a ship called the *Chauncy Maples*.'

'And how do I get him to accept that we can't divert, when the heat's turned on us?'

The point being that the care of any convoy was a responsibility shared, usually on give-and-take terms, between its commodore and the escort commander. Commodores were usually retired admirals, or retired senior Merchant Navy captains. Whatever their previous ranks had been, they were appointed as commodores RNR. They were responsible for the convoy's internal discipline and organisation – for the ships keeping station and observing regulations such as not showing lights at night or making excessive smoke by day, and for manoeuvring, changing formation, emergency turns, and so on. The escort commander's job was defence of the convoy against enemy attack; but a decision to change the route when there was some threat ahead would normally be a matter of agreement, often a request from the escort commander with which the commodore would comply.

Cruance nodded. 'Good question. The answer is you'll be taking the orders down there with you, and he's being warned there are special circumstances applying on which you'll have been briefed. It's been intimated to him that he should accept your decisions, particularly on routing.'

At noon on day two out of Gibraltar, Palma was a hundred miles abeam to port. A noon sunsight provided a position-line to confirm it. Scarr told him, 'We'll be two hundred miles west of Palma at midnight, sir.'

It was what he'd anticipated. 'And our course will then become – one-seven-five, roughly?'

'One-seven-seven, sir.'

The route northward with the convoy from Freetown was already laid off on the chart. For Nick's personal and private use Cruance had provided him with another tracing, a transparent overlay on which all the relevant 'Torch' movements were inked. It was the first system in reverse; while Cruance's chart displayed the 'Torch' pattern and could have SL 320's movements added to it, *Harbinger*'s chart showed only the convoy's line of advance, and Nick could check on the whereabouts of other forces by applying this overlay, with its spreading fan of red-ink tracks annotated with convoy designations, dates and times.

Scarr asked him, 'Is there something special about this lot we're collecting, sir?'

Nick had his glasses up. *Harbinger* pitching to a glassy swell rolling up from the southwest. In these conditions you'd see a periscope a long way off.

'Special?'

Everyone had the same sort of mental disquiet: a feeling of wasting time, being out of things . . . *Harbinger* began to roll as she swung to a new leg of the zigzag, pushing her stem across the lifting mounds of sea.

'Well, sir, seems peculiar being sent such a long way just to bring some convoy back. I mean, why *us* . . . Will we get the group together again some time, sir?'

'That's the intention.' He looked round at Graves, who was officer of the watch. 'I'll be in my sea cabin.'

Scarr's question – 'something special' about the convoy – had put Kate in his mind again. It was a constant, losing battle to keep her out of it.

When *Harbinger* altered course at midnight she'd already passed the Canaries-Azores line. Daylight, when it came, flushed an ocean that was losing its greenish northern tinge, beginning to shade into the blue-black of its southern reaches.

In mid-forenoon Nick was smoking a pipe on the bridge when the HF/DF bell rang. Carlish, sharing the watch with Warrimer, went to the voice-pipe.

'U-boat transmissions on bearing two-four-six, sir!'

'Range?' He looked round at Warrimer. 'Make mean course one-four-seven. Get Gritten on that set.' He knew it couldn't be PO Gritten down there now, because Gritten would never have made a report like that without including a distance in it. Carlish had got one now, though: with an ear still close to the pipe he told Nick, 'Range fifteen miles, sir.'

The alteration of thirty degrees to port was to give the U-boat as wide a berth as possible. At that range and on a bearing that had been almost on the beam to start with it wasn't strictly necessary; but he hadn't known the range, initially, and anyway there was no harm in playing safe. If there was one U-boat around, there could be more.

The bell rang again. Carlish reported, 'Petty Officer Gritten's taken over, sir. Bearing two-four-six, range sixteen.'

Nick moved to the voice-pipe, displacing Carlish.

'Captain here. Sure of that range, Gritten?'

'Yessir. Ground-wave, sixteen – well, say fifteen to seventeen. And – hold on a mo', sir . . .'

Harbinger under helm again, making a zig to port. Binoculars examining the blue horizon, finding nothing. This leg of the zigzag would leave her steering almost directly away from the reported position of the German.

Gritten called, 'Captain, sir – this one's just surfaced. And that weren't no sighting report. He's still transmitting, sir.'

When the transmission ended, Gritten would sweep around and try to pick up any other submarine that might be answering. He'd know this one had just surfaced because he was a very experienced operator and could tell the difference between transmissions over wet aerials and dry ones; in this weather there was no other reason for aerials to be wet. His other conclusion, that the U-boat wasn't passing a report of an enemy seen or heard, came from knowing that German enemy-report calls were always prefixed with a morse sequence called an E-bar.

Once PO Telegraphist Archie Gritten got himself turned to a U-boat's transmissions, he could just about tell you its captain's date of birth.

After half an hour the transmissions ceased. They'd grown fainter before they disappeared altogether, and Mike Scarr's plot of ranges and bearings during those thirty minutes showed that the U-boat had been steering north at about fifteen knots. It wasn't worth breaking radio silence to report it, especially as the Admiralty tracking room would probably have recorded every dot and dash.

'Sub.'

Carlish jumped. 'Yes, sir?'

'Petty Officer Gritten said he was getting those transmissions on ground-wave. Do you know what he meant by that?'

'Ground-wave as distinct from sky-wave, sir.'

'Meaning what?'

'Well, as confirmation that the U-boat had to be within about twenty miles of us, sir. Sky-wave transmissions are bounced off the ionosphere, so they could be coming from hundreds of miles away.'

He nodded. 'Good.'

You couldn't ever be sure, unless you checked. Youngsters tended to have gaps in their knowledge that could be hidden under a few technical phrases, and an introvert like Carlish might be embarrassed to admit ignorance, particularly if he'd disguised it in the first place. Then he'd remain ignorant, and perhaps one day make some daft mistake in consequence.

Nick told Warrimer, 'Resume mean course one-seven-seven.'

Freetown, as *Harbinger* closed in towards it on the evening of the sixth day out of Gibraltar, was a mass of dark-green forest behind a crescent of bright-yellow beach. That beach was to the left of the entrance, the estuary of the Sierra Leone River. Two shabby-looking freighters were just in the process of entering harbour: the pair of trawlers shepherding them in looked as if they were suspended above the surface, a mirage-effect in the low-lying haze of heat. Clammy, mosquito-bearing heat, like foetid breath in your face as you steamed into it.

Graves murmured, beside him and with binoculars trained on those ships, 'Couple of old rust-buckets . . .'

He was right, so far as those new arrivals were concerned. They'd have been brought up from one of the other West African ports, no doubt. But inside, out of sight from here, there'd be thirty or forty others, and among those there might be passenger ships, or anyway ships with cabin accommodation as well as cargo holds.

The signal station flashed a challenge, and Leading Signalman Wolstenholm passed *Harbinger*'s pendant numbers in reply. A longer message then came stuttering over: orders to fuel from the oiler *Redgulf Star* and then berth at Number Two buoy. A glance at the harbour plan showed they were being placed conveniently close to the naval landing-place.

'Close up Special Sea Dutymen, sir?'

'Yes, please. And tell Hawkey about the oiling.'

The *Redgulf Star* was at the far end of the anchorage, which was an estuary about two miles wide and seven long, its steamy expanse littered with moored ships. In there, twenty minutes later, with *Harbinger* forging smoothly through dead-flat, transparently-blue water, Nick was examining ship after ship and finding none in which Kate could possibly have embarked. 'Old rust-buckets' was a fair description. Many of their crewmen were on deck, escaping the heat below and draped limply along the ships' rails to watch the destroyer threading her way up-river. The town – Freetown itself, and the waterfront where the naval headquarters was situated – lay to starboard, on the southern coast of the estuary and about three and a half miles from the entrance.

He took over from Scarr at the binnacle. Stooping to the voice-pipe: 'Slow together.' He was about to take her close under the stern of a freighter of about eight thousand tons: rust-streaked and battered like all the others, she was flying a tired-looking Red Ensign, and on her stern a fat man who appeared to be naked was playing an accordion.

'Port five.'

From the wheelhouse the coxswain, CPO Elphick, acknowledged, 'Port five, sir . . .'

Scarr muttered, with his glasses up, 'That fellow's starkers.' Then he read out the ship's name and registration, which was in faded lettering across her counter. '*Chauncy Maples*. Newcastle upon Tyne.'

Strains of *Rule Britannia* floated across the water from the naked man's accordion. Nick informed Scarr and anyone else who might be interested, '*Chauncy Maples* is our commodore's ship.' He was suddenly quite light-headed with relief. From somewhere at the back of the bridge he heard Harris, a bosun's mate, suggest in a low growl, 'Reckon that's *'im* – bloke with the squeeze-box?' Laughter here and there – and Nick chuckled too, happy because the commodore would have picked the best accommodation that was available, and if the best was the *Chauncy Maples* he could have spared himself some sleepless nights. There'd have been no reason for her to have taken passage in any of these old crocks: they wouldn't have any space for passengers anyway. Scarr reported, 'I can see two Flower-class corvettes, sir. And so far I've counted nine trawlers . . . No, *three* Flowers, there's one under way, over that side.'

He thought, *Any advance on three?*

Nine corvettes and three trawlers would be more like it. He was looking around: at the glossily green hillside above the town, greenery studded with smart-looking bungalows, residences of local bigwigs. The senior officials lived well here – or would have done if it hadn't been for the heat and the rains. The rainy season had ended, obviously, but the land would have been heavily soaked throughout recent months, and the sun would now be steaming it out, maintaining the hothouse atmosphere until the next down-pour . . . He stooped again, to order the wheel amidships. Sliding past yet another war and weather-worn veteran, he was thinking that he was going to have to fight for every ship he could get. And it might not be a battle he could win. If they had only three corvettes here, they'd hardly let him take all three away. And how could you possibly do the job with fewer?

Chapter 5

20 October 1942: Prime Minister to C-in-C Middle East, General Alexander:

'Torch' goes forward steadily and punctually. But all our hopes are centred upon the battle you and Montgomery are going to fight . . . Let me have the word 'Zip' when you start.

Commodore Sandover touched Nick's arm. 'We'll have to start without him, eh?'

Without Baillie, CO of the corvette *Astilbe*, he meant. All the rest were here – thirty-six merchant-ship masters, three trawler skippers, and Guyatt, who had the other corvette, *Paeony*. Baillie had known he was expected to be here in good time for the conference to open at 1400: and time was precious, with only this one day for getting the whole show on the road . . . He asked the commodore, 'Give him another minute?'

The commodore was being very helpful – despite being puzzled, obviously aware there was something peculiar about this trip. The way the convoy of old crocks had been assembled here in dribs and drabs, and he himself kept kicking his heels for nearly a week . . . 'Then they send *you* down to nursemaid us! Practically single handed!' Nick had admitted – last night, over dinner in the *Chauncy Maples*'s dark-pannelled, worn-plush saloon – 'I agree, it's odd.' He'd decided on the spur of the moment to take the bull by the horns: 'Even odder – one point in the verbal briefing they gave me at Gib – is we're not to divert. The route's to be stuck to exactly, come hell or high water. I'd imagine it might be something to do with other fleet or convoy movements.'

'No diversions?'

Sandover had stopped eating, stared at him incredulously. He was about seventy: deeply tanned under a mop of thick white hair, eyes light-blue and lively, a young man's eyes in the seamed brown face. White eyebrows hooped: 'What if we find a wolf-pack smack on the line of advance? Walk straight into 'em, do we?'

They'd come to some useful conclusions about that 'no diversion' rule. But remembering the conversation and hearing the duplicity in his own voice, Nick was uncomfortably aware of double-dealing under the pretence of ignorance and openness . . . Just as now, looking round the packed, smoke-filled conference room, he felt isolated again in that sense of being a Judas. He of all people, the man they all looked to for protection!

Well, they'd *get* protection . . .

Last evening, after *Harbinger* had filled up her fuel tanks and then moved to her buoy, he'd taken a boat ashore, visiting the naval offices with the primary purpose of finding out what ships they'd earmarked for his escort force. The answer was two corvettes, three trawlers. Attempts to get a third corvette added to the force – Scarr had been right, there were three Flowers here at the moment – had been firmly rebuffed, despite the fact that *six* wouldn't have been even one too many . . . But there'd been no point arguing. He'd sent RPC signals instead – 'request the pleasure of your company' – to those five ships instead, inviting their captains to come aboard immediately. Baillie of *Astilbe*, Guyatt of *Paeony*, and Messrs Broad, Cartwright and Kyle of the trawlers *Stella, Gleam* and *Opal* respectively. They'd all arrived in the *Astilbe*'s motorboat, Baillie having rounded the others up. Studying them while his steward poured their drinks, Nick had wished he had a week instead of only part of one day in which to get to know them, impress on them his own ideas of convoy escort tactics, transform this bunch of highly individual characters into a like-minded team.

Cartwright of the *Gleam* was the oddest-looking of them. Rather like Long John Silver, except he had two legs and no parrot on his shoulder. But perhaps the most detached and different of them all was Lieutenant-Commander Baillie of the *Astilbe*. Nick remembered – now that the man had failed to turn up on time – that he'd had an impression of someone shut up inside himself: either aloof, or worried by private uncertainties. With an evasive quality, a way of shifting his eyes elsewhere.

A tall, red-headed skipper with a lantern jaw raised his head and voice above the racket: 'We here to do a job of work, Commodore, or is it just a bloody social?'

He'd won growls of support from all round the long trestle tables. These weren't people to be pushed into a classroom and told to wait. It wasn't only the waiting, either: it was the muggy heat, stifling atmosphere . . . Sandover was explaining, 'One man still to come, Captain. Sorry . . . If he isn't here in one minute, we'll get on with it.'

'Bugger's in the kip, most likely.' Davies, that was, the *Chauncy Maples*'s master . . . And in this climate most of them *would* have been stretched out on their bunks at this time of day. In tropical routine you knocked off at midday and turned-to again in the dog watches when it was slightly cooler: but just today, there were no hours to spare for siesta. It was a case of mad dogs and Englishmen, and it wouldn't have been at all difficult to fall asleep, Nick thought, if you'd been in a position to allow yourself that luxury. Last night's session on board the commodore's ship had been a long and late one. The invitation to dine had come when he'd been waiting for the escort captains to arrive; he'd signalled acceptance at once, because he'd only planned to give his own guests a drink or two, crack the social ice in preparation for a hard day's work to come, and this chance to do the same with the commodore wasn't to be missed.

He'd got through a lot of preliminary work with the other captains this forenoon. And Mike Scarr had been up half the night preparing material for further sessions, as well as some things for this conference. Scarr was here, and so was Tony

Graves, who'd been chatting with the commodore but was leaving him now, pushing over towards Nick while Sandover joined Harry Davies: Sandover taller and slimmer than the stocky Welshman, who as usual had a pipe between his teeth, wide-set eyes narrowed through drifting smoke. Pipe-smoke and cigarette fumes hung blue and pungent in the still, hot air. This was only a hut, a prefabricated addition to the sprawl of the naval base, and its ventilation wasn't up to coping with the climate or the number of human beings crammed into it now. At this end, where a blackboard and easel stood on a small platform, there was even a stove, a black object as grimly threatening as some instrument of torture. Graves reached Nick, and told him, "Commodore says we ought to start, sir, or when *Astilbe*'s skipper does turn up he may get lynched.'

'Serve him right. Except we need him.' Nick shrugged: he hadn't wanted to start before Baillie came, because whatever was said in here needed to be heard by everyone concerned. 'All right. Tell him I agree. In fact he's been very patient.'

'Captain Everard, sir?'

Turning, he found a young RNVR lieutenant at his elbow.

'I'm Marvin, sir, first lieutenant of *Astilbe*. Bad news, sir – my skipper's collapsed and he's been taken to the base hospital. I'm sorry I couldn't get word to you before, sir, but we've been—'

'Anyone know what's wrong with him?'

'Some stomach thing, sir, could be appendix or—'

'Damn.' He looked at Graves: both of them appreciating that there could hardly have been a worse time or situation. Possible alternatives – instinctive reaction was to look at once for answers to a problem that might well become insoluble, in a place like this – might be to arrange for the CO of the corvette they were keeping here – *Calliopsis* – to move to *Astilbe*: or for *Calliopsis* to join the escort instead of *Astilbe*. Two things were certain: first, he couldn't afford to lose one of his only two corvettes, and second, this lad Marvin, behind whose ears you could almost see the wet shine, couldn't conceivably take over the command . . . Another thought was that Baillie had most likely had some illness coming on, had been in pain and trying to ignore it, keep going: so in terms of his own recent thinking he probably owed the man an apology . . . Nick went over to Sandover, to give him the news and invite him to set the convoy conference ball rolling.

He watched the audience, while Sandover reeled off the usual preliminary stuff – importance of effective ship-darkening at night and of keeping funnel-smoke to a minimum by day; restrictions on the ditching of gash – meaning the dumping overboard of garbage – because floating rubbish could provide a trail for a U-boat to find and follow . . . Then signal routines, W/T wavelengths, use of alarm rockets and 'snowflakes', siren signals for emergency turns, and the drill for turns, the importance of maintaining station in the convoy . . .

Many of the captains wore the bored, ironic expressions of men who'd heard it all dozens of times before and knew most of it by heart. The convoy system, to most of them, was an evil necessity; they weren't the sort to enjoy being regimented. Two of the older hands were already asleep, and others dozed occasionally, waking with jerks and grunts . . . You could hardly blame them, in this atmosphere . . . Nick looking at Guyatt now, CO of *Paeony*: he at any rate was awake. A small, dark man with a West Country drawl. The trawler skippers sat in a bunch beside him. Broad of the *Stella* – an RNR lieutenant-commander, a huge man, getting on in years and grey not only round the edges – was next to him, and on Broad's left was the piratical-looking Cartwright of the *Gleam*, one-eyed, sporting a black patch, and always with a black cheroot clamped between his teeth. He was a lieutenant-commander too, the RNR stripes on his khaki shirt as frayed as if a dog had chewed them. Then Kyle of the *Opal*, a complete contrast to that pair – slight, quick-eyed, with greased black hair, a hand-rolled cigarette damp between nicotine-stained fingers.

The proof of that pudding, Nick thought, would be at sea, where all of them belonged. But however good they might be as seamen, as convoy escorts their contribution was likely to be small. You'd often find one trawler, even two, as makeweight in a screen, but to have half the force made up of them was – well . . . He switched his attention back to Sandover, who was referring his audience to the convoy plan, a diagram of which was in each captain's sheaf of papers. Detailing rescue ships: they'd be the *Timaru*, number 35, and the *Leona*, number 65. The figure 65 meant the *Leona*'s position in convoy would be fifth (rearmost) ship in the sixth column from the left. The convoy would be disposed in eight columns, each five ships long, except that in the whole chequerboard diagram there'd be four vacant billets.

The master of the *Leona* was the red-headed individual who'd complained about the delay in starting. He'd begun complaining now about being saddled with the rescue duty, but others were shouting him down. Even one of the two grey-headed captains who'd slept until now had opened bloodshot eyes to rasp 'You might as well lump it an' like it, old son!' – then relapsed into what appeared again to be sleep. It might have been only a way of detaching himself from the crowd while he listened. Sandover announced, 'Vice-Commodore'll be Captain Stileman, *Dongola*, number five-one. All right with you, Captain?' A crewcut, greying head nodded: it had obviously been agreed earlier. 'And Rear-Commodore will be Jack Osborne of the *Ilala*. That's number seventy-one.' Osborne, a bald man with a paunch; raised a hand in acknowledgement. Scarr was taking notes, for Nick, of anything that wasn't already in the duplicated orders. Vice and Rear commodores were substitute leaders, reserves who'd take over the job if it became vacant – if the *Chauncy Maples*, then Stileman's *Dongola*, should be torpedoed.

'Now, gentlemen – before I hand over to Captain Everard, our very distinguished escort commander, I want to mention that it's likely there'll be U-boats somewhere around the Azores-Canaries stretch. That's going by current Intelligence.

So we need to be ready for a dust-up, and I'm warning you here and now that when we get out there—' he waved a hand seaward – 'I'm going to drill you until you can manoeuvre like a platoon of bloody guardsmen. We'll stick to it until I'm good and sure you've got the hang of it: so how long it lasts will be entirely up to you.'

Groans. A grumble from the carrot-headed man, the *Leona*'s master . . . Nick was on his way up to the stand. He introduced himself and then the other escort captains individually, and pointed out on a diagram, which Scarr had prepared on the back of an old chart, the station each ship would occupy in relation to the convoy. With the spread of escorts – for instance, *Harbinger* would be four thousand yards astern of the convoy's rear, *Paeony* and *Astilbe* six thousand yards ahead of its van – the total width of the assembly would be five and a half miles, depth nearer six. More than thirty square miles of sea would be occupied by the advancing convoy. Trawlers would assist in rescue work when necessary and practicable: but the corvettes would not . . .

'I'm telling you this because I don't want you to get the wrong end of the stick and think you're being neglected. I've only my own destroyer and the two corvettes – I *hope* I'll have as many as two – to act as strikers, hit out at the enemy before he's in a position to hit *you*. This is the tactic that will be basic to all our movements.' He saw some nods, some shrugs. He went on, 'Commodore Sandover told you it's likely there'll be U-boats in the Azores area or thereabouts. I'd say it's more than likely, it's damn near certain. On the other hand I've been warned that the convoy must hold to the planned route, with no diversions. The commodore and I discussed this last night, and we decided we'll interpret it as meaning we can take evasive action when we have to, but each time we'll steer ourselves back on to the ordered route as quickly as possible thereafter. I believe—' he held up a hand, asking a questioner to wait – 'I *believe* the reason for that no-diversion order must be other fleet or convoy operations somewhere close to our route. So we do have to bear it in mind: and one thing that's for sure is we can't have any straggling. I do mean *none*. I know, you get told this every time you attend one of these conferences, but this time it's absolutely vital: you *must* all maintain station and hold the convoy tightly together.'

It was about as honest, he thought, as he could allow himself to be. He finished, a few minutes later, with 'That's all from me, you'll be glad to hear. Any questions now, either for me or for your commodore?'

There were a few: but none, thank God, that really put him on the spot. One he'd been half-expecting had been what would happen to a ship with serious engine trouble, total breakdown even, if no straggling was to be permitted? The answer would have been that no ship was to be left afloat astern of the convoy, to attract U-boats into waters that should by that time have been cleared of them. Ships would hold their stations in convoy, or be sunk. It would happen, because without it the whole deception plan would fall to pieces, but these men didn't have to know it yet. And Nick's thoughts were already moving – as the questions petered out – to concentrate on the next essential, to find a solution to the problem of *Astilbe* having no commanding officer. He had just over an hour now before the escort captains were due to muster on board *Harbinger* again: there were still points of tactics to discuss, explain, drive home, and if time permitted they'd move up to the plot, later, and play the convoy-escort game which Graves and Scarr had devised and operated for the group's training up north. Beer-bottle tops for merchantmen, matchsticks for U-boats, paper-clips for escorts . . . But the *Astilbe* crisis had to be settled first.

'Number One – if I'm not on board when they arrive, don't let them just sit around, carry on from where we finished this morning . . . And one thing – get figures for each ship's depth-charge outfit, including how many heavies, if any. The corvettes *may* have some . . . I'll join you as soon as possible – all right?'

* * *

Astilbe's captain was suffering from a strangulated hernia. Or rather, had been suffering from it: the base surgeon had already operated, in time to save Baillie's life, but he'd be out of action for a long time now.

'Can I borrow *Calliopsis*' captain to replace him?'

No, he could not. *Calliopsis* would be the only corvette remaining in Freetown, and she'd be no use without someone to drive her.

'Well, what about letting me take *Calliopsis*, and you keep *Astilbe* here?'

'Really, Everard—'

'If she's only wanted for local patrol work, harbour defence and so on, that first lieutenant of Baillie's might—'

'Out of the question, I'm afraid. In point of fact he's only *acting* first lieutenant, anyway. And before you suggest it, *Calliopsis*' first lieutenant couldn't be transferred, either. You know what demands have been made on us just lately, Everard, though heaven knows what's in the wind: and we're stripping ourselves down to a handful of trawlers and one sea-going corvette, this for a major convoy port of call and with a fairly considerable U-boat offensive brewing!'

'I know . . . But – well, d'you have any officer on the staff here, or anywhere around, who'd be qualified to command a corvette?'

They went through the motions of racking brains, but the answer came up as a flat negative.

Nick argued, quietly and desperately, 'I can't take this bunch north with only one corvette. Even with two, and positive Intelligence reports of a U-boat concentration near the Azores – well, for Pete's sake . . .'

But the convoy had to sail. He knew it. Ironically, he alone of all of them knew why, too. In fact if he'd had no corvettes at all, only trawlers, he'd still have had to start. He was stone-walling, fighting for the best deal he could get, and the man across the desk from him did know *that*. What he did not know – one of a lot of things he had no inkling of whatsoever – was that four days ago, 18 October, 'Torch' advance convoy KX2 would have left the Clyde. Eighteen ships with thirteen escorts, bound for Gibraltar at seven knots: ammunition ships, tankers, freighters with cased aircraft on their decks. Another, smaller convoy would have left the day after. An earlier lot would already have reached Gib – which would be filling up, by now, getting busy – and today, 22 October, the first of the great assault convoys would be setting out. None of which was mentionably Nick's or the Freetown convoy's business: but the need to put a commanding officer into *Astilbe* was – since these people seemed unable to help at all – *entirely* his business.

And suddenly the answer was in his mind. As if it had been there all the time, had chosen this moment to surface . . .

There were complications, of course. Formalities – permissions to be obtained, signals to be made to various authorities – regular, recognised authorities, since it wasn't possible to mention Wishart or A B Cunningham or that rock-lizard Cruance. But he'd pointed out that if Baillie had collapsed after they'd sailed from here, he'd have taken precisely this action without asking for anyone's approval: so what the hell . . .

The muggy heat shortened tempers and patience, perhaps even baked brains a little. Which perhaps explained why he hadn't hit on this obvious solution in the first place.

He was back on board *Harbinger* just as the other captains were mustering. Tony Graves was settling them on chairs around the table in the day cabin, and issuing them with signal pads and pencils while Foster offered cups of tea. Nick began to tell them about Baillie's strangulated hernia, but they knew it already, since Guyatt of *Paeony* had been to the hospital and talked to the surgeon who'd operated. He hadn't seen Baillie, who in any case would still have been unconscious.

'He'll survive, all right, but it was touch and go, apparently. The doc said it'll be a month before he'll be allowed to do more than blink.' Guyatt asked Nick, 'So what happens now, sir?'

'The obvious thing. *Astilbe* gets a new captain.'

He sat down in the armchair which Graves had positioned

centrally for him. An electric fan was whirring and all the scuttles were wide open, but it was still uncomfortably hot. A wise man learnt to sit still, not think about it, reduce physical exertion to a minimum, even desist from mopping at sweat too often. The hot tea made you sweat but in the long run its effect was cooling. Nick looked round at Graves, who'd been hovering, trying to get a private word in. 'What is it, Tony?'

'Would you excuse me from this meeting, for about the first hour, sir? There are a few things I haven't had a chance to get at yet, and if we're sailing at first light—'

'Certainly.' He nodded. 'But whatever's on your plate, pass it to Warrimer. He's to take over as first lieutenant immediately. Chubb had better take over asdics. While you're handing over to them, your servant can be packing your gear. The appropriate signals are being made now, appointing you in command of *Astilbe*. The sooner you can get yourself over to her, the better, but you and I need to put our heads together, so if you care to invite me to dinner tonight I'll accept with pleasure.'

Graves looked as if he'd been sandbagged. An expression of astonishment, then alarm . . . It was disappointing, in fact, to see him looking more shocked than pleased: he should have been wanting this, seeing the opportunity and bucking for it. Instead he was muttering over a buzz of congratulation and good wishes from the others, 'Aye aye, sir. Thank you, sir . . .' Stammering, tongue-tied: 'I'll – do my best to make a go of it. But—'

'But?'

'Well, I'm sorry to be – well, leaving you, sir, even for such a—'

'You won't be leaving me, Tony. You'll be very much with me. The great advantage for me, in fact, is I'll have one CO in this group who'll know exactly what I expect of him.' Nick told the others, 'That's no reflection on the rest of you. The fact is we're still strangers to each other. Which, come to think of it, is why we now have to get down to some more hard work . . .'

* * *

It was past midnight when *Astilbe*'s motorboat returned him to *Harbinger*'s gangway, at Number Two buoy. It had been a well-spent evening: his presence had lessened the potential awkwardness of this sudden arrival of a brand-new CO, and he'd seen to it that his own confidence in Graves became obvious to *Astilbe*'s wardroom officers. Then, alone with Graves after dinner, they'd had a useful session, tying-up various loose ends.

Back in his own ship, he paced the quarterdeck for a while with his new first lieutenant, who'd been at the gangway to meet him. It was no surprise to him that Warrimer, whose elevation had been just as sudden and unexpected as Graves', was taking to it like a duck to water. Warrimer needed no reassurance at all, he was plainly revelling in his greatly increased responsibilities.

Mike Scarr might find the change a bit difficult at first, Nick thought, after he'd sent Warrimer down to turn in. Scarr being RN – as distinct from Warrimer with his temporary commission – and only junior in seniority as a lieutenant by a matter of weeks. Nick realised he'd need to keep an eye on that.

If time permitted any such attention to domestic detail . . . He'd stopped his pacing, right aft beside the depth-charge racks, staring out across the dark but gleaming anchorage. Still, velvet-warm night air under a brilliantly starry sky – which was what gave the flat, black surface of the estuary its shine . . . Well, there'd be a settling-down period, a day or two – even four or five, possibly – before the convoy ran into opposition. With a speed of advance of only seven and a half knots, it would take a week to reach the latitude of the Canaries. That rate of progress was of course dictated by the performance of the slowest ships in the convoy, but in fact the escorting trawlers wouldn't do much better. Ten knots was as much as could reasonably be expected of them. Which meant that if a trawler lagged behind or was separated for any reason, it would take her a long time to catch up, with only a two-and-a-half-knot margin. They were supposed to be twelve knotters: but that had been years ago, thousands of steamed miles ago. The trawlers would provide the convoy's close defence. Each was fitted with asdics, had a four-inch gun on her foc'sl, a couple of machine-guns amidships and a depth-charge chute on her stern. They'd plot along in close attendance on the merchantmen while *Harbinger* and the two corvettes roamed farther afield to act as striking force. Not that the Flowers with their flat-out maximum of 15 knots were ideal for that role, either, when the U-boats they'd be fighting could make a good two knots more; but the Flowers were what he had, *all* he had, and the weaker your defence – he believed – the more necessary it became to take the offensive, smash the assaults before they could be pressed home. He thought Guyatt of *Paeony* fully understood this principle and how to apply it, now; and Graves certainly did.

A faint breeze momentarily dulled the surface shine. The quarterdeck sentry shifted, his rifle-butt thumping against a stanchion. Nick had exchanged a few words with him earlier. Resuming his slow pacing, he noticed the outline on X gundeck of a camp-bed that probably contained young Carlish. It reminded him – he'd meant to tell Warrimer – Mr Timberlake could stand one bridge watch per day, with Carlish to back him up, and for one dog watch each day Carlish could be on his own, although Nick would make a point of being near at hand. If that worked out, by the end of this trip Carlish might rate a watchkeeping certificate, and thereafter earn his pay more usefully than he could at present. This had been Tony Graves' suggestion, this evening.

An interesting character, Graves. Motivated by a desire to serve, rather than by any personal ambition? Nick had seen him more clearly in the last few hours than he had in all the recent months. Graves seemed to be governed by an innate modesty, limitations he imposed on his own opinion of himself: and when you thought about this it was difficult not to see also in your mind's eye that dumpy little wife of his. Because of the – well, 'homespun' quality they shared? They were very much a pair of the same breed . . . Which didn't match Graves' sharp expertise as an asdic man, or the other attributes gained through years of sea and war experience; but Graves was himself unaware of any such qualities – as yet . . . He'd sheltered, always, behind a leader's shoulder: even in civilian life – *assistant* miller, taking little of the kudos but most likely the lion's share of the work, in some factory churning out breakfast cereals, for God's sake . . . As expert in the science of milling as in the art of submarine detection?

He'd learn now, discover talents he didn't yet realise he possessed. Command would change him, probably for life. Nick wondered whether Mrs Graves would mind.

He still didn't feel like sleep. In this single day an enormous amount of ground had been covered, and the echoes of it were buzzing around inside his skull – all the talking, wrangling, planning, instructing and advising . . . That, on top of the upheaval and uncertainties of the past fortnight. And Kate: but he didn't want to speculate about Kate – her whereabouts, anything at all – until this thing was finished. There wasn't room for her, not now: if he let her in at all she'd take more than her fair share. He forced a change of thinking quickly, to the fact – the handicap – that the three trawlers weren't equipped with TBS, the talk-between-ships VHF radio link, so that communications with them could only be conducted through the time-consuming routines of visual signalling, laboriously flashing messages to each ship in turn.

Reaching the stern again, he spoke to the sentry's dark silhouette. 'I'm going below now, Crosby.'

'Aye aye, sir. Goodnight, sir.' Crosby reminded him – as if he might have been thinking it was high time his skipper *did* turn in – 'Not much kip-time left now, sir.'

'I'm afraid you're right.'

Sailing time was set for dawn. In fact the trawlers would be on the move well before the light came, to carry out an anti-submarine sweep offshore. They'd be out there and working when *Harbinger* slipped from her buoy, and *Astilbe* and *Paeony* formed up astern to follow her seaward; the merchantmen would by that time be weighing anchors –

steam capstans clanking, stinking black mud splashing from slowly-rising cables. As daylight flushed the estuary with colour the ships would be crowding west, out past Cape Sierra Leone and into open sea where gradually, after a fair amount of hectoring by the commodore and chivvying by the escorts, the whole motley assortment would form itself into the single entity to be known as SL 320.

Chapter 6

> *23 October 1942: Commander-in-Chief Middle East to Prime Minister:*
> Zip!
> *Prime Minister Winston Churchill to President Roosevelt:*
> The battle in Egypt began tonight at 8 PM London time. The whole force of the Army will be engaged. I will keep you informed.

Max Looff, Kapitanleutnant, dragged out of sleep by the shriek of his submarine's alarm bell, moved instantly by reflex – jack-knifing to hurl himself off the bunk, the noise like a torture in his fogged brain while awareness grew inside like a negative taking form in the developing liquid: this alarm – ten to one it was an aircraft attack – the long, nerve-wracking patrol and his own sick worry growing: but only hours short of docking in St Nazaire now, thank God – or rather, *please* God . . . Main vents had crashed open and before that he'd heard distantly the yell of 'Dive, dive, dive!' The deck was angling by the time his feet landed on it, U 122's bow dropping steeply, men rushing to their action stations skidding and jostling, and Looff glimpsed – as sudden and startling as party-goers caught unaware in camera flashes – fright, desperation, in the pale, drawn, stubbled or bearded faces of men already close to their limits. You saw it only for an instant before the individual reasserted control, faces turning to masks again, and Looff hoping to God that none of them focusing on him one or two seconds ago as he pushed out through the green curtain that shut off his tiny cabin-space might have seen that same fright mirrored: eyes wide, mouth slackened . . . It had drawn tight now, into a slit like a sabre-cut: he was in the control room and the bridge lookouts – and Oelricher who'd been officer of the watch – were sorting themselves out of a heap on the deck, under the lower hatch in a mess of water that would have sloshed down as she dipped into the waves, while Oelricher had still been pulling the lid down over his soused head. Fourteen metres on the depthgauges: Franz Walther, Looff's chief engineer and right-hand man, was busy with the trim.

'Blow Q!'

Q being the quick-diving tank, flooded to get the boat down fast. It had done its job, she was going down *too* fast.

'Brit aircraft, sir.' Oelricher – he was quartermaster, which in the U-boat context meant warrant officer and navigator – answered Looff's unspoken question. 'Bomber – Wellington, I'd guess, but I didn't wait to—' shaking his head, still short of breath: 'Came out of nowhere – well, low cloud, but straight for us, as if—'

The sea began to explode, astern. U 122 like a drum being smashed or a ball kicked point-blank against a wall. Bombs, or very shallow-set charges. Men were being flung about: Looff, hugging the long barrel of the search periscope as his submarine tilted until she was almost standing on her nose, plummeting down, saw the depth-gauge needles jerking to the blasts of pressure. Then realised as the reverberations died away that she was still vibrating, the whole ship trembling violently enough to shake herself apart, and noise from the stern like a giant knife-grinder.

'Stop both motors!'

Noise and vibration ceased so promptly that he knew the men back aft must have pulled the switches of their own accord before that order could have reached them. Either the screws had been damaged – blades bent or blown off – or the shafts had been bent. Or both.

'After ends report bad leaking, sir!'

Eighty-seven metres on the gauges. Ninety . . .

'Get her snout up, for Christ's sake!'

'Blow number one main ballast, sir?'

He nodded to Walther. The engineer was bearded and incredibly dirty, but his brown eyes were calm. Looff envied him: and was more than ever conscious of the degree to which he relied on him. Scruffy bastard though he was . . . He heard the rush of high-pressure air, a noise as harsh as sand-blasting in the narrow pipe. There'd been something said about leaks aft: he guessed it would be the stern glands again, where the propeller-shafts passed through the pressure-hull. They'd had trouble with them earlier in this patrol, first during a counter-attack after U 122 and some others had mauled a convoy south of Iceland, and then again – worse, and with other major damage too – farther west, during a long, very unpleasant depth-charging close to Newfoundland.

Walther had been blowing the forward main ballast tank for nearly half a minute, and she hadn't responded at all. Steep bow-down angle, needles sweeping round the gauges. Hundred and five metres: something as wrong as hell . . . 'Blow two and three main ballast!'

Faces like trapped animals'. Sweating with nerves. Frightened animals, all in the same cage and perhaps about to drown. He himself – inside himself – as screwed-up as any of them, and the worst and deepest fear was the nightmare of this being recognised. Externally at this moment all they'd see would be the straight gash of a mouth, hard eyes, strong jaw. Even a smile – as demanded by his reputation. He was also supposed to smile when ships burned. He'd done so once, apparently, even though he had no recollection of it and could only think it had been a grimace which someone had wrongly interpreted: but whenever he hit a tanker, in particular, they all looked for that grin, for the way they wanted him to be. They were kids, most of them eighteen, nineteen, twenty years old, only the POs and CPOs older than that: they wanted a fable, a skipper they could boast about to their girls. And he'd given them a tanker, this trip, with a grin to match: he'd also knocked down one straggler, and two other freighters out of that convoy close to

Canada . . . The slight smile began to form now as he remembered a little catch-phrase that had gone around and was still quoted: 'For Max Looff it's *always* the happy time!' Then his smile switched off completely: he shouted, pointing furiously, *'Main vents, you fucking idiot!'*

You could see from the indicators on the panel – the vents were still open. All that air had been blown straight out to sea!

Vents thudding shut now. Walther scarlet under dirt and beard. Walther of all people – probably the shrewdest and most conscientious engineer Looff had ever sailed with. Looff glaring at him in white-hot rage: fists bunched, eyes blazing, on the brink of losing control, physically attacking him. It was the sort of carelessness, stupidity, that you'd have skinned some half-baked recruit for: from a man of Walther's experience and expertise it came closer to sabotage, dereliction of duty, *criminal* carelessness . . .

'Stop blowing!'

The boat was levelling, and Walther was directing the two planesmen – on the fore planes, five degrees of dive . . . The gauges showed 130 metres, and the descent had been checked. They'd been deeper than this before now, of course, quite a lot deeper, but the Type VII C was only tested to 90 metres. Besides which Oelricher had called a warning from his chart-table a few minutes ago: 'We're in eighty-six fathoms, sir . . .' 86 fathoms being about 172 metres: so another forty of that headlong rush and she'd have slammed into the bottom.

'I'm—' Walther glancing round, shaking his head – 'extremely sorry, sir. Don't know *how* I could've—' His voice had a shake in it, too. He'd turned back: he had his hands full with the trim, to get her up now out of danger – because with weak spots, leaks such as they had aft and other points of strain from those earlier batterings, this depth *was* dangerous – and to do it in a controlled manner he'd need to get rid of some of that air in the main ballast tanks. The submarine's bow was already rising to an extent that the forward planesman, with maximum dive on now, was finding impossible to control . . . 'Permission to crack number one main vent, sir?'

Looff barely heard. He was still glaring at him . . . Then the engineer looked round again: Looff swallowed, mumbled 'Affirmative', and turned away as if he couldn't stand the sight of him. Walther, the man he'd trusted, relied on, more than any other. All right, so in a U-boat the engineer *was* the man who counted most, after the skipper: but Walther was exceptional in any case. And a minute ago he'd nearly drowned them all! It amounted to nothing less: it you couldn't use your propellers, all you had to get her up with was the store of high-pressure air in the bottles, so if you blew it all out through tanks with open vents in their tops you'd be left with nothing except a one-way ticket to perdition. And yet – it dawned on Looff as suddenly as a cold shower hitting him – by reacting as violently as he had he'd made an exhibition of himself: seeing it, he felt like a man coming out of fever, delirium . . .

Because he did rely on Franz Walther so heavily? Needed his talents and support now more than ever, because of his own . . .

No. He shut his mind to that. It wasn't that his nerves were shot, simply that he was played-out, mentally and physically exhausted, worn through to the bone . . . He needed the leave that was due to him: and afterwards he'd be all right. Berlin, and Trudi: he'd *drown* in her . . . He put a hand on Walther's shoulder, told him gruffly, 'Sorry. Temper's a bit short . . . Look – you're allowed one mistake a year, and I'd forgotten, this year you never drew your ration. So we'll forget it.'

Walther glanced round. White teeth gleamed in a gap in the scrubby beard. Teeth like a rat's, narrow and sharp-looking. Despite which Franz Walther invariably got more than his ration of women. There was surprise in his eyes now, despite the grin: Looff had turned away but he was still seeing that probing stare, a kind of critical speculation – as if Walther had begun to guess . . .

She was coming up nicely now. The engineer was releasing

air from the tanks a little at a time as she rose, still slightly bow-up but not excessively so. It would be necessary to check out the propellers now – one at a time, in the hope that only one of them might be damaged. That was only a very small hope, from his recollection of how it had felt and sounded: but in any case he wanted her closer to the surface before making any experiments of that kind: there was a danger of shaking those glands right out. Imagination saw the spurts of sea, rivets blowing out like bullets, plates bulging, splitting, the Atlantic bursting in . . .

'I want a report on the leaks – after ends.'

'Lieutenant Gebhardt went to deal with it, sir.' That was Grewe, first lieutenant – on his way to the watertight door, to unclip it and go aft. There were only two such doors in the boat, one at each end of the control room, so that the forward and after compartments were very large, so big that in practical terms it meant if one of those subdivisions were flooded, and the boat was in deep water, you'd have had it. And most of the Atlantic – until you came to a shallow coastal strip such as U122 was in now – was very deep indeed.

'Periscope depth.'

He'd decided he'd surface completely, *then* check the state of the screws. A recce of the sky first, of course. That bomber would be a hundred miles away by now, but there could be another: there were far too many of the bastards these days, and the approaches to the U-boat bases were favourite hunting areas for them. Three U-boats had been lost to British aircraft in Biscay in the last few months: and if those bombs had fallen just a metre or so from where they did fall, U 122 might well have made it four.

Looff was at the chart beside Oelricher, using dividers to measure the distance from here to the Loire estuary and the St Nazaire U-boat pens. The quartermaster told him, saving him the trouble, 'Would've been four and half hours' steaming, sir.'

And by this time tomorrow he'd have been on his way to Berlin. To Trudi, whom he'd married only four months ago. Trudi's father was a general, now on the Eastern Front with the Sixth Army, advancing against Stalingrad . . . But there'd be at least a day's delay now, Looff guessed, in his own take-off for Berlin, and more than that if anything else went wrong. The thought gave him a feeling of a barrier erected between himself and Trudi: of Trudi always a little out of reach, like a retreating figure in a dream . . . He turned, feeling the sick depression again as Grewe arrived from aft with the second engineer in tow.

'Reporting on the leaks, sir . . .'

Looff looked at the depthgauges. Thirty-five metres, and she was rising steadily on an even keel. He moved towards the search periscope. 'Stern glands again?'

Gebhardt nodded. Deathly pale, and glistening with sweat – or with spray from those leaks . . . 'The port gland, the one that was bad before, was fairly hosing in. When we were deep it—'

Irritation was sharp, intense: he snapped, 'How is it *now?*'

'It's – less, sir, a lot less, but still – sizeable. Bilge pump will need to be run every ten minutes in thirty, say. But the starboard gland's no more than seepage now.'

'Very well.' He told Walther and Grewe, 'If the RAF have gone home, we'll surface and see what's what.' Turning to the search periscope as the boat rose smoothly towards the ordered depth. This search periscope was operated from the control room, but the attack 'scope you worked from the conning tower, on a saddle-seat that turned with it. He couldn't in fact have used it now because it was jammed solid, one of the effects of those Canadian depth-charges. Looff was busy sky-searching, swivelling slowly around with his eyes pressed against the rubbers while behind him Walther struggled with the awkward trimming job. You needed motive-power, some motion through the water, for the hydroplanes to grip and take effect, like horizontal rudders. Now, with the screws motionless, the engineer was having to adjust his trim by no more than pints flooded in or pumped out: and there was enough motion at this depth to make it a losing battle.

'Can't hold her, sir, we're drifting *up* . . .'

It would be worse to over-flood, blind the man at the periscope by dipping it. Walther's eyes were on the Papenberg, the sensitive water-tube depth-meter between the two clock-face ones. The Papenberg showed depth-changes with great accuracy and was used primarily for periscope work, especially during dived attacks when it was important not to show an inch more stick above the surface than you had to.

'All right.' Looff stepped back. 'Surface.' He told Grewe, 'I want the twenty millimetres manned.' The AA guns, a quadruple mounting abaft the bridge on a railed platform that was known for some obscure reason as 'the conservatory'. He'd have the gunners up there because if you had no motive-power you couldn't dive quickly, and it would be safer to stay up and fight than wallow slowly, defencelessly into the waves, a sitting duck for aircraft bombs or depthcharges. The British aircraft had RDF in them now, which made them much more dangerous than they had been and presumably accounted for the recent losses. U-boats had been promised search-receivers as a counter to this: some kind of device that would give warning when an airborne radar fingered you.

'Blow all main ballast!'

The gunners were standing by. Looff climbed into the tower. Alone for a few seconds he paused with his eyes shut while the sweat broke out like fever and his body shook with the release of tension. Air was ripping into the tanks and his boat tilted, lifted: Walther's voice rang hollowly from below, 'Standards awash . . .'

One whole day lost, was what it boiled down to.

The tug – from St Nazaire – escorted by one Möwe-class torpedo-boat, had taken seven hours to get to them. Another Möwe had arrived before that and stayed with them, and there'd been fighter cover overhead most of the time.

U 122 had been completely immobilised by those bombs. Both screws smashed . . . Looff had sent a diver over the stern, and he'd reported that the propeller blades were all either twisted or shorn off. And one shaft was bent, too. So there'd been nothing to do but wait, with the hydrophones manned to pick up any sound of approaching screws. With air cover to protect them from further bomber attack, the threat to guard against had been the chance of a British submarine finding this easy target.

But it was close to noon now – the attack had been yesterday afternoon – and they were well inside the Loire estuary, the tug making an extra couple of knots in the land's shelter. One torpedo-boat had gone ahead into St Nazaire, and the other hung astern. Air attack was still very much a possibility.

From the partly-raised search periscope, four white pennants fluttered – white because the four ships sunk on this patrol had been merchant-men. When you KO'd a warship, you marked the success with a red pennant. The four streamers looked good, up there: they were the signs a welcoming crowd always looked for and applauded. Looff was dressed for the return to harbour, ready for that welcome, wearing a clean white cap and also his Knight's Cross. The white cap was a U-boat commander's badge of honour and special privilege: they stopped you in the street, women tried to kiss you, and if they were pretty enough you'd permit it.

Max Looff, ace ship-killer. His tonnage sunk had passed the quarter-million mark last time out. The four kills on this patrol added another estimated 33,000 tons to the bag; so a third of a million was in his sights. The old dream becoming fact, the burning ambition he'd had of following in the footsteps and the fame of Prien, Kretschmer, Schepke, Frauenheim, Endras . . .

Endras's nerves had been in ribbons, before he'd sailed on that last patrol. They shouldn't have let him go. And Prien, Schepke and Kretschmer had all been lost in the same month – in March of last year. None of it had seemed to spell out any kind of lesson: those were the tragedies of war and it was always the other guy it happened to. In March of 1941, it seemed to Looff now, he'd been a kid, a brash youngster, new to the white cap and blinded by its glory. In nineteen months he'd aged by – what, twenty years? He could see himself as he had been then when he looked now at the new, young COs: strutting, desperately impressed with themselves, believing in the Reich's destiny and their own involvement in it. Max Looff would look at them and think, *You'll grow up: or you'll drown.*

He'd grown up, all right. And now, he'd *be* all right. After this break, three weeks in Trudi's warm, enclosing arms, he'd be as right as rain. The signs he'd read in himself, all the forebodings and introspection, had been symptomatic of nothing more than exhaustion, over-strain over too long a period. Nerves *on edge*, certainly, but that was an entirely different thing from *nerve lost*. If that had been on the cards it would have happened long ago: there'd been plenty of tough patrols before this one. It was important to bear it in mind: and a question of self-discipline, not to allow the imagination to play such games. Also – and oddly enough – another way of steeling oneself against any such weakness was to think of Trudi: she'd been swept off her feet by a famous U-boat commander, a national hero whose hand had been shaken by the Führer himself: and this same man would be returning to her now – tomorrow, or the day after. The same man, the same lover . . .

What if he – well, talked in his sleep, or—

Christ . . .

Imagination off the leash again: seeing it, the bedside light switched on, Trudi up on one elbow, golden light bathing those perfect breasts, her hand on his shoulder and her voice urgent, waking him from nightmare and the echo of his scream still ringing. The shock, disbelief in her face, tears streaking his . . .

'One man on the bridge?'

He imagined, as he bent towards the voice-pipe, how it would be to have Trudi's sympathy, how long it would be before sympathy became contempt. He answered that request: 'Affirmative.' It was Franz Walther, the chief engineer, who came up, clambering past the helmsman in the tower, emerging into the bridge with an unlit cheroot clamped between his teeth.

'Time for a smoke before we dock, sir?'

'Plenty.'

Walther lit up, then inhaled luxuriously, smoke eventually trickling from his nostrils while he gazed around – at the tug with its mound of churned froth ahead, the torpedo-boat with its clean, warlike lines back on the quarter, the smoothly swelling rush of grey-green water surging into froth along the U-boat's saddle-tanks, her wash spreading in a widening V towards land encroaching on both sides. Looff was glad to have had that sequence of thought interrupted. In fact it hadn't been thought, it had been imagination, the very thing he had to avoid, forbid. It was unreal, a lie, you had to shut your mind against it and *keep* it shut. He asked Walther, 'Looking forward to some leave, are you?'

'Well.' Expelling smoke. Even through its heavy pungency you could smell him. 'I expect I'll stick around the boat, pretty well. Make sure they don't cock anything up.'

Walther wouldn't trust any shoreside engineer farther than he could spit. He was like a jealous husband, with his boat. Looff advised him, 'You ought to get yourself away for at any rate a short while. Pick a stage when they can't do much harm. I don't want you getting stale, or sick, you know.'

He knew the engineer was staring at him: out of the side of his eye he'd seen the black cheroot swing, jutting like a gun-barrel. But silence, no comment at all: Looff remembering the way this man had looked at him yesterday – that doubting, assessing stare. There might be the same sort of question in Walther's face now, if he'd cared to look back at him. The connection being the warning he'd just given him, about getting stale, when yesterday Walther had seemed to be wondering whether his skipper might be going off his head . . . He mumbled, finally, 'I might take a few days. Week, at most – once the work's properly in hand. Maybe Paris.'

Looff smiled. 'Ah.'

'Well, for shit's sake, the local tarts—'

'Quite.' It occurred to him that if one of the local whores took anything like a close look at Franz Walther, she might feel very much the same degree of caution. 'We don't want you with *that* sickness, either.'

'The Maquis' secret weapon.' Walther hawked, and spat to leeward. 'I suppose you'll be off to Berlin, sir?'

'Bet your boots.' Looff was conscious of the constraint between them, and the mutual effort to break through it. It might be quite a while before the incident really faded. He added, partly by way of a fresh, oblique apology, 'Three weeks, and I feel I need every day of it. Every hour. I'm going to forget I ever saw the inside of a U-boat.'

'Fat chance of *that*, sir.' The engineer shrugged. 'They'll have you making speeches, lecturing, signing autographs, taking the salute at parades of Hitler Youth – etcetera, etcetera . . .' Walther belched, and cheroot-smoke seeped through his facial hair. 'Kapitänleutnant Max Looff – in Berlin – ye Gods, they'll be climbing over each other to get their hands on you!'

He was right, at that. It wouldn't be possible to evade it all. The heroes of 'Dönitz's private navy' were a major propaganda asset. Dönitz himself had referred to them as 'the bravest of the brave'. They were the stars, the gladiators . . .

'Knights in shining armour.' The captain of the flotilla's smile had irony in it. 'That was the C-in-C's own expression.' The captain was a large man, about the same height as Looff but much burlier. Duelling scars on his cheeks. 'And you're one of the shiniest, my dear Looff.' He moved round behind the desk. 'Sit down. How about a touch of cognac? Or schnapps?'

'Not just at the moment, thank you.'

'Dare say you're wise. It's early, and you'll be painting the place scarlet tonight, I suppose.' By 'the place' he'd be referring to La Baule, ten or a dozen miles away, to which submarine personnel were transported each evening. This base was too much of a target for bombing, not to mention for British commandos, who'd paid the main port of St Nazaire a highly destructive visit earlier in the year. 'But – I was saying – one of the shiniest. You're very well thought of – which is hardly surprising, the way your bag's mounting and the fact that aggregate monthly tonnages destroyed are the figures by which our lord and master stands or falls. Eh?'

'Admiral Dönitz.'

A nod . . . 'What I'm telling you is he was talking about you, Looff.' The captain pointed at the telephone on the desk between them. 'Over that thing, two or three hours ago.'

Looff fingered the *Kriegsabzeichen*, the gilt U-boat badge on the left side of his jacket. C-in-C talking about a U-boat CO to the flotilla captain could mean very little, or it could mean something like promotion, or – well, something quite different. There was a suspicion in the back of his mind now, a small seed of anxiety. He inclined his head: 'I'm honoured.'

'That's a hell of a long defect-list your engineer's presented, I'm told.'

Abrupt change of subject. But there had to be some link. The seed swelled, a little. Looff explained, 'Most of the damage was done by the Canadians. Or one *assumes* they were Canadians, right on that coast. I was – well, to be frank, lucky to get out of it . . . But there was also an earlier pasting, out in the air-gap, and finally as you know this damn bomber – another *extremely* close shave.' He could hear a shake in his own voice, and he was worried that the other man might detect it too. He thought, *I'm talking too much, running off at the mouth: better dry up* . . . But it was necessary to finish – 'also some of the minor items were held over from our last spell in harbour, if you remember – because that was only a short stand-off, whereas this time—' he smiled, rather uneasily – 'well, personally, I'm off for my three weeks in Berlin, while they put us back in shape.'

He noticed a slight deepening of the lines around the captain's eyes: eyes which did not, now, meet his own. It was out of character: and the seed was active, germinating.

'Not this time, old chap, I'm afraid. As I was saying – or rather, *beginning* to say—'

'But—'

'Wait, let me—'

'Sir – I've absolutely *got* to—'

'I said *wait!*'

A roar: then silence. A slow blink: and now an understanding smile. But the eyes were like steel. Looff staring back at him: Looff's fingers gripping the edge of the desk. The captain's hands moved too, joined each other on the blotter in front of him, linked and seemed to be trying out each other's strength. He murmured, frowning down at them, 'Von Rosenow was a friend of yours?'

Was. So it was true, Horst had gone . . .

'I'm sorry to have to confirm it. But there's no doubt now. We've no idea how or even exactly where, but—'

'That's terrible.' Staring at the motionless, grim-faced man on the other side of the desk, he remembered another question he'd meant to ask – about young Neumann of U 102: Neumann had been out there with him in that first pack attack, and after it there'd been several days of unanswered 'Report your position' calls to him – just as there'd been to Von Rosenow earlier.

'The point is this, now. Rosenow was to have taken over a brand-new boat. U 702. Not only spanking new, but she has the added strengthening, the deep-diving capability. Oh, and a search-receiver. A few other small improvements . . . Anyway – she's yours. This is the personal decision of Flag Officer U-boats, a decision which I personally applaud and also, as you'll appreciate, something of an honour. But it certainly means you'll have to postpone that leave. 702's ready for sea, there's a particular task for her – for *you*, Looff – and you'll sail the day after tomorrow.'

The room was turning, swimming . . . He closed his eyes to stop it. Then wet his lips and found his voice: it sounded like someone else's. 'Special task?'

'Well. You'll get your orders and full details from Operations, of course. But – briefly – and bear in mind this is not to be discussed either here or in quarters, right?'

'Naturally.'

There was far too much talk, and far too many French ears listening to it, and some of them weren't listening by chance or out of mere curiosity, either.

'Intelligence has reason to believe the enemy's preparing a seaborne assault on Dakar. It also happens that a group of boats currently deployed in that general area are being shifted into the Mediterranean: this is a routine change-over that can't easily be cancelled. It's very important therefore that we should deploy a new group down in that Azores-Freetown stretch. As you're aware there's a zone of no air cover, east of the Azores—'

'The Black Pit.'

A nod . . . 'So it's a good hunting ground in any case. Your starting-point will be due east of Santa Maria. It'll take you a few days to get there, of course, and you'll need to get a move on. There'll be seven, possibly eight other boats joining you, to form a patrol line and then move southward towards Freetown. Your pack's been allocated a code-name – which is on the tip of my tongue but for the moment seems to elude . . .' The big hands separated: then the fingers of one of them snapped like a pistol-shot, and the captain smiled. '*Drachen*. You'll command the *Drachen* group.'

Drachen meaning 'dragon'.

Chapter 7

German Naval Staff to Flag Officer U-boats:
In the event of an operation against Dakar all U-boats within reach are to be concentrated for attacks against enemy supply ships. FO U-boats . . . should report number of boats expected to be available for this task.

Eagle, this is Gannet . . . Asdic contact two-nine-five, range three thousand yards . . .

'Gannet' was *Paeony*'s talk-between-ships call sign, and 'Eagle' was *Harbinger*'s; this was the first contact (or alleged contact) with an enemy since they'd left Freetown three days ago.

Ship's time – Nick checked his watch – 1900, 7 pm. *Harbinger* was already at dusk action stations. Asdics pinging, the Type 271 RDF aerial revolving steadily, HF/DF manned and listening, guns' crews and depth-charge crews closed up. Bearcroft, the Chief Yeoman, had acknowledged *Paeony*'s message. There was no need to tell Guyatt what to do: at least, one hoped there was no need. He'd investigate this contact, and if it was confirmed as a submarine target he'd attack it with depth-charges. Then Nick would move over to that side to support him. Not before . . . The convoy's mean course was 335 degrees and *Paeony*'s station was six thousand yards ahead of the left-hand columns, so the reported bearing of 295 degrees and distance of one and a half miles indicated that the U-boat – if it was that, not a whale or a patch of denser water – was well out on the port bow.

A classic position for a dived attack, incidentally.

Harbinger was alone at the convoy's rear, zigzagging four thousand yards astern of it. The convoy's own zigzag would cease now, as darkness fell and made such manoeuvring dangerous for ships so cheek-by-jowl. *Paeony* and *Astilbe* were leading from up front – roughly six miles between then and *Harbinger*, in fact – with the trawler *Stella* between them but farther back, two thousand yards ahead of the front rank of merchant-men. *Opal* was a mile to port of the convoy, *Gleam* the same distance to starboard. And Guyatt should have been telling *Opal* now by morse light – because the trawlers had no radio-telephones, and in this half-light probably would not have been able to read flags – what he was doing. That was *Opal*'s side of the convoy, and if there was a U-boat there the nicotine-stained Kyle ought to know about it. *If* . . . Nick wondered, *Seconds out of the ring? This soon?* However much you prepared for it, that sudden TBS call had still been totally unexpected. He was resisting the temptation to take *Harbinger* across to that side of the convoy. There was no confirmation that it was a U-boat *Paeony*'s asdics had picked up, and if there *were* some around anything could develop in any other direction too; with so few ships you could be badly caught if you committed too much of your defence too soon to one single threat. He was suppressing another urge as well: to call Guyatt on TBS and check that he was keeping *Opal* in the picture. He was holding back on this because he wanted to be able to assume it was happening, not set a precedent by reminding them of procedures he'd spent hours drumming into them in Freetown, and which in the last couple of days they'd practised half a dozen times.

He'd check afterwards. And rub Guyatt's nose in it if he hadn't.

As the light went, the ships ahead were becoming indistinct, merging like phantoms into the dirty-water shades of dusk. The horizon to port was still bright, but cloud had been gathering during the afternoon and that small area in the west was the only clear sector now. Admiralty weather forecasts, supported by falling barometric pressure, made it obvious that the tropic calm and heat astern could be forgotten; not far ahead the Atlantic was becoming more like its old self, and you could feel the breath of it already. *Harbinger* was learning how to roll again as Carlish brought her round, maintaining a zigzag across the convoy's rear.

The only reason for not having expected U-boats this far south was that the Intelligence reports had laid stress on the Azores-Canaries as primary danger area. Their logic would be, Nick guessed, that the enemy believed (as Cruance had been confident they would) that surface forces were moving against Dakar, and to disrupt any such move the Azores air gap would be the obvious place to picket. There was a long haul yet, moreover, before the convoy would be anywhere near it – the Cape Verde islands were at this moment 120 miles abeam to port, Dakar about 150 on the starboard quarter, the Canaries something like 700 miles away and the Azores more like 1250. And the convoy was making a bare seven knots. So the longer action could be postponed, the better. Once the U-boats found them and concentrated, SL 320 was going to start losing ships; no matter how efficiently this handful of escorts was made use of, it was inevitable.

Behind Nick in the creaking, jolting bridge, Chubb observed to Warrimer, 'Hell of a long investigation by friend *Paeony*. Ask me, they've lost the bloody thing.'

TBS crackled into speech, *Eagle, this is Gannet: contact confirmed, attacking!*

Warrimer murmured to Chubb, 'Now perhaps you'll understand why we very rarely *do* ask you.'

'Bring her round to three-oh-oh degrees, Sub.'

'Three-oh-oh – aye aye, sir . . .'

To get over to that side, where he might be able to help *Paeony* and where an attack might be expected if the U-boat evaded Guyatt, now out to the west of the convoy as the mass of ships, near-invisible now in gathering darkness, forged on northwestward. If the contact remained firm and seemed worth staying with, *Harbinger* might take it over from *Paeony*, allowing the corvette to start clawing back up to her station in the van. *Harbinger*'s higher speed would enable her to catch up again afterwards much more quickly: which was why she was going to have to do most of the leg-work.

'Course three-oh-oh degrees, sir!'

'Very good.'

Depthcharges rumbled: *Paeony* had made a first run over her target. The light of the western horizon had faded almost to extinction. The trawlers had no RDF, consequently needed to remain inside visibility range of the convoy; this meant that in darkness or bad weather conditions they'd be on very short leashes. Yet another limitation . . . And if the balloon was going up now, and the convoy did stick to its route and timing – which would mean it wouldn't have crossed that fan of 'Torch' convoy tracks until about 6 November – and it was now 25 October . . . *Ten days?*

It probably was *not* starting now. This would almost surely be a loner they'd stumbled on. But that was all it needed for the homing-signals to go out . . .

Eagle – this is Gannet. Guyatt's tone was flat; you could guess what was coming, before he said it. *Contact lost. I've searched all round but we don't seem able to pick it up. I suppose it could have been non-sub – although my operator swears it was the real McCoy . . . Over.*

Nick took the microphone.

'Gannet – Eagle. Resume station. I say again, resume station.' He told Carlish 'One-eight-oh revolutions.'

Speeding up so as to get out there faster, on the off-chance of picking up the contact or catching the bastard if he tried to surface. From where he was supposed to have been to start with he might have been intending to make a dived attack, with just enough light at that time to do it by; now his alternative would be to surface and run in on the beam or quarter. He might, if he heard *Paeony* chugging away, and thought he'd been left to his own devices.

If he existed at all.

In *Astilbe* Tony Graves would have listened to the TBS messages. He'd have moved his ship across to cover some of *Paeony*'s ground, earlier, and this would have put him in the centre of the van. Now he'd know she was on her way back, so he'd adjust again. But during *Paeony*'s absence the screen ahead of the convoy – eight columns of ship with a thousand yards between columns making a front three and a half sea miles wide – had consisted of one corvette and one trawler. A U-boat commander's idea of happiness . . . Nick lowered his glasses. 'Come to three-four-oh, Sub.'

To scrape out closer to that corner of the convoy. Asdics pinging, searching the churned water. He'd decided to make a wide sweep out to port and then round astern. Knowing full well there might be nothing there at all, that *Paeony*'s depth-charges had probably only killed some school of fish: but knowing also that if there was a U-boat nearby, it would be vital to deal with it before it could whistle up its friends. He thought it *would* have been a single enemy: there'd been no HF/DF transmissions, none of the chatter you tended to get from a patrol line. And it was in line with the policy of aggressive defence, to leave the convoy for an hour or so, go out in search . . .

Burning oil, meanwhile. He'd need to fuel again tomorrow. *Harbinger* and the two corvettes had topped-up their tanks this forenoon, from the oiler *Redgulf Star*. She was number fifty-four: the other tanker was the *English Ardour*, in position sixty-three. It was important to keep fuel tanks as full as possible; there might come a time when it would be difficult, under pressure, to find the lull in which to do it. When you were linked by the umbilical cord of an oil-pipe to a tanker you weren't much use as an escort.

'Course three-four-oh, sir.'

'Good . . .'

Harbinger lurching, taking the sea head-on, her stubby bow smashing black sea into streaming sheets of white. It felt good to be on the move: like flexing muscles that had been rested for too long.

But the hour's search found nothing.

It probably *had* been fish . . . He'd taken her out westward and then curved back and across the convoy's rear in a wide half-circle: the kind of off-chance, elliptical sweep he'd once or twice struck lucky with before. Asdics pinging, radar circling, a dozen pairs of binoculars probing the dark. There was a slight radiance now where the moon was lifting behind fast-moving cloud thin in patches; the wind was westerly and there was enough of a sea to be putting a corkscrew motion on the ship as she pounded up north-westward to rejoin. The convoy was a pattern of blips on the 271's 'poached egg': holding together pretty well, so far, judging by the evenly-spaced line-abreast of the rear rank. Evenly-spaced except for one gap in it, a spare billet at the back of column five, immediately astern of the *Redgulf Star*. It was a convenient arrangement: in her present position as number fifty-four the oiler was well tucked into the protection of ships around her, while for refuelling operations it was easy for her to drop astern where she became accessible to her customers.

Nick told Scarr, through the voice-pipe to the plot, to let him know when they were back in station. He went back to his high chair. 'Number One?'

Warrimer came forward. A hand on the torpedo-sight for support as the ship pitched bow-down, jabbing her stem into solid sea. Warrimer's arms were about five feet long, but as his legs were also very long he tended to lose his balance. Nick told him, 'You can fall them out from action stations. Relax to second degree . . . Your watch now, is it?'

Weapons would still be manned, guns' crews sleeping on the gundecks and the depth-charge party in whatever shelter they could find aft; one man at each station would stay awake and ready to alert the others. Not too uncomfortable, in present conditions – and they were used to a great deal worse.

'Kye, sir?'

The dark shape at his elbow was the bridge messenger, Harris.

'Good idea. I'd like it in the chartroom, in five or ten minutes, please.'

Alone in there – *Harbinger* back in station, motion and vibration much reduced once the speed was cut, he took

Cruance's transparent overlay out of an inside pocket, and fitted it to the chart. Needing to keep the wider picture in mind . . .

Convoy UGF1, the big American outfit, was at sea now, gathered out of several US ports into one eastbound armada. Fifty-six escorts covering thirty-eight ships was a proportion that put *this* little circus into perspective . . . And convoy KX4A, which included some Tank Landing Ships, would be out from the Clyde, southbound. KMS(A)1 and (0)1 would also be at sea: more than sixty ships in that contingent, the first wave of the assaults on Algiers and Oran.

'Captain, sir . . .'

He pocketed the transparency as he turned to find the doctor, Mackenzie, bringing him a signal.

'Just deciphered this one, sir.'

Holding it under the yellowish chart-table light . . .

MV 'Burbridge', straggler from convoy TDF1, now in position 14 degrees 05 north 31 degrees 28 west, steering 045 at 12 knots to R/V with convoy SL 320 noon October 30 in position 23 degrees 38 north 24 degrees 05 west. 'Burbridge' to report any further speed reduction or other change affecting R/V.

TDFI was the convoy that had left Freetown routed for Trinidad and thence up through the American convoy system before re-crossing the Atlantic via the northern route. Cruance had mentioned it. Nick looked up from a second reading of the signal as someone else slid in and shut the door. It was his navigator, Scarr.

'All right, doc. Thank you.' He told Scarr, 'Check a steamer called *Burbridge* in the register, will you. *Burbridge* with a "u".'

While Scarr was getting the register out and thumbing through it, Nick checked those positions and the given course and speed. It was correct, just where this convoy should be at that time and where the *Burbridge*'s route would bring her to rendezvous with them. Presumably she'd had some kind of machinery breakdown – the words 'any further speed reduction' indicated it – and had dropped back too far to have any hope of catching up on her own convoy.

Mike Scarr had his finger on the entry. 'She's nine thousand, eight hundred tons, sir, passenger ship, London registry nineteen-thirty-eight.'

He was reading the signal, which Nick had passed to him. Nick thinking, *Passengers* . . . All under the impression, no doubt, that by making a rendezvous with convoy SL 320 just west of the Canaries and south of the Azores they'd be kissing their troubles goodbye? They'd be in considerable danger now: alone, defenceless, watching the sea for the white feather of a periscope cutting through it: telling each other, *Three days, we'll be back in convoy* . . .

Was it possible that the genius who'd ordered this rendezvous had not been told what SL 320 was *for*?

Well, sure it was. It was *possible*. You didn't pass this sort of information out to authorities that didn't need to have it. And she *could* be in that ship . . .

The odds against it would be – what, two hundred to one? At least that much. So forget it. He'd been through all that . . .

But he'd have liked to have had Cruance here now, in *Harbinger* or in one of those blacked-out freighters up ahead: there'd have been justice in putting the planner of deceptions where he'd helped to put all these people . . . Cruance who'd had the cheek and insensitivity to try to strike a pally note – who'd asked him, when the briefings had been finished and he was strolling out through the long, dripping tunnel at Nick's side, 'No doubt your submariner son will be playing some part in "Torch". Even though he would probably not know it yet. You've good news of him, I hope?'

Paul was his son by his Russian-born first wife Ilyana, and he was in a submarine in the Malta-based flotilla. But in the next breath, barely waiting for any answer to the question, Cruance had mentioned Jack too – Jack Everard who'd been taken prisoner at St Nazaire and was now in some German POW camp.

'He's your half-brother, am I right?'

It hadn't been necessary to confirm it. Cruance knew as much about the Everards as Wishart had been able to tell him: which could *not* have included the fact that Jack was Nick's son, not his half-brother. The lie, and Jack, were both twenty-three years old.

'Two tough eggs, eh? A submariner and a commando?'

Jack was not a commando. He'd gone on that raid *with* commandos, for some special task. But he was a tough egg, all right. And Cruance had obviously been at pains to commit all this family background material to memory: as soft soap, what in navalese was called 'flannel'.

If Jack Everard, at this moment about two and a half thousand miles northeast, was carrying a torch of any kind, it was for a girl called Fiona: whom he'd stolen from the man he thought of as his half-brother – from whom he'd also acquired, if nothing else, the maverick quality to a high degree . . .

'My God. Talk about brass monkeys . . .'

Frank Trolley grunted, from the cubicle next to Jack's. There were three of them at this end of the latrine. They had swing-doors without locks or bolts, a smother of multi-lingual graffiti and very small, barred window-holes up near the ceiling for ventilation. The place needed all the ventilation it could get, but winter was starting early in south Germany and from the 'brass monkeys' point of view – meaning the freezing blast of a northeaster – one might have settled for the stink. Despite having two sets of clothes on – German uniform on the outside and what might pass for civilian gear under it. Trolley's rig was that of a *Sonderführer*, while Jack was dressed as a private soldier. In the morning – if they were still here by morning, and not frozen stiff, stuck to the rims of the seats – the others would be bringing a rifle with them, to go with this uniform.

'Think we've got a prayer, Jack?'

'I've said mine.'

'I mean d'you reckon we've any real chance of getting clear?'

'Why the hell shouldn't we?'

But they'd thought they had a good chance *last* time . . .

They were going to have to spend several more hours – the rest of the night – in this freezing, foul-smelling lavatory. Jack thought, *What we do for England* . . . Except that in his own case it wasn't primarily for England he was doing it. As a sort of background motive, perhaps it was; but the real spur was Fiona, to get home to her and hold her to her promise – that if he came back at all, she'd marry him.

He appreciated a number of things about Fiona Gascoyne. Such as the fact that, based in London and quite exceptionally attractive, she enjoyed the company and attentions of men, was very much flesh and blood and in her own chosen ways extremely – well, the word might be 'unconventional' . . . Jack knew he could hold her, given half a chance, he was completely confident of it; but he did *not* have half a chance while he was in Offlag VIIB.

For the simple reason that *she* didn't have a chance. There'd be no question of blame, none whatever.

But there'd be even less chance from Offlag IVC, to which it had been rumoured he and Trolley and the others who'd been with them on their last escape attempt were soon to be transferred. This news had galvanised them into making a fresh attempt at once, as it was known that IVC – a castle, some place called Colditz, but known to POWs as the *Straflager* – was particularly difficult to get out of.

Not that this dump, Eichstatt, was easy. Although this time he did have a feeling they might make it. Wishful thinking to some extent, because it was essential they *should* get away. If they were caught now it would mean the *Straflager* for certain, with the distinctly possible alternative of a firing-squad. There'd been some highly realistic threats of 'execution' last time: and the fact was, you never knew, with Krauts.

He murmured, 'I do believe we'll make it.'

'Huh?'

Trolley might have been dozing.

'I said I think we'll make it. Get away.'

'Hope you're right. But why?'

'Just a feeling. Because it's spur-of-the-moment stuff, perhaps, instead of that careful planning. Last time we may have been a bit too clever. *And* there were too many helpers.'

There were a few helpers involved in this one too, but only to cover up the absence of two prisoners at roll call in the morning. The other two would be there to answer their names, but they were already listed for sick parade and they'd be coming straight here from the 7 am muster. Jack and Trolley had needed to be here in advance, on account of the German uniforms; there wouldn't have been time to change into them, otherwise, and it would have been tricky to smuggle them down to this place in daylight.

Trolley murmured, 'Thought we weren't going to talk.'

'Can't do much harm, if we keep it quiet. D'you think? It's going to be a hellish long night.'

'OK. We'll hear anyone coming, anyway.'

This was the out-patient department; there was no reason for anyone to be around at night, not inside the building. Outside there were guards, and dogs, and every twenty seconds the glare from circling perimeter searchlights flared across the latrine's ceiling through those high, barred apertures.

Trolley, like Jack, had been caught at St Nazaire. He was a commando, and before the raid he'd helped to train Jack and his small naval team in commando methods. Jack remembered that in the training period, at Cardiff, he'd detested him, summed him up as a self-satisfied prig. Crazy . . . Old Frank was solid gold. But at that time he'd seemed to be like some young Cromwell. Super-fit, iron self-discipline, no drink, no smokes, no girls, blond hair like the bristles of a toothbrush and – worst of all – contemptuous disapproval of Jack's weekends in London. Weekends with Fiona, of course.

All this effort wasn't *only* for the sake of getting back to her. There was also the hatred of being cooped up, and with that the hatred of bloody Germans. For one's own sake, let alone any duty aspect, you longed to get back where you could kill some.

'Know any word games?'

'No . . . What's the betting on guards using this bog?'

'Walk up a flight of stairs, when they can piss on the wall outside?'

'Wouldn't be difficult to sneak out and clobber one, while he was at it . . .' He changed the subject. 'One thing that bothers me slightly, Frank, is if the goons notice my beard. I mean guards at the gate.'

'You're going to keep your coat collar turned up, aren't you?'

'It's still a risk. There isn't a single bearded postern in this camp.'

German guards were 'posterns'.

The other prisoners who'd be joining them here after roll call were 'Barmy' Morrison, a Rhodesian Air Force flight lieutenant, and a Greenjacket known as 'Cockup' Cockrace. Those two were getting a sound night's sleep in their own bunks, the lucky devils. There were dummies, rolled bundles, in Jack's bunk and Trolley's. Jack, hunched into his German greatcoat, pulled its collar up around his ears. He wore a beard not to hide the pink, burn-scarred areas of his face, but because in the early days shaving had been impossible, and he'd got used to it. He'd been very lucky, in fact; there were deep scars, real lacerations, elsewhere on his body, but the facial burns had been only skin-deep. The French doctor had said it would be because his clothes had been smouldering on him for some while before he went into the water. That Frenchman had done a marvellous job – on him and the others – in a hospital not far from St Nazaire, under German supervision, guards in the ward with automatic weapons trained on men semi-conscious in their beds.

Bloody idiots . . .

He wasn't worried about Fiona's reaction to his discoloured face. That was another thing he knew for sure about her. But she might like the beard, anyway. It was short, trimmed with scissors close to the outline of his jaw. The coat-collar would hide it, all right.

'Frank.'

'Bitte?'

'When we get back—'

'Ah . . .'

'You sound like a Bisto Kid. Frank, seriously – I want to ask a favour.'

'Oh?'

'What you're supposed to say is "Certainly, old boy, anything at all".'

'All right. Certainly, old boy, within reason – *my* reason – anything at all.'

'*Very* generous . . . Look, all it is, is I'd like you to act as best man at my wedding.'

'Oh, crikey, I'd be delighted!'

'Hurray.'

'Really, I'm – well, honoured, flattered, whatever . . .'

'You'll get as pissed as a skunk, is my guess. Bachelor party, I mean, night before, ancient tradition and so on. For the wedding itself I'll make sure Fiona picks the prettiest bridesmaid in London. Pretty and willing?'

'Didn't you tell me your girl was married before? Some old codger who snuffed it?'

'So what?'

'Well, I'm no master of etiquette, as you know, but I *believe* the second time round she'd have a matron of honour, not bridesmaids.'

'If she's a smasher and not *too* bloody honourable, d'you care?'

'Not a hoot in hell, old boy . . . But seriously, I'd be as pleased as Punch to . . .'

'Let's not get *too* serious about it. We have to get there, first. We ought to keep our thoughts on the minute-by-minute stuff, not daydreams. The wedding idea's just something I've had in mind and meant to ask you about before.'

'We'll get there, Jack. The whole *Wehrmacht* won't keep me from *that* party . . . Hey – that's the door downstairs!'

And boots now, stamping up the stairs . . .

Unmistakably German army boots. A guard too fastidious to spray the *outside* of the building?

Trolley whispered, 'Don't even breathe . . .'

The latrine was long and narrow with its entrance at the far end, *pissoirs* down its full length on one side with a few washbasins facing them, and these cubicles filling the whole width at the end. Boots getting louder as they climbed the stairs, getting near the top now. He might, of course, turn the other way – into the waiting room or the dispensary where he could park himself for a quiet smoke?

He turned *this* way.

Much louder, on the plank floor out there. A tired man's heavy heel-dragging, echoey in the empty building. Searchlight sweeping by: by its brief light Jack saw his own clenched fists on the thick grey apron of the *Wehrmacht* coat over his knees. The light had gone again. The door at the end banged open, and the light-switch clicked: a bare bulb in a cobwebbed metal cage flared over this central cubicle in which Jack crouched. The knuckles of his fists were white.

A loud, long yawn: then a mutter in German. Talking to himself. Trolley might have understood it; it was because Frank spoke some German that he was playing the part of the NCO, in tomorrow morning's charade. Also, he had blond hair, and with that bony face could easily pass for a Hun. He was the only one who'd need to open his mouth, tomorrow. The heavy boots, scraping along the latrine's composite floor, were coming down towards *this* end.

Stop. Take a pee. Please?

Still coming, ignoring telepathic instructions. Jack resisting a natural inclination to gather himself into a position like a runner's before a race, so as to be able to propel himself forward and grapple with the German as he pulled the door open. But to do it would mean shifting his feet, there'd be the risk of making some small sound. If the man was alert then he'd rush out, raise the alarm . . . *Just* – Jack told himself – *be ready* . . . The alternative might be to sit fast, glare up at the intruder, a fellow-German interrupted in the performance of a natural function?

In the dark? An unknown, bearded face, and clothing plainly intact? The only practical thing would be to hit him, hard and fast, while he was still off-guard, easy meat – as good as dead.

Better not kill him, though. That *would* justify the firing-squad.

The German had stopped. Muttering to himself again. Sounds of a coat being pulled open, buttons wrenched, heavy breathing . . . Perhaps after all he just preferred this end of the urinal: like a regular in a pub having his customary place at the bar . . . There was a rattle, then another semi-metallic sound. A thud – rifle-butt grounding. Leaning his gun against the wall? And now he'd begun to whistle between his teeth, a hissing with a vaguely familiar tune in it . . . Jack caught on to it suddenly – Harry Roy's band, a year or two before the war: *The Music Goes Round and Round* . . .

And it comes out here . . . Here, the dénouement coming, boots clomping this way again. *All right, you clown, I'm ready for you!* The pacing had stopped again: there was a heavy flopping noise. Greatcoat being dumped on the floor: and it was *not* a leak this Bosch had come for, he was heading for the cubicles.

Tensed, and waiting: whichever door the bastard picked, this or Trolley's, he or Trolley would go for him like a bull while the other one shot out and grabbed the rifle. Trolley would be on the same wavelength, just as ready for it . . .

The door of the cubicle on Jack's right banged open, bounced against the wall. Jack frozen, motionless. The German had picked the empty cubicle, the *only* empty one, the one-in-three chance you hadn't dared hope for!

The seat banged down. Boots scraped as he shuffled round. More movement of clothing: a belt-buckle or key-ring knocked against the partition, so close it was as startling as a shot. There was a heavy sigh as weight descended on the seat.

Then – if he'd dared move his hands, he'd have liked to have blocked his ears. And my God, not only noise . . . Ears and nose: you'd have needed two pairs of hands. And how long might it be before he leant far enough forward to see feet in the adjoining cubicle? The partition ended about nine inches above the floor: if Jack had turned his head in this crouched position he'd have seen Trolley's boots. He wasn't moving a muscle, though, not a finger, he wasn't even blinking.

It would have been even nicer if he hadn't needed to breathe.

What would the goon do, if he suddenly realised he had company?

Scream? Fall off the seat?

Screaming would have been preferable to the racket he was making. He must have been on guard-duty for the last week . . . Jack envied Trolley for being one booth further removed . . . But a new sound now: the scrape of a match. And a degree of silence, broken only sporadically, staccato-fashion while cigarette-smoke drifted up blue against the caged light, dissipating when it met the air-stream from the ventilators. Whistling again, and shifting round, grunting, then another burst of action. Jack thought, with his face screwed up and cramp in the muscles of his calves, *He's a one-man band . . .*

A continuing lull now, though. Without any indications of departure or preparations for it. Just sitting: not even whistling, sitting as quietly and as still as Jack and Trolley.

Enjoying the end of his cigarette? Or listening?

One might have made some sound, without being aware of it. He shut his eyes, concentrated on not moving, on maintaining the total, universal silence.

Until Trolley sniffed.

The sound had been quite distinct. Nobody, Jack thought, could have doubted there was someone in that cubicle and that he'd sniffed. Except that to the German it might have sounded loud enough to have emanated from this nearer one.

Could have spotted his feet by now, under the partition? Might be sitting contemplating them, trying to work it out – why anyone should have been squatting in here in the dark and had stayed quiet, or tried to . . . Trolley's slip astonished him: if he hadn't heard it, he wouldn't have believed it could have happened. But as it had, and the German must have heard it, why hadn't he spoken up, demanded to know who was there?

Suspecting the truth? This was, after all, a POW camp, and there'd been escapes and escape attempts before . . .

Years ago, Jack had developed a technique for soothing the soul while waiting to be beaten – at Dartmouth, the Royal Naval College. Beatings had been commonplace, mere routine: it was impossible *not* to be beaten, from time to time, and it was not at all unusual to have red weals, even broken skin, high on the right-hand ribs, more or less under the armpit. It was the way the tips of the flexible canes whipped round. If the cadet captain or house officer wielding the cane happened to be left-handed, you'd have the sores under your *left* arm. The habit Jack had developed involved the mental recitation of poetry to oneself. As he'd spent four years at Dartmouth he'd stored quite a lot of verse away, and much of it seemed to have scored itself indelibly into his brain. At random now he dredged up William Cowper's *The Solitude of Alexander Selkirk* . . .

I am monarch of all I survey,
My right there is none to dispute;
From the centre all round to the sea
I am lord of the fowl and the brute . . .

From next door came a sound of paper being crumpled. He continued with his eyes shut . . .

O solitude, where are the charms
That sages have seen in thy face?
Better dwell—

The German was on his feet, dressing himself. The belt-buckle clinked. Jack's eyes were open: he was reminding himself that this wasn't necessarily the end of it, it could be that the man was putting himself into a state enabling him to take action of some sort. A few minutes ago, when Trolley had let out that sniff, obviously he hadn't been in any such position. But now, as he suddenly thumped the door open, he began to sing in a low growling tone: *Under the lamplight, by the barrack gate* . . .

Jack murmured, a minute later when the door at the other end had slammed shut and the boots were crashing away towards the stairs, 'Better dwell in the midst of alarms, than reign in this horrible place.'

'Come again?'

'Frank, you could have finished us off with that sniff!'

'Sniff? Me? *I* didn't—'

'Christ Almighty, you *did!*' they could hear the boots clattering down the stairs now. 'For all we know he's gone to report there's someone hiding here – get help, bring 'em back and—'

'Balls . . . But I say, didn't he *need* that?'

'I'd say he needed a vet.'

Trolley sniggered. 'What's time? Three-thirty yet?'

'Getting towards four.'

Three hours to wait . . .

Then he was waking up – confused, and Trolley's voice booming hollowly, like part of a dream he'd been having – 'Awake, are you?' Jack was on the floor with his back against the lavatory bowl: he'd been there a long time – although he didn't realise it immediately – and his back and neck were painful when he moved. Trolley's voice again, sounding anxious: 'You awake, Jack?'

'Of course I'm bloody well awake.'

Filthy taste in the mouth. Plus an ache in the skull . . .

'No "of course" about it. And I've no watch, you know. How's the time?'

'You asked me that about ten minutes ago, damn it.' Squinting at his wristwatch, which had suffered no harm from its immersion in the St Nazaire Basin a few months back. 'Seven minutes past six.' He did a double-take. 'Hell, it can't be!'

'Last time I asked you it was four thirty-five. Hour and a half, you've been snoring and mumbling to yourself.'

'Haven't you slept?'

'Maybe ten minutes . . . We've been darned lucky, you know, only that one customer.'

'Well.' Still getting his mind together. 'Might be a rush soon, between now and roll call.'

Roll call was at 0700. The other two ought to get here by about ten past. They were already on the sick bay detail, so as soon as the parade was dismissed they'd hurry down here; if they were intercepted and questioned *en route* they'd say they wanted to be first in the queue for treatment.

They were both scatty, though. Each about as crazy as the other. A short-notice scheme like this would only attract loonies.

'Why should anyone use this place so early in the day?'

Jack was easing himself up on the seat. He growled, 'I'm not saying they will. It's possible, that's all. All I'm saying is we can't afford to relax.'

'Listen who's talking about *relaxing* . . . Actually, I was thinking it might be a very good idea to limber up a bit. Don't know about you, but I'm as stiff as buggery. If we want to be fighting fit in an hour's time . . .'

Exactly at seven, as always, the hooter sounded. Then you could hear distant yells. The prisoners would be tumbling out of their huts, staggering out still half asleep to fall-in by platoons. Jack, listening to the distant sounds of a familiar routine, sang quietly, '*Raus, raus*, bleedin' well *raus* . . .' He'd been trying to loosen up: toe-touching, arm-swinging, doubling on the spot. He stopped it now, and began to tidy up his uniform. Incredibly, the night had passed. Within minutes now, they'd be on the move.

'Think we could use the basins, freshen up?'

'You're the *Sonderführer*. But I'd say wait a couple more minutes.'

'OK . . . What if we do get visitors? I mean now, before the others—'

'Trust to luck, Frank, that's what!'

You either planned every step along the way, or you played it off the cuff.

HM Submarine *Ultra* had surfaced one mile from the St Elmo lighthouse an hour after the Mediterranean dawn, and forty-five minutes later she'd slid her slim form alongside at Lazoretto, the Malta flotilla's base on Manoel Island in Marsamxett Creek. Her Jolly Roger, the black skull-and-crossbones flag, was flying from the slightly-raised forward periscope with two new white bars sewn under a whole batch of others in the top-left corner; she'd sunk two ships out of a convoy of five bound from Italy to North Africa, and another boat of this flotilla, acting on her signal, had knocked down another of the surviving three before they'd reached Benghazi, which wasn't bad – although quite recently the flotilla had destroyed one entire convoy and part of its escort as well. There were rumours of an impending offensive in the desert, so there couldn't have been a better time for making holes in the Afrika Korps' supplies.

Paul Everard commented – dodging out of the throng that was now milling through the submarine's narrow gut – 'Seems there's a slight flap on, around these parts.'

Two boats were on the point of sailing, and one had been on her way out as *Ultra* had been entering the creek. For a lot of submarines to be pushed out all at the same time did suggest there might be something brewing. McClure, *Ultra*'s diminutive navigator, growled, 'What's the betting we won't get more than one night in?'

It would be enough. You only needed a few hours: essentially to refuel, and embark water, stores, torpedoes and ammunition.

'You two got nothing better to do than stand around like stuck pigs?'

Hugo Wykeham, first lieutenant. Beside McClure he was like a giraffe looking down at a monkey. Paul said, 'Only wondering how long we'll be in for.'

Their captain, Ruck, was still 'inboard' – up on the first floor of the old stone building with its many bomb-scars – communing with Shrimp Simpson, who commanded the Malta submarines. Paul, looking past Wykeham, saw Creagh, the gunlayer, slinking away as if he didn't want to be noticed. Paul was gunnery as well as torpedo officer. He called, 'Hey, Layer, got those figures yet?'

Figures for ammunition expended. It had to be an exact figure, since magazine and ready-use locker space was extremely limited, and you didn't want to sail with one less shell than there was room for. You couldn't take one *more*, either, unless you kept it under your pillow . . . Creagh told him, 'Can't get down there, not just this minute, sir.' Because the hatch to the magazine was in the gangway, there wasn't a hope of opening it up.

'What a bloody shambles!'

James Ruck, lieutenant-in-command – shouldering through, staring around at the rabble . . . Wykeham, who'd been leaving with McClure in tow, turned and came back as Ruck moved sideways into the wardroom, edging in between the table and his own bunk on the forward bulkhead. In this space you could *not* have swung a cat round, not without annoying it considerably. Ruck, straddling the bench seat and opening a drawer to find cigarettes, muttered, 'Some bastard's been at this drawer . . .' He swung round with a cigarette in his mouth, and gestured to them to gather round. 'Listen. News for you.' He struck a match. 'It's started, at last. Came over the BBC half an hour ago – the Army's attacked, at El Alamein. Started last night with a super-colossal artillery barrage – about a thousand guns all opened up at once and then just carried on. Big advances, fierce battle raging, etcetera. This looks like the big one we've been waiting for. And so, as the Italian fleet might just conceivably find reason to come out—'

Laughter included a cackle from CPO Logan, the coxswain, who was standing in the gangway, listening. Ruck threw him a glance, then went on, 'In case they do, it's Iron

Ring routine. All boats away to patrol off Taranto and suchlike places. In fact this flotilla's being reinforced for the purpose, a couple of boats joining us from Gib and two or three from Beirut.'

'How long have we got, sir?'

Ruck told Wykeham, 'Believe it or not, four or five days. Better allow for only four. But there's no panic, anyway, far as we're concerned.' He glanced over his shoulder again, at CPO Logan. 'Want me for something, Cox'n?'

'No, sir, not really—'

'Then don't let me detain you.'

He watched him move reluctantly away; then told his officers quietly, 'Reason we aren't joining the madding crowd is we're earmarked for a special job. Cloak and dagger stuff, there's a lot of it about at the moment.' He looked at Paul. 'We'll be taking two torpedoes less than usual, Everard, so as to have room in the reload stowages for canoes. Folboats. Consequently we won't embark torpedoes until the last day, in case it gives anyone ideas.'

'Two-four-oh revolutions.'

'Two-four-oh revs, sir . . .'

'Steer three degrees to port.'

Nick had taken over at the binnacle from Chubb, to con *Harbinger* up between columns two and three. Now it was just about full daylight, the commodore had signalled for the zigzag to be renewed, but the plunging, wallowing freighters, agleam from spray and seadew, were on their mean course at this moment. Columns were one thousand yards apart, but ships in column had only four hundred yards between stems and sterns, and combing through them like this – *Harbinger*'s bow-wave curling high, wake spreading in foam as she drove ahead at twenty-two, rising twenty-four knots between the tall-funnelled *Harvest Moon* to port and the shabby little *Timaru* to starboard – you had to watch out for that zigzag, the sudden, simultaneous change of course by this whole mass of ships. He was driving her up through them so the merchant navymen could see her at close quarters and be reminded they did have some warships in attendance. In any case he wanted to take a look around, and eventually have a chat with Tony Graves, up ahead there. Graves had reported over TBS that *Astilbe*'s radar, RDF Type 271, was on the blink. Apparently it had been out of action for some periods during the night, and they'd taken it to pieces now in the hope of having it in operational order before sundown. Nick was prepared to send *Harbinger*'s RDF mechanic over to *Astilbe* by seaboat, if Graves wanted him.

He raised the loud-hailer, aiming it at two figures in the port wing of the *Timaru*'s bridge. The *Timaru* was one of the pair designated as rescue ships. He called, 'Morning, *Timaru* . . . Did you hear the BBC news?'

A wave, and the other man lifted his cap – straight up, then down again, in Charlie Chaplin style . . . The news being that three thousand miles to the east the Eighth Army's offensive was going well: Kidney Ridge was being held against frantic Panzer onslaughts, while the Seventh Armoured and Forty-fourth Divisions of the XIIIth corps smashed into enemy defences facing them. Every news bulletin was being listened to intently in anticipation of the great break-through.

'Zigging to port, sir!'

A warning from Chubb, who'd been watching out for it and spotted the beginning of the swing. Nick stooped to the voice-pipe's copper rim. 'Port ten.'

That desert offensive had opened with a barrage from nearly a thousand guns. He remembered Cruance telling him, 'Don't forget we have an army poised at the Egyptian end as well . . .' Under Generals Alexander and Montgomery they'd launched that one first, on 23 October, while over in the west the huge forces for 'Torch' were massing and converging. The scope of the entire strategy was staggering: and so were the risks, the cost of failure. He couldn't think that in the history of the world there'd been anything of such dimensions. And this – he was looking out over lively, white-streaked sea as the solid block of freighters swung to a new course and *Harbinger* dodged through them like a dog through a herd of cows – this mob, unknown to itself, was part of the same far-reaching plan, might even be the key to its success.

'Midships, and meet her.'

Slanting away now, course nearer west than north, a vacant billet to starboard and the *Colombia* just ahead to port. 'Starboard five . . .' He'd brought her over too far: he was aiming her now for the midway point between the *Sweetcastle* and the *St Eliza*. And – in terms of what was happening here – even if to Cruance and Aubrey Wishart and no doubt a whole team of other planners whose minds were geared to immensely broad strategic concepts, even if to those backroom brains the *raison d'être* of SL 320 was to entice U-boats to attack it, SL 320's escort commander had a much more straightforward object. It was embodied in standing orders in the well-worn phrase 'safe and timely arrival of the convoy', and it was simply to get as many of these ships as possible home to UK ports. That was the job, and you could forget the rest: they needn't even have explained it to him. His preoccupation at this moment wasn't what was happening in the Western Desert or how many convoys might be on their way to Gibraltar, it was this worry about the defective RDF set in *Astilbe*. No *small* worry, either. With only three escorts possessing radar, and night attacks on the surface being the U-boats' favourite method of assault . . .

'Steady as you go.'

'Steady, sir . . . three-three-four, sir.'

Lancing through between that next pair . . . He used the loud-hailer again, to wish them good morning. No response from the *Sweetcastle*, but there were waves from a group on the stern of the *Omeo*, her next ahead. And he saw the turn to starboard just developing now: in every one of these ships a zigzag bell would have rung, telling the quartermaster to put his wheel over. 'Starboard five . . .' Putting a foot wrong here might be rather like being trampled by a herd of elephants. Coming up between the *Omeo* and the *Coriolanus*, whose single squat, blackened funnel was emitting rather too much smoke. Not *all that* much, though; he decided to be tactful, leave it to the commodore to deal with it if it worsened. 'Increase to ten degrees of wheel.'

'Increase to ten . . . Ten o' starboard wheel on, sir . . .'

The commodore – the *Chauncy Maples* – was the next ahead to starboard now, as all ships settled back to the mean course. The next leg would be out to starboard . . . 'Midships.' The leading ship in column two, abeam to port of the commodore, was a Dutchman, the *Toungoo*. 'Steady!'

'Steady, sir . . . Three-three-seven.'

'Steer three-three-five.' He put up the loud-hailer, aiming it at the *Chauncy Maples*. 'Morning, Commodore!'

Sandover was in the bridge wing already, and ready with his loud-hailer. He got in first: 'D'you reckon the Eighth Army's bogged down, at Alamein?'

Harbinger pounding forward through the gap, pitching and smashing through the waves, white spray streaming and green water slamming into the forefront of the bridge and the gunshields down below it. Nick said no, he thought the breakthrough would come pretty soon now. Then they discussed the *Burbridge*, the passenger ship due to join up with SL 320 further north. And some domestic detail: for instance, the full recovery of a man who'd been ill with stomach poisoning in the *Baltimore Cross*, number seventy-two, one day out of Freetown. *Harbinger* had ranged up alongside her in loud-hailer distance so that Mackenzie, the doctor, could give the freighter's captain advice on how to treat the condition. None of the merchantmen carried doctors.

Harbinger was drawing ahead now, and Nick let Chubb take over again at the binnacle. Astern of her, the convoy slewed away to starboard. Ahead, the trawler *Stella* was fine to port while broader on each bow the masts and superstructures of *Paeony* and *Astilbe* swayed more distantly against grey-gleaming sky.

'Come round a bit, Sub. Leave *Stella* some sea-room.'

'Aye aye, sir.' The Australian didn't need to bend his stocky frame far, to reach the voice-pipe. Asdics pinging monotonously as *Harbinger* thrashed on to overhaul that trawler. Whose captain's name was – Nick made the effort, and won – Broad . . .

'Signalman: make by light to *Stella*—'

The HF/DF bell rang, interrupting him. It was the first time it had rung since they'd started northward. Nick was closer to the voice-tube than anyone else, and he answered it. 'Bridge, captain.'

'U-boat on bearing one-seven-one, range eighteen, transmitting sighting report, sir!'

Like a swift kick in the stomach . . .

And there'd be no mistake. That was Gritten, the PO Telegraphist, on the set.

'Anything more than that, Gritten?'

'I'd say he's just surfaced, sir. Not positive, but – he's repeating it now, sir. On 4995 KCs, and the usual prefix. He *is* just up, sir – unless it's very wet where he is . . . I never heard this operator before, sir. Clumsy, like. Not long out of training-school, I'd guess . . .'

Straightening from the voice-pipe, thinking it out. Distances, and times . . . The German was eighteen miles from here . . . say about seventeen astern of the convoy. It might easily be the one *Paeony* had had a sniff at and then lost: it would have stayed down and trailed the convoy from astern, using its hydrophones, listening all night to *Harbinger*'s screws, for God's sake. It probably hadn't intended to attack, before *Paeony* had happened to stumble on it – they weren't normally supposed to, when they found a convoy, their standing orders were to shadow, report, so that Flag Officer U-boats could order this, that and the other bastard to converge, form a pack for a concerted assault . . . Well, the German would be travelling in this direction, if he was following, so you wouldn't have to cover eighteen miles to get at him. Ten to one he'd dive before you reached him; but say half an hour to get there, another half-hour to hand out some discouragement . . . Getting back to the convoy would take longer, since it would have moved on during that time: say an hour and a half, or two and a half altogether. It was almost certainly too late to silence those signals: by the time *Harbinger* got into striking distance, U-boat headquarters at Kernéval would have a convoy position, course and speed . . .

Nine minutes past seven. They'd been out of their kennels, used the cold-water washbasins and holed-up again. Jack leant with a shoulder against the thin wood partitioning, wondering how he'd ever thought for a moment this scheme had a chance of working.

Trolley muttered, 'They've ballsed it up, don't you think?'

'I don't see how they could have been here *before*—'

'Hey!'

The outside door – at the foot of the stairs – had crashed open. Feet were pounding upwards. Too noisy – he thought, too *many* – to be them. So . . . what, guards, sent down here to round them up?

'Better keep out of sight in case it isn't them.' Trolley offered, 'I'll open my door a crack. No point *both* of us—'

'OK.'

It sounded more like six people, than two. And they were off the stairs now, on the plank flooring, coming this way . . . It could be a group of goons coming to use this latrine before going on duty: in which case—

The door was flung open, and a voice called loudly, 'Everard? Trolley?'

Jack pushed his door back. He saw Barmy Morrison, with Cockup Cockrace just behind him, both of them startled for a moment by the sight of German uniforms. Jack asked Barmy, 'What d'you think you are – the town crier?' Trolley snapped, 'Shut the bloody door, at least!' Cockup limping forward with a smile on his pale, moustached face as he opened his coat and tugged at the waistband of his trousers. Pulling the rifle out awkwardly: it had been down his leg like a splint, but he limped anyway from having been shot in the knee at some stage, and no-one would have seen a difference without looking closely. Morrison, beaming, crowed, 'Piece of cake, *mein Herren, keine* bother whatsoever!'

'We haven't even started yet.' Jack took the rifle from Cockup. 'Frank, you ready?'

'Yes. Let's move.' Trolley told the other two, 'Act as you would if we were real Germans. Forget it's us, just be yourselves being escorted to the dentist and nothing special about it. And for God's sake keep your traps shut, will you?'

Cockrace asked, 'One point . . . If the gate sentry's clued-up enough to remember the dentist goes off on the toot on Wednesdays, what's the drill?'

'I try to bluff us through. This Wednesday he must be working, for a change. If I see it isn't going to work–' Trolley was moving towards the door, herding them – 'I'll act as if I'm fed up, someone's given me the wrong orders. I turn you about and we march back here, abort the operation, dump the rifle, slope off . . . Now come on!'

Out, and clattering down the stairs. The building was still empty, so that much of the gamble had come off. Jack slung the rifle, goon-style. The Escape Committee had had it in their keeping for several months; some idiot had pinched it somehow, from a drunk or otherwise unwary guard, and there'd been a tremendous hue and cry, searches and mass punishments. It was said the guard had been accused of selling it and had been shot, and the Committee had been only too glad to get rid of it.

The cold drizzle was a good enough excuse for turning up greatcoat collars. Cockrace and Morrison marched in file – POW-style marching, which meant shambling – with Jack as armed guard to one side in front of Tolley as the NCO strutting behind. Along behind the hospital block and then left to join the road leading to the gate. Where they'd be stopped, of course; and possession of the rifle would make the offence extremely serious, might even justify the firing-squad with which they so much enjoyed threatening would-be escapers. Otherwise it would be another dose of solitary, then transport to the *Straflager*: which not only was said to be escape-proof but was also miles from anywhere. Unlike this dump, which wasn't *so* far from the Swiss border . . . Trolley asked in a low mutter, 'Got your train tickets, you two?'

'Yup.'

'Money?'

'Rolling in it . . . Permission to sing *Land of Hope and Glory*, sah?'

'Will you shut up, for Christ's sake?'

Cockup murmured, 'Zey have vays of mekking us shot op.'

They'd wheeled on to the road now, and the gate was fifty yards away. It was because there was never a dental party on Wednesdays that it had seemed feasible to mount this excursion. If there'd been a real dentistry session you couldn't have done it. The snag was that the gate sentry might be smart enough to know which day of the week this was.

Thirty yards to go. The sentry was standing squarely in front of the gate, this side of it, gazing at them as they marched towards him. Not many yards to his right, at the corner of the wire, was one of the tall lookout boxes on stilts, with a machine-gunner in it. Jack was careful not to glance upwards, because such a movement might have displayed his beard.

Barmy began gabbling over his shoulder, 'Hey, fellows, I forgot to mention—'

'Shut up!'

'Yeah, but listen – news bulletin on Hut Four's set, crack of dawn: the dingdong in the desert? Well, sounds like we're about to hit 'em for six!'

Trolley bawled in German, 'Talking is forbidden!'

A dozen yards ahead, the sentry moved. Swinging the gate open . . .

Chapter 8

From 'The U-boat War in the Atlantic' – official German account:
In spite of the sighting reports by radio from the U-boats, convoy . . . coming from the south, maintained its course and . . . passed through the centre of the patrol line.

'Red two-oh, sir, beam-on!'

CPO Bearcroft had sighted the *Burbridge*. They'd been searching for her, and had had her on the 271 screen for some time, but it was pitch dark under low cloud and although the wind was still only force four it was out of the northwest, right in their eyes and with spray in it. Altogether a lousy night, with a shadower astern of the convoy piping up from time to time, plus this errant passenger ship who'd failed to make the rendezvous yesterday at noon, failed again at dusk after yet another engine breakdown. They hadn't received her signal until after she'd missed the first one; her master obviously wouldn't have wanted to break radio silence unnecessarily and advertise his ship's position, but it had caused headaches. A ship on her own in the Atlantic could easily disappear without trace; when she hadn't shown up for the third rendezvous Nick had left the convoy and come out to get her.

Every hour counted now. By midnight you'd be counting out the minutes. He told Bearcroft, 'Call her up, say, "Please follow me. What is your best speed?"'

Then he'd know what course to steer, to rejoin as fast as possible. He was anxious to get back, for the obvious reasons but also because at midnight SL 320 would be in position A, where mean course would be altered to 042 degrees, a northeasterly slant to take it between the Canaries and the Azores.

They'd relaxed from dusk action stations an hour ago, and Chubb had the watch. Nick, with his glasses focused on the *Burbridge*'s dark profile, was telling him to turn on to a converging course, closing in obliquely on the passenger ship's bow. His object was to take *Harbinger* up fairly close to her, and let them see her at close quarters so they'd know what they were following. The *Burbridge* was lucky to be afloat, to have come this far alone and unscathed. Yesterday there'd been calls for help from another straggler – a tanker, according to the register – who'd been attacked several times, fought off the first one with her gun – that had been a U-boat on the surface – then suffered only minor damage from one torpedo hit some hours later, and finally been hit again and sunk, or had been sinking, early this afternoon. She'd been too far away for there to have been any chance of helping, but she'd been in this general area of the Atlantic, and apparently three different U-boats had each had a crack at her: while this *Burbridge* had come through completely untouched. *This* far.

An answering stab of light sparked, then died again, from that substantial-looking superstructure. She looked bigger, he thought, than her registered 9800 tons. From behind him in *Harbinger*'s jolting, swaying bridge a blue-shaded Aldis lamp had begun to clack out that message, with a flash for each word from the *Burbridge* as her signalman took it in.

'Come five degrees to port. One-three-oh revs.'

The name of the ship who'd been under attack had been *Anglo-Maersk*, 7705 gross registered tons. Not that one had needed proof of the presence of U-boats in the area. SL 320 still had at least one shadower – or had had, up till dusk this evening.

'Message passed, sir.'

'Very good.'

'Course three-five-five, sir.'

Wind and sea were on the bow now, *Harbinger* performing her corkscrew dance, spray sheeting over and away to starboard while she closed in towards the *Burbridge* – whose crew and passengers might well be heaving sighs of relief, in ignorance of the fact they'd be joining a convoy which must by this time have become a focus of interest at U-boat headquarters. SL 320 would have been on Admiral Dönitz's plot for several days now: from the morning when he'd taken *Harbinger* tearing southward in the hope of catching that U-boat on the surface, perhaps even with a chance of stopping him before his transmissions were picked up at Kernéval. Fat hope: the transmissions had been acknowledged – not by FO U-boats, Gritten had said, but by some other U-boat a long way north, who'd have passed it on – and had then ceased, and there'd been no submarine on the surface when they got down there. An asdic sweep had produced nothing either, and new sorties in recent days had also drawn a blank.

There was a hope now, though, if he could get this *Burbridge* back and tucked into the convoy quickly enough. It was a slim chance, admittedly, and only of throwing the shadower off the scent for a while, giving the convoy another day's grace, perhaps, before the sharks gathered in strength. The hope rested on this course alteration that was due to be made at midnight, a swing sixty-two degrees to starboard; if while the convoy wheeled he could keep the shadower away – dived and busy saving its own skin – there might be a chance of fooling it, winning a breathing-space before the next one picked them up.

But obviously he had to get the *Burbridge* into the convoy first.

Flashing, now . . .

He read it for himself: *Will follow you at 9 1/2 knots. Deeply grateful for this assistance.*

'Number One, tell Scarr nine and a half knots. I want the course to rejoin and how long it'll take.'

Warrimer went quickly to the plot voice-pipe, long arms reaching spiderlike to drag his lanky frame up the slope of bridge. Then she was teetering on a ridge and he was folded against the bridge's side, clutching the voice-pipe for an anchor as she swung over, whacking into a trough, sea flying up and over . . . Nick told Chubb, 'Come down to one-one-oh revs!'

It would take them slowly past the big merchantman, slanting across his bow to take station a few hundred yards ahead. Holding the carrot of deliverance visibly in front of the donkey's nose. A spurious deliverance though it might be. You certainly couldn't envy passengers in the situation they'd be in: helpless, aware of how vulnerable their ship was, that a torpedo might strike at any time, day or night. They'd have slept fully dressed and wearing lifebelts and with any valuables in their pockets . . . He heard Warrimer taking Scarr's answer through the voice-pipe: 'Course to steer three-five-three, for two and a quarter hours.'

'Chief Yeoman: make to the *Burbridge*, "Course three-five-three. Expect to join convoy at—"' he checked his watch's green-glowing dial – '"twenty-three ten".'

So if all went well he'd have her there fifty minutes before the convoy reached position A and altered course. Not much margin . . .

This was close enough to the *Burbridge*. He checked his ship's head and the lie of the other ship, and told Chubb, 'Come three degrees to starboard.' Glasses up again: he could make out figures along her rails. Dark shadows, and no chink of light anywhere, but – hands waving?

One white cloth or handkerchief . . .

Chubb reported, 'Course is three-five-eight, sir.'

'Very good.'

Overhauling the passenger ship very slowly while the Aldis clacked, passing that signal, and the light's bluish radiance flickered spasmodically across the bridge. You had to take care not to look round at it, or you'd lose your night vision for a while; but the destroyer's racy profile and that occasional faint illumination over her swaying bridge would be easily visible to the people looking down at her across sea swelling and tumbling between them like rapids. Nick heard the morse symbols AR, the end-of-message group, and read the *Burbridge*'s K acknowledging. Then as the clicking stopped, he heard cheering.

Warrimer moved up near him. 'Sounds like they're glad to see us, sir.' The two ships were as close as they'd come, at this stage. Warrimer added, putting his glasses up again, 'Why, quite a few of 'em are women!'

There was no reason to be surprised at it. Passengers, whether civilian or uniformed, did come in two sexes. *Harbinger* was drawing ahead, and she was well enough clear to steer the course ordained by Scarr; Nick told Chubb, 'Bring her to three-five-three.'

At ten forty-five they had the convoy on a steady bearing on the bow, the nearer corner of ships and the trawler *Opal* painted clearly on the RDF screen. In twenty-five minutes he had to have the *Burbridge* in her billet. She was on *Harbinger*'s port quarter now, at two cables' distance. It seemed they'd be cutting it very fine.

'Signalman.'

Wolstenholm came slithering from the starboard for'ard corner as the ship rolled to port . . .

'Take this down. To *Burbridge* from *Harbinger*.'

Wolstenholm ducked under the canvas hood of the bridge chart table, where he could use a light. Nick dictated, '"Convoy is in eight columns of five ships, columns one thousand yards abeam, ships in column two cables apart. Course is three-three-five, no zigzag until daylight, speed six point seven five knots. You are allocated vacant billet number three-four. I will lead you between numbers two-five and three-five. Course will be altered at midnight to oh-four-two by signal from the commodore who is in MV *Chauncy Maples* number three-one. We are being shadowed and attack by U-boats must be expected soon. Time of Origin – whatever . . ." Read that back, now.'

He thought, when the lamp was clicking again, calling up, that the last sentence of the message might make them feel less like cheering. But it was necessary to warn them, and in any case they'd soon have the comfort of being surrounded by other ships.

Ten minutes later he had *Opal* in his glasses. He'd been searching for her, knowing her bearing already from RDF, and now there was more work for the signalman. He called him over and pointed out the trawler.

'Call him up, and make, "Pass to commodore, from *Harbinger*: am leading *Burbridge* into her station from astern. Have informed her master of your scheduled alteration."'

The HF/DF bell rang: he told the signalman quickly, 'Go on, send it.' Warrimer shouted from the huffduff voice-pipe, 'U-boat transmitting on one-five-oh, nine miles, sir!'

Still astern of the convoy, but closer. In a shadowing position and possibly doing no more than shadowing; but with its high surface speed – compared to the convoy's – it would only take it an hour to catch up, if that was its intention.

Warrimer passed another piece of information from Gritten: 'It's calling some other U-boat, sir, and getting no answer.'

He saw an answering flash out there – from *Opal*.

He couldn't do a damn thing about that U-boat while he still had the *Burbridge* on his hands: she had to be put into safe storage . . . And as she had only two and a half to three knots margin over convoy speed, it was going to take a little while still. Leaving the German out there on his own, meanwhile, calling to its friends, passing them details about the convoy. He might even be telling them, *The rear of this outfit is wide open*. There wasn't anything he could do about that either: the two corvettes had to be in the van, and the trawlers didn't have the speed, or RDF . . .

HD/DF bell again, and Warrimer's answer of 'Bridge!' Wolstenholm was still rattling out that signal, drawing splintery glints of acknowledgement from the trawler. *Opal* wasn't taking it in very fast.

'U-boat on bearing three-three-nine, range seventeen, in contact with the one astern, sir!'

Damn . . .

'Number One – put the messenger on that voice-pipe. You see to it the plot's getting these ranges and bearings.'

He had it visually charted, though, in his mind. Ranges and bearings when plotted down there by Scarr and his assistants would eventually provide enemy speeds and courses; but meanwhile he was picturing it for himself and reckoning that this one ahead, now seventeen miles on the convoy's port bow, must be roughly seven miles the other side of position A, where the convoy would be changing its course. But the German wouldn't be sitting still: and if it was closing now, it would be attacking well *before* the turn was ordered. But then again, it could be maintaining its distance, keeping pace while it waited for others to join it.

Time would tell. The snag was that time was rather short.

'Number One. That contact on three-three-nine – ask Scarr for its range and bearing from *Paeony*.'

Because *Paeony* would be the striker to be used against it – and before the convoy turned. The one and only major course alteration SL 320 was to be allowed . . . He decided he'd send Guyatt out *now*: in the hope he'd be able to keep that one at a long arm's length.

'Message passed to *Opal*, sir!'

Plunging on, convoy shapes growing, clarifying. *Opal* was visible to the naked eye now, mostly because of the froth of white around her. Warrimer reported, 'Contact range and bearing from *Paeony* is twelve miles on three-two-eight, sir!'

At last . . . 'Chief – TBS to *Paeony* – "Investigate surface contact bearing three-two-eight twelve miles from you".'

It would take Guyatt half an hour to get close enough to that one to do anything useful about it.

Neither of the corvettes had HF/DF. But at least *Astilbe*'s radar was functioning now. *Harbinger*'s RDF mechanic, who'd been transferred to her by boat three days ago, had fixed it. Nick had left him there, to make sure of it.

Paeony had answered, and Bearcroft was passing that order to her. Nick checked the time: six minutes past eleven . . .

'Now call Fox, Chief. Captain to captain.' He had his

glasses on the convoy's tail-end ships. It was time to edge over and pass close under the sterns of the *William Law* and the *Harvest Moon* before turning up between the columns.

'Bring her ten degrees to starboard, Sub.'

The *Burbridge*'s master would see the bend in his wake, and follow.

'Commander Graves on TBS for you, sir.'

He went over and took the mike. 'Tony, here's the picture. I'm about to lead the *Burbridge* into her billet in column three. Then I'm going to investigate a huffduff contact last heard of nine miles astern. As you'll have heard, *Paeony*'s on to the one ahead of us. When we're in position A we may both be able to keep 'em busy while the convoy turns. So you'll be on your own . . . All right?'

Graves's voice crackled, *Roger, sir. Out*.

The *Burbridge* had followed *Harbinger*'s adjustment of course to starboard. Passing astern of the *William Law* at this moment . . . 'Come five degrees to port.'

HF/DF bell: the messenger, Wragge, was answering it . . . 'U-boat transmitting on one-three-nine, seven miles, sir!'

So the bearing had drawn left and the range had shortened: which meant the shadower was moving up on the convoy's starboard quarter and talking to one of its colleagues while it did so. If it had been sensible it might have kept its mouth shut: Scarr would be able to produce a course and speed now, from two well-separated fixes and if the German held on as he was an interception wouldn't be difficult – even if he did not appear soon on the 271 screen.

'Course three-five-eight, sir.'

Harbinger thrashed through the wake of the *Harvest Moon*. Nick was fidgetting with impatience to get out after that U-boat which, if it was making its full surface speed of seventeen knots, could be in a position to attack in roughly – the figures sorted themselves in his mind as he turned to see where Wolstenholm had got to – in say thirty minutes; which would be the worst possible time, as the convoy would be on the point of making its turn then. You needed to hit him well before that . . .

'Signalman, make to the *Burbridge*, "I have to leave you now. Please take station ahead of the *Timaru*, rear ship in column three".'

From this angle the *Timaru* was a black end-on shape underlined in white. He heard the Aldis lamp begin its calling-up routine, rapidly repeated letter As: impatience growing, thinking, *Come on, come on, wake up* . . . Then the plot/RDF voice-pipe was calling, and Warrimer was there to answer it: 'Two-seven-one contact bearing one-three-oh, five and a half miles, looks like a U-boat!'

'Tell them it *is*.'

What the hell else it could be, short of the Flying Dutchman, who might not register on RDF . . .

The *Burbridge* had answered – thank God. His message was stuttering out to her. He called to Chubb, 'Starboard wheel to one-one-oh. Three hundred revolutions.' The picture in his mind, each feature in it moving in relation to all the others, was of the convoy steering northwest and only forty minutes short of position A, *Paeony* forging out on its port bow to meet one threat, *Astilbe* shifting towards the centre to cover as much as possible of that wide front, and his own ship now turning east – just south of east – to intercept the threat from astern. It might well be the German who'd been shadowing them for several days – if it had now had permission or orders to attack: if that was so one might assume the shadowing job was done and the pack had gathered.

Harbinger heeling to the turn, gathering speed, turbine and other noise rising as the revs increased. Warrimer asked, close beside him, 'Close the hands up, sir?'

'Yes!' He thumbed the alarm button: annoyed at having had to be reminded they weren't already at action stations. Getting old – or stale . . .

'Three hundred revs on, sir, course one-one-oh!'

He left the high seat, took over at the binnacle. Relief at no longer being nursemaid to the *Burbridge* was diluted by sober recognition that the battle for convoy SL 320 was about to start: it was likely to be a long, exhausting one . . .

Looking round the bridge he saw Chubb busy at the depthcharge telephone, Warrimer talking over the line to his guns' crews. Carlish, having seen that Nick was conning the ship himself, went to look after communications with the plot and the 271.

'U-boat bears one-three-one, five miles, sir!'

'I want a course to intercept.' He called down to the wheel-house, 'Three-forty revolutions.'

'Three-forty revolutions, sir . . .'

That was the coxswain, CPO Elphick, on the wheel now. *Harbinger* at full stretch, hurling herself across and through the combers. It was dry in the bridge now though, because the wind was almost right astern. Warrimer's voice was pitched high over the mix of noise: 'Four-inch and point-fives closed up, sir!' Chubb followed suit: 'Depthcharge crew closed up, sir!'

'Course one-one-oh, sir.'

What was needed now was news from Scarr. From the U-boat's course and speed he'd work out – should have, by now – a course to intercept it. But a TBS call was coming in: *Eagle, this is Gannet: U-boat has dived one mile ahead of me. Attacking!*

'Target bears one-two-eight, four point one miles. Plot suggests course to intercept one-one-four degrees, sir.'

'Steer one-one-four, cox'n.'

She was fairly flying now. But there were no orders to pass to Guyatt: if he had a U-boat diving only two thousand yards ahead of him, he might have a chance . . .

'Enemy course now three-three-nine, speed sixteen, bearing one-two-one range three point four!'

Six thousand four hundred yards . . .

'Load A gun with starshell, the others with SAP.'

Warrimer intoning into the telephone, 'A gun with starshell, B and X with SAP, load, load, load! Target will be right ahead, U-boat on surface, set range oh-six-oh!'

And then the one thing you dreaded . . . A deep, hard crash, from way back on the quarter, the convoy's starboard wing. The sound had all its usual, sickening implications.

No flash, only the sound of the torpedo striking, exploding. Then – ten or fifteen seconds later, a second one. Fleetingly in the back of Nick's mind there was recognition that there *were* more than two attackers; also that *Gleam*, the trawler on that side, and perhaps also the *Leona*, the rescue ship with the red-headed, argumentative skipper, would look after the victims. Although *Gleam*'s priority would be to counter-attack first – if he had any idea where the torpedoes had come from . . .

'Target's dived, sir!'

Meaning it had vanished from the 271 screen. 'Last range and bearing?' He told Chubb, 'Shallow pattern, stand by.' He wasn't going to start hunting this one with asdics; by the time he got there and then slowed *Harbinger* enough for the set to be operable the German could be a mile away in any direction he chose. So – one wild swipe . . .

'Diving position now bears one-one-six, three thousand four hundred yards, sir!'

'Steer one-one-six.' He straightened from the voice-pipe: that distant rumble was from depthcharges – *Paeony*'s . . . 'Sub – I want to know when we've run three thousand yards.'

Blind chance, but some rough method in it. Three thousand yards was one and a half nautical miles: at that point he'd order port helm, count on the turning-circle carrying her to the U-boat's track, and steady on 340 degrees, the course it had been steering until it dived and might (or might not) still be steering now. He'd run up what he'd assume to be its continuing track, and drop one full pattern.

Then search. For long enough to keep the bastard down while the convoy made its turn. Which he guessed would be in just minutes now.

He'd ordered shallow settings on the charges, but second thoughts prevailed now . . . 'Set charges to one-five-oh feet, Sub!' Fifty metres, that would be in the German reckoning. His gamble was that the U-boat's captain would want to go deep enough to hide but might be hoping to surface again and press home his attack when this danger had passed, so would not – probably – have gone *very* deep. Chubb had passed the new order aft to Mr Timberlake, who would undoubtedly be turning the air blue with curses while his team worked fast to change the settings on the pistols. You did it with a special spanner, but in the dark and on a bouncing, canting deck it wasn't all that easy.

'One thousand five hundred yards, sir!'

Three-quarters of a mile . . .

Astern, light sparked, grew, flooded its whiteness across the seascape. You didn't have to blind yourself by looking to see what it was. Snow-flake, the merchant ship's equivalent of starshell, an illuminatory rocket they fired to light up attacking enemies. And if there was another U-boat that close to the convoy, the turn to starboard wasn't going to help, because the damn thing would be there to see it and report it. There was a call on TBS, at the same time as Carlish passed on a warning from Scarr that there were one thousand yards to go: this was *Astilbe*, Tony Graves reporting he had an RDF contact six thousand yards ahead – attacking . . .

'Five hundred yards!'

One quarter of a mile. At thirty knots, they'd cover it in thirty seconds. No great accuracy was involved in this: in fact it was so hit-or-miss that an apparent error like turning too soon or too late might happen to be lucky; and if anything came of it other than keeping the U-boat down and preoccupied – which was the main object – it would be *pure* luck. He put his face down near the voice-pipe: the plot, echoed by Carlish, called '*Now*, sir!' and he told Elphick, 'Port fifteen.' As the wheel came on *Harbinger* leant hard to starboard, pitching and slamming through the turn as her rudder hauled her round, lying on her ear and slicing the sea into sheets of flying white: and the commodore's siren wailed like a distant banshee – so SL 320 was in position A, altering course to north-east, the herd of ships swinging their stems to point at the gap between the Canaries and the Azores . . . 'Midships!'

Those two torpedo hits had been widely enough separated in time to have been hits on two different ships. First blood, anyway, and much too soon . . . 'Meet her!'

'Meet her, sir . . .'

Elphick, down in the wheelhouse, would be spinning his wheel to put on reverse rudder and check the swing. Nick told him as the rate of turn slowed, 'Steer three-four-oh.' At this speed it was just a hope that *Harbinger* could be over the top of the U-boat and depth charges floating down around it before its captain caught on to what was happening and dodged away.

'Course three-four-oh, sir!'

Hammering into the sea, meeting it more or less head-on now: 'Stand by!' He glanced round, saw the white of Chubb's face turned towards him, Chubb crouched against the depthcharge panel with one hand grasping the telephone and the other on the firing buzzer. Back aft, Timberlake's men in their streaming oilskins would be waiting to send the first high-explosive cannisters splashing down from the stern chutes. And now was as good a time as any: he shouted, '*Fire!*' Then, turning to look ahead again, saw a lick of flame from where the convoy would still be making its wheel to starboard. A very small spurt of yellow fire and then a glow that brightened, blossomed; the sound came afterwards, muffled by distance but clearly another torpedo crashing home.

One of the oilers?

The blaze astonished Looff. He'd thought when the flames first gushed out of her, *My God, I've hit a tanker!* But he hadn't: it was the freighter he'd aimed at, a snap shot with two torpedoes when suddenly and surprisingly he'd found the easy target in his master sight perfectly set up and at ideal range; he'd loosed off two fish and struck this blazing gold with one!

He guessed the other would have missed astern. U 702 swinging fast now, under maximum wheel. '*Full* ahead both engines!'

The convoy had altered course, he realised: that was how the target had suddenly presented itself to him as it had. Not just an emergency alteration with all ships turning simultaneously, but a wheel, a real change of course with the convoy's formation maintained by inner ships slowing down, outer ones increasing by a knot or so . . . But that freighter must have had some highly inflammable cargo in her. She was alone, stopped, burning from end to end, and U 702 was turning her tail to the inferno, skidding out of the dangerous light of it . . . 'Steady as you go!'

Trimmed down low, lancing through the waves, as low as a surf-board and about as wet. Diesels pounding: the air-intake was only a few feet behind him, virtually under the lookouts' feet, and the roar of it was loud at this full speed. Sea was coming over green, half a ton a minute. And those were depthcharges, somewhere far astern of the convoy, he thought. Werner Knappe getting it in the neck? He shouted, 'Ship's head?'

Oelricher told him, 'Zero-zero-seven, sir!'

To all intents and purposes, north. So the convoy's wheel must have been to about northeast. It would make sense, too: he'd check it later on the chart, but he guessed it would be normal enough for a convoy on this route. In fact he might have anticipated it: *should* have . . .

There was an escort of some kind, he saw, moving in close to the burning ship. Small, its profile etched black against the flames. It looked like a tug . . . Nosing in there . . . He wiped the front lenses of his glasses, put them up again quickly. Trawler? If *that* was what they were trying to guard this convoy with . . . 'Reduce to half speed!'

He'd bring her round to starboard in a minute, to a course parallel to the convoy, out on its bow. For the moment his main concern was to get clear of that burning ship, which was lighting up a square mile or more of sea. An escort destroyer in the wrong place now would have U 702 silhouetted against her own kill: and there could be one out there, too, if the ship he'd run into earlier had turned back. They certainly weren't *all* trawlers. He called over his shoulder, 'Keep your eyes peeled, you lookouts!'

There were only two of them. He'd have four on the bridge in normal routine, but when you might have to dive in a hurry that was too much of a crowd. Four men in all – himself, those two, and Oelricher – were more than enough. He'd brought the quartermaster – and Franz Walther his chief engineer too – with him from U 122 to this new command.

'Come to zero-four-zero!'

Oelricher passed the order down into the tower. Heusinger was there, as well as the helmsman and two others. Willi Heusinger's job as first lieutenant was to operate the torpedo-fitting calculator, the machine that told you about such things as deflection, aim-off, based on the courses, ranges and speeds you fed into it. He also triggered the firing of the torpedoes from there. It had been very smartly and quickly done, this shot at the target that was now ablaze: and right after a distinctly nerve-jarring encounter with that escort out in the deep field. It had materialised out of nowhere, belting straight at them: Looff had crashdived and made use of his boat's deep-diving capability, taking her right down fast and steeply to two hundred metres while depth charges were pooping off right up near the surface. He'd kept the batteries grouped-up and pushed on at full speed for a while – hearing more charges burst astern, and laughing at them – the sort of thing a crew of youngsters, brittly nervous, admired and responded to with enthusiasm . . . Then he'd brought her up again, at slow speed and with great caution, while the escort was still hunting them three or four miles away.

Looff felt good again. His old self. Only exhaustion had led him to confuse that drained, hopeless mood with loss of nerve. And he'd recovered quickly from the deep shock and despondency at being deprived of his Berlin leave. Trudi's admirably stoic reaction had helped a lot: Trudi was a lot more than just a pretty face and a sensational body, she was her father's daughter too!

'Escort vessel red one-zero, sir!'

Oelricher's sharp eyes and strident voice . . . Looff swung like a gun-fighter – except it was binoculars he was aiming. Focusing – on a corvette in profile, white turmoil around her hull making her easy to see. She was travelling from left to right at about twelve knots.

'Port twenty!'

The corvette hadn't spotted them: and he was turning stern-on to it, to reduce the chances . . . Turning the long way round, actually, because this suited his plans and also because he guessed the corvette would be heading for the convoy's van. If this was the one who'd charged him earlier on, and had since been wasting a lot of depth charges, it would almost certainly have come from the front of the convoy and would therefore be returning to that station now, with a longer distance to cover because of the change of course. Alternatively it might be the ship he'd heard hunting *Drachen* Three earlier on. *Drachen* Three – U 208, Gustaf Becker – hadn't put in an attack yet, so far as Looff had heard.

'Midships.'

Depthcharges. A long way off. You felt them, more than heard them. The helmsman span his wheel, down in the tower. Looff asked Oelricher, 'Where is it now?'

'Just about astern, sir.'

'Steady as you go!'

According to the shadowing *Drachen* Four's reports – that was Knappe in U 580 – the convoy consisted of about forty ships with six escorts. Knappe had been riding herd on the convoy for several days, having found it and stuck with it since before Looff and U 702 had got down here. But there'd been nothing about trawlers. Tomorrow when they all compared notes it should be possible to make a more accurate assessment. Meanwhile two of the convoy had been accounted for: he'd heard two hits some time ago – they'd been on the convoy's starboard side, so that must have been *Drachen* Two, Hans Köning's U 54 – and now he'd polished off this incendiary. It was a start, anyway.

'That Brit's out of sight, sir.'

'Good. Port twenty.'

'Port twenty, sir!'

'I'll take her round in a circle, settle on about northeast

and close in again. Give tubes three and four a chance, maybe.'

The flames in the southwest had been extinguished, and he guessed his target had sunk. U 702 might have been alone now in an empty sea. Darkness and wind and the sting of salt water, rumbling growl of diesels and the hoarse sucking of the intakes . . . Wondering what had happened to Becker and Knappe, and whether they'd realise the convoy had altered course. During these night rough-and-tumbles you couldn't keep track of everything: you had a certain picture in your brain and you could touch it up with a certain amount of guesswork, but things rarely went just as they'd been planned and boats that hadn't shown up in the sectors allotted to them could be just about anywhere until torpedo hits or depthcharging provided clues. He'd have them all concentrated and organised again tomorrow, and there'd be some others joining too. Four were on their way. The original intention had been for them all to be here before U 702 arrived, but there'd been some hitch connected with the redeployment of one whole group into the Mediterranean. Anyway, with eight boats altogether and escorts few and far between, there'd be easy pickings to come.

The thing was, undoubtedly, to play it by the book – Flag Officer U-boats' book. Use the pack *as* a pack, go for the hammer blow. At this stage, before he had them all together, reconnaissance was more important than sinking a ship here or there; as leader, it was one's primary task now to organise and concert the action. While naturally, if opportunities like the last one did present themselves one would take advantage of them.

'Convoy's in sight to starboard, sir!'

'Ship's head?'

'Zero four five, sir . . .'

'Steer zero-five-zero. Open three and four bowcaps. Revs for five knots.'

He was reducing speed in order to make less wash, show less bow-wave, and keep peace with the slow-moving convoy. Sliding quietly and very nearly invisibly along, gradually closing the range while taking the opportunity to make a detailed inspection. Sweeping round with his binoculars now as his boat edged in closer, converging by a few degrees on the enemy's course, he could see no escorts at all.

None. It was quite extraordinary.

'Seems it's open day here!'

Oelricher grunted. He was searching too. The masts and upperworks of the nearer column of merchantmen growing taller and clearer as distance slowly lessened. U 702 was trimmed down so low she'd get almost alongside those ships before they'd see her: and with her tanks already half-full of water she could crash-dive like a ton of bricks if she needed to . . . The quartermaster suggested, 'Might be the little widger that was standing by that ship we hit, when it was burning, should've been this side?'

'Right. And when the cat's away . . .' Looff chuckled. 'Even if it's only a little, toothless one!'

But – one trawler, to guard the whole flank of a convoy this size?

'Three and four bowcaps open, sir!'

It felt like being in a zoo with a game-rifle. The whole bag of tricks was in his lap! It made him feel slightly drunk – such fantastic luck! And there was a lot more of it than his immediate situation . . . He asked Oelricher, 'Did you ever hear of anyone destroying an entire convoy?'

'Not *yet* sir.' The quartermaster grinned. 'But there's always a first time . . . Big fellow in there, sir. Two wide funnels on heavy-looking upperworks: looks like a liner, passenger ship!'

'I don't see—'

'Just abaft our beam – there's a vacant space in this line, no ship astern of the one abeam now?'

'Check.'

'But in the next column there is. And if you look past that one's stern – at what must be column three?'

'Ah. Yes . . .'

It would be a tricky shot from here. And there were so

many easy ones. There was also a week or so in hand, and four boats joining the pack tomorrow.

'I'll take this near one.' He thought, just *one* torpedo. Why waste more, when a blind halfwit couldn't miss, and when you were going to need all the torpedoes you had? To knock a target down with a single fish was also rather stylish, and would look well in the patrol report . . . 'Target speed six knots, range nine hundred metres. Stand by number three tube. I'll fire from ninety degrees on his port bow, and his course is – zero-four-zero. Starboard five!'

Oelricher set the night-sight, as she began to swing towards the firing course. In the tower, Heusinger had worked out the director angle, aim-off: he called up to her skipper, giving him the course to steer, and at the same time removed the safety clip from the trigger of number three tube. Oelricher was reporting he had the sight set when both men heard the soft *whoosh* of a rocket, then another, and a snowflake burst: the entire surroundings were suddenly as bright as day. Looff shouted, 'Increase to ten degrees of wheel!' In order to come on aim and fire more quickly: but then he saw his target beginning to swing, turn towards him, the freighter's length shortening, bow-wave lifting against the steel walls of her massive stem. She'd seen him, fired those snowflakes, turned to ram . . .

'Hard a-starboard, full ahead both, shut bowcaps!'

Running: but what the hell else? You couldn't hit a ship bow-on; and lit up like this he wasn't in command of the situation any more, he was vulnerable, with a vision printed on his imagination as U 702 swung away – picking up speed, diesel and intake noise rising, roaring: the vision was of that towering black stem looming over, shutting out the sky as it bore down on him, explosively destructive as it hit, ploughed in, crushing and ripping through steel . . .

It was all right. She'd outrun that old hooker, easily . . .

Another *whoosh*, another light flooding from the sky . . . 'Midships!'

'Midships, sir. Wheel's—'

'Destroyer starboard! Green one-zero-zero, bow on!'

He had it in his glasses. Corvette, not destroyer. But *close.* A gun on its foc'sl fired: a yellow flash, and a noise like ripping canvas as the shell passed overhead. Looff wrenched himself out of the paralysis of shock – screamed at the look-outs, 'Down!' He'd shoved Oelricher towards the hatch. Then: 'Dive, dive!' Where the hell that thing had come from: *out of the convoy?* It had just fired again. They were piling into the hatch before he realised he'd blundered. The corvette was too close, there wasn't going to be *time* . . .

Trolley stopped suddenly in the middle of the road. It was so dark that Jack almost walked into him. The road – or rather lane – curved and dipped just ahead, and there were lights glimmering through trees down in the hollow.

At 2am? In this rural wasteland? Two previous nights' observation along the way had suggested that bedtime in these parts was about 8pm.

'Village,' Trolley muttered, 'We'd better skirt round it. What d'you think – left or right?'

This was the third night's walking, after some nerve-punishing but in fact uneventful train journeys: first to Munich, and then to Ulm, where they'd changed for Tuttlingen, which was only about twenty miles from the Swiss frontier. Three nights was what they'd reckoned on, after they'd decided – with good reason – to hoof it over this last section. The plan was to walk by night and hole-up by day, living frugally off the remains of their food and keeping away from people or habitation; and this third night should bring them close enough to the border to make some sort of reconnaissance of it, either in daylight tomorrow or after dark. Depending on how it looked, they'd cross either tomorrow night or the one after.

By which time, they realised now, they'd be starving. Frugality was one thing: having bugger-all to eat was another.

The other two had taken a train from Tuttlingen to Singen, which was bang on the frontier, but the odds were ten to one that by this time they'd be wishing they hadn't. Jack thanked his own and Trolley's caution, that earlier decision to travel in two separate pairs. The reason they'd advanced for this was that four scruffy-looking characters in one bunch would have been more noticeable, more alarming or suspicious to the eyes of respectable citizens or officials. This was a valid point, too, but there was another – that Morrison and Cockrace, who seemed to regard the whole thing as a lark, might well become a liability.

Which, as things had turned out, had been putting it mildly.

The moon had gone down an hour ago, and except for those lights down in the dip it was as black as pitch. Jack said, having thought about it, 'I think this time we should keep to the road. Just sneak through quietly. Otherwise it'll be daylight before we're near the frontier. That'd mean another night, and we'd have to get food somehow.'

'What if the border guards have been alerted?'

It seemed a *non-sequitur*. The guards would be alert anyway. Unfortunately . . . 'Oh, you mean if they've caught the others?'

'I mean border villages would have been warned too.' He nodded downhill. 'This one included. Could account for lights burning.'

They were both tired as well as hungry – and knew it, made allowances for it when they got on each others' nerves. The next step but one always looked as if it would be easy, but when you got to that point you found the snags, unexpected problems. The really colossal hurdle, of course, was going to be the frontier: back in the camp, planning this break, *reaching* the frontier had been the main worry.

'The place we do have to avoid is Singen. The odds are that those two are in the bag by now, probably have been for days. The Bosch know there were four of us, and it was Singen they were heading to, so that's where they'd expect *us* to turn up. Sense?'

Trolley seemed dubious. Or slow-witted . . . 'Could be. But I don't see what—'

'This lane takes us wide of Singen: that's one thing we

know. So I say if we keep to it – not in daylight, obviously – we'll be OK, with a bit of luck. But if we make a detour now and can't get back to it – we could be blundering right into Singen before we know it!'

'Should have followed the railway line.'

'Straight through Singen?'

'Oh, *damn* it . . .'

Trolley sat down on the grass. Jack suggested, 'If you're certain you could hit this lane again the other side – then let's detour. But personally, having seen how they loop around – and we might get on a different one . . .'

'We stick to it.' Trolley got up. Then: 'Hey, the lights've gone out!'

'Well, that settles it.' Jack stared down into the hollow: and there wasn't a glimmer now. 'They've run out of booze, all hands pissed, turning in.'

'Let's take a *shufti*.'

In file, quiet-footed on the verge. Trolley had the hedge on his left for guidance.

Until the railway-station incident at Tuttlingen, the whole thing had been quite easy, except for the strain on nerves. Every uniformed official had seemed a potential danger, but in fact their papers hadn't once been asked for, and the forged rail tickets – Escape Committee again – had been accepted without a second glance. From the camp gate they'd marched past the dental surgery, round behind a row of houses and off down a side-road to a wood, where they'd buried the uniforms and the rifle. Leaves showering down would quickly have covered all traces. Then they set off in their separate parties and by divergent routes to the railway junction, from where a slow train left in mid-forenoon for Munich; in the camp they'd been tutored on train routines, and one of the tips was to travel only on slow ones, where papers were rarely inspected. The documents they were carrying might not have stood up to close scrutiny.

It was still nerve-racking. Every time a German so much as glanced at them; or when some solid-looking *frau* left a carriage you'd imagine she was off to fetch a guard . . . Jack tried to convince himself that it was less dangerous that it felt: two men travelling by rail in wartime England dressed as he and Trolley were, would never have been stopped and questioned, so long as they had tickets. They'd simply have been ignored – in the good old British manner.

On the other hand, four prisoners had escaped. Wouldn't they be broadcasting appeals to look out for them?

In Munich they dozed in a cinema until it was about to shut, then walked about the streets until the early hours when the train for Ulm was due to drag itself away. Slowly, like the first one. Cockup and Barmy were there on the platform: they looked as if they might have passed the time in some bar, and Jack and Trolley kept well away from them. It was about eighty miles westward, via a place called Augsburg; then from Ulm to Tuttlingen was southwest and slightly less far. They both catnapped, and looked surly when any fellow-traveller seemed disposed to chat. If the alarm had been raised this far afield, Jack hoped, nobody could have guessed these two unshaven, slovenly-looking creatures could be British officers. Touch wood . . .

The intention had been to take one more train journey, a short hop from Tuttlingen to Singen. The main object had been to get to the Swiss border as fast as possible, and the Escape Committee had agreed that the Germans probably wouldn't anticipate such rapid movement. They'd be expecting men on the run to be making slow progress across country, keeping out of sight and probably heading for the frontier farther east, nearer the camp. Another advantage of using trains was that if they'd been able to go straight through as planned, their food would have lasted out well enough.

It was Cockup Cockrace who put the kibosh on it, on the platform at Tuttlingen.

He might have acquired a bottle of Schnapps or something, in Munich. Not that Cockup needed liquor to make him behave like a clown. He and Morrison were standing together on the platform, well away from anyone else; hunched against a cold wind, but talking and laughing,

Cockup's bray – it had been famous even in his own regiment, apparently – rising now and then to a pitch that made Jack and Trolley cringe. It also made some German heads turn – including those of a group of *Luftwaffe* a short way down the platform. Jack and Trolley turned to stroll further away, but Trolley, glancing back, froze like Lot's wife.

'Oh, *no* . . .'

Cockup was doing the Lambeth Walk. Dragging Barmy by an arm, trying to force him to do it with him. Barmy protesting, pulling back, and – worse – glancing worriedly over his shoulder at the watching Germans. At this point there was an ear-splitting shriek as the train arrived: it was steaming in as Cockup finished his dance, the traditional shout of 'Oy!' almost drowned by the chuffing and clattering and leaking steam, and the platform filling suddenly with people who'd been sheltering inside the station building. Cockup was roaring with laughter, helpless with delight at his own lunacy. Jack thought he'd probably been relishing the prospect of the story becoming legendary back home and in the Greenjackets' mess – how Cockup Cockrace, on the run, had danced the Lambeth Walk on a German railway platform. This would be Cockup's dream of immortality. But Barmy was yanking him along, making for the nearest carriage door as the train came to a stop: three of that *Luftwaffe* group had detached themselves from the others, were shouldering their way through the throng, obviously making for the same carriage.

Trolley muttered, 'He's round the bend. I'd say they've *had* it.'

'So've we, if we get on that train.'

Wild horses wouldn't have got him on to it. And with further consideration they'd decided to forget railways altogether. It might have been for the best, anyway; Singen was really too close to the border, there'd surely be identity checks on passengers. In the long run, Cockup might have done them a favour.

Ahead of Jack now, Trolley stopped. The road still curved and ran downhill into that dark hollow.

'Smell it?'

Cooking. Meat frying or grilling. Steak and onions? Pork? Delicious, mouth-watering . . . But at two in the morning – or it might be nearer three now – hard to explain.

'Not for us, Frank.'

'Wot, no fatted calves' heads?'

'Try not to sniff. If we don't press on, we'll have another foodless day and night.'

'OK . . .'

Moving on down the hill, passing occasional farmsteads or cottages set well apart. At the bottom there was a tight cluster of dwellings, set around one larger building. The only light – Trolley's hand rose to point as it, but he didn't stop – was a thin streak of yellow between curtains in an upper window. Then a narrow, rutted lane led away to the left, with a smell of manure and animals in it: the entrance to a farmyard, probably. Trolley had paused: Jack murmured, 'Keep going, Frank.'

'Roger . . .'

Cobbles under their feet now. And a black-and-white building leaning out over the lane so pronouncedly that only the willpower of centuries could have been holding it at such an angle. The smell of food was stronger here. They walked on – more slowly, finding it less easy to be quiet on cobbles. Around the side of the black-and-white building – the corner, as it happened, where the bend in the road was sharpest – was a wide opening: a yard, also cobbled . . .

The darker objects in it were tables and benches. Old, heavy timber. Feeling the edge of one gingerly, careful of splinters. Then goggling – at plates and mugs on the table. They weren't all empty, either!

It was impossible not to stop. Nobody on earth could have been that strong-minded. Jack found a beer-mug that was half full: and the plates had bones and other debris on them. He had that mug in his hand, could hear Trolley gulping, and he was reaching with the other hand for a chop-bone that had a lot of meat on it when his elbow hit another – empty – mug. It span off the table, smashed loudly on the cobbles.

He'd gasped: and they were both still, listening, poised to run – But hoping anyone who'd heard it might assume it had been a cat. Leaving food lying around like this: didn't they have rationing here? He was beginning to think they'd get away with it, there hadn't been a sound. His hand moved again, and he'd just grasped that bone when the lights came on – all around the little yard, blinding . . . A voice bawled in German, and the last three words Jack recognised, having heard them before somewhere or other: '*—oder Ich schiese!*'

Meaning, 'or I'll shoot!'

Four other men – in front and to the left – two quite old, two middle-aged, and the fifth, the one doing the yelling, young but crippled, leaning sideways on a twisted leg. They all had sporting guns trained on Jack and Trolley, the one in the doorway had been issuing further threats, and Trolley had his hands up.

'Better give up, Jack. Chap says if we're good boys they'll give us a meal while we're waiting for the transport, but if we're bad they'll shoot us.'

In the past hour there'd been HF/DF transmissions from U-boats both ahead and astern of the convoy. Two of them Gritten had identified as operators he'd heard last evening, but there was one stranger . . . *Harbinger* was out ahead of the convoy, pushing northeastward at twelve knots, taking the starboard bow position with *Paeony* roughly on her port beam and the re-formed convoy nearly three miles astern. *Astilbe* had dropped back to the rear to oil; *Harbinger* had already done so, and it would be *Paeony*'s turn next.

He'd shifted *Stella*, Broad's trawler, from the front of the convoy to the rear. In daylight *Harbinger* would be spending a lot of time up front here, or chasing shadowers.

Wind NW force four: sea moderate, visibility good. The promised bad weather seemed to be a long time coming.

Chubb told Mr Timberlake, at the binnacle, 'We're almost there. Skipper'll say when to cut revs.' He dropped his voice to a low murmur. 'A touch short-tempered. Overdue for a crashing of the swede, I'd say.'

Variation of 'getting the head down', sleeping . . . the gunner's only answer was to glance across the bridge at his skipper's back, then at Chubb again. Expressionless gaze out of red-rimmed eyes in the stubbled, long-nosed face. 'All right. I've got 'er. Go and get *your* fat 'ead down.'

'Brekker first.' Chubb grinned, and smacked his lips. 'If you left any, you old shite-hawk!'

'Eff off, Aussie.' Anywhere near the skipper, Timberlake's language tended to be restrained. He bent his scrawny body to the voice-pipe. 'Port ten.'

Independent, irregular zigzag was called for, while getting her up into the station vacated by *Astilbe*. You simply ordered the wheel this way or that, from time to time. It would be much more confusing to a U-boat that was drawing a bead on you than a regular zigzag would be, one that could be timed with a stopwatch and its turns anticipated.

From where he stood, Timberlake had only a three-quarter rear view of the captain, who was on his high seat with his glasses at his eyes; hunched, uncommunicative . . . Down below over a snatched breakfast, Matt Warrimer had made some similar observation to Chubb's – that the skipper ought to be getting some kip now, before the next lot of trouble started. The sods might hold off till dusk, but on the other hand they might not, and right now they were doing a lot of talking. *Harbinger* and her captain had done three hours' hard work since dawn, on top of a sleepless night; now there was nothing to be done for a while – at least until both corvettes had finished oiling – but he seemed rooted to that chair.

Timberlake took the wheel off, steadied her on due north. He hoped the skipper was going to remember to tell him when to reduce speed. Something about the way the old man was hunched suggested he might bite your head off if you interrupted his thoughts unnecessarily.

There'd been a lull in the action after about 2am, and in fact nothing more of any significance had happened, except the odd contact and a few depthcharges dropped here and there; but they'd remained closed-up at action stations until after dawn. Timberlake had had a couple of hours' rest between then and breakfast and taking over this watch, and during that time the convoy had been re-organised into seven columns instead of eight. *Harbinger* had been tearing round like a sheepdog, pausing here and there for the skipper to have loud-hailer conversations – with the *William Law*'s master, for instance, congratulating him on the way he'd turned out of his column and put the fear of God into an attacking U-boat: he'd asked the *Law*'s skipper, 'Want a job in the screen? We're a bit thin on the ground, you know . . .' He'd been full of praise for Kyle, captain of the *Opal,* then mildly critical in a discussion over TBS with Guyatt of *Paeony*. Two ships had been sunk during the night: the *Sally Joy,* number eight-four, who'd been hit by two fish early on, and the *Dragoman,* whose highly incendiary cargo of chemicals had ignited and burnt her down to the waterline in less than half an hour. She'd loaded the stuff in Port Elizabeth, was all Matt Warrimer knew about it. Three-quarters of the *Sally Joy*'s crew had been picked up by the trawler *Gleam* and the rescue ship *Leona,* but only seven crewmen and one junior engineer had survived from the *Dragoman*. They owed their lives to the *Opal,* who'd pushed in so close that her own paintwork had blistered and some of her crew were suffering from burns. Most of the freighter's boats had been incinerated on their davits, and the survivors had all been in the one boat that reached the water, its timber already smouldering. Kyle had since transferred them to the *Malibar,* whose master had been advised by *Harbinger*'s doctor on how to treat their burns.

'Starboard ten.'

'Starboard ten, sir . . .'

'Guns.' The skipper spoke without lowering his binoculars. He'd have heard the watch changing over, but he hadn't once looked round. 'Come down to revs for nine knots. And make the zigzag more frequent and erratic.'

'Aye aye, sir.'

'Don't hog the whole watch, either. I want Carlish to get his hand in.'

'Midships.' The gunner glanced round. 'Take her now, Sub, if you want.'

The convoy had started with four vacant billets. One had been taken last night by the *Burbridge*, but with two ships lost there'd been five holes in the pattern, which had also become somewhat straggly, by dawn. So one column had been done away with. The skipper had ranged up alongside the commodore's *Chauncy Maples* to discuss the reorganisation, then plugged up and down moving ships like pieces on a chessboard.

The *Burbridge* should really have had red crosses on her sides. Warrimer had been on the bridge when the skipper and commodore had been chatting, and Sandover had told him that the passengers were mostly convalescents or wheelchair patients being repatriated from a military recuperation centre near Durban. The commodore's reason for mentioning it had been that the *Burbridge*'s master had offered to take on board any wounded survivors in need of medical care; he had a doctor and a team of nurses looking after those convalescents.

Harbinger's firing on the U-boat astern of the convoy hadn't achieved anything, except that no subsequent attack had developed from that quarter, so it might have been scared off. And *Paeony* had come near to being rammed by the *William Law* when the freighter had charged out at the U-boat. *Paeony* had been going after it at the same time, rushing down close to number one column. Guyatt had picked up the U-boat on his 271 when he'd been returning to station after losing the contact he'd been chasing out on the bow; he'd spotted the U-boat in the glare of the *William Law*'s snowflakes, and altered course to ram. He'd been so close that his four-inch gun had time to get off only two shots as he tore in: he'd passed right over the top, he'd said, couldn't have missed by more than a foot or two, but the German had crash-dived remarkably fast. The skipper had told Guyatt he shouldn't have tried to ram. With so few escorts, and the fact that ramming invariably damaged the rammer as well as her victim, it was now forbidden. Guyatt should have held off and used his gun to better effect than he had: and if he'd been as close as all that, why on earth hadn't his shallow-set depthcharges been effective?

Astilbe had depthcharged a U-boat that had dived in front of her, too. Graves had said his asdics had lost contact almost as soon as he'd picked it up, after the disturbance of the explosions had faded; he suspected it might have been one of the deep-diving boats. He did have some 'heavies' in *Astilbe*, but there'd been no chance to use them. He'd made two other contacts during the night, but with no end result. So – summing it up – with only three or four U-boats at them, they'd lost two ships and nothing to show for it.

Hardly surprising, Mr Timberlake thought, that there was a slight air of grumpiness up here.

'Signals, sir?'

CPO Bearcroft was at the skipper's elbow, with the log for his perusal.

'Anything of interest?'

He'd taken the log, and was leafing through the night's messages.

'Not really, sir. We got a BBC news, though – more 'eavy fighting in the desert. Aussies made a big advance, it said.'

'Good for them.' He handed the log back. 'Thank you, Chief.'

The news bulletins still weren't revealing much, though. So little, in fact, that he wasn't feeling as optimistic as some of the announcers sounded. If the Eighth Army didn't break through soon they'd run out of steam, and then it might be Rommel's turn. Glancing round as the HF/DF bell rang, Nick saw Timberlake with his beak in the pipe: listening, and scowling . . . Then he looked up, and met his captain's stare. 'U-boats transmitting on oh-two-seven, oh-four-eight and oh-six-one, sir, ranges nineteen, sixteen and eighteen miles.'

'Ask him if they're the same ones he heard earlier.'

Apparently two of them were not. One, Gritten said, had been around yesterday, but two were newcomers, probably just arrived and getting their orders and the convoy details.

Convalescents embarked at Durban. Would their nurses have embarked there too?

He heard Carlish order 'Starboard fifteen!' There was no reason to imagine one of the nurses might have reached Durban from Australia; there was *every* reason not even to consider the possibility.

'More of 'em with us now, sir, I'm told.'

Warrimer, at his elbow. Nick looked round at him.

'Now you're here, Number One, I'll take an hour's rest in my sea-cabin.'

'Good idea, sir. Why not make it *several*—'

'*Paeony*—' the skipper pointed, as he cut Warrimer short – '*Paeony* is to oil as soon as *Astilbe* finishes. I want a shake when she's done it. Alternatively wake me if there's any contact within twelve miles.'

'Aye aye, sir.'

Carlish ordered, 'Midships!'

Mr Timberlake watched the skipper slide off his high seat, hang his binoculars over the back of it by their strap, and turn aft to leave the bridge. Nick Everard was a thickset, hard-looking man, with dark hair greying at the temples. The scar he'd collected in some fracas out East was camouflaged by an embryo beard. He'd stopped, and he was looking quizzically at the gunner.

'All right, Guns?'

Timberlake nodded. 'Top line sir.'

'Plenty of depth bombs in hand?'

The red-rimmed eyes blinked. No smile: Mr Timberlake knew when his leg was being pulled. 'Dare say they'll last out, sir.'

'Let's hope so.' A gesture of one hand – northeastward, where the U-boats were chattering to each other. 'I'd say we're going to need all we've got.'

Chapter 9

From 'The U-boat War in the Atlantic' – official German account:
Allied methods of spreading large numbers of different rumours served to confuse the minds of our Intelligence officers. It must be admitted that our enemies showed themselves to be masters of deception.

From 'Monthly A/S Report' (British) for October 1942:
This month the U-boats made all their assaults by night . . . The rough weather during the month, by reducing the efficiency of R.D.F., was to that extent at least in favour of U-boats attacking by night, but it may interest the escorts to know that . . . [it] . . . has also been a severe strain on the Germans.

'This mission is of very high importance, you see. Perhaps even so much as to win the war, I think.' The Count's brown, spaniel-type eyes were fixed gloomily on Paul Everard across *Ultra*'s wardroom table. He added, 'There is much danger, consequently, for yours truly.'

Paul sipped at his mug of cocoa. *Ultra* was on the surface and it was shivery cold inside her. For ten hours the diesels had been drawing cold night air down through the control-room hatches – ever since she'd slipped out of Malta before dusk last evening, and turned west. She'd be diving soon, before daylight, to spend the day motoring through the minefield known as QB 255, along the southwest coast of Sicily. It would be Paul's watch at about the time they dived, which was why he'd turned out now to be ready for it.

The Count was of medium build, dark-haired, with a Mediterranean complexion, sad eyes, and soft, well-cared-for hands. Wykeham had expressed the opinion that he was no more a count than Alfred Shaw the wardroom flunky was a bishop; and the Count had only smiled and reminded him, 'My friend, I do not request you should call me "Count". Did I not request you call me Peter?'

His way of turning the other cheek added to a certain charm of manner. But 'Peter' would have been one name too many. According to the patrol orders, his name was Carlo Paoli, according to *himself* he was a count, but on top of this he had a Greek prayer-book which he dipped into quite often, with the name Christos Venizelos on its flyleaf. Paul had asked him about this: why an Italian would read Greek from a Greek Orthodox Church prayer-book, and who was Venizelos?

'Christos is myself. Although I have once been Selim Zorlu, a Turk, and once also a Hungarian. But Venizelos—' he patted himself on the chest – 'mine own family name. My father highly important man of course, you know, *everybody* know.' At this point he'd crossed himself, and Paul had let the matter drop, only exchanging glances with others in the circle; the gesture had implied that further questions might intrude on holy ground. But the Count had raised the subject again himself, in the wardroom mess in Malta, yesterday, by telling Wykeham, 'You will know the name of Venizelos, I may assume?'

'Well, no, Count, I don't believe—'

'Was Prime Minister, in Greece. In Great War.'

One had met men before who seemed to be arrant liars but whose stories, if you bothered to check up on one when there was some chance to do so, seemed to stand up. And apparently Venizelos *had* been Greek premier during the other war. Questioned by a Greek submarine officer, moreover, the Count had been completely at his ease in detailing his own birth date and place, and the names of brothers, sisters, uncles . . . it wasn't proof of his own membership of the family, but it had convinced that Greek. The fact remained that Carlo Paoli came from Naples and was going to be put ashore in two days' time on the north coast of Sicily. It was complicated all round, and settling for 'Count' was an easy way out.

He asked Paul now, 'After this war, you go back to America?'

'I don't know. Really, no idea at all.'

Paul's mother, Nick Everard's first wife, was a White Russian. After her divorce from Nick she'd married an American industrialist, and Paul had been at college over there until 1939, when he'd ducked out of it and come over to join up.

'You give me your address, maybe I look you up one day, in Connecticut?'

'Why, sure, I'd like that very much.'

He'd make damn sure to do nothing of the sort. A man like the Count might be invaluable in wartime, but in peace he'd be a con-man, to be given a wide berth. Paul felt two-faced himself as he nodded again: 'Be delighted.'

The brown eyes looked sadder than ever. Might a master of duplicity see through an amateur's deceit?

'I think you do not know, what for this business?'

'Not really.'

'You like I tell you, Paul?'

'Perhaps you better not.'

'Why for not?' When the Count shook his head like that, his jowls trembled. 'Who you tell? The fishes?' He lifted his arms. 'Birds?'

'Go ahead, then, let's hear it.'

'On your chart, I show you.'

The way he pronounced 'show', it rhymed with 'plough'. Paul leant out, reached across the gangway and pulled the chart over. 'Here we are. What's the story?'

They were alone in the wardroom. Hugo Wykeham had the watch, and the skipper had gone up to the bridge ten minutes ago. Bob McClure had moved out of the wardroom to make room for the Count; there was a small bunking space, more like a shelf really, in a caged section of electrical switch-gear opposite the wireless office, and this had become McClure's berth. He didn't like it being referred to as his cage, especially after Paul had offered to keep him supplied with bananas in there. He'd been indignant anyway, at having to move out, despite the fact that his small size suited him to that restricted space and that it would only be for two nights. They'd be sending the Count off in his canoe on the night after this next one.

'But then taking the sod off again?'

'And straight back to Malta. Another couple of nights, that's all.'

McClure hadn't argued with the captain, but to Wykeham he'd expressed strong resentment at having to surrender his bunk to a 'fat Greek'.

'He's Italian, not Greek.'

'That's worse.'

'Well, he's got guts, all right.'

'Phoney as hell. I wouldn't trust him a bloody inch!'

'He's the kind they get for this sort of thing, that's all. I agree, I wouldn't lend him a fiver – or leave my sister alone with him for two minutes!'

'Right.' McClure had nodded. 'She'd eat him alive, I expect.'

The Count's soft-looking hands moved across the chart.

'Here I land. You see?'

Paul nodded. It would be his job to get the folboat up to the casing and launch it. They were carrying two, but only in case one got damaged. The operation of surfacing in the dark, getting the fore hatch open and the canoe out and the hatch shut and clipped again while it was being launched – timing had to be split-second, so as to have the hatch open for only a minimal time, in case of enemy interference and a need to dive – had been rehearsed in Malta, in Marsamxett Creek at night. The Count would go up through the bridge hatch and climb down to the casing, and by the time he got there Paul's team would have the canoe in the water alongside, ready for him to step into it. In fact none of these arrangements pleased the Count, who'd claimed that on previous occasions he'd been provided with a commando boat-handler to do the paddling for him, taking the folboat back to the submarine and bringing it in again a few nights later to pick him up. This time he was required to hide the canoe on shore, and do his own paddling both ways.

The landing spot was near Termini, about fifteen miles east of Palermo.

'You want I should tell you what for I risk my life in this business?'

The Count did seem to be acutely aware of his own intrepidity. Paul shook his head. 'Not unless you want to. Naturally I'm curious, but it's your neck.'

'Make no difference, you see . . . So – here. Other side Palermo, that is Golfo di Castelammara. And my place for landing – here. Now – you see this coast between Capo Zafferano and Capo Cefalu? For landings, both sides Palermo. Many, many men. With tanks, guns. Big, big army, both these places. Battleships, many ships – bombarding first – and aircraft carriers with fighters over . . . So then very quick is Palermo captured, then all Sicily – huh?'

'My sainted aunt . . .'

'You are surprise, huh?'

'How the heck do all the ships arrive at those places without the enemy getting wind of it and being ready for 'em?'

'Problem for others.' The Count brushed it off. 'Me, I land, meet with Resistance leaders – friends . . . But wait: as yet I do not tell you all . . . *Here*, also!'

'Sardinia?'

'I know this, but private, is not my official informations. True, however – at the same time, landings here also, southwest, with this port Cagliari between – you understand?'

He'd closed his hands like pincers.

'Here Palermo, here Cagliari. Sardinia, Sicily – huh?'

'I'll be damned.'

He was rather flattered, that the Count should have chosen him to tell this to. Paul did like him, despite a certain caution in his attitude; perhaps because he was such an original, but also because there was a loneliness about him that drew one's sympathy. Drew *his*, anyway. And what he'd described made sense, all right. With Palermo and Cagliari in Allied hands, both islands could be invested and captured quickly. With those ports and airfields then you'd leapfrog into Italy, or the south of France even.

'Please not to remark I am telling you these matters. Is not so important, but I am not *suppose*—'

A voice behind Paul exploded: 'Now where's the bloody chart, for shit's sake!'

Bob McClure. Like an angry gnome bristling in the gangway. Paul handed him the chart. 'Who let you out of your cage?'

'Diving any minute now. Cape Marco's ten miles abeam.'

'How's the shelf?'

'No more than painful, long as you don't raise your head. If you do, you get electrocuted.' He asked the Count, '*My* bunk nice and comfy?'

'I am most appreciating—'

The diesels cut out. In the suddenly contrasting silence McClure muttered, 'Here we go.' There was a rush of movement down the ladder into the control room, then Ruck's voice funnelled down the pipe: 'Open main vents!' He was diving her quietly 'on the watch' so as to allow men who were off-duty to continue sleeping. Paul heard Wykeham order, 'Eighty feet.'

It was a well-established route through this minefield. You divied to eighty feet and then spent fifteen hours at four knots on a course of 300 degrees, passing five miles off Cape Granitola. Then you surfaced off Marettimo – in darkness again by that time – and went wherever the patrol orders directed you: in this case north and then east, around the western end of Sicily.

Ruck arrived as Paul was edging out into the gangway, on his way to the control room. He'd take over the watch as soon as Wykeham had caught a trim – as soon as he'd got the boat in balance and neutral buoyancy at that depth. For the ten hours' dived passage there'd be nothing for officers of the watch to do except watch the trim, making adjustments now and then by pumping a few gallons this way or that. It would be a warm, quiet, sleep-ridden day: as long as nobody'd moved any of the mines since they'd last passed through.

'Well, Count.' Ruck was shedding bridge clothing and hanging it behind the water-tight door. 'We're right on schedule. This time tomorrow you'll be ashore in Sicily.'

'Yes.' The Count had his Greek prayer-book open again. He nodded, licked his lips. 'Thank you.' The troubled look in his spaniel eyes was perhaps habitual. They flickered up now as McClure came in and squeezed on to the padded bench, bringing some paperwork with him. The Count asked Ruck, 'How far from the shore—' he shook his head – 'How *near* distance to the shore will you take me?'

'Half a mile.' Ruck swung up on to his own bunk. 'Half a nautical mile, that is. One thousand yards.'

'Thousand yards.' Opening his hands, looking at their soft palms. Then closing them into fists. 'Why is it I am not allow a soldier for the boat?'

A canoe-handler, he was griping about again. Ruck sighed. 'I gather there were no commandos available. Until now we've had a squad attached to the flotilla – for impromptu raids and sabotage – well, as you know. But they've been whisked off somewhere.'

The Count nodded. 'I can guess what is that purpose.'

'Then you know more about it than I do, Count.'

'Is possible.'

Ruck lay back, and shut his eyes. The answer he'd given had not been the true one. And the orders concerning this part of it had been given verbally. Nothing on paper, and the explanation had been strictly private, offered over a glass of gin. He heard Count Peter, alias Carlo Paoli, alias Christos Venizelos and Selim Zorlu, explaining, 'It is not only for the work of paddling the boat that I am concern. On other times the commando have also tommy gun for protecting me. You see . . .' He'd turned to McClure now, for want of a better audience. 'I leave my boat – this time not, I must hide him – I am saying times *before* this . . . So I have sand or rocks I must pass over. But on the sea the boat is not difficult for persons on shore to be seeing: so when I come on land I am – how you say—'

'Exposed.'

Ruck had offered this, without opening his eyes.

'Yes. This is why it is much better, infinitely, for having other man with the tommy gun, you understand?'

McClure nodded, without looking up from his work. 'Have to take your chances.'

'Yes. Yes . . .'

'You volunteered for it, didn't you?'

McClure disliked him, quite apart from the trivial business of the bunk. He'd made it obvious before this, and Wykeham had pulled him up about it . . . The Count hadn't answered that last question: only frowned slightly as he looked down at the prayer-book. Ruck's head had swung over, though, and his eyes were open.

'That's an extremely brave man you're talking to, McClure. Takes a hell of a lot of guts, his kind of work.'

The Count's eyes shifted. He murmured, 'Thank you, captain. You are very kind.'

It was noon before the truck reached Singen. It pulled up outside the police station, the tailboard crashed down, and there was a ring of soldiers in the roadway with levelled rifles. The two who'd brought Jack and Trolley from the village ordered them out, and the soldiers hustled them inside, where they were separated and locked into one-man cells.

Now there'd be some interrogation, Jack guessed. Or a firing squad. In principle you didn't believe in that outcome – not *really*, that the Germans would flout international law and the Hague Convention to that extent: but having been threatened with it more than once by men who clearly would have enjoyed doing it, you were aware it could happen. If, for instance, the Gestapo took you over: if they decided it was the thing to do, and reckoned they could get away with it.

Perhaps not this close to the Swiss border. People gossiped, and they'd be sensitive to the risk of publicity. Which only meant they might transport them elsewhere first . . .

The meal of leftovers in the village last night had been excellent, and their captors had been quite pleasant. They were some variety of Home Guard, and pleased with themselves for having pulled it off. But the food had been splendid. Here, it was thin soup and black bread, the soup tasting as if floor-mops had been wrung out in it. It was early evening by this time. Jack was considering the discomfort that the night ahead now promised – a plank bed and a single blanket, no pillow, under the glare of an unshaded bulb – when a guard unlocked the cell door and ordered him out, pushed him into a room where Cockup and Barmy, standing at ease and with a rifle covering them, brightened at the sight of him. He noticed that they both had cut lips, black eyes and bruises.

'Hey, Jack's the boy!'

'Wotcher, me old cock sparrer!'

'You stupid buggers . . .'

'Barmy – *what* did he say?'

An officer at a desk in the corner had taken notes of this conversation, although it couldn't have made much sense to him. And now Trolley was marched into the room. The seated officer scribbled a signature on a piece of coloured paper, banged a rubber stamp on it and then handed it to a sergeant. Then he rose, came over to stand in front of them with his hands clasped behind his back.

'Speak German, anybody?'

Nobody seemed to have heard him.

'Very well. I tell you this in English. You will be returned to your camp now, on the train. You will of course be under guard, and they will have orders that if you attempt escape, or disobey or cause other trouble, they are to shoot you dead. Is this now understood?'

Jack began, 'Shooting unarmed prisoners, in terms of the Hague Convention—'

'Silence!'

The officer's face thrust close to Jack's.

'When you escape from the Offlag, was not one of you armed?'

Cockup said, 'I don't even *know* anyone called Ahmed.'

Jack said as the laughter ended, 'Old drill rifle. Rusted solid, and no ammo.'

'We could shoot you for this.' A slow nodding. 'If you give more cause, we will!'

Jack said stolidly, 'We're unarmed prisoners, and it would be murder.' He heard Barmy suggest, 'Tell him to take a running jump, old boy.' Then Trolley muttered, 'I'd let it ride, Jack, if I were you.' The officer was chuntering away in German to the sergeant and corporal; when he'd finished and they'd both shouted *'Jawhol!'* he turned to glare at Jack again. 'Understand what I say to them?'

'How the hell could I?'

'I say if you make trouble, he must shoot to kill, and shoot you the first. You understand *this* perhaps?'

Cockup drawled, 'Fellow's English is really quite good, you know.'

They were marched to the railway station through dark, deserted streets. Trolley urged Jack in a murmur, *en route*, 'Shouldn't push 'em too far. I mean they're Nazis, remember?'

Barmy Morrison said, 'Knocked us about something shocking. Whole pack of 'em on that train.'

'Serve you damn right.' Jack meant it. 'Of all the bloody stupid things to do!'

'We most likely wouldn't have got through anyway, Jack.'

Trolley, pouring oil on troubled waters. But the plain fact was, Jack thought, that as a direct result of Cockup's lunacy he and Barmy had been bagged, and then the Bosch had started looking for two more in the same area. Consequently he was not now on his way to London and Fiona. It had been vitally important that he should be, but instead he faced incarceration in the *Straflager*, which as likely as not would mean for the duration of the war.

In a way, it would be preferable to be shot. He began to sweat, at the thought of it. The prospect of years in Offlag IVC, with Fiona on the loose in London; or rather, Fiona alone in London and half a million men on the loose around her. She wasn't the sort to sit at home and knit seaboot stockings. He knew exactly how she was, and he was crazy about her. There was no question of blaming or judging – any more than he'd blame himself for being the way *he* was. He'd pinched her from Nick – who'd ratted on her, admittedly, but she hadn't known it at the time – and he was quite certain in his understanding of her. She was his, and exactly as he wanted her.

'Frank.'

Trolley's head turned slightly. A minute ago the sergeant had yelled at Barmy to shut up. Jack whispered, 'Make a train-jump, if we get a chance?'

'What sort of chance?'

'A slowish stretch, and soft ground to land on. The others could start scrapping or something, to divert the goons.'

'Then what?'

'We jump. Hours of darkness left – with luck – to get hidden . . . Frank, we're out now, but once they lock us in the *Straflager*—'

'Halt!'

They were outside the station. There was a military checkpost at its entrance and the sergeant was showing them the movement order. Jack told Trolley. 'If you don't want to, I'll go it alone.'

'Three-four-oh revolutions!'

'Three-four-oh, sir . . .'

No sinkings *yet*. But the night was young, and only in the last half-hour had the U-boats stopped talking to each other and begun to close in around the convoy. A few of them seemed to be held back in reserve, much farther ahead, but they'd no doubt be moving in when they considered the time was ripe.

The skipper was at the binnacle, taking her straight up

the middle, *Astilbe* angling out to starboard and *Paeony* to port as *Harbinger* drove up between them. The contact they were going after happened to be on the convoy's course, the course they were steering now. Trying out new tactics, Warrimer appreciated, in keeping with new orders issued earlier to the other escorts: he hadn't discussed any of it with his first lieutenant – as he usually had done in the past with Graves – and now he wasn't talking much at all. Just hunched there, grim-faced, binoculars at his eyes – to keep them open, maybe, Chubb had suggested. Warrimer said into his telephone, 'Very good . . .' He called, 'All guns loaded, sir, starshell in A, SAP in B and X!'

The odds were it would dive before they got a shot at it. Not that anyone was likely to run short of targets; there were certainly no fewer U-boats around them than there had been last night. Only one on the 271 screen so far, but Gritten had identified about six different ones ahead of the convoy and there was also one out to starboard and a shadower back on the port quarter. The ones ahead had been talking fit to bust, then abruptly fallen silent, and there'd been a tense wait before RDF had picked up this one that *Harbinger* was now thrashing out to find. If the skipper had anything like a proper escort group at his disposal, Warrimer thought, and if it hadn't been for the 'no-diversion' rule, he'd have deployed several escorts ahead while the convoy made a big emergency turn. By leaving the convoy and tearing out like this – he'd moved *Stella* to guard the rear – he was actually breaking the rules he'd laid down himself at those sessions in Freetown: but since last night and the night before the system hadn't paid off, it was reasonable to try another one.

'Bearing is oh-three-eight, range five miles, sir!'

That was Carlish, tending the plot voice-pipe. Warrimer heard the skipper order, 'Steer oh-three-eight, cox'n.'

A gun's crew would already be soaked to the skin, at this speed and on this course. Wind and sea were still from the northwest and about the same as they'd been for the past three days, but even with it on the beam at thirty knots the stuff was fairly sheeting over.

Warrimer was guardedly aware of a growing feeling of hopelessness. In himself and also, he thought, in others. Nobody admitting to it . . . Last night they'd lost four ships: the *Carl Jansen*, the *Timaru*, the *Lord John* and the *Tarcoola*. The *Timaru* had had half the *Carl Jansen*'s crew in her when she'd been blown in half. The trawler *Stella* had claimed to have scored a direct hit with her four-inch gun on a U-boat which had then turned away and dived, and Tony Graves had been sure he'd been close to finishing one off with depth charges when the skipper had had to order him to resume station ahead of the convoy. This had been unavoidable because at that time *Paeony* had developed some defect in her asdic training unit, so that for a while there'd been no asdic cover at all in the van of the convoy. In normal circumstances this would have been unthinkable: especially when one remembered how professional and successful they'd been with their own escort group up north. In fact if you thought too much about it, it was heart-breaking.

Thank God, Guyatt had reported at dusk this evening that his asdics were now operable. Not one hundred percent reliable, but working, pinging.

There'd been another reorganisation of the convoy this morning. It was still in seven columns but the outer two columns on each side were now of only four instead of five ships. So the rearmost line-abreast was of only three ships, on the three centre columns only. That trio consisted of the *Harvest Moon* in the centre, flanked by the *Leona* to starboard and the *Mount Trembling* – she'd taken the *Timaru*'s job of rescue ship – to port. The *Burbridge* had moved up to become third ship in column three, and the two oilers were also in billets well surrounded by other ships. The tankers were the ones you could least afford to lose, and the *Burbridge* with her wheelchair patients and crowd of nurses had to be given as much protection as possible.

'Bearing is oh-three-six, sir, range four miles!'

'Steer oh-three-six . . . Starshell stand by.'

Warrimer told A gun's sightsetter, 'Stand by starshell.

Target U-boat on the surface right ahead. Set range oh-seven-oh.' He heard the sight-setter repeating the order in a high-pitched yell; the telephone line also carried the noise of sea battering that gunshield. Behind him, Chubb was telling Mr Timberlake over the depthcharge telephone, 'Shallow settings, Guns.'

Guesswork: chancing his Australian arm.

'Bearing right ahead, range oh-seven-three, sir!'

All over the bridge, binoculars moved slowly, sweeping the white-streaked, camouflaged surface.

'New contact oh-oh-eight, six miles, sir!'

'I only want to hear about the first one.'

'Aye aye, sir . . .' Carlish was passing that down to Scarr. Then: 'Bearing oh-three-five, range oh-six-eight, sir!'

Six thousand eight hundred yards, that meant: just under three and a half miles. The skipper lowered his glasses. 'Tell the plot to keep up-to-date bearings and ranges of other contacts from us and also from *Paeony* and *Astilbe*, for passing by TBS if they get by us.'

Carlish stumbled over the words as he rattled that off to Mike Scarr. It made good sense to Warrimer – who *needed* to make sense of it, to interpret for his own satisfaction what was not being explained and had not been discussed in advance . . . If *Harbinger* was busy with this contact and another U-boat moved in past her to become a closer threat to the convoy, warning could be passed to the appropriate corvette before the blip actually showed up on her 271 screen. In this way *Harbinger* was an advance scout as well as a striker. The snag, of course, was it might not be just one, it could be four or five of them, *Harbinger* tied-down here while the pack moved in behind her. But you couldn't be there *and* here, you had to make a choice . . .

'Range oh-six-three, sir, bearing oh-three-three!'

'Steer oh-three-two.'

It ought to be possible to spot the U-boat before it saw the danger coming. As one knew exactly where to look.

'Range oh-six-oh!'

Harbinger shouldering up white foam that flew arcing

across the bridge. Binocular lenses needing to be dried twice a minute, however much you tried to shield them.

'Range—'

'Starshell open fire!'

The skipper had caught sight of his target: Warrimer yelled 'Starshell, fire!' and with less than a second's interval A gun had crashed and recoiled, Warrimer ordering 'B gun, range oh-five-six, open fire when you bear. A gun with SAP load, load, load!'

'Range oh-five-five, sir!'

'Set range oh-five-three, target right ahead!'

The starshell exploded, a white brilliance suspended on its parachute, drifting slowly downwards as its light spread across the sea's crests and slopes, darkening the hollows in between. B gun fired, a lightning-flash and the metallic, ear-thumping crack of it, then A gun like an echo and the clang of shell-cases on iron gundecks, sea swamping over and the ship bow-down with a lurch to port. As she recovered, lifting, Warrimer had the U-boat in his glasses, a ray of that starshell's last glimmer on wet black steel bedded in foam . . . 'A gun, one round starshell, fire!'

'Range oh-five-oh, sir!'

'Set range oh-four-eight.' He heard the skipper order, 'Come ten degrees to starboard, cox'n.' Both the for'ard guns had fired again; one of those rounds would be a refresher to the illuminations. The U-boat could be seen to be altering course, swinging to port, a shell spout springing up just short and new crashes from both guns as the starshell opened. Warrimer saw the German's conning-tower tilting – diving, or it could be only pitching, its stern to the sea now. A gun cracked, then B again: it was very chancy shooting, on those moving platforms. Carlish yelled that the range was down to oh-four-eight: and that yellowish flash was a *hit!*

'Set range oh-four-six . . .'

Closing less rapidly now, because of the enemy's change of course: but still closing, *Harbinger* galloping in – and hope in the heart at least, because that hit had changed the picture dramatically . . . 'A gun, one round of starshell, fire!' The U-boat still wasn't diving: if it had been punctured, of course, it couldn't, and its captain would be wishing to God he'd done it three or four minutes ago when the first starshell had lit him up. Perhaps he'd thought he'd be able to run for it, get around this interference and still press home his attack. Both the for'ard guns were still firing and Warrimer had seen a number of shell spouts poke up around the target, but nothing from the last five or six. The new starshell opened, showing the German almost stern-to and rocking bow-up, its stern buried in the sea as it lifted to a wave; he told his gunners, 'Down four hundred!' as he passed the order Carlish shouted 'Range oh-four-one!' So the correction had been overdue and shots would have been passing over him. Not that there was all that much science in it, shooting as it were from horseback at the gallop, the layers and trainers sighting through salt-washed telescopes . . . *Hit number two!*

'Range oh-four-oh, sir!'

'Down two hundred . . .'

But it had *not* been a hit. It had been the enemy shooting back at them. He'd have a 37 mm, something like a Bofors, on the back end of his bridge. But he couldn't dive, obviously; he was at bay . . .

'X gun, point-fives and searchlight stand by!'

The order came from the skipper, who'd shouted it without taking his glasses off the U-boat. Preparing to turn his ship so those other weapons would bear – from this range, instead of running in close to the U-boat's lighter weapon. Weapons, plural: he'd have a 20mm AA gun as well as the other, if he was U-boat Mark VII . . . But now that *had* been a hit! And in the background a TBS call from 'Fox' – *Astilbe* – announcing excitedly, *Contact: attacking* . . . Bad reception, crackly: CPO Bearcroft was acknowledging the message in a tone as calm as a butler's announcing luncheon served. There'd been a flash and some bits flying: bits of U-boat or bits of men, or both. Warrimer had passed the stand-by order to the guns aft, and Leading Signalman Wolstenholm was at the searchlight sight, talking over that intercom to its two-man crew on their raised platform abaft the torpedo tubes. The two for'ard four-inch guns meanwhile still belting out shells, while the German had fired only twice. It was on the cards that the second hit had knocked his guns out; they'd be within a yard or so of each other, on railed platforms at the back of his bridge. But this could be a kill, all right – please God . . . Shell spouts just short again, one quickly after the other, in time with the sequence of the guns' firing: now a third hit – flash, and a cloud of muck obscuring the target for a moment before the wind cleared it. *Harbinger* still racing in, so the after guns and the searchlight weren't getting a chance yet; the skipper would have changed that intention because of the enemy ceasing fire, he could go in close now without danger to his own people, and his object would be to finish this as quickly as it could be done. Because there'd be work elsewhere . . . Warrimer was not only attending to his own job, but also casting himself as understudy, needing to see the reasons and motives: it was a habit he'd acquired when his immediate senior had been Tony Graves, and it explained why he hadn't been at all flummoxed when he'd been given promotion at a moment's notice.

The U-boat, its engines stopped now, was slewing broadside on; and its bow was lifting, the long fore-casing rising to point like a gleaming, accusing finger at the last starshell's dying light. Range closing fast, since the enemy was no longer running: was in fact finished, by the look of him.

'Port ten. One-eight-oh revolutions. Searchlight *on* . . . Midships.'

Just enough of a turn to expose the light. It sprang out like a knife, a silver lance that caught the U-boat – a speared fish, dying. Men were coming out of it in a ragged stream, diving or sliding over, puppets that appeared, struggled with the blinding light and the sea breaking over, then vanished. Their ship wasn't allowing them much time: its bow was nearly vertical now and it was visibly slipping back, stern-first. There'd be a lot of men still inside that thing.

'Cease fire!'

X gun hadn't fired at all. Warrimer intoned, 'Check, check, check . . .' He still had his glasses on the U-boat, and saw it disappear in a quick, drowning slide: the white turmoil where it had vanished lasted only a few seconds. The skipper was telling Carlish to take over at the binnacle, and he'd already moved to the viewing slot that looked down on the plot table and the 271. 'What have we got, pilot?' Scarr told him, 'They're all over the place, sir. Nearest bears two-three-oh, seven thousand eight hundred yards, and *Paeony* must have it on her screen – this blip here is her, moving to intercept it.'

'So we'll leave it to her.' He raised his voice. 'Pack up that searchlight!' Back to Scarr and the PPI . . . 'What's that to the southeast of us?'

A TBS message from *Astilbe* about losing one contact and moving to intercept another was interrupted by an explosion from the direction of the convoy. On its heels, white rockets soared. Warrimer thinking for a moment – as the searchlight beam cut off, seeming to withdraw inward along its own length as if it was being sucked back into the ship – about the Germans in the water, the ones who'd got out of the U-boat before it sank. And obviously with the convoy under attack, your people's lives being lost and every ounce and minute needed in their defence – and that had been another torpedo hit – there could be no question of risking British lives for German . . . 'Sub – three-four-oh revs, come to starboard to one-two-oh!'

Warrimer was telling A and B guns to train fore-and-aft, clear the decks of empty shell cases, refill ready-use lockers. More white rockets fizzled up, a few miles south. The skipper finished his conference with Scarr and took over at the binnacle while *Harbinger* was still under helm, turning to a south-easterly course. Distantly, a rumble of depth charges . . . Chubb was muttering at Timberlake over their private line, 'Certainly the bastard sank!' Then, 'Of course not, for Pete's sake, their pals are all over the bloody shop, didn't you hear those two *whumpfs*?'

There was another *whumpf* now: the third torpedo hit in

as many minutes. It was the sharp edge to the sound that distinguished it from others, usually; a *knock*, like a hammer on iron, contained inside the boom of the explosion, all of it muffled by distance and submersion.

And *another . . .*

TBS call, *Eagle, this is Fox. I have no contact now. Convoy is under attack astern of me. Resuming station. Out . . .*

Wanting permission, obviously, to turn back and help. But by the time he got there it would be too late, and in the meantime new attacks could be coming in from ahead.

'Where is he, Sub?'

Carlish, learning to comprehend cryptic questions, passed it to the plot. *Harbinger* steadying on 120 degrees, wind and sea astern, funnel-fumes following and hanging over the bridge – acrid, irritating to eyes and lungs. The skipper had interrupted some confusion between Carlish and Mike Scarr: 'What I want is the range and bearing from *Astilbe* of the contact ahead of us now.'

'Aye aye, sir!' Back to the fount of all knowledge . . . While a new TBS call came in: it was *Paeony* reporting she was in asdic contact and attacking a U-boat which *Opal* had engaged on the surface and forced to dive. *Opal* had reported having hit the U-boat's periscope or standards with her forefoot as she ran over it, but apparently sustaining no damage to herself. Warrimer heard Chubb telling Timberlake, 'Jesus, Guns, it's a bloody rough-house!' Chubb would have to be sat on, Warrimer decided. But you could understand the skipper's frustration, his wanting to be in six places at once: with so many holes to plug, and so few ships to do it with . . . Carlish told him, 'From *Astilbe* the bearing's oh-one-three, range eight thousand two hundred yards.'

'Take over here, Sub.' The skipper had lurched back to look down at the 271 screen. 'Chief Yeoman. Call Fox, tell him "Surface contact bearing oh-one-three range oh-eight-two from you now. Leaving it to you." Pilot, where are the deep-field specimens?'

'Bearings are oh-three-seven, oh-four-one and oh-four-four,

sir, ranges between six and eight miles. The nearest's the one on oh-three-seven.'

'Come round to oh-three-five, Sub.'

Bearcroft finished passing the order to *Astilbe*. 'Message passed, sir!'

'Good. Now by W/T to the commodore, repeated to all escorts: "Request immediate emergency turn port while we try to break up second wave of assault now ten miles ahead of you."'

The train rattled and swayed through cold German night. It was made up almost entirely of goods trucks, and even its three passenger carriages were more than it needed. They had this one to themselves – the four of them, and their escorts.

Jack observed, 'Right sort of country for it. Nice grass bank to land on, lot of the time. Have to dive well out to reach it, remember.'

Trolley murmured, 'Not at *this* speed, if you don't mind.'

It was a slow train, but when you thought about leaping off it into the darkness its slowness was less obvious. On the other hand, the longer you stayed on it the farther you were getting from the frontier. Every clank of the wheels meant another few yards of Shanks's mare: and yards built into miles, while the rhythm sent words whispering through his brain: *With me along some strip of herbage strewn* . . . He suppressed it: thoughts couldn't be allowed to wander. The chance would come suddenly, if it came at all, you needed to be ready to act on the spur of the moment. Trolley would follow, all right. Frank Trolley, Jack had heard from other people, admired him for his verve and decisiveness. He was himself no sluggard: but he was disciplined, principled, which Jack was not. To Frank, prison was irksome and escape a duty: he'd think 'I ought to' and 'I'd like to' but not as Jack did, 'I *have* to, *now!*' Partly of course because Frank had no Fiona, no daydream of arriving at her flat in Eaton Square and throwing some swine out, damaging him somewhat in the process . . . It was what he *wanted*: far better than finding her alone. You'd get it over with, she'd see the physical proof of it, it would be over, exorcised . . .

He and Trolley were on the right-hand side, facing the engine, while Cockup and Barmy were beyond them on the left, facing the same way. The escorts, one corporal and one private soldier, were facing them from the other bench, backs to the engine.

Neither of the Germans understood English. The prisoners had checked this quite thoroughly by insulting them in both personal and national terms, smiling pleasantly at each other while commenting on the guards' appearance, lack of intelligence, criminal tendencies, probable sexual deviations, etcetera, and also discussing Nazi leaders in similarly offensive terms. Even if the corporal had been trying to sit it out, he couldn't have remained so completely unmoved if he'd known what was being said. And it had provided passable entertainment for an hour or so.

Jack said, with his eyes on Trolley, 'Listen, you two. Don't look at me or seem interested. Don't want these cretins to guess we're planning anything . . . But the thing is, Frank and I are going to jump off this puffer. All we need is a soft landing and an uphill bit so the thing slows down a little. When we're set to go, we'd like you two to oblige us with a bit of a diversion. Would you mind staging a fight and making it realistic?'

Trolley murmured, 'If they're going to start hitting each other, I'd rather stay and watch.'

Cockup addressed Barmy. 'They'll break their bloody necks. Don't care much, do you?'

'Not a hoot. But I'd say the best thing would be to get rid of one goon first, then lay on some diversion for the one that's left. What I have in mind is I might decide I need to get to the PK in a hurry.'

'Do talk English, old lad.'

'The shithouse. PK stands for *piccanin kaia*, meaning "little house". We Rhodesians are brilliant linguists, you should realise.' He nudged Cockup. 'What you could do is start peeing at the chap that's left. *That*'d occupy his attention, wouldn't it?'

'Make him a bit too cross, though.' Cockup had considered the suggestion, and dismissed it purely on practical grounds. 'Tell you what, though. I could lay on one of my epileptic fits. Used to do it at school sometimes – in Scripture classes, that sort of thing. Though I say so myself, it's pretty damn good.'

There was a silence. Then Trolley suggested to Jack, 'We need to see our spot coming from quite a distance, if Barmy needs time to lead his stooge away before Cockup gives his performance?'

'Good point. We'll need a long uphill stretch.'

'*Essentially* uphill. And with a sharp eye out for telegraph poles. If you've noticed the way they flash past?'

'That's all fixed then.' He told Trolley, 'If I say "Golly, but I'm as tired as hell", Barmy gets the ball rolling at once. Then when we're down to one goon, and if the terrain still looks right for it, if I let out a loud yawn then Cockup does his act. If the position's changed I won't yawn, so Cockup must restrain his natural instincts until he does get that signal – because if we postpone, Barmy could get another belly-ache later. Now total silence from all concerned will tell me you all agree.'

The silence lasted long enough. After a while Jack said, 'Good. Thanks, you two . . . But I'm afraid we've lost our grass bank now, Frank.'

'Too fast anyway.'

It was about an hour before there was a similarly promising landing ground beyond the rails. And a bit longer still before he realised there was an incline coming. He decided to stop looking out of the window, to ration himself to just an occasional glance. He sat back, shut his eyes. It was an uphill section, all right. But there was no way to be sure it was going to last. You could see the ground in the immediate vicinity of this carriage, but for only a short distance up the line. The rhythm of the wheels undoubtedly was slowing, though; and if you waited for absolutely perfect conditions you might never move at all. Except into the *Straflager*.

The train was beginning to labour on the gradient. Jack stretched. 'Oh, golly, I'm as tired as hell!'

He saw a flash of fright on Trolley's face. Barmy was staring in front of him, wide-eyed, as the penny dropped. Now he'd clasped his hands to his belly, gasping as he half rose. The corporal moved too, lifting his rifle.

'I gotta *go*, me old Kraut.' He groaned, made gestures, pointed . . . 'Help!'

Cockup had been dozing. He was visibly in the early stages of catching-on to what was happening.

The other guard escorted Barmy away, on the corporal's instructions. Barmy moaned as he mooched away without looking round, 'Good luck, you chaps.' The train was crawling. Jack sweating, with his eyes shut, knowing it might reach the brow of the hill at any moment and pick up speed down the other side; but he had to give Barmy time to take that soldier well away. He opened his eyes, and Trolley, looking a bit white around the gills, nodded to him. Jack squinted sideways, saw the grass bank still there. Have to clear the down-line to reach it, unfortunately. And jump right after a telegraph pole flashed by, otherwise you'd be smashed by the next. He yawned, loud and clear. Cockup wailed, slipping forward on to his knees on the dirty floor: then he was on his face, writhing, flailing with arms and legs, high-pitched animal sounds coming from between clenched teeth, eyes bulging. The corporal looked scared; he got to his feet, rifle in one hand, obviously having no idea what to do. Cockup was slobbering, banging his forehead on the floor and making sounds like cats fighting. The German began to shout down at him: then he was banging his rifle-butt down repeatedly near Cockup's head, presumably in an attempt to attract his attention. Cockup's arms whipped up, wrapped themselves around it, clung to it: there was a tug of war going on and Cockup still screaming, spittle flowing down his chin, as Jack moved fast, flung the door crashing back into rushing, cold, dark night, heard the *whoosh* of a telegraph pole rushing past, and dived . . . The night revolved and the noise in his ears was as if the train was passing over him, then something hit him in the face with carthorse strength while another agency tried to prise his left arm out of its socket. He thought as he somersaulted with bright lights bursting in his skull that his back might have been broken. He had his hands linked at the back of his head, forearms jammed against his ears: pain burnt like fire in that left arm. He was on his back, across a low wire fence which he hadn't noticed before the jump: the train's noise was dwindling, the lights in his head had stopped exploding and the world came joltingly to rest.

Wire twanged as he rolled off it. Two strands, taut between low concrete stanchions. Signal gear, most likely. He seemed to be all in one piece, and no bones broken, except possibly on his left side where a rib or two might have gone. Or it could just be bruising. Everything seemed to work, muscles and joints obeyed under initial protest. He guessed the bruises would be agonising tomorrow. Unless it was tomorrow already. He peered muzzily at his watch's luminous face, holding it up close: it was still ticking, and the time was 3-40. He asked himself, staring round and probably only just becoming more or less fully conscious, Frank Trolley?

Even if Frank had jumped immediately behind him, he'd be as much as thirty or forty yards up the line.

'Frank?'

The train was no more than a far-off murmur. Cockup had done marvellously: he'd pay for it now, they'd really have it in for him, he'd be in solitary long enough to get sick of his own jokes . . . Jack stumbled up the slope, keeping to the line of the wire. 'Frank, you there?'

Might have knocked himself out. An alternative – Jack's mind was clearing fast now – might be that Frank hadn't jumped. If the corporal had seen what was happening – if Frank had given him time to . . .

He nearly fell over him.

'Hey, Frank, what's—'

One hand had come into contact with what had been Frank Trolley's head. It had smashed against one of the concrete uprights that carried the wire: the post was plastered in brains, blood, shattered bone.

SL 320, clearly visible to port as dawn surrendered to the day, was a rabble which its commodore was working to re-form. Groups of ships here and there: half a column out on its own, a scattering of individual ships over a wide area. *Astilbe* a cable's length abeam of one straggler, her morse lamp winking.

They'd fallen out from action stations but the skipper was at the binnacle and *Harbinger* was hurrying south, because the worst straggler of them all was the *Burbridge*, who was now several miles astern with the trawler *Stella* in attendance. This information had only just come, by light signal from the commodore, and the skipper had immediately ordered the wheel over and increased to full speed. The thought of that easy target alone down there – or almost alone, and she was down to about half the convoy's speed, Sandover had said – was distinctly scary. Wheelchair patients, women passengers . . . Warrimer heard the note of urgency in the skipper's voice as he called down, 'Midships . . . Steer one-eight-five . . . Here, pilot, take over, will you?'

'Sir.' Mike Scarr got up on the step. He was pale, from a whole night spent in the plot; and once again cloud-cover had made morning stars unobtainable.

Four ships had been lost during the night. The *Ilala*, whose master was the rear-commodore, and the *Bannerman*, had been the first two hit. They'd taken one torpedo each out of a salvo that must have been fired from well forward on the bow of the convoy. The *Ilala* had gone down quickly but the *Bannerman* remained afloat but stopped, causing the first disruption to that side of the convoy as ships astern put their helms over to avoid her. She and the *Ilala* had been the leaders of the starboard columns. Then another U-boat altogether had given her the *coup de grâce*, she and the rescue ship *Leona* – again, two birds with one salvo – when they'd been lying close together, the *Leona* with two boatloads of *Ilala* survivors alongside. The last casualty had been the Dutchman, the *Toungoo,* another column leader; she'd been hit by two torpedoes soon after the convoy had made its emergency turn.

Which at least had saved it from further losses at the hands of three U-boats which had been waiting out ahead. They'd have had an easy job – the convoy in disarray, some ships isolated, trawlers already fully occupied with survivors and getting ships back into line. But now the diversion was being paid for: course was almost due east, to return to the track which according to the 'no-diversion' order should never have been departed from. For three hours SL 320 had slanted away 40 degrees to port, so for the same length of time now it had to shift back to starboard. But without that diversion there mightn't have been twenty-seven ships surviving now: it could have been nearer twenty. Even twenty-seven was bad enough: mental arithmetic made it about twenty-five percent losses, in what, three nights? With the lack of sleep and nights of constant action, much of it repetitive, days ran together and you lost track of time . . . But the skipper's tactics last night, Warrimer thought, had probably been as good as any could have been, losses notwithstanding. He'd told *Gleam* and *Opal*, the flank trawlers, to increase speed by a knot or two and zigzag more widely, covering more ground and making themselves more obvious, by way of deterrence; he'd moved *Stella* to the rearguard station, with similar orders, and given new instructions to the corvettes, restricting each of them to a radius of four miles from her own front corner of the convoy. This allowed them to shift round to the flanks in support of the trawlers if necessary. And *Harbinger* on her own had become the striking force – and had scored, once.

The skipper, up on his high seat now, had his glasses on the *Burbridge*. It was full daylight by this time. He told Scarr, 'Pilot – bring her round ten degrees to port . . . Signalman – by light to him, "What is your best speed now?"'

Wolstenholm went for the lamp. Daylight was revealing tired, whiskered, anxious faces. They'd sunk a U-boat but lost too many of the ships in their charge for that to be a sufficient cause for joy. From *Harbinger*'s pitching, swaying bridge *Stella*'s upperworks were visible, some way out on the *Burbridge*'s starboard bow, whenever she rode up on a wave, but otherwise she was still hidden.

'I'll reduce speed in a minute, Chubb. Who's on asdics?'

'Leading Seaman Garment, sir.'

Garment was the HSD, Higher Submarine Detector, the operator who'd made such an effective partnership with Tony Graves. The skipper's question had been in reference to the fact that as soon as he slowed the ship to something less than twenty knots he'd be relying on asdics as the defence against any dived submarine attack – a shadower closing in from the beam, for instance, and finding this very attractive target. She'd answered now, and the message was being passed. The sea was livelier, Warrimer thought, than it had been yesterday. The rough stuff coming at last: it had been promised days ago.

The *Burbridge*'s answer was, *Making eight knots at the moment but doubtful this can be maintained. Machinery problems snowballing. Sorry to be a nuisance.*

The skipper grunted: he'd read it for himself. 'Make to *Stella*, "I will look after this. Rejoin convoy."'

It would take Broad a while to do it, but not as long as it was going to take the *Burbridge* and *Harbinger*.

Warrimer saw the captain staring at the passengers who were lining the rail of the *Burbridge*'s main deck, one level below the boat deck. Promenade deck, they'd probably call it. The nurses were easily distinguishable, in their cloaks. Queen Alexandras', Warrimer thought they might be. The skipper half-raised his glasses; then lowered them again to hang on their strap – as if he'd been about to take a closer look and for some reason decided not to. Frowning, then glancing aside and finding Warrimer's eyes on him.

'When one corvette's refuelled, she can take over from us here.' He added, in a lower tone, as if talking to himself as much as to Warrimer, 'Just hope to God this fellow *can* keep going.'

'What if he can't, sir?'

A baffled look – as if he barely knew who he was, or the question didn't make sense . . . He told Mike Scarr, 'One-eight-oh revs, pilot. Come round to port now.'

Asdics began to ping, as the ship slowed. And *Stella* was drawing away, making her best speed up the convoy's wake.

Chapter 10

2 November 1942: General Montgomery to Chief of the Imperial General Staff:
I think he [Rommel] is now ripe for a real hard blow . . . It is going in tonight and . . . if we succeed it will be the end of Rommel's army.
Same evening. Adolf Hitler to Field Marshal Rommel:
I and the German people are watching the heroic defensive battle waged in Egypt with faithful trust in your powers of leadership and in the bravery of the German-Italian troops under your command . . . You can show your troops no other way than that which leads to victory or to death.

'All right, then.' Max Looff glanced up at Franz Walther, Willi Heusinger and the quartermaster, Oelricher. They were round the table in the wardroom – Oelricher by invitation, since he messed next door with the engine room artificers and the coxswain. Looff said, 'Comments of a constructive nature will be welcome.'

U 702 was rolling heavily on the surface twenty miles north of the convoy. It was afternoon now. They'd spent the forenoon reloading one torpedo tube and bringing in the spares from the external stowage in the casing. Most of the reload fish were carried internally, except for those two outside the pressure-hull, one for'ard and one aft, but they'd now been moved in through the hatches and secured in the racks. The weather hadn't made it an easy operation, by any means, but as they were bound to need all their torpedoes and conditions weren't about to improve, Looff had opted to do it while it was still just feasible: one fish at a time, first stemming the sea with a stern hatch open, then turning stern-to for the same job for'ard. He'd advised the other *Drachen* group captains who'd used any torpedoes to do the same. Looff had expended three so far, which left him with eleven.

He was steering northeast at six knots, which was the convoy's present rate of advance – according to *Drachen* Six, Ernst Pöhl, who was shadowing from the quarter. Pöhl estimated the Brits were making seven to seven and a half, but with a zigzag taken into account it came down effectively to about six. And at this low speed, with wind and sea on the beam, U 702 was behaving like a drunken cow. It was tempting to dive, get under all the rough stuff, but he wanted to keep a lookout for other members of the group who were close by, and it could be put up with at least until the battery was fully charged. It was rather a luxury, too, to be operating in this zone where there was no chance at all of being jumped on by aircraft. Meanwhile there were signals to be sent and received, and after he'd finalised this plan of action for tonight and passed precise orders to each of the other COs he'd take her a bit farther along the convoy's track before he dived. The peace and quiet was something to look forward to: and you could still use wireless, by shoving the mast up.

'The first point to note is that the convoy has been regrouped, during the forenoon. Six columns only – so it's a somewhat tighter formation covering a smaller area. Not exactly to our advantage, I admit, but – well, can't help whittling 'em down, can we?'

It was a blow that Knappe, *Dracken* Four, had been lost last night. Werner Knappe had managed to get part of a signal out, just before the end: he'd been hit by gunfire from the escort's only destroyer, and hadn't been able to dive, and then another hit had blown off the diesel intakes and swamped the engines. So he'd had to stop and take his punishment: the signal had cut off in the middle of a word.

Ernst Pöhl had missed a wonderful chance, early this morning. Probably because of increased wave-height limiting his periscope vision. The passenger liner had dropped right astern of the convoy; she'd been on her own, a sitting duck, and Pöhl had been just too late catching-on to this situation. The convoy had slowed to allow the straggler to catch up, and before Pöhl had been able to get inside torpedo range the steamer had been enfolded in the convoy's embrace again: worse still, the destroyer, having got her there, was starting an A/S sweep back southward, directly towards him. As he was there primarily to shadow, not to make single-handed attacks, he'd got out of the way, swiftly. It had been an intelligent bit of guesswork on the part of the escort commander, Looff considered, to have realised that the odds were a U-boat *would* by that time have been trying to get into position to attack.

Pöhl and his *Drachen* Six had had a lucky break two nights ago. A shell from a trawler had hit him as he dived, very close to the convoy: the hit had been right aft, on the casing. It had scared the daylights out of everyone with its noise and percussion, but had done no damage to the pressure-hull or anything else that mattered, only tangled some steel up there. It was pure luck that Ernst wasn't playing a harp duet with Werner Knappe, right at this minute: and lucky for everyone else up there too, since the only songs he'd ever known had been dirty ones. But there was a lesson in that experience – not to dismiss trawlers too lightly.

'So.' Looff's pencil tapped the diagram he'd been working on. 'Here's the convoy, and these are the escorts as they were deployed last night. We can see it now, well enough – their stations and *modus operandi*. Corvettes: here, and here. These two stick rather closely to their own corners. And these three objects, the trawlers, are similarly limited. As, of course, they'd have to be, and it would be easier for us if they were not . . . The exception to the rule seems to be that when ships are torpedoed, the trawlers hang around them for rescue purposes, at least for a while, and this of course leaves certain sectors open to attack. My idea last night was based on this factor: to have one assault by several boats create alarm and confusion, and then three more of us coming in to reap the harvest. Unfortunately it didn't work out as well as I'd hoped – and tonight, therefore, we'll make one simultaneous attack, as shown here.'

From each bow of the convoy a U-boat would approach at an angle of about thirty degrees to the line of advance. It was a reasonably good bet that these two – they'd be *Drachens* Eight and Five – would draw the full attention of the two corvettes, who'd romp out after them. This would leave the centre open except for the destroyer, which if it stuck to last night's system would be placed centrally and poised to rush out ahead to break up attacks before they got in close. So for the entertainment of the destroyer – whose captain was obviously the escort commander – *Drachens* Two and Three would attack the convoy head-on, midway between *Drachens* Eight and Five and with about three thousand metres between them initially. Whichever the destroyer picked on, the other would go on through, while the one attacked would dive and be ready to surface and press in again as soon as the destroyer diverted to the other.

'This way I believe we can't fail to get at least one boat into the front of the convoy with a free hand to pick targets, and no escorts to interfere – they'll be busy elsewhere, at least for some time. And of course if they cease to be busy, *those* boats can then surface and wade in, help themselves . . . Meanwhile *Drachen* Eight and *Drachen* Five, who've come in on the bows, will either dive and re-surface, or dodge round their attendant corvettes – they'll have the speed advantage – and come in again on the flanks. Simultaneously with this, *Drachens* Six and Seven will sweep in from port and starboard – here, and here – to attack from the quarters or astern. If the flank trawlers – *these* boys – should be drawn towards *Drachens* Four and/or Five, then the quarters will be undefended; otherwise the rear would be the place – just one trawler in the way shouldn't be much of a problem for the combined talents of Oberleutnants Pöhl and Horsacker . . . Eh?'

'Excellent, sir.' Heusinger nodded. 'You'll have 'em by the balls. But may I ask—'

'Yeah.' Franz Walther had been about to speak when the first lieutenant had annoyed him by jumping in first. 'You didn't say what we'll be doing, sir.'

'I've saved that until last.' Looff pointed, with the pencil's tip. 'We start up here, somewhere between Koning and Becker.' Those were *Drachens* Two and Three, coming in frontally, from the northeast. 'My intention is to move in wherever the door's open, depending on which way the cat jumps. We'll be just far enough out to control the start of it, then to take advantage of results as they show up. I would guess this scheme should give us at least six kills tonight: and what I would *hope*—' he raised a hand with two fingers crossed – 'is that the convoy will be opened up so well that I can get right inside it. I want that passenger ship. Also, there are two tankers in there.'

Franz Walther murmured, 'Passengers.' He wrinkled his blunt nose. 'The Dönitz doctrine?'

It was a kind of joke, from the U-boat men's angle. Flag Officer U-boats' orders in the context of killing human beings as well as the ships they sailed in had been cleverly ambiguous; this was what made it mildly amusing, to the sea-going cynic. The issue was whether crews as well as ships were legitimate targets, and the admiral had contented himself with pointing out that without crews, Allied ships couldn't sail. The logical conclusion was that for men to drown couldn't be at all a bad thing. It pleased some U-boat captains to take it a few steps further: for instance, when time and circumstances permitted, to destroy a ship's boats on their davits by riddling them with machine-gun fire before torpedoing the ship. Others felt differently, sharing the traditional instinct of the seaman that a man in the water was a life to be saved.

Looff told Walther, 'What I'm thinking of is my score. That liner's a fair size.'

Heusinger suggested, smiling, 'Thinking of bonfires too, sir?'

That old fable . . . Looff had a suspicion that Franz Walther knew the truth of it – that it was rubbish. Walther was smart, and saw *through* things: whereas this self-ingratiating Willi Heusinger was really still a boy, and typical of the kind who'd enjoy having a CO who laughed when he watched tankers burn . . . How would he like to know, Looff wondered, that the same CO, alone in his bunk at nights, often woke shaking like a man in fever – in a helpless, mother-seeking funk?

As likely as not Franz Walther knew it. Or guessed. He'd been around, seen other captains in similar shape. You tried to disguise it, but – well, nobody *else* succeeded. And the top brass ignored it, because they wanted you at sea, wanted the last gasp out of you . . . This was something that Looff had come to recognise and cling to during those few days in the base just recently: that practically everyone had trouble with his nerves. After a while . . . Not the new boys, who were so busy being heroes: but after a certain stage, when you'd come to the conclusion that you were *not* a hero and saw the stark reality – that the odds were you'd drown . . . If there was any heroism at all, he'd decided, it was being like this and carrying on, putting up with the shakes and the mental screams and assuring yourself between whiles that you were OK, could see it through . . . Walther's brown eyes were on him, thoughtful, understanding: and if he was aware of that aspect of it too there'd be no contempt in such insight.

Oelricher cleared his throat, and spoke for the first time. 'If I might make one comment, sir. It's –' he nodded – 'excellent . . . But wouldn't it be more effective – that's to say, really *guaranteed* to succeed – if we postponed it twenty-four hours, so we'd have the other two as well?'

There'd been a signal from Kernéval to the effect that two Sixth Flotilla boats who'd been on their way from Brest down to the Mediterranean were being diverted to join the *Drachen* group. Otto Meusel and Klaus Ziegner were travelling in company and had been ordered to rendezvous with *Drachen* One as soon as possible. They'd be here some time tomorrow and they'd become *Drachens* Nine and Ten. It would have been inviting bad luck, Looff thought, to have re-allocated Werner Knappe's number in the group.

He agreed with his quartermaster, up to a point.

'You're right, of course. But there's no reason to wait for them. After all, our lord and master is crying out for blood: and time isn't completely unlimited.'

The rest of that signal from U-boat headquarters had said, *This convoy with its weak defence should be annihilated. There can be no excuse for even one ship emerging from the air gap. The Black Pit must swallow it.*

'Tomorrow night, if this plan has proved itself – and mind you, we may learn some lessons and find it can be improved – well, we'll repeat it, only in a more elaborate form with nine boats instead of seven. I've already considered this, in fact. All things being equal, I'd employ the newcomers as back-ups to *Drachens* Eight and Five – two more attackers going in on the bows at the same time as the two – or three, counting ourselves – from ahead. Well, Oelricher?'

The quartermaster nodded. 'I would say there's no doubt at all you'll be giving the C-in-C exactly what he wants, sir.'

'But don't we *always*?'

Franz Walther chuckled at his own humour. Black-rimmed nails, greasy hair over his collar, face as fuzzy as a dog's and with discoloured teeth that could have been a dog's too. Even his eyeballs looked as if they could do with a good rinse. And he was as efficient a chief engineer as you'd find afloat. Heusinger was looking at him with a mixture of curiosity and revulsion in his expression: he wasn't used to Walther yet, and they were such contrasting types – Heusinger youthfully fresh, well groomed and clean . . . Loof, who was neither as scruffy as his engineer nor as immaculate as his first lieutenant, said, 'I *intend* to give him what he wants. Even before that signal I had decided—'

'Signal, sir.'

He glanced up – at Kreis, the PO telegraphist. Kreis said, 'From *Drachen* Six, sir.'

Looff read, *Convoy reduced speed to four knots at 1515.*

'Well, I'll be – *damned* . . .' He looked up at Walther, who was squinting in an attempt to read the scrawl upside-down. 'We even have a few extra days now in which to make a job of it.'

Jack Everard lay in a depression that was no more than a fold in the ground, in roughly the geometric centre of something like four acres of sloping stubble. Beside the slot he was lying in was a low outcrop of rock and some gorse and nettles; the rock would account for the fact that these few square yards in the middle of the field had never been ploughed. He was wet, cold, hungry, and his left ankle wouldn't support his weight. He'd used Frank Trolley's knife to cut and trim a stick, in the woods where he'd hidden before daylight came and from which he'd moved only a few hours ago; using the stick he was able to hobble along, slowly. The knife had been under the edge of a platter on the table in that village where they'd had the meal: it was the kind you'd expect to be kept in a sheath, but someone must have used it earlier that evening for cutting meat, and Trolley had managed to liberate it. Frank's word for surreptitious acquisitions, that was. Jack had pulled it out of Frank's sock, in the early hours of this morning beside the railway line, and now it was in his own.

This was a good hide, as hides went, because it didn't look like one. A platoon of soldiery had been through the wood where he'd been earlier; that *had* been the sort of place you'd search for a man on the run. They'd reappeared on the road down there at the bottom, re-embarked in their trucks and gone off to draw some other covert a long time ago now. There'd been no reason for them to have beaten over this field: only someone unusually astute or experienced in such matters would have guessed there could be cover for a man here, even though from the road below the gorse must have been in plain sight just as the crossroads was from up here. There were some small houses around it, and several times military vehicles had stopped, soldiers getting out for a smoke while others knocked on doors. Now, the crossroads was deserted, and the occupants of the houses weren't visible.

He wondered again whether the sensible thing might not be to give himself up. He had one lump of hard bread in his pocket and no idea where the next bite after that might come from . . . The worst aspect was he hadn't got far enough from the place where he'd jumped – and where they'd have found Frank Trolley's body, which he'd had no time or way of doing anything about. The reason for this, of course, was the sprained ankle, which had slowed him down so much.

There was still no movement below: but smoke rising from a chimney and a bicycle propped against a gatepost showed there were people around somewhere. If he just stood up now, hobbled downhill, surrendered?

What made him reluctant to do so was the fact it would be so irreversible an action. Here and now he had his options open, to some extent. There was no guard with a rifle trained on him, no wire, lights, machine-guns on towers. If he got up and staggered down to the houses, there damn soon would be. Earlier when he'd considered this there'd been troops about, and he'd stayed put for fear they'd shoot if he moved: it would have saved them trouble. But giving oneself up to civilians might provide some small measure of insurance: there'd at least be witnesses to the fact he *had* surrendered. On the other hand he'd be putting himself back in their trap, possibly for years. And Fiona alone in London: or before long *not* alone . . .

Hold out for just a day, he told himself. Then maybe another – until the leg was back in commission and the local hue and cry might have died down. *They* might give up, thinking he'd got away? Then it would only be a matter of moving south until one hit either the frontier or Lake Constance. Which could be negotiated – somehow . . .

But that was it: the state of freedom, uncomfortable as it was at the moment, had taken a lot of achieving and did not have to be thrown away if it could be (a) prolonged, (b) endured. The priority had to be Food, Acquisition of: then some kind of shelter, and eventually, mobility.

Move *north*, initially? Which the searchers would not

expect? If one could move at all, go north, lie up for a few days and then slip southward to the border?

Having come this far – and cost old Frank his life?

Frank Trolley wouldn't have made the train-jump if he – Jack – hadn't been so set on it. Even then he'd had his doubts about it. Jack remembered sitting there beside him and thinking while the train beat out its drumbeat rhythm for mile after mile, *He doesn't have the compulsion that I have: with him it's only duty . . .*

He'd have been alive now, if one hadn't—

Aircraft. He turned his head slowly, carefully, and saw it flying into sight over the wooded shoulder of the hill on a course parallel to the south-leading lane. On that course it would pass almost right overhead, and it was at no more than – he guessed, having turned his face down and pressed himself into the trough of muddy weeds – three or four hundred feet.

From the air, he supposed this *might* look like a hide. And perhaps a man on his face in a shallow groove in the middle of a field of stubble would be seen from up there for precisely what he was. The din was growing, a loud bang-banging from the light plane's engine: it was a monoplane, small, khaki or green in colour, clattering through the sky. A military spotter-plane, probably.

Getting fainter now . . . *Turned away*?

He didn't move. No point at all in moving . . . His quick glimpse of the plane was imprinted on his brain, and to get rid of it he turned his thoughts to the road below and the pasture on its other side – and wondered whether if the flyer had seen him he'd find some place to land. But of course, he'd have a wireless . . . Definitely receding now, in any case. Thinking of the road, crossroads and houses, he saw again in his mind's eye that bicycle leaning against a gate.

The plane was flying south. On a weaving, searching course – which accounted for its swing away just at this point – but definitely leaving. For the moment, anyway.

A bicycle wasn't a difficult thing to hide, even in open countryside. He was thinking ahead, to a time when he'd need to get rid of it . . . If at dusk it was still there: and if one could crawl to the far hedge and then down in its shadow to the lane, then – hobbling – over to the gateway where the bike *might* still be. Then, if it was, the question would be whether an ankle you couldn't walk on might be sound enough to push a pedal.

Mike Scarr, swaying to the ship's wild motion and with his sextant at his eye, yelled '*Now*!' The bosun's mate's bark into the voice-pipe matched that shout, and in the plot Scarr's assistant recorded the chronometer time to within half a second. Scarr peered closely at the sextant, to read off the altitude of Deneb, the last of the three stars he'd shot; he'd get position lines from the three of them that would intercept to give *Harbinger*'s precise position. He knew already that Madeira was roughly 170 miles on the starboard bow, but until he'd worked these sights out he couldn't have guaranteed the dead-reckoning position within ten miles or so.

He looked around now, lowering the sextant and holding it against his belly to keep it out of the intermittent spray. The horizon was almost invisible as the last of the daylight leaked away. Half a minute after taking that last sight he couldn't have taken another, for that lack of an horizon. The ships of the convoy, spread from right ahead to broad on the starboard bow, were becoming indistinct, so that each looked exactly like its neighbours and all of them merging into darkening seascape, encroaching night.

'I'll go down, sir.'

They were still closed up for dusk action stations. The skipper – on his high seat, and as usual with binoculars at his eyes – only grunted. It was about as much as anyone was getting out of him, at present. He'd seemed to come out of his shell – or try to – twice during the first dog watch, though: once when he'd told Carlish, 'After this trip, Sub, I can see no reason why I shouldn't sign a watch-keeping certificate for you' – and Carlish had been overjoyed – and then a bit later he'd asked Matt Warrimer whether everything was all right below; meaning in effect whether

Warrimer felt he'd got control of things in his new role as second-in-command. Warrimer had assured him quickly that there were no problems: and he'd been noticeably glad to be asked, to be putting on record the fact he'd slipped so effortlessly into that very demanding job. Scarr had seen and recognised this; and as a rather easy-going RN officer himself, Warrimer the Volunteer Reserve man's go-getting attitude rather amused him. Scarr thought Warrimer would probably be just the same when he was back in the City in his bowler: a thruster, dedicated to a kind of cheerful one-upmanship.

The skipper had a deckchair set up behind his tall seat now, and he'd been taking cat-naps in it during the day. Since dawn this morning he hadn't been off the bridge for more than a few minutes at a time.

Starsights had been possible because a rising wind had ripped holes in the cloud-cover, permitting glimpses of the heavens. The wind was about force five, with a sea to match, and the forecast was for an increase to force six. Scarr realised, taking another glance upward as he left the bridge, that there'd be some patchy moonlight later. It might be a factor to the advantage of the U-boats, who'd been doing a lot of talking, up ahead and on the convoy's beams. Gritten had come to the bridge earlier and told the skipper, 'Never 'eard so much yacking from one pack, sir!'

They'd be planning their night's tactics. And a moon *would* help them – if they used it carefully – by reducing the advantage of the escorts' RDF.

He was in the chartroom, working out his sights with the aid of logarithm and cosine tables, when he heard the order passed to relax from action stations. So it would be dark up there now: the ship's company would get down to a hasty supper, getting it finished and the messtraps cleared away as fast as possible, before the night's troubles started.

There . . . He had the position. A neat intersection, and the DR estimate hadn't been far out either. Having pencilled the date and time against it on the chart, he entered the latitude and longitude in his notebook. At the moment, SL 320 was pretty well up to schedule – thanks to having been a few hours ahead of it yesterday. He was shutting the notebook, finishing, when the door slid open and the skipper came in.

'Know where we are?'

'Close to where we reckoned, sir.' Scarr moved over. 'And where we're supposed to be.'

'That won't apply much longer.'

At four knots, the *Burbridge*'s best speed now, they'd be losing something like seventy miles a day. Even without any more diversions. He was checking it out on the chart, walking the dividers up the marked track. He muttered, 'Just how late we'll be getting to position B . . .'

'Shall I—'

'No. Go and get something to eat, pilot. Or some fresh air. You'll be stuck in the plot again all night.'

Scarr glanced at his captain again, as he turned away. Telling him *he* needed this, that or the other, for God's sake! Everard looked about ten years older than he had a few days ago. Warrimer had mentioned it to Ian Mackenzie, the doctor, and Mackenzie had reacted irritably . . . 'If he doesn't sleep, won't eat, and worries himself sick, what can *I* do about it?'

Scarr had never thought of his captain as a worrier.

The door slid shut. Alone, Nick found the answer to that question of arrival at position B, the point where they were due to alter to port again: and the answer was they'd be twelve hours late. Instead of midnight tomorrow, noon the day after. So – and here was the vital aspect of it, on top of the fact they'd be in U-boat territory for several days longer than intended – he took Cruance's tracing out, to check how far astern of SL 320 'Torch' convoy KMS 1 – the main assault force from the Clyde and Loch Ewe – would be crossing. Whether indeed there'd be any margin at all . . .

Well, there would be. And it would be adequate. But nothing like as much of a gap as had been intended.

Cruance, and others, who by now would have read a signal despatched from *Harbinger* four hours ago, would be having kittens. The signal gave them SL 320's position, course and reduced speed, losses to date, estimated strength of the U-boat pack and the destruction of one of them, and it had ended with a request for reinforcement of the totally inadequate escort force. Cruance and company would be biting their nails down to the knuckles: they wouldn't have any escorts available for reinforcement, and they'd be sweating at the danger to their 'Torch' convoys. And understandably . . .

The Americans would be all right. This convoy's track for the past three days had coincided almost exactly with the route the US assault force would be following after its loop southward. UGF 1 with its escorting Task Force 34, carrying 34,000 troops under Lieutenant General George S Patton and aiming for beaches around Casablanca, would be ploughing this very patch of ocean at midnight on the fourth – two days' time – and they'd have a clear passage, U-boat-free water right up to the Moroccan coast.

He'd pulled out a pipe, and he was filling it when the chartroom door slid back again. PO Steward Foster edged in, balancing himself and a tray against the ship's gyrations. And talking before he was even through the door: 'Got the buzz you was off the bridge at last, sir. Thought you might care for a bite before you goes back up. Coffee, this is – strong, way you like it, sir – and in this dish 'ere . . .'

'Thoughtful of you, Foster.'

''ave to keep body an' soul together, sir, don't we?' Charley Foster put the tray down on the chart. Rattling on . . . 'Specially since they say our playmates is about to 'ave another go at us.' He was keeping up the patter, Nick appreciated, so as to get him to start eating before he remembered he wasn't hungry. Like a nanny with a small child: except for some of the terminology . . . 'Right lot of sods as they are . . . You'll find this is quite a tasty drop of corned-dog 'ash, sir . . .'

'Stand by to surface.'

'Stand by to surface, sir.' Wykeham glanced round. 'Check main vents.'

The Count was dressed as a Sicilian peasant. Loose trousers, rough shirt, sheepskin jacket that smelt of sheep, and a shapeless hat. He was sitting at the wardroom table, waiting, and very nervous now that the moment had almost arrived.

'Depth?'

'Forty-one fathoms, sir.'

They'd spent the last few hours of daylight making a periscope reconnaissance of the area. There'd been nothing about, either afloat or on shore, to suggest the enemy could have been expecting a visit.

The Count had asked again, this morning, 'Why, truly, I do not have commando this time, for the boat and so forth?'

Ruck had spread his hands 'Count, I do not know!'

'Before, you say there is no commando available for me?'

'I was guessing, that's all – what reason there could be. I know a lot less than you do, Count. Didn't you put this question to whoever gives you your orders?'

The Count had only shrugged. But it was obviously bothering him a lot. Paul had suggested privately to Ruck that he, Paul, might take the job on. 'Wouldn't be much to it – just paddling one of those things half a mile and bringing it back again?'

Ruck had snapped, 'The hell you will!' And no explanation.

Paul was up for'ard now in the torpedo stowage compartments, chatting to CPO Ron Gaffney, the TI. The folboat had been hauled out of its rack and lay on the deck, with a line from its after end which would be taken up through the hatch when they'd surfaced. Paul and the second coxswain, Leading Seaman Lovesay, were the only two men who'd go up top; from down here the torpedo-men would manhandle the canoe up into the open hatch, and Paul and Lovesay would drag it up and launch it, while the hatch was being shut and clipped again.

The Count was carrying papers identifying him as Carlo Paoli, and a medical certificate proving he was a consumptive, which would explain his not having been enlisted. He also had a sealed package of documents taped to his ribs inside the shirt. Paul had shaken a hand that was far too soft to be either a canoer's or a peasant's, and told him, 'See you in a couple of nights, Count.'

'Perhaps.'

The quiet hero, going to his doom. But the brown eyes were definitely scared.

'Ready to surface, sir.'

Ruck was at the periscope, circling, taking a last look round. He pulled his head back from the lenses and asked Newton, the asdic operator, 'Anything?'

Enemy propellers, Newton was listening for. Patrol boats: E-boats or MAS-boats, in ambush. It had been known.

'Nothing at all, sir.'

Ruck snapped the handles up. 'Surface!'

Air roared into the tanks, and hydroplanes swung to hard a-rise. The signalman pushed the lower hatch open then came down off the ladder to make way for Ruck, who climbed up into the tower – in seaboots and waterproof Ursula suit with its hood up, binoculars slung round his neck. The depthgauge needles were circling fast now: twenty-five feet – twenty – fifteen . . .

'Ten feet, sir!'

At Wykeham's yell, Ruck pulled off the second clip and flung the top lid open. Salt water rained down into the tower as *Ultra* lifted herself into the dark offshore silence, sea still sluicing away through the holes in her bridge deck as he climbed out of the hatch, dragged the voice-pipe cock open and took a preliminary all-round look with the naked eye. Then a more careful sweep around with glasses, while the signalman and a lookout emerged behind him. Two thirds of the surroundings consisted of black coastline; *Ultra* had been brought up with her stern to it, bow pointing at the open sea, but land enclosed her from beam to beam, Cape Zafferano to port and around the stern to Cape Cefalu on the other side.

Wykeham had stopped blowing. The submarine lay at rest in slightly loppy but well sheltered water. Weather-wise the canoeist should have few problems. Ruck called down, 'Open fore hatch, up folboat. Ask our passenger to join me in the bridge.' The signalman and the lookout moved like automatons, slowly and steadily turning with their glasses probing the darkness. Ruck had turned his attention to the shore.

They were getting the fore hatch open: he could hear the clangs as they worked at the clips inside. Then the Count arrived, shouldering against him. At that moment Ruck saw the two blue flashes.

'There's your man.' He pointed. 'Bang on time, and in the right place.'

They had to wait a full minute before the flashes were repeated. They came from the deepest recess of the bay, right astern, well to the east of the village of Termini.

Pitch dark, and very quiet. Aware of the closeness of that enemy coast, men kept their voices low . . . The Count didn't speak at all. He'd been in such a sweat of anxiety all day that Ruck had been wondering how or why he'd ever got into this kind of work. But he did know a certain amount of Carlo Paoli's background – a lot more than the Count knew he knew – and his sympathy was limited.

It *had* to be.

He heard the slam of the fore hatch shutting. So they'd already got the boat up on the casing and they'd be easing it over the side. He told his passenger, 'Go on down, Count. Just keep your boat pointing at those flashes, whenever they show up, and you can't go wrong. Same when we come back to collect you, aim for *our* flashes. And please be on time – I'm not allowed to hang around for long after I've shown a light. OK?'

Everard's voice floated out of the dark: 'Boat's in the water, sir.'

'He's on his way.' He took the Count's arm, to help him over the side of the bridge, where footholds led down to the catwalk that ran around it. 'Over you go. Good luck . . . See you in two nights' time, Count.'

Carlo Paoli climbed over without answering. Ruck heard

a murmur down there where Everard would be meeting him, leading him for'ard around the gun while Lovesay held the canoe alongside.

Paul murmured, 'Easy does it. A bit slippery here.' The Count's heels were noisy on the casing. He was wearing farmers' boots, while Paul was sure-footed in rubber soles. Lovesay, in more traditional seamanlike fashion, crouched barefooted on the casing's edge, steadying the boat and also holding the double-bladed paddle. Paul found the Count's hand, and shook it: it was inanimate, unresponsive, like shaking a dummy's hand. He said, 'Good luck. See you soon. I'll have a tot of rum poured ready for you.'

'Goodbye.'

It was all he said. He was shaking, panting with a shortness of breath induced by fear. They helped him into his boat: *Ultra* was lying low in the water so the transfer wasn't difficult. Lovesay passed the paddle to him: 'OK, sir?' He didn't answer. They angled the canoe out, and sent it clear of the submarine's side with a push. Half a minute later it was moving shoreward, the paddle circling rather clumsily, with too much splash, and the course erratic. Darkness swallowed it. Paul and Lovesay climbed up into the bridge, where Ruck had just passed the order for three hundred revolutions on the diesels with a running battery charge both sides.

'Well done, you two. Go on down now.'

The diesels rumbled into action. *Ultra* was to move east, dive off Cape Milazzo before daylight and spend a day and a half patrolling north of Messina. Then back here, to pick up the Count on the following night.

Paul said later, over a mug of tea at the wardroom table, 'Wonder what our friend's doing at this moment.'

Ruck glanced at him: after a pause he remarked, 'It's a fairly extraordinary operation, this.'

'I know.'

'*What* d'you know?'

'The Count told me. He's contacting local partisan leaders to alert them for very big landing operations both sides of Palermo – and in Sardinia, near Cagliari. Whole armies, tanks, the lot. I suppose this'll mean the beginning of the end – particularly if we're about to roll 'em up in the desert now.'

Ruck swallowed, put his mug down.

'That what he told you?'

Paul nodded. 'He warned me he wasn't supposed to talk about it. But as it's going to start any minute now it can't make much odds. I suppose this is what all the flap was about in Malta, rushing everyone out on patrol?'

Ruck shook his head. 'I'll be damned.'

Wykeham asked from his bunk, 'Didn't you know this, sir?'

'There's one thing I know for sure.' He wagged his head again. 'They're pretty damn smart, our lot. My *God* they are.'

Jack's right leg had done all the work while the injured one just suffered. He'd got down to the crossroads by crawling down the length of the hedge at the far side of the stubble-field: it had been dark before he'd risked moving out of the hide. Crossing the road, hobbling on his stick, had been the dangerous bit. But the bike had still been there: if it hadn't, he didn't know what he'd have done. There'd been no lights showing from the houses – blackout regulations, no doubt – and he'd got away without a sound except for the nerve-twisting squeak of the turning pedals. He'd turned into the lane that led north – north by west, to be accurate – using the Pole star for a leading mark.

He'd stopped now because there was a muddy track and a random-looking collection of farm buildings around it, just off this lane. In the glimmer of starlight the place looked deserted and neglected. There was a farmhouse – a cottage – and a barn with a sagging roof, and sheds that might have been old chicken-houses. No lights anywhere: but you wouldn't have expected any.

He'd eaten the lump of hard bread while he'd been lying in his wet hole in the field. Hunger, as well as the ankle and the fact he was completely played-out, was a problem. At some periods he'd been wondering if he'd been stupid, whether if he was capable of travelling at all – which he was now proving he *was* – he shouldn't have steered directly for the frontier, to get out as quickly as possible; whether this wasn't a bit too clever . . . He'd covered about six or seven miles, he thought: it hadn't been exactly fast travel, but it had been a lot faster than he'd have managed on foot. There'd been only one stop, a panic blundering into the ditch, bicycle and all, when a lorry without lights had come trundling round a bend. In the past half-hour or so nothing had moved except rabbits and scared pigeons making as much row as pheasants when they took off.

Ride on a mile or so, find a place to hide the bike, then hobble back and lie-up in one of those sheds?

Woodsmoke. He sniffed the air, and knew the farm *was* inhabited – which had been likely anyway, but which one could think about in two ways. For a hide pure and simple, an abandoned place might be safer . . . He wondered, forcing his tired brain along, *Would it*? Wouldn't they tend to look twice at empty places? Well – anyway, the other aspect – there'd be food around. A farm that was being worked would surely have a few edible items: potatoes, swedes, corn – you could chew corn, blowing the chaff out . . .

He was probably more exhausted than he'd ever been. This was a factor one had not only to contend with but also to take into account – recognising that the urge to stop, rest, *give up* was part of that tiredness. One was not in a condition to arrive at major decisions: so postpone them, just hang on, and something might turn up . . . He told himself, as if he was addressing a subordinate, to ride on for a mile: if he didn't come across a better place in that distance he'd hide the machine and come back here. As long as one didn't bite off more than one could chew, allow daylight to catch one in the open: by dawn he had to be well hidden. Ditto bicycle: and not in the same place. He pushed off, began the painful one-footed pedalling again: *squeak-squeak, squeak-squeak* . . .

* * *

Astern, the sky glowed red over SL 320. A ship on fire: several torpedoes had found targets in the last quarter-hour. That blaze could be one of the two oilers.

'Port twenty!'

Harbinger had just put one U-boat down – charged it, seen it dive and then plastered it with a shallow-set pattern of depthcharges. She was turning back now because the battle had closed in around the convoy. Both corvettes were chasing RDF contacts – fresh ones, having had some before and lost them – most likely when they'd dived. The picture on the plot was a full one and fast-changing but what it amounted to was the U-boats were all around and attacking simultaneously: the chatter that Gritten had listened to during the day would have been the planning of what was happening now.

'Midships.' Warrimer saw the skipper checking ship's head on the gyro repeater. 'Steer two-one-five.'

At full revs, plunging southward. The moon was a glimmer through driven cloud: at intervals it had been giving quite a lot of light. Depth-charges burst in deep, muffled thunder – a long way off; another torpedo-hit was like a vicious answer to that sound. The blaze surely had to be an oiler, although it didn't look quite like that sort of fire: the two of them had been right in the centre of the convoy, they and the *Burbridge* placed like the kernel in a nut, encased . . . TBS stuttering in, Bearcroft taking it, *Eagle, this is Fox, U-boat surfaced after depthcharging, engaging – out.*

The bastards were everywhere . . .

'Course two-one-five, sir!'

Explosion. A flash: like ammunition going up, or a tank of gasoline. And TBS again, *Eagle – Gannet . . . Convoy's slightly out of shape, sir, but Opal's in there somewhere trying to organise them. The one on fire is the Malibar, and Stella's standing by her. The Springburn's gone down and so has number twenty-four – the Harvest Moon. I have a new contact on three-five-five, three miles – investigating – out . . .*

Two sunk, one burning, but no oiler . . . About five minutes ago, Warrimer remembered, the skipper had asked Guyatt for a report on what was happening on that side of the convoy; this had been his answer. But the five minutes had felt more like half an hour.

'Range and bearing now, Sub?'

Wolstenholm bawled, 'U-boat surfacing – red oh-five, sir!'

Against the glow from that burning ship – and close, easy to see . . . Warrimer was passing orders to his for'ard guns. Black, wet-gleaming hull emerging from the whitened waves: the German imagining the field was clear here, so he'd come up and cruise in undetected, draw some blood? Warrimer had his glasses on the filthy, predatory thing as A and B guns both fired and the skipper shouted, 'Stand by the port thrower!'

The range was too short for anything except ramming: so he was about to lob a depth charge – like tossing a huge grenade . . . Guns rapid-firing, but the ship was bucking like mad and shellspouts had gone up right, left, short, over . . . Chub called, 'Port thrower ready, sir!'

Harbinger with the sea on her quarter, corkscrewing: there was a danger at high speed in these conditions that the screws might race in thin surface water as her bow dug in and she stood on her head like some old duck. When they'd first spotted the U-boat there'd been no-one visible in its bridge: the German captain would have become aware just about now that he wasn't alone here. Shellspouts lifted short again: and the thing was diving . . . The skipper was leaning over the wheelhouse voice-pipe, judging his moment to start a turn and have her swinging as he lobbed the charge away into the patch of churned foam where the enemy was vanishing like a snake into its hole . . . 'Starboard ten!'

Torpedo hit – distant . . . *Harbinger* responding to her rudder's drag . . . 'Thrower stand by . . . Fire!'

Looking aft, Warrimer saw the black cannister – the size of a tarbarrel but packed with 750 lbs of high-explosive – flung out on a high, curving, forward-inclined trajectory, thrown that way by the ship's own forward and swinging motion. Chubb's voice echoed the skipper's as he thumbed the firing button: now he was telling Timberlake to reload the thrower, and Warrimer guessed Timberlake would be snarling at the unnecessary instruction. *Harbinger* plunging with her head down as she turned . . . 'Midships – meet her, cox'n . . .'

Warrimer had all guns loaded and trained out on that side. If the single charge had the extraordinary luck to hit the jackpot, bring the U-boat up, X gun and the point-fives would be in it too, this time. But if the skipper had driven his ship straight at the target so as to drop a shallow pattern, at such close quarters it would have been impossible not to ram; *Harbinger* could have staved-in her bow, or wrecked her screws as she ran over the submarine, and an incapacitated *Harbinger* was too high a price to pay for one dead U-boat, at this stage of the losing game.

A white mountain rose with thunder in its base. A great cauliflower-shape of sea flinging up . . . Warrimer told his guns, 'Set range zero, point of aim that explosion, stand by!'

It was a toss-up: but the U-boat *could* suddenly be there, floundering . . .

'Midships. Steer one-five-oh. One-eight-oh revolutions.'

Carlish called from the plot voice-pipe, 'Surface contact bearing one-seven-five, four thousand one hundred yards, sir!'

Another one: two miles away. The froth was subsiding, sea boiling as it fell back into itself, wind-driven spray lashing away for several hundred yards and whipping the surface as white as if it had been painted. Guns trained and loaded, gun-layers' fingers on the triggers, layers' and trainers' eyes against the rubber eye-pieces of their sighting telescopes. But no target yet.

'Stand by one full pattern with settings one-fifty and two-fifty feet.'

He was altering course again: to run over the same spot, assume the U-boat would have held on towards the convoy: he'd drop a pattern, and *Harbinger* would be on course either to rejoin the convoy or to chase after that new RDF contact. The Germans were like fleas on a dog's back tonight: except their bites were lethal. 'Asdics?'

'Nothing yet, sir.'

The water would still be churned-up, from the explosion of that charge: it was too lively a sea in any case, for good A/S results. If it got much worse there'd be interference to spoil the performance of the 271 RDF, too . . . Leading Seaman Garment yelled from the asdic cabinet, 'Torpedoes approaching, port beam!'

A split second, for that to sink in . . . Then Nick's shout – 'Hard a-port, full ahead together!'

Looff swore. He was in the tower, on his seat at the attack periscope, and the destroyer's racy profile had begun to shorten. She was swinging her bow into the direction of the attack, sea cascading like white fire as her engines flung her into the turn. Moonlight glittered diffusely through spray around the top lense of the periscope. There was still a chance, one of his three fish *might* still hit . . .

If in the next few moments the destroyer wasn't blown to bits, she'd be counter-attacking with depth charges. Within seconds, he was going to have to go deep.

'Torpedoes still running?'

'Running, sir!'

They wouldn't have run to that range yet, though . . .

Looff groaned in his mind, *Please – one hit*?

When he'd climbed out into U 702's streaming bridge and found he was being shot at – one shell streaking overhead and another sending a column of white up close to starboard – he'd crash-dived to fifty metres, put his helm hard a-port and taken her right round in a fast spiral with full grouped-up battery power on the starboard screw. The single explosion had rocked her: it must have been close, considering that shallow-set charges were less effective than those in deeper water. But there'd been one over-riding thought in his mind: that this was the destroyer, its captain was the escort commander, and if he could be eliminated – after all, here he was, for God's sake, out here on his own and there *was* a chance! – the rest of the job of butchering the convoy would present very little difficulty. It was the kind of opportunity that revealed itself in a split second, and part of Max Looff's success as a U-boat captain had been to recognise such openings and take instant advantage of them.

The destroyer was bow-on now: being aimed so accurately at U 702's periscope that you could imagine the Brit could see it. Which was an impossibility in this sea . . . He'd known where the torpedoes had come from, that was all, he was charging down the tracks. Looff's hands were tight on the periscope handles and there was an incipient tremble in his taut muscles: if there was going to be a hit he wanted to see it, and it could come at any second!

But you'd hear it anyway. And he ought, he knew, to be taking her down *now* . . .

Holding his breath. Mesmerised. Shaking. Lips drawn back, teeth clenched . . .

He'd gasped, as if something inside had snapped, and his right hand had moved without being told to, depressing the lever that sent the 'scope down. Its motor humming as it sank, shaft glistening with grease and saltwater droplets. It was as if the decision had been made *for* him, some voice other than his own rapping out 'Flood Q, two hundred metres, full ahead both motors, starboard twenty!'

Going deep – to *safe* depth – and turning away from the direction of the convoy because the Brit up there – who'd be over the top and shovelling out depth bombs at any moment – would expect him to turn towards it . . . Climbing down into the control room as his boat angled steeply, spiralling to starboard with Q quick-dive tank flooded to drag her down all the faster, he saw questions in several pairs of eyes. He shrugged, muttered, 'Can't win 'em all.' A glance from Franz Walther, at the smile on his captain's sweat-gleaming face: Walther had turned back again, busy with the trim, but with a faintly sardonic look as if the astute brain behind that oil-smeared, hairy countenance had recorded the phoniness of the smile, seen the quivering of nerves behind it . . . Screws raced overhead, churning like a meat-grinder. Looff felt a dryness in his throat: he glanced instinctively at the depth gauge and saw the needle swinging past the hundred-metre mark. The deep-dive capability that would take them right down to two hundred metres was a life-saver. He told Heusinger, who'd been gazing at him with that blank, really rather stupid expression he tended to assume in times of crisis, 'It was worth a try.'

A nod: with surprise, at having been favoured with such an explanation. Even an apology, it might have been! There was interest in Oelricher's covert glance as well. But it *had* been worth trying: if it had come off, the success would have been of major significance. It would also have been regarded as a tactical master-stroke, knocking out the one really effective escort, and escort commander, as a prelude to massacre.

Depthcharges thundered – astern, and well overhead. One all on its own, a maverick deeper than the others, burst close enough to make the lighting flicker. Looff crowed, with his head back and his hands on his hips, 'We've heard hundreds much closer than *that*, my friends!' Then – 'Slow ahead both motors.'

Three torpedoes had been expended. Leaving eight. Only two tubes had torpedoes in them, though, one for'ard tube and the single stern tube. Depth gauge needle passing the hundred and fifty mark . . . Walther, working at the trim, was taking some of the angle off the boat, to slow the rate of descent, and pretty soon now U 702 would be below the effective range of British depthcharges. There'd be no point trying to get to the convoy now to join in the action: there was tomorrow night, and the one after, and a few more after that . . . He told Heusinger, 'Prepare to reload those three tubes.' It had to be done, and it was a good reason to stay deep for a while: you couldn't safely move heavy torpedoes around when you were being flung from beam to beam.

At 0200, by which time the U-boats seemed to have withdrawn, *Harbinger*'s W/T operator took in a cyphered reply to the signal she'd made earlier. It read: *It is essential that you keep to the timetable. Ships unable to maintain station should be abandoned and sunk. Reinforcements will be sent to join you as soon as ships are available.*

The skipper – he was on his high chair, Carlish at the binnacle now – had grunted at Bearcroft to read it out to him. He gave an impression, to Warrimer, of a man in isolation, a man with a slow fire smouldering and liable to erupt. As it had, at one point . . . *Harbinger* was two miles ahead of the convoy, zigzagging broadly across its front. The corvettes were stretching their areas to cover the bows and beams while the trawlers rounded up stragglers and chivvied others back into formation. But taking *Harbinger* through the middle of the herd during the worst period of its disruption, when both rescue ships – the *Mount Trembling* and the *Archie Dukes* having this duty now – had been stopped, transferring survivors, the ships as weather-breaks creating shelter in which their boats could work, by no means without danger to their crews – the eruption had come when he'd found the *Burbridge* also stopped, with a boat alongside and tackles and jumping-ladders rigged, hoisting a wounded man in a stretcher. He'd stormed at the *Burbridge*'s master, over the loud-hailer: by stopping he was putting all his passengers at extreme risk – which didn't equate with the benefit to a few survivors – and by dropping astern he was adding to the problems of the escorts. Survivors, wounded or not, could be taken into any ship *except* the *Burbridge*: why in the name of God did he think he'd been kept in the centre of the convoy, cossetted like the oilers? The *Burbridge*'s master had called back, when the tirade ended, 'All right, captain, keep your wool on . . .' *Harbinger* had surged on, ranged in close to the *Chauncy Maples* to request the commodore, in coldly formal terms, to order the *Burbridge* not to stop again.

Warrimer had never heard his captain rave like that before. He hadn't known him or served with him long but he wouldn't have believed he was capable of such loss of temper. You could almost feel the heat of anger still radiating from the hunched, brooding figure while Bearcroft read out that signal: there was a moment or two of silence, and then a quiet, 'Put it on the log, Chief.' He raised his voice: 'Bring her round, Sub. Starboard wheel, back over to the other wing.' Asdics pinging: an accompaniment to the noise of wind and sea and the ship's creaking, jolting, slamming progress. He'd taken another bite at his sandwich – Warrimer had organised kye and corned beef for distribution to all hands at their action stations – then tossed it away to leeward . . . 'Chief – take this down!' Shouting over the general racket . . . 'Same addressees. "Your – whatever that time-of-origin was – MV *Burbridge* passengers include wounded men and nursing sisters. Transfer to other ships in present weather conditions is impossible. Following this night's sinkings convoy now has twenty-three ships surviving but pending arrival of reinforcements further losses are inevitable." Ask the doctor to code that up, Chief.'

The night's losses had been the *Malibar* – who'd burnt because she'd had two hundred tons of palm oil in her number two starboard D tank, and when she was torpedoed abreast numbers two and three holds it had ignited and engulfed the bridge – and the *Springburn*, also in column one, the *Harvest Moon* and the Danish *Tylland*. Four losses seemed to be the nightly quota – 'par for the course', Bruce Hawkey the engineer had called it . . . *Harbinger* was rolling like a drunk as she turned her port beam to the thrust of wind and sea; the moon was a filtered radiance, but it would be setting soon. Carlish called down, 'Midships. Steer oh-seven-five.'

'Oh-seven-five, sir . . .' CPO Elphick's low, phlegmatic tone . . . And in sharp contrast to that drawl, an explosion – torpedo-hit – somewhere down there on the beam. Then you could see *exactly* where – flame spurted, lighting in silhouette a black tracery of ships' masts and upperworks, fire reaching skyward, widening and brightening so fast that there could be no doubt they'd got one of the two oilers – and they'd been in the centre . . .

White rockets rushed up to burst flaring under low black cloud. And a snowflake now, back over the convoy's other quarter . . .

The trawler *Gleam* had been plugging up between the slightly crooked columns three and four. For a time there'd been only three ships in column four, since it had had a vacant billet at the tail end to start with and then the leader, the *Tylland*, had dropped astern, sinking, and had been abandoned. Cartwright, *Gleam*'s one-eyed skipper, had led the *Orangeman* from column six to the rear of column four, and he'd been trying to get the others ahead of her to close up – as much as anything in compliance with the escort commander's orders to get the oilers and the *Burbridge* surrounded again. The *Cressida* had taken the *Tylland*'s lead position, but there was a large gap into which the next two had to be persuaded to shift up. Cartwright, chewing one of his black Burmah cheroots, had been on the *Redgulf Star*'s port beam, between her and the *Burbridge*, addressing the oiler's master by loud-hailer, when the other one – the *English Ardour*, in column five – went up in a crash and a blast of flame. Cartwright immediately put his wheel hard a-starboard, rang down for maximum revs from his ship's single screw, and turned under the *Redgulf Star*'s stern to get to the stricken, blazing ship. But the rescue ship *Archie Dukes*, the *English Ardour*'s next astern in column five, had put her helm to port, simultaneously stopping engines – partly to avoid running into the burning oiler but also to come up on her windward side and stand by for rescue work. Collision between the trawler and the *Archie Dukes* was narrowly avoided by Cartwright holding full starboard wheel on and just grazing under the rescue ship's counter, so closely that he had to reverse his rudder in order not to swing his stern into the *Dukes* as he swept by. In this way he ended up three cables' lengths astern of the burning, exploding tanker, on her starboard quarter and in the still-overwide gap between columns five and six. He was turning again, to get up there and risk the flaming leeward side of the *Ardour* – likely as not there'd be crewmen in the drink on that barely-approachable side – when he saw the U-boat diving, no more than a cricket-pitch length ahead of the trawler's bow. There was no time for the *Gleam*'s gun to fire: it couldn't have been depressed far enough to hit, at such close range, and the *Cimba* in column six was directly in the line of fire;

Cartwright's first lieutenant was yelling at the gun's crew to get off the foc'sl and hang on . . . This was only seconds before the trawler crashed into the submerging U-boat. *Gleam* had been rising to a wave: her forepart swung down into the German's hull abaft the conning tower, smashing into the engine-room section like a huge axe-head. Flames from the oiler lit the whole scene in flickering red and yellow, showing the two ships locked together at right-angles and Cartwright leaning out of an open window in the front of his bridge with the black patch in place over his left eye and the cheroot jutting from between his teeth; he'd stopped his engine just as he'd struck, and then put it astern. He had to spit the cheroot out before he could bawl down for all hands to get up on deck.

As *Gleam* withdrew her stem from the enormous hole it had carved, the U-boat rolled over and sank. But *Gleam* wasn't going to float long either. Cartwright's first lieutenant came back to the little glassed-in box of a bridge to tell him that the crew's quarters down for'ard were rapidly filling. It was a big compartment and it meant there wasn't a hope of saving her. Cartwright rang down to stop the engine – knowing that while it was still running his chief stoker would not have obeyed the order to come up – and ordered the dinghy and the two Carley floats to be cut loose from their stowage. Most of the convoy had drawn clear by this time: there was only the sinking trawler, the blazing tanker, the *Archie Dukes* with her boats in the water picking up bodies in some of which there might yet be life, and *Astilbe* nosing up into the flames with hoses gushing from her foc'sl.

Chapter 11

4 November 1942: General Alexander to Prime Minister:
After 12 days of heavy and violent fighting the Eighth Army has inflicted severe defeat on the German and Italian forces under Rommel's command. The enemy's front has broken . . .

A cock woke him with its crowing: he'd been having a dream with that noise in it, listening to it in his sleep. He knew immediately where he was, and why, and that he couldn't have slept for more than about an hour. He could see it would be daylight soon. He'd drunk water from a ditch, and eaten a carrot and the centre of a rotten onion; he was very hopeful that before long he might find an egg or two. They'd have to be eaten raw, but with the number of hens that were roosting in at least one of the other sheds there'd have to be some, somewhere. The problems were going to be (a) moving around in daylight without being seen, (b) getting to the eggs before someone else did; the two requirements in combination might prove difficult to accomplish.

He'd disturbed the hens, when he'd tried that hut first: there'd been a lot of flapping and squawking, and he'd been expecting someone to come running from the house – with a gun for a fox, perhaps . . . But the hens had gone back to sleep and no-one seemed to have heard. He'd found this broken-roofed, open-sided shed, full of old timber and sacks, straw and other rubbish – kindling for the house fires, he guessed. The straw and sacks were wet, but he'd made a bed of them, a nest that might be improved on when it was light.

Dawn was spreading from behind the house, which from as much as he could see at this stage seemed to be semi-derelict. Well, say in bad repair . . . He could see that its roof was uneven, and the surroundings over-grown. The house had shutters on its windows, all of them fastened. To the left was a clump of trees in a circle that might surround a duck-pond.

He'd hidden the bicycle in undergrowth half a mile up the lane. It was well covered, and he'd be able to find it again when he was fit to leave and head south. He felt that his decision had been the right one, that he did have a chance and it would have been stupid not to try. If it didn't work and he was caught, at least he wouldn't spend the next couple of years in Offlag IVC wishing to God he'd had a bit more staying-power. Meanwhile he hurt more or less all over and he knew he'd be black with bruises. He'd massaged the sprained ankle, and he'd been trying to keep it propped up so that it ached less. He had the thought of eggs in his mind quite a lot: an egg was nourishing, he was extremely hungry, and he knew he was going to need all the strength he could gather. They would be raw, of course: he'd shut his eyes and try to believe he was in the flat in Eaton Square, in bed with Fiona, swallowing Prairie Oysters.

She'd still be indulging in such pleasures, he guessed.

Because of the way she looked, and the way she was.

Break some bastard's bloody neck!

He'd heard the actual words, and knew he'd muttered them aloud. Talking to himself, with his eyes fixed like a wolf's on the silent house. Shack, whatever . . . And with muscles taut – as if he'd been about to do exactly that – spring out, break a neck . . . But forcing himself to relax now, to be sane: and with a resolution in mind, a vitally important one – that if he came face to face with the farmer or anyone else and couldn't get away, he'd surrender, not try to escape by using violence. That would be fatal, you'd have the whole countryside out looking for you, and the hunt would have only one end. You had to stay sane and cautious, despite that kind of image in the mind: images and desperation driving one to the brink of madness. He told himself he *could* stand it: he'd been on the run before – in Crete, eighteen months ago. Of course, that had been quite different, in a lot of ways: for instance, it had been mostly warm, during the first months, and he'd had plenty of companionship, and the locals had been well-disposed . . . But thinking about himself as he'd been such a short time ago was like thinking about a younger brother. That girl in Alexandria, for instance – how shocked he'd been when he'd discovered she had a husband! Really only months ago, and he'd been so innocent and naïf . . .

A door had opened. Alert, straining his ears, he heard a female voice call out in German. Then the same door banged shut. Silence now. The sounds had come from somewhere on the other side of the house, probably the back of it. So it was, after all, inhabited. Well, it would have to be – *someone* had shut the hens up, last night, before he got here. The house's front door, in the middle on this side facing him, was still shut, and by the look of the grass it wasn't used. There was a cart lying half on its side, one wheel missing and a shaft broken: he was looking at that corner of the house when a child appeared – a boy. Short pants and a thick wool jacket. That was a well he'd gone to: he'd tossed a bucket down, and the winch-handle clanked over. Jack smelt woodsmoke, a new fire starting. The boy was winding the bucket up now. You could imagine the fire in there, warmth, food . . . He heard the boy grunt with the effort of lifting the full bucket over the well's brick surround: then, leaning sideways almost horizontally to balance the weight, he'd gone staggering round the corner of the house and out of sight.

At least he knew where to get a drink. It was light now, more or less. He could make out a few rows of what must be cabbages, and a stack of logs. But it was coal-smoke he was smelling now: some ground-floor shutters were being pushed open from inside.

The sun came up red, angry-looking, between the house and the clump of trees. Nobody else had appeared. He'd heard a woman's voice, and a sharper one which was probably the boy's, and after about half an hour he saw them both – mother and son, or big sister and little brother – as they appeared around that same corner. The boy wore a coat and cap now, a cap with a shiny black peak, and he was carrying a school satchel. The girl was in a woollen dress with a shawl around its upper part. They were coming this way and she had a hand on the boy's shoulder. Mother, Jack decided: it was the proprietory, affectionate attitude of a parent. The path they were following – a beaten track through orchard-length grass with patches of nettle in it – would bring them close by this shed. He kept absolutely still, with his eyes half-shut in case their whites showed: he guessed, seeing her at close quarters, that she was in her middle twenties. She was fairish, though not exactly blonde, with a round face and a rather solid figure – broad-hipped, heavy-thighed. Her hips swung attractively as she walked with a long stride that made the boy trot now and then to keep up with her. She was swinging a bucket too, and doing most of the talking – in German, of course, which he didn't get a word of, but at the end of the track leading to the lane it was obvious she was calling parting instructions after him: 'Work hard and mind you come straight home!', something of that sort.

He heard the hen-house being opened, and the noise of birds stampeding out. She'd be feeding them from that bucket: he could hear her talking to them while she did it. Then the sound of a car engine: it came down the lane and stopped, a door opened and shut and then it moved on again, no doubt with the child inside it. The girl was in sight again, and she'd stopped to listen. School bus, he guessed, or neighbour.

He watched the girl go back around the side of the house. Then there was nothing to watch for a long time, except the sun's slow rise into cloud. A cold wind from the north bent the chimney-smoke away to his right. He wished the girl would reappear, but she didn't. While she was hidden in the house, he couldn't make any move: all he could do was wait. She might live alone in the house with the boy – there might be no farmer, father: or there was one and he could be sick, or lazy . . . But she was young: a husband of her own age-group would almost certainly be in uniform and in the war, wouldn't he?

After a while the door at the back of the house was opened, and it was about five minutes before it shut again. Stretching his imagination to account for all the circumstances as seen or heard, he guessed there might be an outside lavatory, a privy at the back. As they had no running water here, used that well, there'd have to be, he thought. He was in need of it himself – which was probably what made him think of it – but to move out of his shed would have been foolhardy and to relieve himself inside it unwise: he'd no idea how many days and nights he'd be spending here, and it was uncomfortable enough without that. The length of his stay had to depend on whether he could get some food: but for the moment, having eaten and drunk so little recently, the other urge was controllable.

An hour might have passed. Hens pecked close by without taking any notice of him, and the morning turned greyer, colder. He was thinking he was going to have to creep away and prospect elsewhere when the door at the back opened and shut again and a few seconds later the girl appeared round the side where the wrecked cart was. She was wearing what looked like a man's overcoat and a woollen hat, and she was carrying a basket; she walked straight down the path towards the muddy entrance from the lane, and disappeared.

Jack lay still, watching the house and listening. Only the hens moved, muttering to themselves. The cock might have turned in again. There was no sound from the lane.

He'd had various kinds of rubbish on top of him: he pushed it off now, extricated himself as quietly as possible, and crawled out. The hens eyed him suspiciously and moved away. He was against the corner of the shed, crouching with his weight all on one leg while he looked around. Nothing moved. He hopped around to the back, leant one shoulder against the planks and did what he'd been wanting to do for quite a while.

It seemed he had the place to himself. Unless there *was* some inactive, housebound husband, parent, grandparent, grandparents plural . . . But there'd been no voices. The only times he'd heard the girl's voice had been when she'd had the boy with her and when she'd teased the hens. But the one thing there *had* to be inside the house was food.

Eggs – he remembered that intention, suddenly, and stopped. Then thought – try the house first. Eggs as fallback, last resort . . .

The back door was locked. A path of cinders led from it between unweeded vegetable patches to the brick-built lavatory he'd expected. A rickety fence beyond it separated vegetable garden from orchard. No gate, so that land didn't belong to this house. Turning back, he saw that all the shutters, upstairs and downstairs, were closed and fastened; but he knew she hadn't shut the ground-floor ones in front. He went back – through nettles and brambles on the other side of the house, so as not to walk right into her if she happened to be coming home at this moment – and tried the front windows. Sash windows, with heavy frames in bad condition. The first one he tried wasn't latched, didn't need to be because it was stuck solid: the next moved easily. He slid it up, climbed in, shut it again behind him. Despite his clumsiness – the sprained ankle made him less agile than he might have been – he'd made very little noise, but probably enough to be heard by any inmate who wasn't stone deaf. He waited for a few moments, listening: he was in a bedroom and it was obviously the child's. No sound from anywhere: the house *felt* empty, he just about knew it was. He crept out, into a passage. Dead-end to the left, two doors in the facing wall, an open end to the right: he went that way, into a central hall that was evidently the main living area. The front door, the one she didn't use, was on his right now, there was a heating-stove in an alcove with wood piled near it and heavy, ugly furniture grouped to face it, and a flight of stairs leading up above a door that led into the kitchen. The passage he'd come through was continued on the other side of this living room, with a drab-coloured curtain covering it.

The upstairs rooms had to be out of use: the staircase was blanked off with stacked packing-cases, furniture, some rolls of carpet and other stuff. It was the kitchen, anyway, that drew him. He'd started towards it before caution made him stop, warned him to check the other rooms first: there *could* be old people here, or a bed-ridden husband . . . He hesitated: then thought that if he did find someone in the house and have to bolt for it – *without having had anything to eat . . .*

Kitchen.

Entering it, he was facing the inside of the back door, the door they used. On a dresser on his right, three-quarters of a loaf of bread. And a smell of soup or stew: it led him to a covered pot simmering on a coal stove. He tore off an end of the loaf, dipped it in the steaming tureen, and ate.

Like a dog. *Feeling* like a dog. Grunting, gobbling, with his eyes fixed on the rest of it . . . Gasping, then, out of breath, leaning against the wall with his injured foot stretched out in front of him. Two things stopped him wolfing the whole lot: he needed to check the other rooms and didn't know how long he'd have before she came back, and two, if he didn't take too much she mightn't be sure any had gone. If she did realise she'd been robbed, he might not find a meal here tomorrow. But leaving any of it at all wasn't easy. He stared at it, swallowing, licking his lips, shaking . . .

In the other downstairs wing the rooms contained some furniture but were obviously not in use. Junky furniture was layered in dust, and beds had only mattresses on them. There'd be room for a large family in this place, and most likely there'd have been one here not so long ago. Dispersal would have come through males being called up, females drafted to services or factory work; just as the war had split families in England. He limped back into the living-hall, through it and into the other section of passage, looking into the other rooms. One contained a wash-stand, tin bath, drying-rack and ironing board, another contained only an iron bedstead, and the third was the girl's. Standing, looking round – and on the dressing-table one object held his eye: a photograph frame with no photograph in it. An empty frame, wood with silver corners, placed where you'd expect the portrait of a husband, lover, or parents: prominent, yet empty.

There was a wireless beside the bed: it had a fern design in fretwork on its front panel. His eyes followed a twist of dangerously frayed flex to the lamp on the dressing-table. Moving closer, glancing again at the empty frame, he saw his own face in the mirror.

He stood rooted, horrified . . .

The creature staring back at him out of red-rimmed eyes was nearer beast than human. Bearded, filthy, mad-eyed, with multi-coloured bruises showing through dirt and beard. He could hardly believe it was himself: it wasn't only hideous, it was actually frightening. If you were searching for a prisoner on the run and you came face to face with *this*, wouldn't you pull the trigger?

He muttered, 'Christ . . .' And the creature's lips had moved . . . He turned his back on it, with the thought that if the girl who slept in that bed caught as much as a glimpse of him—

She wouldn't. The guards at the frontier – Swiss – would be the first to have that pleasure.

Clearly – he shut the bedroom door behind him – the girl and her child were the only occupants of this house. With the stairs blocked, there couldn't be anyone using the top floor. He decided he'd take a look up there, anyway, make sure . . . He crawled over the pile of junk: then he was on bare boards, climbing, hauling himself up on heavy bannisters draped with cobwebs.

There was a wide landing, but since the ends of the house sloped inward there were only two rooms to the right and two to the left. Electric wiring slung from nails hung in dusty loops. From the front room on the left a badly-fitting shutter allowed him a wide view of the front area – the hen-house, the broken cart, the semi-collapsed shed where he'd spent some hours and to which he'd have shortly to return: he reckoned he'd last a day and a night, all right, on that hastily gulped snack. Then he'd look for more: by that time his ankle might have mended well enough so he could take off again, unearth the bike and pedal swiftly south . . . Beyond the sheds he could see right down the track to the lane, and it was all empty. He thought of the eggs again: he'd have time, it wasn't likely she'd be back all that soon, he guessed. She'd gone out dressed for outdoors and carrying that basket – for shopping, or to deliver or acquire something – and there was no shop or dwelling within several miles. Perhaps the basket had been full of eggs? But even then, he'd find one or two . . .

Unless she got a lift back, from wherever she'd been going. Then she might *not* be long.

Just one more *small* piece of soup-soaked bread?

Negotiating the furniture on the stairs again – one might assume it had been cleared out of the upstairs rooms – he noticed in passing that it included some mattresses. They were in the middle, surrounded by other stuff. The thought of them was in his mind while he devoured his second helping, thinking also of the discomfort to which he was now returning – to be there, hidden, before she got back. With a few hens' eggs to keep him going . . . But the idea of a mattress to lie on, to rest the ankle on: what a dream! Impractical, of course: even if he could have dragged one out there it would be too big for the space, it would show up.

He stopped chewing.

Drag a mattress *upstairs*? Into the empty front room with the view, over the empty downstairs wing?

Harbinger, zigzagging across the convoy's rear, was climbing mountains, shooting rapids, hurling herself from beam to beam. The wind was up to force six, with a sea to match it and a bite in the air more like winter than autumn. The convoy ploughed on ahead, at the reduced speed of four knots and in six columns with only three ships in columns one and six, four in the central ones, and the *Burbridge* and the *Redgulf Star* as second ships in columns three and four respectively. The corvettes were out ahead, trawlers at the sides; the corvettes and *Harbinger* had refuelled this forenoon.

Mike Scarr had the afternoon watch, and Nick was slumped in his deckchair under an oilskin. Scarr thought he was asleep – and he was, off and on, but it was a light, fitful sleep with two figures jostling around in his brain. Twenty-two and five. Twenty-two was the number of ships left in convoy, five the number lost to U-boats last night. If you divided one by the other, even through the fog of semi-consciousness you had to see that in four or five days' time SL 320 would have ceased to exist.

It was unthinkable.

But – you *had* to think about it. Because with the destruction of the convoy the whole operation would be aborted too. The U-boats would be right where the 'Torch' convoy routes converged into the Gibraltar Strait: they'd have run out of targets, but maybe not out of torpedoes . . . And the conclusion was that in the interests of 'Torch', quite apart from keeping as much as possible of this convoy alive, it was entirely up to SL 320's escort commander to pull something new out of the bag.

But how the hell . . .

The prospect was so terrible that it only belonged in nightmare. But he was awake now, and it was real: and the core of the reality – like an uncovered nerve in a tooth, agonising every minute of the days and nights – was the *Burbridge*. Even if it was all in the mind: the coincidence of a ship full of nurses – plus one's own cowardice, not daring to ask, or even *look* too closely . . . There was a degree of sense in it as well as cowardice, moreover: because if fate – fate assisted by Cruance and company – had played such a filthy trick on you *and you knew it*, you'd then be facing the dilemma, practical and moral, of protecting that one ship even at the expense of others.

He heard Scarr call down for an increase in revs. He had a vague recollection of having heard a similar increase being ordered only minutes ago. *Harbinger* must have dropped astern of station, perhaps held to one leg of the zigzag for too long. He was trying to force his mind back to the problem of new tactics – which there could not be, with a four-knot convoy, like a mouse already crippled in a room full of cats – when the wireless office bell rang, and a signalman shouted into the voice-pipe, 'Bridge!' There was a gabble, hollow-sounding in the tube: then the signalman – it was Bloom – telling Scarr, 'Signal from the commodore, sir – *Burbridge* has completed temporary repairs, convoy speed now seven knots!'

'Very good.' Scarr hesitated, deciding whether or not to wake his captain. He came to the right conclusion. 'Captain, sir?'

'Yes, pilot.' He spoke without opening his eyes, or moving. His brain was doing all the movement, in these few seconds. 'I heard it.'

It made all the difference in the world!

He pushed off the oilskin, sat up, nearly fell out of the chair as the ship lurched hard to port: then he was on his feet. He put his glasses up, training them on the rear ships of the convoy – which was in the act of zigzagging, slanting over to starboard of the mean course. There were only four ships in that rearmost line abreast, since columns one and six lacked tail-end charlies. Grey hulls were sheathed in white and rolling ponderously as they turned, masts and upperworks rocking against the backdrop of pale-grey sky, *Harbinger*'s bow slamming down into an advancing cliff-face of green water, burying itself in its white explosion, the ship jolting solidly from the impact, sea and spray sluicing over. Then she was climbing again, and the convoy's grey, slow-moving mass was back in sight . . . He pointed, called to Scarr, 'Take her up to pass between columns two and three. I'm going down to the chartroom, but I'll be back before you get there.'

'Aye aye, sir!' Scarr's thin face, running wet, dipped to the voice-pipe. 'Starboard fifteen! One-eight-oh revolutions!'

Nick slid the chartroom door shut. The outline of a plan was in his mind, but its detail needed checking, on two levels. First in terms of the convoy and the U-boats trailing it, and second in relation to the 'Torch' convoys approaching from the north and northwest. And it wouldn't be good enough to get SL 320 away from the U-boats, even if that were possible; for better or for worse, he accepted the obligation to keep the sharks with him, draw them north. *As Aubrey Wishart would have known he would: which would be why he'd picked him for this lousy job* . . . All he could hope to do was keep their teeth from closing on his convoy's throat – for a night, or even two nights. It wouldn't be an escape, it would be a respite. Those U-boats had tasted blood, they knew there was plenty more: it would only be necessary to provide them with the scent and they'd keep their snouts to the trail.

The bad weather ought to help.

Working swiftly: extending the convoy's progress by two-hourly intervals from its present position. But at four knots, not seven. Until – say – 11 pm tonight . . .

Midnight would be the German's optimum time to attack. Say 2300, then, to make the move. The commodore might take some persuading, to reduce speed now, return to the four-knot crawl. But it was essential the Germans shouldn't know SL 320 was now capable of almost doubling its speed of advance. With that card to play, and the heavy weather, plus a strike by *Harbinger* and the corvettes well out ahead – leaving the convoy with only two trawlers as close escort when it turned and put on speed?

Then, if it worked tonight – a repeat tomorrow, only the other way, back on to the ordered route?

He slid the parallel rule across, on its ribbed brass rollers. Having increased to seven knots tonight, there'd be no point in slowing again. That cat would be out of the bag . . . Now, Cruance's overlay: this was the acid test, whether SL 320 could make this diversion and still cross those

'Torch' convoy tracks far enough ahead to take the U-boats clear of them.

Well . . . Checking them off, one by one. If the *Burbridge* could maintain seven knots from here on, it looked as if it would be all right. *Just* all right. No worse than holding a straight course at the lower speed would have been. There'd be a finer margin than Cruance would have liked, obviously: but this was compromise, an attempt both to achieve the vital success of that huge invasion operation and have a few ships of this convoy survive. Those few to include the *Burbridge* . . .

He checked over his workings again, more slowly and very carefully. Courses, times, distances: and the likely spread of U-boats at 2300 when they deployed for their night assault. HF/DF reports during the forenoon indicated that by now all except one shadower would be ahead of the convoy's beams; a few hours ago there'd been one – the pack leader, in Gritten's assessment – out ahead, and the rest on the beams and quarters but moving up. The usual tactics, in fact, clawing up ahead while one remained astern to report convoy alterations and snap up any straggler. You had to trust to luck that the convoy's simultaneous change of speed and course, with darkness and bad weather to hide it, would throw that shadower off the scent. If there'd been just one more corvette, he'd have sent it back to cope with that threat. The fact was, he hadn't, and lack of escort vessels was the big difference between this ploy and one he'd used in that last North Atlantic trip, when he'd used smoke to obscure a very drastic emergency turn. Tonight, bad weather would do the smoke's job. But that last time he'd had six corvettes to leave as close escort with the convoy: there was a hell of a big difference between six corvettes and two trawlers.

The speed trick would be something new. *If* the commodore agreed to it.

When he got back to the bridge, the convoy was returning to its mean course and Scarr was aiming *Harbinger*'s stubby, foam-drenched stem at the gap between the *Mount Trembling* and the *Bonny Prince*.

'Steady!'

'Steady, sir.' The quartermaster's voice floated from the voice-pipe. 'Oh-three-nine, sir.'

'Steer oh-four-oh.'

'Steer oh-four-oh, sir . . .'

Nick told Signalman Bloom, 'I'll need the loud-hailer in a minute.'

He'd used it earlier in the day when he'd talked to Cartwright, skipper of the sunk trawler *Gleam*: Cartwright, who was now Graves's guest in *Astilbe*, had bawled over to him – Yorkshire accent booming over the welter of foam between the two ships as they steamed side by side – 'Weren't supposed to ram, I know that, but truth is I didn't neither, bugger bloody well impaled himself on me!'

Chubb had muttered vulgarly to Warrimer, 'Sounds like a bugger's defence, to me . . .'

Practically every ship had survivors from others on board. *Astilbe* had the entire crew of the *Gleam* plus some survivors the trawler had picked up previously, and five men from the *English Ardour*.

The *Mount Trembling* and the *Bonny Prince* were abeam. The *Mount Trembling* being one of the rescue ships now. Asked how many survivors he was accommodating, her master replied, 'Too bloody many!' He amplified this to 'More'n I have crew.' She was only about 1400 gross registered tons; the smaller ships were always picked for the rescue job, since they tended to be more manoeuvrable. *Harbinger* pushed on up between the columns, between the *Columbia* and the *Omeo*: from both of them there were waves in answer to the destroyer's hail. Looking at the plodding, plunging merchantmen as they fell astern, Mike Scarr wondered which of them might be afloat by tomorrow's dawn. It was like musical chairs, or Russian roulette: and when you thought of ships that had been here a day or three days ago it was like recalling, not without effort, the names of acquaintances from a distant past. To port now was the *St Eliza*, and coming up to starboard the taller, bulkier shape of the *Burbridge*. Scarr saw his captain move over to the port for'ard corner of the bridge, taking the hailer with him and plugging it in on that side to talk to the *St Eliza*, his back to the passenger ship as they overhauled her. He was asking the *Eliza*'s master what survivors he had on board: the answer was twenty-one, all from the Dutchman, the *Toungoo* . . . While on the other side the *Burbridge* loomed over them, her rails crowded with waving passengers of whom a fair proportion were women, *Harbinger*'s captain was the only man on her upper deck not waving enthusiastically back to them. Then it was the *Corialanus* to port, and the *Chauncy Maples* to starboard; with the convoy beginning a turn, altering to a port leg of the zigzag.

'Come down forty revs and close in a bit, pilot.' He'd crossed over, plugged the loud-hailer in on that side. 'Hello, *Chauncy Maples*. Commodore to speak by loud-hailer, please, if he'd be so kind.'

Sandover had seen him coming, and was ready for it.

'Good afternoon, Everard. What can we do for you?'

'I want to suggest you reduce convoy speed, Commodore. Back to four knots, until eleven o'clock tonight. Then crack on to seven again, with a sixty-degree emergency turn to port. I'll be up ahead to keep the U-boats busy with this ship and both corvettes, while you speed up and turn away. I hope we might get a fairly peaceful night this way.'

'What about the no-diversion rule?'

'It'll have to be broken again. Otherwise you'll soon have no convoy left. We could get back on track by another turn tomorrow night – if the *Burbridge* can keep her end up, now . . . But I don't see much alternative, Commodore.'

Pause, as he lowered the hailer. Weather-noise, ship-noise, and Scarr's orders to the wheelhouse . . . Sandover would be thinking it over. Knowing nothing of those 'Torch' convoys, the great armada that was on its way, the reason behind the no-diversion rule . . . But he'd realise something did have to be done, if any part of SL 320 was to have a chance of getting through.

'All right, Everard. Tell me what you propose in detail.'

The herd was lumbering round again, zigging the other

way. Nick threw a glance over his shoulder and saw that Scarr was on to it, only waiting for the right moment to pass the helm order. The destroyer needed comparatively little rudder to match her turn to that of the more cumbersome freighters: but she'd need extra revs now, being on the outside of the turn, to stay up close to the *Chauncy Maples*.

He raised the loud-hailer. 'I'd propose reducing to four knots *now* – before they notice we're capable of more. Now – right away, sir?'

'Very well.'

He resumed – seeing a flag signal for the speed reduction flap multicoloured to the *Chauncy Maples*'s masthead while he was talking – 'Zigzag would cease at dusk as usual. At 2300 – or earlier if they start moving in before that – we'll go out and attack them, well out ahead. At the same time you'd turn to three-four-two degrees and increase to seven knots – or better . . . Hold that course and speed for six hours – and we'd be cutting the corner slightly on position B, which would help.'

He looked back at the *Burbridge*, wallowing astern of the commodore. This whole scheme depended on her being able to maintain the seven knots. If she found she couldn't, if she broke down during the hours of the diversion, SL 320 would be stuck right across the 'Torch' convoy routes. The risk, when you thought of that, was terrifying in its implications: but taking a risk was surely better than facing certain disaster and doing damn-all about it?

By dusk, when as usual the ship's company was closed up at action stations, he'd added – in one sense – to those risks. He'd been thinking hard about the shadower astern. The point being that by leaving the convoy with only two trawlers to guard it while he rushed out ahead with his other three ships he'd be taking quite a chance: but by leaving the shadower loose astern he'd be compounding it. The solution was to detach one trawler to turn back and deal with the shadower, keep it dived during the crucial period, deafen it with depth charges.

The disadvantages consisted of leaving only one trawler

with the convoy, and the fact that the one that did this job astern would be back there on its own with a very long way to go and only a small margin of speed for rejoining afterwards. Also, in rejoining it would have to pass through the U-boat line.

Nick briefed Kyle of *Opal* for the task. He was to force the shadower down and keep him down, and he'd add to the deception by seeming to chase after the convoy on its previous course. And he would do a bit more than that, too, by way of deception. Broad of the *Stella* would meanwhile stay with the convoy as its sole protector.

As dusk thickened into night, the shadower was nine miles on the starboard quarter, and Gritten estimated there were six U-boats between sixteen and twenty-one miles ahead.

'All in a bunch, sir. Been doing a lot of yacking, last hour or so.'

Making *their* plans for the night . . .

In the hour between dusk action stations and closing up again for the night's exertions, he explained his intentions to Warrimer and Scarr, and invited comments.

Scarr said thoughtfully, 'I'd say it adds up to as good a chance as we'll have, sir.' He was going to have to do some smart work in the plot, pinpointing each contact as *Harbinger* moved up towards them – so that none would be left to slip through and find the convoy wide open to it. It was a point that Warrimer touched on too: 'If we can keep all the U-boats at arm's length, sir, I suppose the lack of close escort can't really matter.'

That 'if' was a big one. The fact the U-boats were bunched together now didn't mean they would be in a few hours' time. Nick turned to his engineer, Bruce Hawkey, whom he'd also summoned to this briefing.

'I'm going to need a lot of high speed, Chief. Twice as many enemies as escorts means we'll have to be fast on our feet. Force six or no force six . . .'

Jack lay on his mattress in the dark, cold, silent house. It wasn't as cold as the wrecked shed would have been, and he'd brought up an old carpet for a blanket, but the mattress was damp from disuse and the carpet smelt of cats.

The girl had come back at about four in the afternoon, and the child had returned an hour later. A car or bus had brought him. Jack had heard it approach and stop, then the slam of a door, and after a minute the boy had appeared and gone round the side of the house where the cart was. After this there'd been voices downstairs, and music – from that wireless in the girl's bedroom, perhaps, although it had sounded as if it came from the central living-room. He'd heard them moving about too, doors opening and shutting, and footsteps. He stayed on his mattress, wondering whether she'd have noticed the shortfall of bread and soup: and knowing that she *must* . . . He didn't move about at all, because he could have been heard, and it wasn't worth the risk, and there wasn't anywhere to go . . . With luck he'd have the place to himself again tomorrow, it was as good a hideout as anyone could hope for, and there was the possibility of another snack down there tomorrow. All he had to do was lie doggo for a couple of days, while the ankle mended, then skedaddle.

It was dead quiet, and he guessed they'd gone to bed. The child would have, anyway. He could imagine the girl sewing – making clothes for herself, or patching her son's. He supposed she might be as much as thirty: or say twenty-eight. The boy would be about seven, he thought. He'd spend his days at some village school, presumably, while she either had a job or went to visit friends or family. As long as she did so every day, he didn't give a damn, the important thing was that her daytime absences should be routine, invariable. Otherwise it could become difficult for him, up here. The thought of a weekend was a worry: he had no idea what day of the week it was and if tomorrow was Saturday it might mean two days with no school, perhaps no outings at all. If that happened he'd simply have to grin and bear it, but one way and another it could get to be uncomfortable.

He told himself that it was better than the shed, anyway.

And to stop worrying: think about Fiona, then if he was lucky he might dream about her . . .

He was dozing when the troops came.

A roar of engines: a glare of headlights on the shutters. He was awake: the engines cut out but the lights still blazed and a voice was yelling orders in high-pitched German. Jack on his knees on the mattress, squinting down between the wooden slats, eyes narrowed against the dazzle; he could see what looked like a staff car and also a larger, open-topped vehicle, personnel carrier, the kind he'd seen when he'd been lying on the hill. Men had jumped out of this one and vanished around both ends of the house, while others combed through the sheds, pulling doors open and kicking through the piles of litter: hens squawked and scattered. If he'd been in that shed they'd have had him cold, by now he'd either have been standing with his hands up, or dead.

The soldiers were hammering at the back door, but here in front two of them only stood and watched the house – so they must have known the place, known the front door didn't open. Jack thought the officer who'd given those orders was still in the car; its headlights were full on, lighting the whole house-front, and he couldn't see much past them, but he had an impression of someone sitting in there. It could have been only his imagination, stemming from the way one of the men facing the front door had twice turned towards the car as if in conversation.

He heard the back door open, and the girl's voice, then a male one, and heavy boots on the plank floor of the kitchen.

If she'd noticed that some of her food had gone, would she tell them now?

Not that it would make much odds. They were obviously about to search the whole place.

Earlier on, before she'd come home, he'd made sure these shutters would open so he could bale out this way if he had to. Now, of course, this was out of the question. If they came up here, he'd be trapped. And the girl would be in trouble too, he realised. They wouldn't believe she hadn't known he was in her house. He was surprised to find this bothered him. Surprised and pleased. Touched by an impression of loneliness, perhaps, the joint loneliness of woman and child alone, unprotected? Self-analysis had never been a habit, or even an inclination, but he was aware of this feeling of sympathy, concern for her predicament as well as for his own. The emotion was short-lived, replaced by a kind of fatalism: boots were clumping around downstairs, going from room to room, and at any moment they'd finish and come to check up here. More shouts from down in front: it looked as if they'd searched the grounds and the searchers were returning to their transport. He'd been right about the man in the staff car: light gleamed on the peak of his uniform cap as he climbed out and stood with his fists on his hips, staring around. Then he swung to face the corner of the house and Jack had a bird's eye view of the girl and the child, with a soldier escorting them, walking into the brightness of the car's lights. She was wearing her overcoat and a scarf round her head, and the boy had a blanket round him. The officer didn't move, just watched them approach, and the soldier made some kind of report; the girl began to complain – the tone was complaining, anyway – with an arm resting on the boy's shoulders. They'd stopped, in the headlights' beam. Behind the officer, the other searchers were clambering into their vehicle: dark, overcoated figures in forage-caps and with slung rifles. There was an exchange of questions and answers now between the officer and the girl: her answers, brief and flat, sounded like denials. Finally he turned away, gesturing to the escort to let them go.

All over?

But he'd thought it too soon. The officer had stopped, turned, and he was looking at these upstairs windows, the blank shutters facing him. Jack pulled his head back . . . The German had called out some new question: the girl turned her head, moved one hand wearily, a gesture accompanied by words that might have asked 'Why don't you go up and look?' The officer still staring upwards . . . Then the boy squeaked something and some of the soldiers laughed. It seemed to break the tension, down there and in here, too:

Jack had been in no doubt at all that a search party had been about to be sent up. Instead, the officer lifted his hand in a cross between a farewell gesture and a salute and the child spoke again, his arm jerking out of the blanket's folds: 'Heil Hitler!' As sharply as if the officer's casualness had offended the little brat. The girl's hand stroked his yellow, close-cropped hair. The officer was staring at her now, as if waiting for something: but she was looking down at the boy, ignoring all the rest. He shrugged, swung away abruptly as if he was sick of hanging around here, wasting time; he barked an order and soldiers came hurrying from around the ends of the house and piled into the personnel carrier. The staff car's door was being held open by its driver: the officer slid into it, and the show was over. Engines revving, headlights flaring over tumbledown sheds and darkly looming trees, the car led and the bigger vehicle followed through a tunnel of light that narrowed towards the lane then weakened, vanished as the lights were cut. The house stood silent in the darkness now, listening to the receding sounds of the two engines: then the back door slammed shut and its bolt rasped over, and Jack heard the girl's voice faintly as she led her child back to bed. He lay staring into darkness, wondering whether that perfunctory search would have satisfied them, whether he might be safe here now for the few days he needed. Or – less optimistically – whether it meant they had some reason to suspect the prisoner they were hunting might have turned north instead of south . . .

If, for instance, they'd found the bicycle?

Opal, with wind and sea on her quarter, rolled and pitched like nothing on earth. Tom Kyle, her skipper, leaning out of an open glass panel in the lee side of his bridge, bawled through a tin megaphone, 'Starshell, *fire*!'

He'd acquired the knack of pitching his voice up so that it was audible even in these conditions. And Potts, down on the foc'sl, would have had his ears pinned back in any case.

The four-inch cracked, flashed, recoiled. That was the second starshell on its way to replace the first one, which was low now and fading. Having no RDF, Kyle had nothing to go on except the position he'd been given just before he'd turned his ship and pointed her back down the convoy's track. His orders were not to try and take the shadower by surprise – that way he might very easily have missed the bastard altogether – but only to force it to dive and then give it as hard a time as possible. Nine miles on bearing 207 degrees had been the shadower's position at 2225: you had to allow for his steering the convoy course, 042, at slightly more than convoy speed – because he'd been creeping up during the last hour, gradually shortening the distance between him and his night's targets – so in half an hour you could say the thing would have made about two and three quarter miles, while *Opal,* making ten knots the other way, would have covered five. This left a gap between them now of one and a quarter miles, 2500 yards, and it was over roughly the mid-point of this patch of ocean that the illuminants were being projected now.

The gun's crew, in oilskins and sou'westers, were hanging on for their lives down there. It wasn't as bad for them on this course as it would be on most others, but it was bad enough, and you'd never pick a man up in this sea. Once he was in it, you wouldn't even see him. That starshell burst blossomed, lighting the ragged underside of cloud and throwing a hazy radiance over several square miles of sea. Any U-boat there would – one hoped – assume it had been detected, and pull the plug.

Kyle had pulled his head inside for long enough to light one of his hand-rolled cigarettes. He used Admiralty-issue tobacco, 'Pusser's', flavoured with Scotch whisky. A tot of Scotch cost threepence nowadays, at sea, and it was enough to treat a half-pound tin. Kyle rolled his cigarettes one-handed, without having to look at what his blunt fingers were doing, and each one ended up as a perfectly symmetrical tube. Over the flare of the lighter, squinting past the coxswain at his asdic operator, he asked him, 'Working, is it?'

'Won't get bugger all in this lot, though.' The operator

nodded. In these sea conditions, he meant. He was hunched over his set, bald and unshaven, chewing gum, the headset clamped over his ears and two fingers delicately twisting the knob that trained the quartz oscillator in its dome under the trawler's forefoot. The coxswain – a short, stocky man, with one side of his face scarred purple by burning – had glanced sideways at him, then away again, eyes returning quickly to the compass card, feet straddled against the violent rolling, wide-palmed hands on the wheel's brass-capped spokes constantly adjusting this way and that. Ahead, the starshell light was dimming: it had sunk too low and its parachute was travelling laterally on the wind. Kyle pushed the megaphone out again and screamed on that same noise-cutting note, 'One for his knob, lads – *fire*!'

He muttered – inside again by the time the gun fired – 'Sod'll be down under by now. Less he's bloody cracked.' The trawler hit a waveface so hard you'd have expected damage: Kyle staggered, grabbed for support at a nest of voice-pipes, muttered, '*Bastard* . . .' The asdic operator nodded, agreeing with the sentiment: pings singing away loud and clear, regular as the ticking of a watch, and he was turning the control knob minutely between each one, a degree or so each time, directing the impulses from broad on one bow to broad on the other. Any U-boat down there would be hearing the transmissions through its hydrophones, waiting for the probe to find it, hoping to God it wouldn't, and manoeuvring to get clear. The German would know this was a trawler hunting him, because the sound of the single screw driven by a reciprocating engine (as opposed to turbines) was quite distinctive; but he would *not* be in a position to know that several miles northeast convoy SL 320 would at this moment be swinging 60 degrees to port while a dozen miles beyond it *Harbinger* and the corvettes would be running down on their U-boat contacts, forcing them down, plastering them with depth charges, keeping them blind and deaf and busy while those twenty-two merchantmen and their single trawler escort turned away.

'Contact! Green one-nine!'

The operator sounded and looked amazed . . . Kyle too. But he'd heard that echo: he snatched up his depthcharge telephone and yelled at the team back aft to stand by . . . 'Two hundred and fifty-foot settings: got that?' Kyle *always* set the same depth on his charges: his view was that whatever settings you chose it was a toss-up, so there was no point messing about. He told his coxswain, 'Come twenty degrees to starboard.'

'Aye sir . . .'

Wheel spinning as he flung it round. All three men in the stuffy little bridge were plainly astonished at having picked up this contact, on a set they'd had no faith in for weeks now. But you could hear the echo plainly, the sharp, clear return of each impulse bouncing back off the U-boat's hull. Kyle had never heard a contact so clearly in all his time at sea: and tonight he'd never expected to hear any at all, with these conditions and a set that only worked when it felt like it . . . That last starshell was low to the water and a long way off: the U-boat would have dived at sight of the first one, he guessed. Harris, the A/S man, was the ship's eyes now: he asked him, 'Got a range yet?' Harris flinching from the whisky-scented cigarette-smoke, blinking and puffing his own breath out to clear it . . . 'Green two-four . . .' Despite the trawler's swing to starboard, the target had drawn to the right: it had to be travelling fast . . . Harris nodded: 'Range fourteen hundred yards.' As *Opal* turned her beam to the onslaught of the weather the degree of roll was frightening – would have been, to anyone but a trawlerman. Down below, if anything breakable hadn't been lashed or jammed in its stowage it would have been smashed by now. Kyle grated to his coxswain, 'Keep the wheel on her. Steer two-five-oh.'

'Two-five-oh.'

But he couldn't keep men on that gundeck now, not unless they used both hands and a strong set of teeth as well to hang on with – and even then you might lose a few. He'd got his megaphone out again; he yelled, 'Clear the upper deck! All hands below!' A flash of a torch from the foc'sl acknowledged it. There was a telephone connection to the gun, but it hadn't been working lately: Kyle had meant to tell Potts to fix it, but it had slipped his mind.

'Course two-five-oh, sir.'

'Lost contact!'

Several pings had gone out and found no submarine to bounce off. Harris looked dismayed: he was twisting his beam this way and that, covering a wider and wider arc and getting nothing . . . Jumbo Potts, Kyle's first lieutenant, arrived from for'ard looking as if he'd been swimming: the torch in his hand was enclosed in a French letter. He was a fat young man with a round, bright-red face and small, narrow eyes. Harris muttered, glancing at him but speaking to himself, 'Lost the bugger good an' proper.' Potts said, 'No wonder. Fucking thing never did work more 'n two minutes at a time.' It was a fact; the set was anything but reliable. *Opal* staggered to a big sea that walloped her beam-on, then rolled away from it so hard you'd think she was going right over: she hung there on her side for a moment and then came whipping back, at the same time burying her stem in a mound of foam and shaking like a duck with Parkinson's Disease. Potts shouted, 'Force eight, I reckon.'

'Could be rising seven.' Kyle had a new cigarette waggling in his mouth; the grease on his hair gleamed in the faint light from the binnacle; his face was bony, hollow-cheeked, a nervy drinker's face . . . 'Bloody asdics. Got him by the knackers one minute, then—' he shook his head. Potts commiserated, 'Fluke gettin' anything at all, sea like this. Eh, skipper?' Harris nodding, agreeing, but still searching, finding nothing, pings going out unanswered: Potts, who'd done an A/S course quite recently, suggested, 'Could've turned towards us, run under us, run out of the beam and away astern?'

They stared at him: and he was right. The U-boat had been travelling to starboard, might easily have been circling: then, heading directly for its hunter, it *would* have passed out of the elliptical beam, vanished . . .

'Starboard twenty. Bring her round to oh-seven-oh.'

Reciprocal course: if she could get round across this sea without actually bashing herself to pieces . . . Kyle checked the time: the escort commander's orders had been to sit on top of this one for at least thirty minutes, but it was only 2314 now and this meant it had to be badgered for another twenty yet – and it could be a couple of miles away, or at least, *half* a mile . . .

'Depthcharges, sir. Northeast, long way off.' Listening, twiddling the knob, not pinging now, listening to the rest of the U-boat pack getting clobbered up there while the convoy slid away northwestward. Kyle told him to get on with it, never mind bloody depth bombs, this bastard here was the sod that mattered, he had to be kept deep and nervous. *Opal* fighting her way round . . . He shouted at Potts to go aft to the depth-charge party, have them stand by to drop single charges at one-minute intervals. *That* might entertain the Hun for half an hour . . . Then for an hour after that, plugging northward at her best speed, *Opal* would try to make herself look and sound like a whole convoy. She'd drop a depth charge now and then and fire off some rockets. U-boats up ahead, already confused by the other escorts' attack on them, might not be too difficult to fool, in this blinding weather. But finally, Kyle faced the task of getting his ship past them – through them or round them – and the long haul from there to rejoin the convoy – with a top speed of just over 10 knots, no bloody RDF, weather going from piss-poor to flaming awful and SL 320 already God only knew how far away, getting itself hidden in the night.

Chapter 12

> *Prime Minister to General Alexander:*
> I send you my heartfelt congratulations on the splendid feat of arms achieved by the Eighth Army under the command of your brilliant lieutenant, Montgomery . . . 'Torch' movements are proceeding with precision and so far amazing secrecy . . .

Ultra paddled slowly, quietly, in towards the beach near Termini where at 0200 she was due to meet and embark the Count. She was still a few miles offshore, with Cape Cefalu a dozen miles away to port. Ruck was taking her in at periscope depth: he was at the periscope himself, straining his eyes into the dark, and he had Newton – *Ultra*'s senior asdic rating – on the set. The submarine's motors were running at slow speed, grouped down, meaning that the two sections of her battery were connected in series, as opposed to parallel which gave greater power. This way she was getting about one and a half knots and keeping propeller noise to a minimum. On operations of this clandestine kind you had always to be on guard against the possibility of ambush, which accounted for Ruck's extreme circumspection.

The ambusher might be a U-boat, or E-boats, or destroyers. A U-boat lying dead quiet and listening through its hydrophones would be the most dangerous: the first you might know of it could be the sound – detected too late – of torpedoes racing at you. You could imagine it visually, here and now: a submarine's black shape somewhere between this point and the shore: tubes ready, bowcaps open, captain motionless at the periscope and hydrophone operator nodding as he picks up the sound of approaching screws . . . It could be real. Happening at this moment – if, for instance, the Count had been caught and talked to save his life: or if there'd been a leak elsewhere . . . Ruck was on his toes and being very, very wary, more so than usual: he was entering the enemy's back yard, and if the enemy had known he was coming they'd have had it staked out.

Bob McClure was at the chart table, watching points for Ruck, checking the boat's slow progress on the automatic log. The log's constant clicking was the loudest sound in this midships area of the submarine: otherwise there was only the soft hum of the motors and an occasional quiet movement from Ruck or one of the control room watch-keepers. A planesman putting on a few degrees of angle; the helmsman fractionally shifting his wheel; the messenger clearing his throat. It was very warm, to match the stillness: *Ultra* had spent the whole of the day motoring westward along the Sicilian coastline, and electric power made for central heating.

It also drained the battery. In normal patrol routine they'd have been on the surface now, running a diesel charge to top it up.

It was 1 am, 5 November. One hour to go to the rendezvous. Paul was flat on his bunk, sleepless, listening to the small sounds from the control room, trying to figure out an answer to a problem that was bothering him, and hearing pages turn – Hugo Wykeham, at the table, reading Edgar Wallace . . . Wykeham had been into the control room a short time ago, offering to look after the trim for Ruck, but the skipper had told him not to bother, McClure could handle it.

Paul wished he could see the Count now, this minute, wherever he might be. On the beach, perhaps, already there and waiting for *Ultra*'s blue light to show. Or in some farm-house with a bunch of cut-throat partisans . . . He might have a good yarn to tell when he came back on board: and he'd be in a better frame of mind, one might hope, better than the blue funk he'd been in when he left.

The puzzling aspect of this situation was what the routine was going to be for the re-embarkation. Paul had asked Ruck about it: for instance, space would have to be cleared for the canoe in the torpedo stowage compartment before they surfaced, and it should have been happening now – with only an hour to go, and the TSC resembling the Black Hole of Calcutta, crammed with all sorts of gear that would have overflowed into the rack-space formerly occupied by the folboat. Moving stuff around wasn't easy, because the compartment was so full of it: to reorganise it you'd have to pile a mountain of stuff out in the gangway first. But Paul had also wanted to get a decision on the drill with the fore hatch: for instance, whether he'd go up that way himself, or use the bridge hatch so as to be available on the casing before they got that for'ard one open.

Ruck's answer to all of it had been, 'I'll let you know.'

'But all that clobber for'ard, sir—'

'Plenty of time. Don't worry.'

He could hear Ruck circling with the periscope, the shuffle of his tennis shoes as he moved round the raised sill of the periscope well. Then his voice asking his navigator, 'How far to go now?'

To the rendezvous position, he'd mean. Wykeham had stopped reading, and was waiting to hear the answer. McClure provided it from the chart table, which was just across the gangway from this space: 'Two point four miles, sir.'

Ruck grunted acknowledgement. Still circling. Faint clicking from asdics as Newton trained around with his ears turned to any whisper from the black surrounding water. Paul looked over the edge of his bunk, down at Wykeham, the slightly balding top of that Old Etonian head. 'D'you understand the form with the canoe? What the hell I'm supposed to do with it?'

Wykeham glanced up. 'I wouldn't dream of making a suggestion, Sub.'

Ruck's voice: 'How much water under us, pilot?'

'Hundred and ninety feet, sir. Not shelving much yet.'

Paul said quietly, 'I told the Count we'd have a tot of rum for him, when he gets back.'

'And where will that come from?'

He hadn't given it much thought. He said, 'I'll ask the coxswain.'

'Easier to give him a slug of Scotch.' Nobody drank at sea, in the wardroom, but there were some bottles in the wine locker. Wykeham pushed his novel aside, and reached for the poker dice in their leather cup. '*If* we get him back . . . Want a game, Sub?'

'D'you think there's some doubt?'

'I've no idea at all . . . Come on, turn out, let's roll 'em.'

He slid down on to the bench. 'Are you thinking he might not make it?'

'Agents have gone adrift before, haven't they.' He passed him one of the dice, to spin for starters. 'Ace up, king towards . . .'

'At this rate we won't be anything like in position by oh-two-double-oh.'

'Doesn't look like it, does it.' Wykeham murmured, 'Skipper knows what he's doing, Sub . . . That's a queen to your miserable ten, so I start. Here come five aces.' He threw a low straight, in one, the rattle of the dice startlingly loud in the surrounding quiet. 'I'll leave it at that, this time. But let's have that cloth on the table.'

'Hope to God we do get the old twister back.'

'"Twister" is about right . . .'

At 0140 Ruck ordered Diving Stations, and when the hands had settled down at their posts and Wykeham had adjusted the trim he had one motor stopped. Making the boat's propulsion even quieter. He'd already decreed 'silent running', so the order was passed to the motor room by word of mouth instead of by the noisy telegraph, which was loud enough to be heard miles away, under water.

McClure told him, 'At oh-two-double-oh we'll be two and a half-thousand yards short of the R/V position, sir.'

Ruck took his eyes off the periscope lenses, looked at McClure, and nodded. Then he resumed his slow, concentrated search. Newton, on asdics, had his eyes half-shut as he trained all round, listening intently, his entire concentration out there in the cold blackness with the fishes.

'Signalman.'

Jannaway started . . . 'Sir?'

'When we surface I want you behind me on the ladder, carrying the Aldis with the blue shade on it. But you're to stay on the ladder, right in the hatch. I'll take the lamp from you when I'm ready, and I'll do the flashing: all you have to do is plug it in and pass it to me, and stay where you are. Clear?'

'Aye, sir.'

'If we have to dive, I may throw you the lamp. Just get the hell out of the way and make sure the lamp's lead is clear of the hatch rim. Shout down any "dive" order that I give, as you drop down. I do mean *drop*. It'll need to be the fastest dive anyone ever saw.' He pulled his head back from the periscope again, to address Wykeham now. 'Point is, Number One, I don't intend opening the voice-pipe. Nor do I want her fully surfaced. I want the top lid a few feet out of water, that's all. Get the idea?'

Wykeham nodded. 'Eight feet on the gauges?'

'That'll do. We'll stay on the motors. On the order "dive", full ahead grouped up, and flood Q. You can *expect* that order, so be ready for it.' He'd put his eyes back to the lenses again. Nobody understanding much yet. The orders were clear but the reasoning behind them wasn't. To be surfacing at least a mile short of the position, and expecting to stay up for no more than seconds, and yet needing the blue lamp as if the Count would be there to see it, *in range* to see it . . .

Perhaps Ruck was hoping to get the Count started on his canoe trip, then to run in dived and surface again in the right place, not having had to hang around and wait after the first showing of the light? But the Count had been told to steer for it: and if after one lot of flashing it didn't appear again he'd have no mark to guide him.

'Depth?'

'Twenty-nine feet, sir—'

'Keep her up, for Christ's—'

'Sorry, sir.' Wykeham was fiddling with the trim. With so little way on her, it needed to be a very accurate one. Also the closer you came to land the more uneven the salinity and therefore density might be, if there was any mix of river water.

'Twenty-eight feet, sir.'

'Hear anything, Newton?'

'No, sir.'

McClure prompted, 'Five minutes to oh-two-double-oh, sir.'

'Port twenty.'

'Port twenty, sir.' The helmsman span his wheel. Wykeham told the second coxswain, 'Put some dive on the fore planes, Lovesay.' Under helm, the bow tended to rise. The helmsman reported, 'Twenty of port wheel on, sir.'

Paul was thinking that as a canoeist, the Count was very much an amateur, and without the light to steer by he'd panic, go any way except the right one. He'd miss the rendezvous, and he'd be invisible in the dark. And Ruck wouldn't risk his ship by hanging around.

'Steer north.'

'Steer north, sir . . .'

Swivelling her right around, turning her stern to the beach. So he wasn't intending to go any closer in, wasn't taking her even within a mile of the pick-up position?

'Stand by to surface.'

Wykeham ordered, 'Check main vents.' And a minute later, when the reports were complete, 'Ready to surface, sir.' Paul decided that this must be intended as a test surfacing, to make sure the bay was empty. When he was sure of it, he'd go on in and find the Count. Well, he *had* to: it was what he'd brought *Ultra* in here for, the only reason for being here at all!

Questioning Newton again: the asdic man shaking his head in that goofy way of his, repeating, 'Nothing, sir . . .' Ruck looked across at Wykeham, and nodded. 'Half ahead together. Surface!'

'Blow one, three and five main ballast!'

Quinn, the bearded artificer on the blowing panel, wrenched the valves open. Jannaway had opened the lower hatch, and he had the Aldis ready with its rubber-covered lead coiled over his shoulder. Ruck started up the ladder as air blasted into the tanks: Jannaway followed close behind him. Hydroplanes were at hard a-rise and the boat was lifting, depth-gauge needles circling slowly and then faster round their dials and Wykeham intoning, for Ruck's information up there under the hatch, 'Twenty-two . . . Twenty feet, sir . . . Eighteen . . . Sixteen . . .' At twelve, one clip swung off, clanking as Ruck released it: at ten feet, second clip, and the hatch flung back, water cascading down and Wykeham yelling at Quinn over the racket of HP air coursing through the pipes, 'Stop blowing!' Cold night air wafted down. A lot of sea had come down too, ladder and hatch-rims still dripping into a pool of it on the corticene-covered deck. *Ultra* wallowed, rolling sluggishly in low waves, really only partly surfaced and in just a little better than neutral buoyancy; there'd be very little of her in sight above water. Enough to show up on direction-finding apparatus, of course: and any enemy with hydrophones would have heard her surfacing, which was a very noisy process . . . Ruck would be displaying the blue lamp now; a second ago he'd shouted for it, to Jannaway, he'd be pointing it in the direction of the beach and giving three blue flashes – pause – three more – pause – three more . . . Wykeham ordered, 'Stop together. Group up.' To be ready for the 'dive' order if it came.

Newton instigated it – wide-eyed, bawling: 'HE right astern, fast turbine, closing!'

'HE' stood for hydrophone effect. Propeller noise. He'd howled it like a dog affected by the moon and Jannaway had heard it up there in the top hatch and repeated it, a booming, echoing cry of alarm in the steel drum of the tower. Ruck's shout followed instantaneously: 'Dive, dive, dive!'

'Open main vents, flood Q, full ahead together!'

Paul thinking, in the rush of movement as the vents banged open all along her length, *He was right . . .*

The signalman dropped like a ton of deadweight with the lamp clutched against his chest. He was crashing through the lower hatch when the top lid slammed shut and Ruck called 'Hatch shut, one clip on!' An OK that it was safe to continue to dive. By this time, two seconds later, the top hatch would be under water anyway: and as it would have been distinctly unsafe *not* to take her down, the alternative would have been to shut the lower hatch, trapping the skipper in the tower. Fortunately that had not been necessary. Jannaway was on his back in that pool of water, then scrambling aside, getting out of the way of Ruck's equally fast but less uncontrolled descent.

'Sixty feet. Well done, signalman.' Ruck was soaking wet, and panting. He asked Newton, 'How close? I saw *some* damn—'

'Here.' Newton's eyes were wide, his body upright, rigid on the stool, and the long forefinger of his left hand was pointing directly upward. 'Coming over – *now* . . .'

Enemy screws raced over, fast and loud, a singing churn that had barely passed before it was repeated – a second one close astern of it. Passing very fast, though, and already fading seaward. Newton said, his torso seeming to shorten as he relaxed, folding down into his customarily slumped pose again, 'E-boats, sir.'

'Group down, slow ahead together. Port twenty. Blow Q.'

There *had* been a welcoming party.

But no depth charges. Not yet, anyway. They might not be carrying any: they might have been expecting a clean kill on the surface with torpedoes, or their guns.

'Going round to starboard, sir. Circling, I'd say.'

'Midships.' Ruck told Creagh, the helmsman, 'Steer three-three-oh.'

The Germans had known exactly where to find them, Paul realised. Except for the fact that *Ultra* had been a mile to seaward of where she should have been, and Ruck handling her as if he'd known beyond doubt they'd be here. If he had *not* been so extremely cautious, *Ultra* would almost surely have been blown apart by this time.

'Course three-three-oh, sir.'

'Very good. Stop starboard.'

One motor only: to take her softly, softly out to sea north-westward.

Newton reported, 'Enemies bearing green seven-oh, moving left to right, sir.'

Heading back inshore, then. Ruck murmured, mostly to himself, 'Thought they had us on toast, I'll bet.' He looked at Wykeham and told him flatly, 'They've got the Count. That's the only way they could have known precisely where to jump us.'

'Couldn't there have been a leak somewhere else, sir? The planning end, shoreside?'

Ruck shook his head: a decisive jerk. 'I and the Count fixed the position and the time after we left Malta. That's the system, you see.'

Wykeham nodding slowly. 'So what now, sir? Home to Malta?'

'Doubt it. But let's find out.' He told McClure, 'Let's have the sealed envelope, Sub.'

He didn't seem in the least disturbed by his certainty that the Count had run into trouble.

McClure opened the safe and took out a brown, red-sealed envelope. He gave it to Ruck, who took it to the chart table and slit it open. Newton reported, 'They're inshore of us, sir, slowed down a lot. Bearing green one-five-oh, distant, drawing right. No transmissions, sir.'

McClure muttered to Paul, 'At least I keep my bunk now.' Ruck's murmur of 'Callous little swine' was fair comment, Paul thought. An agent caught as Paoli – alias Venizelos, etc – had apparently been caught, was liable to be tortured, probably shot after they'd squeezed all they could out of him. The sad little guy who'd sat at that wardroom table only three days ago and proposed visiting in Connecticut after the war was most likely either dead or in agony. While *Ultra* turned her back on him, tiptoed discreetly away . . . Ruck finished skimming through whatever orders were in that package: he'd folded it all and stuffed it into the hip pocket of his old grey flannel bags. Pulling out a fresh chart now, one covering the whole of the western Mediterranean. Paul and McClure, sharp-eyed for any clues, watched him slide it over the Sicilian chart and begin to check distances from here westward, setting dividers against the latitude scale and then walking them across the chart.

'E-boats have turned seaward, sir. Green one-five-five, moving right to left, about half speed.'

'Very good.' But they'd missed out, and they'd know it . . . Straightening from the chart, Ruck came back into the control room. 'We'll stay as we are for half an hour, Number One. Then if we're still in the clear we'll surface and pump some amps in – about three and a half hours of darkness left. But we now have nearly five hundred miles to cover, in—' he checked it out on his fingers – 'in three days and two nights. So we'll need to get a bit of a wriggle on.' It was a fact: mental arithmetic told one that with the need to be dived, slow, throughout the daylight hours, you'd need every minute of it . . . But Ruck looked happy – even jubilant: you could see that the events of the last half-hour had brightened him enormously. Whereas Paul had an uncomfortable feeling of treachery, desertion . . . Ruck was reaching for the microphone of the Tannoy broadcasting system: he switched it on, tested it by slapping it with his palm. Then, 'D'you hear, there? Captain speaking . . . Unfortunately, we have not been able to pick up the agent. The opposition was waiting for us, and that's certain proof they've nabbed him. Too bad . . . Now, however, we're off westward, for a different but very special job. There'd be no point telling you at this stage what it is, but we'll be in transit three days and two nights, and what we'll be doing is something very important, probably a turning-point in the war. We can feel honoured to have a key role to play in it . . . But anyway – that's it for now. I expect we'll be surfacing in about half an hour.'

McClure had been at the chart. He whispered to Paul, 'Five hundred miles west takes us either to Majorca or Algiers.'

The Count had said Sicily – Palermo – or Cagliari in Sardinia. No . . . he'd said both those places. And he'd had secret papers taped to his ribs: and he'd been caught. But he might have got rid of the papers first. Except he'd told them *this* much . . . Paul felt sure it wouldn't be Majorca, anyway: Majorca was Spanish, and the Spaniards were still neutral – just . . .

An hour later, on the surface, drinking cocoa round the wardroom table while the diesels rumbled, charging the battery and driving the ship westward while they sucked cold night air down through the hatch, Ruck told them, 'You might as well know it now. Our so-called Count was a double agent. That's to say, he took pay from our side and sold information to the Italians too. Our people knew it, and they've been keeping him on ice for something of this sort.'

Wykeham spooned sugar into his cup. He was dressed for the bridge, due to relieve McClure up there in about ten minutes.

'Are you saying he was intended to be caught?'

Ruck nodded. 'Complete with detailed information in which he believes. The Italians and Germans will believe it too. It's all balls, of course.'

'Palermo and Cagliari?'

'Exactly, Sub.' Ruck added, 'Sorry as I am to disillusion you. You thought he was rather a nice chap, didn't you? The truth is that on at least one earlier stunt, a commando expedition to the Eyetie mainland, he sold our blokes down the river and none of them came out of it. Whatever's happening to him now is poetic justice, you see, as well as serving a very important purpose.'

'I wonder if he suspected something of the sort. He was pretty scared.'

'Mostly at having to paddle his own canoe, wasn't it?'

Paul asked Ruck, more on the off-chance than in any expectation of getting an answer, 'When we were in Malta, sir, you said the flotilla had some other cloak-and-dagger jobs on. Are they jobs like this one?'

'Not really.' Ruck rubbed his jaw, nails grating on the

stubble. 'Well, it'll be all wrapped up by now, so there's no harm telling you . . . No, those were all to do with generals. Mostly from Gib, though, not Malta. There was a Yank general by the name of Mark Clark to be put ashore in Algeria and then brought off again, and a frog one plus some of his family to be lifted from a beach somewhere near Marseilles. He was to be transferred at sea to a Catalina and flown to Gib. General Giraud . . . *Seraph* was earmarked for those jobs, then *Sybil* was to run in and pick up Giraud's staff, on the next night.'

'Big stuff, by the sound of it.'

Ruck nodded at Wykeham. 'About as big as you can imagine.'

Paul thought, putting two and two together, *Algiers* . . .

But there was another question annoying him . . .

'If we knew the Count would have been caught, sir, why risk this ship by coming back to the place where they'd be pretty certain to be waiting for us?'

'Two good reasons.' Ruck asked Wykeham, 'Suggest what they might be?'

'Well.' Wykeham gave it a few seconds' thought. 'One you mentioned. The fact the E-boats were there proves they caught him. Since the R/V details were only settled at sea and no-one else could have known them?'

'Right. What else?'

Paul had stretched his mind to it . . . 'If we hadn't shown up, they'd have guessed we planted him on them?'

'See what you can do when you try.' Ruck tapped the signal log. 'And the news we sent out ten minutes ago, regretting the rendezvous couldn't be kept owing to enemy interference . . . If the Wops can decode it, all it'll tell them is what we want them to believe. Whereas to our backroom boys it says "operation completely successful". Right?'

The early morning BBC bulletin confirmed a much bigger success – continuing exploitation of the Eighth Army's victory in the desert. The RAF had achieved total air superiority and Rommel's forces were in full retreat.

* * *

'Another bloody day of it . . .' Tom Kyle muttered it to himself: barely loud enough for the helmsman or young Chalmers, his OOW, to have heard. He scowled out through salt-stained glass at a sea that was down to about force six again now. It had certainly exceeded force eight during the previous day and night. But this was the second dawn in which *Opal* had found herself alone, rolling northwestward and still separated by miles of ocean from convoy SL 320.

The rendezvous was set for noon today. Kyle had wirelessed yesterday, giving his own estimated position, course and speed, and a couple of hours later he'd received the escort commander's answer, establishing the R/V position at a certain point on bearing 030 degrees from position B. Obviously he'd expressed it that way, instead of in terms of latitude and longitude, because the Germans wouldn't have the slightest notion where position B was, so that even if they were able to break the cypher they wouldn't be getting anything of use to them.

All days looked horrible to start with. In years now he hadn't seen one that didn't. He lit a cigarette.

On the night of the second, running into early morning of the third, after he'd kept the shadower down for the requisite period of time and then left on a northeasterly course – up the track from which by that time the convoy would have turned away – Kyle had seen no fewer than four U-boats on the surface and at comparatively close quarters. One had fired a few shots at him and then dived, and the last of them had been about a mile ahead of him and steering the same course, gradually drawing farther and farther ahead, for more than an hour before he'd lost sight of it. It had been too rough on that course to man the gun; if the U-boat had ever looked astern and spotted *Opal* it must have thought she was one of its own crowd. In fact in those conditions the German might well not have seen her. The U-boats had been all over the place, obviously at sixes and sevens after that pasting by the other escorts and then the disappearance of the convoy; Kyle had been intent – having finished his performance with rockets and depth charges farther south – on getting through them, getting through the night, joining up with SL 320 as early as possible next day. *Yesterday* . . .

Sub-lieutenant Chalmers observed brightly, 'Could be worse, sir . . . Gone down quite a bit during the night, wouldn't you say?'

Kyle felt his head drawing in like a tortoise's. He wasn't saying a bloody thing. Or even glancing round. Cheerfulness at this time of day set his teeth on edge. Only five minutes ago he'd been asleep, on the horsehair settee in his cabin-cum-charthouse, and it took a lot more than five minutes, in his view, for an Atlantic dawn to acquire a silver lining.

Potts would still have his great fat head down, of course. Potts slept like a hippo, no matter what the weather was doing. Slept like a hippo, ate like a wolf. Kyle drew hard on his cigarette, and turned his thoughts to the midday rendezvous. Since *Opal's* course and the convoy's could be only just converging, probably with no more than a few degrees between them, and since the intersection of their tracks was – theoretically, anyway – less than six hours ahead, you could reckon there was probably not so great a distance between them now. SL 320 might not be far over that western horizon. 030 degrees from position B was in fact the original track, the path the convoy should have been on all the time, and *Opal* was right on it while the convoy was in the process of crabbing back towards it after that diversion. They'd be well astern of schedule, but Kyle couldn't say by how many miles or hours – or days – because he was going purely by dead reckoning, having had no chance to use a sextant in recent days.

Wind and sea were broad on the bow. *Opal*'s rolling was prodigious. But they were so used to it by this time that if it had stopped they'd have gone on staggering.

Kyle had seen enough of the dismal-looking seascape. He turned his head and pink-rimmed eyes on young Chalmers.

'I'm off below for breakfast. I'll give Potts a shake for you.'

'Thanks a lot, sir!'

Chalmers' chirpiness was intensely irritating. Twenty

years old, clear-eyed, clean and smart even at sea, and too sharp-witted for his own good. He was a very reliable watchkeeper, his celestial navigation was fast and accurate, and his ship-handling was better than most – Kyle thought – he handles her better than bloody Potts does, any road . . . But the young bugger was always so bright and willing: that was what grated, that and the fact he was so good at his job that it was difficult to find justification for kicking him up the arse, which was what Kyle found himself wanting to do several times a day . . . He was asking him now, 'When the escort commander replied to your signal, sir, wasn't he giving away his position to the U-boats? I mean, having gone to such lengths to get away from them?'

Kyle had given some thought to this, too. He wouldn't have been surprised – only fed-up – if there'd been no reply for a day or two. *If* the diversion had worked well, and the U-boats had been thrown off the trail, he wouldn't have blamed Everard for clamming up.

He pinched out his cigarette. 'Depends. If there was one of the bastards still shadowing, wouldn't have made much bloody odds, would it?'

'No. I see . . .'

Kyle had his hand on the sliding door at the back end of the bridge when the first shell scorched overhead. A scrunching, ripping noise, like tearing canvas . . .

The first shots from the 37mm had gone over, but Emsmann, the man on that gun, had the range now and was hitting. Hartwig on the 20 mm had incendiaries as well as armour-piercing rounds in his pans, and every sixth round was tracer: he used his gun like a hose-pipe, aiming with the fall-of-shot more than with the weapon itself, and at this close range it was easy and quite devastating. His orders were to go first for any close-range weapons that might be firing at them, then for the dinghy on the trawler's stern and then the liferafts. The trawler was turning: rocking up on a big roller as it ran under her, displaying the full depth of her hull for'ard, and at the same time her length was opening as she swung to starboard. Looff saw men pouring out of the accommodation hatch in her for'ard welldeck, rushing to man the gun on her foc'sl: the 37mm hit the foc'sl ladder when the first of them were on it, and he knew then for sure, seeing parts of men as well as ladder flying and the foc'sl-break opened, gaping jaggedly and smoking, that he had an easy killing here. In a second or two that gun itself would be smashed, and the trawler didn't have a hope in hell. A fire had started in her bridge, and its starboard side was already partly wrecked. He called down to his helmsman, 'Port fifteen, up five knots!' To counter the trawler's turn. Surprise had played its part, but basically this was a very simple tactic that could hardly fail to succeed. He'd surfaced U 702 right astern of his target, and with the trawler on a bearing of red 30, thirty on the port bow. This enabled both the U-boat's guns to engage, and also put them in what was a blind arc to the trawler where her only weapon – that four-inch on the wave-swept platform on her bow – couldn't bear, was utterly useless. Now as she swung to starboard so that it *should* bear, his guns raked that exposed forepart while at the same time he turned his submarine to port to cross the Brit's stern again, seeking cover while he engaged her now over his starboard side. Looff had just happened to be approaching on the *Opal*'s beam, closing in towards the convoy with which *Drachens* Three, Six and Nine were currently in contact. He'd ordered them to spread out ahead of it, and he'd been steering to join them, re-establish the pack in a position to make up, tonight, for what had been lost in the past two nights: and there right ahead of the U-boat, twenty minutes ago during Leutnant-zur-See Kurt Schwieger's watch, had been this little hostage to fate all on its lonesome . . . He had the bastard cold. He had the speed advantage, and the weapons, and he'd caught him completely on the hop. There'd be a red streamer among the white ones all right, when U 702 returned to base: this might be a tiddler, but it *was* technically a warship. It made up – partially, and for the moment – for the maddening, highly frustrating past forty-eight hours during which Looff and most of the *Drachen* pack had lost the convoy, through a combination of foul weather and tricky manoeuvring by the Brits . . . Who'd still, anyway, lost two ships last night, one to Gustaf Becker in *Drachen* Three and one to young Meusel in *Drachen* Nine . . . There'd been a slight pause in the action while U 702's bow had been pointing directly at her target: but she'd swung on round and now the guns were trained out to starboard, finishing the job off, the quick-firing 37mm maintaining its steady rhythmic pumping crashes and the lighter, high-speed 20mm roaring harshly, hosing its lethal stream to and fro across the already badly mauled and dying ship. When any human figure moved, even on its hands and knees, the stream shifted, found it. The trawler had got one shot off – *one*, with two men manning that gun for less than half a minute – before Looff had tucked his submarine back into the safe sector again: and those two men had been dead by that time. The target was still circling: its bridge was a nest of flame, smoke pouring away down-wind, shells bursting constantly in that mess of destruction, a few missing now and then – mostly because of the motion, the way the weather was flinging the submarine around – but never for long, the gunners always came back on target very smartly. U 702 was like a prize-fighter with a heavily-outmatched opponent on the ropes and groggy but somehow still on his feet: you just went on hitting, destroying, smashing . . . Looff, near-deafened by the racket, most of which was from the lighter gun, the snarling 20 mm which was on the rear end of this same bridge deck; the other one was farther aft and a step lower, on the railed circular platform known to U-boat men as the 'conservatory'. He shouted in Oelricher's ear – his own voice inaudible to him, but the quartermaster heard it – 'Tell Emsmann, aim for the waterline!'

To puncture him, and sink him. That little dinghy had been blown to pieces, ditto the liferafts. But now, extraordinarily, a gun was firing at them – a light machine-gun firing in short bursts – from the confusion of smoke and fire amidships, up in the wrecked bridge. He saw it because there was tracer in it, the glow seemingly slow-moving, lifting with bright balloon-like slowness then speeding into the wicked whipping crack of bullets flashing over: he yelled, 'Hit that gun!' but Oelricher was already shouting in Hartwig's ear and pointing: and he needn't have bothered anyway – it happened, at that moment. With the trawler virtually lying on her side, locked in the circling turn, wheel most likely jammed, Looff guessed; but all he had to do was circle too, stay astern for near-total safety while his guns cut her to pieces. The 37mm had gone for the Bren or whatever that gun was, and it ended in that whole side of the little ship's upperworks disintegrating. She *was* on her side, listing, not righting herself any more, lying on her beam with her forepart higher than her stern: but, *incredibly*, a man, erect, with a gun, struggling to fit it to a mounting . . . Another machine-gun, on some raised part in the middle of that slope of wreckage abaft the trawler's funnel: the gun hadn't fired when Looff saw this happening and raised his glasses, focusing on that figure and screaming a warning back to Oelricher—

Tom Kyle had sent Chalmers down to get the old water-cooled Lewis out and mount it on its stanchion on the engine-room hatch back aft. Potts meanwhile had finally managed to get the Vickers GO set up on the signal deck on the starboard side of the bridge. Taken him a bloody age, at that. The Lewis hadn't been used in a year or more: they'd been in the Med then, on the Tobruk run, and it had been salvaged out of a dump at Mersa; all the trawlers stuck extra weapons on, whatever they could scrounge from the dumps, for AA defence on that desert coast. It might have been a fine weapon in its day (in 1914, say) but it turned out to be a pain in the neck on board *Opal*, jamming solid the moment it saw a Swastika or those black crosses. So it had been stowed down for'ard in the bosun's store. Kyle had sent Chalmers for it partly to get rid of him and partly because the radio operator, amongst others, had been killed, and he considered it important to get a signal out before the aerials and the set went to blazes, to let the escort commander of

SL 320 know what was happening. He mightn't be aware there was a U-boat this close to him, and Kyle flattered himself at being a dab hand with a morse key: he managed it, too, despite having been hit in the shoulder and having a useless arm that hung dripping, luckily without any feeling in that side at all. As soon as he'd got the message away he went down to help Chalmers – Potts had been killed by then, and the Vickers and that bit of signal deck had gone with him. There was no steering, no control, no purpose that Kyle or anyone else could have served up here: the coxswain was draped across his wheel, dead and smouldering and with cortisene all burnt away around him, reeking. Kyle found the boy dead too, his skull smashed by a cannon shell like an exploded egg, in the for'ard welldeck, with the Lewis gun under him and some belts of .303 ammunition wrapped round his shoulders. The only men alive now were dying, and *Opal* was sinking by the stern and listing too, perhaps about to turn turtle, by the feel of her. Kyle pulled Chalmers' body off the gun, hefted it in his good arm and staggered aft to the engine-room hatch, which was blackened and blistered but intact, although the mounting for the gun was slightly askew and he could see he'd have a problem. There was nothing else he could usefully have been doing, though, not the slightest point in trying to help such men as might still be living, since there was no hope at all of survival. There were no rafts, and U-boats never bothered with survivors. He knew this so well that he didn't think about it: the only practical thing to do was take a few Germans with you, make it slightly less joyful an occasion for them. The gun in its cylindrical water-cooling jacket was a heavy, awkward load, and one-armed it was a hell of a job to get it up on the slanting hatch-cover. Cursing it steadily and fluently, a growling noise that sounded like someone else beside him swearing and grunting in his ear. The ship was low in the water, sluggish as if the sea was glue. He got the thing up there finally, then remembered – cursing himself for it, a loud shout of profanity – that the ammo belts were still draped round Chalmers' torso. He was turning to ease himself down from the hatch-top when U 702's 20mm sewed a straight line like explosive stitchwork right up the trawler's slanting centreline, bursting the old Lewis into flying scrap a second before it sent Tom Kyle reeling scarlet to his Maker.

Instead of a cross, the albatross / About his neck was hung . . . The effort of recall passed time, and occupied the mind. His greatest accomplishment so far had been to recapture half Swinburne's *Forsaken Garden*, which when he'd memorised it in the English class at Dartmouth had been considered somewhat *outré*. But now the Ancient Mariner was going to have to wait a while, as it was time to go down and reconnoitre for some grub.

The child had gone off to school and the girl, wearing the same clothes and carrying the same basket, had left soon afterwards, as she had on the previous two days. Before these departures there'd been the standard early-morning routine as well – the boy to the well with a bucket, sometimes several buckets – his mother opening shutters and seeing him off to school before she fed the hens. Peering down between the slats of the shutters, Jack saw too – as he had yesterday – that she also went into the henhouse and collected the morning's eggs. Yesterday she'd done it twice, morning and evening, and during her absence in the afternoon he'd gone out there and found three still warm in the straw nests. He'd considered boiling them in a pan of water on her stove, but he'd baulked at taking such a liberty: it had seemed excessive, for some reason. He'd thought better of it since: eating the eggs raw up here later, he'd wished he'd gone ahead and cooked them. There'd have been no traces for her to have seen, just from a pot having had water boiled in it. And he could have used the heated water afterwards for washing. He'd taken some bread yesterday, and a mutton bone with meat on it, and drunk some milk from a jug. He'd also washed himself, without soap, in a bucket of ice-cold water, and his appearance afterwards in the mirror in the girl's bedroom had been somewhat reassuring. He'd approached it with trepidation, remembering the shock he'd given himself that first day; but yesterday the eyes had seemed less crazy, the expression altogether less savage. As a result, he supposed, of having had some rest and a certain amount of sustenance, and shelter.

The ankle was less painful, too. Sprains did heal themselves, given time and rest. Moving out of his room now and down the stairs, negotiating the heap of junk that blocked them lower down, he hardly put any weight on it at all. He'd become adept at hopping on the sound foot, and taking weight on his arms against walls and so on; and feeling generally better now, stronger in spirit as well as physically, he wanted the ankle to mend quickly so he could be on his way. He thought the bike would still be in the place where he'd hidden it. There'd been no further signs of the military, which there surely would have been if they'd found it; they'd been searching for an escaped POW at the very time it had disappeared, and they'd hardly have failed to connect the two phenomena. They might well have assumed their quarry had taken off in a southerly direction, and that search would have been a formality, compliance with an order to check all buildings within a certain radius. Something like that. It had seemed perfunctory, at the time.

Today, his programme was to go out and get some eggs, then heat water in a saucepan and boil them. He'd been over-cautious yesterday, and raw eggs were fairly unappealing even to a very hungry man. Whereas hard-boiled ones, with some bread if he struck lucky again—

He stopped dead, in the kitchen doorway.

She'd laid a place at the table. A setting for one. Knife, fork, German sausage and a peeled, hard-boiled egg, two thick slices of black bread, a tumbler with a jug of milk beside it.

He stood frozen, gaping at it. Scared stiff of it. It was like looking at a baited trap. He was as shocked as he might have been if there'd been someone sitting there with a pistol pointing at his head.

But as his mind began to unfreeze, he realised that she might have set it for herself. Or for the child . . . *That* was it! The child would be coming home early from school – before she was expecting to get back herself – so she'd left his meal ready for him.

It was the obvious solution. But for a moment he'd been really frightened. Nerves on edge: he hadn't appreciated what strange tricks solitude could play. Staring at the setting on the table, actually *frightened* . . .

She'd left it for the child. Obviously. And he'd better make it snappy now, he realised, because if that was the boy's lunch he might be trotting up to the door quite soon. Nasty little Nazi that it was: Jack remembered that bony little arm shooting up, the rapped '*Heil Hitler* . . .' But now . . . *move*. Egg-hunt first. No – visit to the outside WC first, *en route* to the egg collection. Via a window, since as usual the back door was locked. The child would have its own key, presumably: unless she hid one for it somewhere outside – which might be worth investigating . . . It was most likely a half-day at school – a Saturday, probably. In which case tomorrow would be Sunday, they might not leave the house at all and he, Jack, might therefore be confined to his room. Facing, among other deprivations, foodlessness. So the thing would be to gather quite a few eggs and hard-boil them all. Then straight back upstairs, before the return of junior. Eat a couple of the eggs today, save the others – and perhaps take one of those two slices of bread?

The child would hardly complain at getting only one slice. If it did, its mother would tell it not to talk nonsense. Might take a slice and a half, in fact: cut one slice neatly in half with that knife, and keep the half-slice in case tomorrow *was* a Sunday?

He set a pan of water on the stove to start heating while he was outside. And he found five eggs. Good for him, bad luck for the girl. He felt sure it was eggs she took away with her every morning in the basket. Probably traded them for other items such as bread, milk, sausage . . .

The child did not come home for its lunch. Jack was lying on his mattress several hours later when he heard someone approaching and knelt up quickly, peering through his shutters: it was the girl. At about the same time as she'd returned on the last two days, and as usual carrying a loaded basket. She went round the side of the house to the back, and he heard the back door open and bang shut.

Then – distantly but clearly, echoey through the half-empty house – he heard her laugh.

In London, Rear-Admiral Aubrey Wishart slammed a black 'phone down and snatched up the red one.

'Wishart.'

Listening . . .

'I know. As a matter of fact I've just been on a visit to the Tracking Room. It's true he's a long way astern of station, and it's also quite plain the U-boats are homing-in on him again . . . Yes, agreed, SL 320's in for some more rough stuff, at least two or three more nights of . . .'

Listening again. Impatience in his manner.

'Close, yes. But he's back on the rails again now, and he'll know as well as you and I do that he'll have to stay on them. He knows the score, he'll handle it.'

Wishart reached for a cigarette, put it in his mouth, groped for a lighter. The voice from the other end of the scrambled line continued for a while, then ended with another question. Wishart drew smoke hard into his lungs.

'I can tell you positively that he would never have intended *losing* them. He'd have seen he had to do some damn thing, though, and what he's just done may have saved half a dozen ships. Or more. But if there'd been any likelihood of actually losing the U-boats he'd have put the kibosh on that when he answered the first call from *Opal*, wouldn't he?'

Another interruption . . . Then, 'I agree.' Smoke gusted round the telephone. '*Very* sad. And that's two of his three trawlers gone, which rather brings one back to his request for reinforcements. As I said before, it seems perfectly justified – especially now his primary task is damn near completed – *and* that convoy's going to be lucky to survive even in single figures!'

He rocked back in the chair, scowling at the ceiling. 'Yes. Admiral Ramsay *has* been kept informed.'

Admiral Sir Bertram Ramsay was running the London end of 'Torch', as Deputy Allied Naval Commander – deputy to A B Cunningham. Sir Andrew Cunningham and his staff were already in Gibraltar, and General Eisenhower would be joining them in the tunnel some time today. Not that convoy SL 320 came into the scope of *their* enormously complicated plans: the red-herring operation was entirely peripheral to the main one.

'No.' Wishart frowned into the red telephone. 'Nobody can send him orders now without risk of blowing the gaff and wrecking the whole bloody thing – just when it's on the point of accomplishment. And if I know Nick Everard, he'd ignore your orders anyway. *My* worst time, let me tell you, was three days ago *before* he took matters into his own hands. I've known him more than twenty years, he's there because I knew damn well that if anyone could . . .'

He'd been interrupted again. He listened for only a few seconds this time. Then he cut in: 'I'm sorry, Joe. I'm very busy, and this isn't getting us anywhere. The only way you could possibly help is by sending him the reinforcements he's asked for. What the hell would *you* propose – a PQ seventeen?'

Chapter 13

From a German intelligence appreciation dated 4 November 1942:
The relatively small number of landing craft and the fact that only two passenger ships are in this assembly at Gibraltar, do not indicate any immediate landing in the Mediterranean area or on the northwest African coast.

'Four hundred revolutions. Port fifteen . . .'

Nick Everard was at the binnacle with a sliver of moon beyond to silhouette his dark, duffel-coated shape as *Harbinger*'s rudder went over and revs increased; she was moving out to support *Paeony*, who'd put a U-boat down at close quarters and now had it in asdic contact. It was the first one tonight and as yet there was no pressure from elsewhere; the Germans had been holding off, keeping the defenders on edge in the knowledge that they were out there and might move in at any moment, had only two or three nights left in which to finish the butchery.

Unless they were intending simply to maintain contact, and wait for the rest of the pack to join?

It wasn't likely.

'Midships!'

'Midships, sir . . .'

Paeony's RDF was out of action – which was a good enough reason for *Harbinger* to move in that direction. Guyatt was busy with this U-boat, and his sector would be unguarded by RDF or even visually. Not that any sector could be covered as it should be, with escorts spread so widely: *and* the only remaining trawler having some trouble with her asdic set. Broad had made a signal about it this afternoon. Even *Harbinger* wasn't totally without problems: the weather had been foul for days on end, and the rough handling had left a host of defects including one serious one, a leak on one condenser. Hawkey was in a state of agitation about it, but there wasn't anything to be done, at sea. The prospect of *Harbinger* breaking down was one you didn't have to entertain.

'Steer oh-one-eight.'

'Oh-one-eight, sir . . .'

The convoy's mean course now was 030. They were back on the ordered route, and nearly two days astern of schedule. It would have been worse if they hadn't cut the corner, by-passed the dog-leg of position B. But there could be no more diversions, not at any rate until all the 'Torch' assault convoys had passed astern.

SL 320 consisted of twenty ships, after losing the *William Law* and the *Bonny Prince* last night. The *William Law* had been hit by two torpedoes and had gone down quickly, but the *Bonny Prince* had straggled, dropped several miles astern, and she'd been hit while *Stella* had been struggling back to see what the trouble was and persuade her to rejoin. Then she'd been torpedoed twice, with an interval of about ten minutes between the attacks. Nick had known there were two U-boats ahead at that time, a dozen miles away, but not of any other until those two ships were hit, within about half an hour of each other.

So thirty-seven ships had been reduced to twenty. And the fewer ships were left in convoy, the shorter the odds became on any individual being the next to go. But those odds would also be affected by the number of U-boats involved. HF/DF contacts during the evening and early hours of the night had indicated that four were keeping pace with the convoy, and a Tracking Room signal received at dusk had stated, *In addition to those in your immediate vicinity, transmissions on 4995 KCs between 1500 and 1800/ A indicate 5 U-boats now ahead of you will have joined by noon tomorrow.*

Bearcroft had read that message out from the W/T office voice-pipe, when they'd been at dusk action stations, and Chubb had broken an ensuing silence with an enthusiastic 'Oh, *good*!'

Chubb's ebullience was undiminished. Warrimer had settled down, become more intent on the job he was doing and less conscious of his own value to it. Mike Scarr was quieter than he had been. For all of them – except Chubb, apparently – it had been a telling, formative week.

The *Omeo* was being left astern as *Harbinger* surged forward and diverged from the left-hand column. Next ahead of the *Omeo* now was the *Colombia*: then the *Sweetcastle*, and the *Tolworth Tide* as column leader. The *Chauncy Maples* led the whole pack of them from the centre, the head of column three, with the *Burbridge* astern of her. The oiler, *Redgulf Star*, was abeam to starboard of the *Burbridge*. *Harbinger* driving her narrow hull across a sea that was definitely easier now, lower and longer and with moonglow highlighting the crests, spray glittering as it came whipping across the bridge. The moon was only a brightness behind cloud, most of the time, with occasional leaks of brilliance through gaps: the wind was distinctly colder, to make up for conditions having improved in other ways.

A call from the plot . . . Carlish took it. 'Surface contact oh-four-one, seven miles, sir!'

'Translate that into range and bearing from *Astilbe*, and pass it by TBS.'

Scarr would probably be doing it already: he'd have sent the initial report up to the bridge while he got on with it. Although Graves should have it on his own screen by now: he was closer to it than *Harbinger* was. But RDF as well as asdic performances were erratic in bad weather. Nick had his glasses up, looking for a sight of *Paeony* somewhere ahead: and TBS was calling, Gannet informing Eagle that she'd lost her contact. Then, *Captain to captain, please?*

'Bring her to oh-three-oh, cox'n.'

Convoy course – until he'd drawn clear of the *Tolworth*

Tide, to be able to cross ahead of her. He took the microphone from Bearcroft: 'Everard here. What's the problem?'

Just for the record, sir, the one I just lost would seem to be a deep-diver. Went straight down and out of my beam at a range when I should have held him. Over.

'Could be so. We thought we had one a few days ago.' Or more. Time ran into itself: two days, seven, ten . . . 'I was coming to join you, but I've a contact now on oh-four-oh, seven miles. I'll be passing between you and the convoy. Out.'

Whether it was one of the Germans' new deep-diving boats or not, Guyatt would try to sit on top of it long enough for the convoy to pass clear. But with so few escorts that even this small group of attackers outnumbered them, no rational system of defence was really viable. All you could do was keep at them, attack wherever one showed up.

'Course oh-three-oh, sir!'

The *Tolworth Tide* was abeam: a long, low shape wreathed in white, kingposts like topped tree trunks black against the moon. Half a mile beyond her, moonlight permitted a glimpse of the *Coriolanus* leading column two . . . Bearcroft in contact with *Astilbe,* tipping Graves off about that 271 report: but Graves's telegraphist came back smartly with a report of their own – they had that one on their screen and were chasing after it, but another as well, broader to starboard.

Making three in all. You had to keep the picture in mind and constantly updated, the whole moving scene as the convoy ploughed steadily onward and the enemy's position shifted in relation to it. It was a picture that so far was incomplete, although it did look as if they were moving in now. They *might* have held off tonight, waited until there were nine of them instead of four, but SL 320 was emerging from the Azores air gap and the Germans would have this very much in mind. They weren't to know that with the 'Torch' convoys to protect and then invasion beachheads to cover the RAF and Fleet Air Arm were going to be stretched to their limits, so that air patrols out here weren't necessarily to be counted on . . . *Harbinger* crashed explosively into a trough, whitened sea leaping to enfold her, swamping her before she recovered, got her snout up and began to climb the oncoming slope, its crest an uneven, toppling horizon with moon-washed cloud behind it. Survival was the objective now: the 'Torch' commitment would soon have been completed. He'd kept the U-boats either close to him or ahead – spreading, scouting to pick him up again – and only the last of the assault convoys had yet to slip by astern. The first would have been passing through the Straits of Gibraltar just after sunset this evening: tonight and tomorrow night there'd be a stream of them sliding past the Rock, with darkness hiding them from Spanish and other eyes.

'Starboard ten. Steer oh-four-oh.' To cut across, now. He straightened from the voice-pipe. 'Range and bearing of that contact?'

Depthcharges rumbled. From *Paeony*'s direction, and not far off. Perhaps the alleged deep-diver had been less deep than Guyatt's A/S man had thought.

'Oh-four-seven, five point two miles, sir!'

'Steer oh-five-oh.'

Starshell: on about that same bearing. And TBS calling: Fox – *Astilbe* – was reporting *U-boat on surface, engaging* . . .

'Starboard ten. Steer oh-eight-oh.' Because Graves had said he had another contact, out somewhere in that direction. Graves was attacking the one in the centre because it happened to be the one in his sights . . . 'Tell RDF to sweep from about oh-five-oh to oh-nine-oh.' Guyatt was still in contact with *his* German – a fresh outbreak of depthcharging had just confirmed it – and *Astilbe* had this other one while *Harbinger* headed eastward to hunt a third. It left one card still wild. The fourth might be slinking in at this moment, unmarked, nothing between it and the slow-moving merchantmen, nothing to prevent it slipping in between the columns and getting at the *Burbridge* or the oiler, or both . . . Nothing down there except *Stella*: and Broad could only be in one place at a time, didn't have the speed to transfer quickly to meet a new threat developing elsewhere, didn't have RDF or even an asdic set he could rely on.

There wasn't anything you could do: except make do with what you had, and hope for some lucky breaks. This wasn't a real defence, it was a token one.

Timberlake asked Chubb, over the depthcharge telephone, 'Tell us what's 'appening, Chubby lad?'

Chubb hesitated: he loathed that form of address, which was why the gunner used it. Then he decided to ignore it: he said quietly, with one hand cupping the 'phone against his mouth, 'Chasing a two-seven-one contact. *Paeony*'s bollocking one, and *Astilbe*'s got another on the surface, and – there, gunfire . . . See it? See that starshell?'

'Well, I'm not bloody well blind, boy!'

'Pete's sake, you *asked* me, you quarrelsome old turd!'

He'd told Timberlake earlier this evening, 'I got myself a Sheila. Would you believe it?'

'Not in a thousand years!'

'Gospel truth. In the *Burbridge*. In the first dog we were up close – doing the old social round, you know – and what d'you think? Well, I'll tell you – she blew me a kiss! Tall number, very sexy-looking . . .'

'Carrying a white stick, was she?'

'What's that?'

'She'd 'ave to be blind, wouldn't she?'

'You're jealous. Because you're past it, eh?'

'And you can kiss me arse.'

'Ah, well now, I don't like to offend old men, Guns, but I have to admit I'd as soon not even *look* at it.'

He asked Timberlake now – still smarting from being called 'Chubby lad' – over the depthcharge link as *Harbinger* plunged eastward across the convoy's van, 'Cold, is it?'

'*Bloody* cold.'

'You want to wrap it in a sock, then. Or keep it in your hand.'

He chuckled as he put the 'phone back on its hook. Definitely one up . . . Carlish yelling, 'Surface contact oh-seven-one, three point seven miles, sir!'

Another version – range and bearing from a different position – was coming in from *Astilbe*. There'd been more gunfire on the beam, and more depthcharges on the quarter. A starshell from *Astilbe* broke high to port.

'Starshell stand by!'

Warrimer reported, 'All guns ready, sir, B with starshell, A and X with SAP.'

'Contact lost, sir!'

Meaning it had dived. Hopes nose-diving with it. The German had most likely been alarmed by that starshell from *Astilbe*, which had been intended to illuminate the other one.

'Steer oh-seven-three.' The skipper called, 'One full pattern Sub, hundred-foot settings, stand by!'

Chubb busy now: Timberlake too, back aft, preparing for another blind attack, a frightener more than much chance of doing any damage. All you could do was blast a section of ocean and pray the German might be in it. But there was still a fourth U-boat – somewhere . . .

U 702 had been forced to dive, by the corvette on this bow of the convoy. Looff had taken his boat down to 175 metres, and started his stopwatch in order to time a slow paddle under the convoy, allowing those juicy targets to chug over the top of him while he pottered gently southward. He didn't object to having been put down: if anything he was pleased to have pinpointed the position of one corvette. You could guess the other would be at the same distance out to starboard, and the destroyer fussing around between them: it gave him the pattern, the escort commander's best answer to the insoluble problems he was facing. You could be almost sorry for him: whatever happened tonight, tomorrow would see an end to it.

The sound of screws in that easterly direction was confused, and covered further by rough conditions, but the general picture was clear enough. He wasn't sure where the trawler was, but he guessed somewhere astern. The whole thing was a gift, now: he'd assured FO U-boats, in reply to a terse signal from Kernéval, that annihilation or near-annihilation of this convoy was guaranteed.

The deep-dive capability was a blessing – in terms of tactics, but also to Max Looff personally. It had virtually solved his personal problem, all by itself. He could thank his stars – thank Admiral Dönitz and Flotilla, anyway – for having deprived him of that Berlin leave in order to shift him to this boat. All right, so the effects lingered, he could still wake shaking and sweating, close to screaming, but then he'd remember this – like reaching to some magic touchstone – and his nerves would steady.

Steady as rock now. And he'd planned this dip under the convoy. He'd have run through on the surface if he'd met no opposition, but this was the alternative he'd had in mind: to duck down, swim under, then surface and attack from astern. He grinned at Franz Walther, his scruffy-looking engineer, and promised him, 'We'll have that liner now. And/or the tanker. Tonight, I'll settle for either or both.'

'Tanker would be the most useful, tactically?'

'Escort's lost contact, sir!'

He nodded complacently. It was no surprise to him that *Drachen* One had dived through and out of the scope of the corvette's asdic beam. It was the beauty of the deep-dive trick. Seen as a diagram in profile, an asdic beam was more or less elliptical; as an escort approached its target, the submarine even at shallow depths was lost to it as it passed out through the sloping near-edge of the beam. This was why an escort making an attack always lost contact shortly before it was in a position to drop charges, and the short interval gave the submarine time to take evasive action in that last minute; it was also why A/S vessels tended to hunt in pairs, so that one ship could hold the contact while the other attacked. But at this depth, to maintain contact the hunting ship would have to stay back at a considerable distance – where it didn't have a hope of doing you any damage: and on top of this, you were actually below the effective range of their depthcharges!

Looff checked the stopwatch time. It was going to take a while . . .

Depthcharges thundered. The explosions were above

them, and out to port. The boat had quivered: the charges had been close enough for her to feel their shock-waves, but not nearly close enough to hurt.

'Chancing his arm.' Looff shrugged. '*And* wasting his depth bombs.' He looked up, and called, 'Come on, my little dears, waste some more!'

Smiles, here and there around the control room. This was the Max Looff they admired, the ace they boasted about to their girls!

The hydrophone operator jerked his head up. Staring at Looff, from his little cabinet. Opening his mouth . . .

More depthcharges: eight – nine – ten . . . The operator looked down, frowning. Having said nothing at all, just shut his mouth again. Reverberations dwindling . . . Heusinger murmured, 'Only about a mile off-target. Silly bastard!'

A nod or two: a chuckle from the coxswain. Looff was puzzled, though, at the continuing waste of depthcharges. He knew they'd be getting short of them by this time. He noticed that the hydrophone operator had finally decided he *did* have something to say . . .

'Escort's in contact, sir!'

Looff continued staring at him. Other faces, too, registered surprise and doubt. 'How in hell can—'

'Not with us, sir. One of the others, it's got on to.'

Walther, busy with the trim, muttered 'Well, *well* . . .' Heusinger sucked in a noisy breath. Looff said, 'Must be Pöhl. Ernst Pöhl, for God's sake, taking the heat off me!'

Not that there'd been any heat. With this darling of a boat, the real heat might be a thing of the past. But there might be some coming to Pöhl, he guessed. Heat like – *that* . . . Another pattern of charges blasting off. Knowing what it was like to be in the middle of a battering of that kind, nobody here envied Pöhl or his crew. Looff was checking his watch again, thinking the convoy should be audible pretty soon. The operator exclaimed sharply, 'Sir – would you – listen?'

He went over, grabbed the spare headset. Puzzled: then

grimacing, and eyebrows lifting in surprise . . . 'What the hell is it?'

'Well – one of our's, sir. Whichever's getting clobbered.'

Drachen Six?

Pulling the headphones off, he remembered that *Drachen* Six had been hit by a shell from a trawler about a week ago, and how lucky Pöhl had been to have survived it with only exterior damage of a completely unimportant kind. It might be that the damaged after casing had been further loosened by depth charges, those first ones; but whatever the cause of it was, Pöhl's boat was making a noise like a brass band now. You'd hear it a mile off!

It wasn't a bit funny, either. That corvette could hardly lose him, now.

Go to his assistance? Attack the corvette while it was concentrating on him?

Looff held on. More depthcharges booming: and Pöhl was in for a pasting, obviously. But when you'd made a plan and embarked on it, it was best to stick to it. The hydrophone operator confirmed him in this decision – pointing upwards, announcing, 'Convoy, sir . . .'

Guyatt had reported over TBS, *I think I've hurt him, sir. Could be a propeller blade.*

That wasn't likely. If it had been a blade he'd have stopped using that screw. Of course, it could be that *both* had been damaged – screws, or the shafts bent. It was that kind of racket, and it had to be something the German couldn't stop, or something external he couldn't get at. It would be an agonising experience, to know about it, just have to grin and bear it . . .

But these characters deserved a few agonising experiences.

Nick told Guyatt to stay with his target, finish him. The U-boat was running westward on a dead-straight course, and the only uncertain factor was its depth.

'Chief – call Gannet again, say, "I suggest you try three hundred foot settings".'

Because wounded and running, the German would be likely to have gone deep. And Guyatt had it in contact at normal asdic ranges, so this was *not* a deep-dive merchant. He decided he'd give Guyatt his head, for the time being: if there was a good change of reducing the U-boat force by one, it was a chance worth taking.

Astilbe and *Harbinger* had both lost their contacts. Nick had told Graves to cover the convoy's whole front while he took *Harbinger* round to the starboard side. It was more hunch than science, but it fitted the pattern indicated by those three U-boats' original dispositions – right, left and centre. And Germans were reputed to have orderly minds.

Number four, then – astern?

Harbinger's course was 180 now, with 180 revs on as well, to give her fifteen knots. Asdics pinging, like a blind man's stick poking into darkness. On the bow, in faint moonlight, he could just make out the *Dongola*, leader of column five, smashing black sea into white emulsion with her high, sheer stem. He knew all these ships pretty well, by this time.

'Surface contact ahead, four-one-five-oh yards!'

He'd ducked to the pipe: 'Four hundred revolutions!' Then over his shoulder to Warrimer, 'Starshell stand by!'

Asdics were out of it now, as speed increased. And this contact just might be *Stella*, swanning out on her own. Although Broad oughtn't to be that far out . . . Nick decided, no, he wouldn't.

'Range four thousand, sir, bearing right ahead still!'

Harbinger was getting into her stride, and the motion was easier on this course. She was still making hard work of it and digging up a lot of ocean, but her lunges were longer and more regular; the guns' crews would have an easier time of it, if they got to grips with this one.

'Range three thousand, seven hundred, bearing one-seven-seven, sir!'

'Steer one-seven-five!'

Every second counted: because if this was a U-boat and not the trawler, it would be in a position to fire – now – with the whole flank of the convoy open to it, unless Broad's trawler was there as well, and she might be . . . But he couldn't risk waiting any longer. 'Starshell, fire!'

B gun crashed. In the echo of its noise Warrimer passed the order to reload with semi-armour-piercing . . . 'Range oh-three-five, target right ahead . . .' The starshell ignited, light spreading in concentric halos from the ragged underside of wind-driven cloud. Bearcroft howled, 'U-boat dead ahead, sir!'

'Target in sight! Open fire when you bear!'

Nick had it in his glasses: and it was turning away. It had been in profile, moving in towards the convoy's side, but now it was turning away to port. Half-lost in foam: at moments, completely hidden . . . The light was drifting down this side of it: and he thought the German was diving. One gun down for'ard had fired – B, the greater height of eye from that raised gundeck giving it an advantage over A gun – but it *was* diving, it was already half under, only the upper part of its tower visible: the sea closed over, piling, just as from the side of the convoy they all heard the harsh explosion of a torpedo. *Harbinger*, bow-down, sea sheeting up all round – and a second torpedo-hit . . . In the nearer column, he thought, with a flood of that sickening sense of impotence that had become familiar lately . . . As she climbed again, her motion more violent now because of the higher speed, he tried to see which ship had been hit: guessing the U-boat would have been firing as it swung, spreading a salvo across the convoy's flank when he'd actually had his glasses on it . . . Another thought was that it couldn't have been the *Burbridge*, not from that angle.

Looff was dieseling up into the rear rank of the convoy, nosing U 702 in between the tail-ends of columns three and four. He'd surfaced her a few minutes ago, having turned her already on to the convoy's course; then he'd searched for and spotted the trawler – roughly a mile away, close to the convoy's port quarter, nicely removed and ignorable. So he'd accounted for all the escorts well enough, and he had his submarine trimmed right down, as near invisible as she could have been. His intention was to pass right up between these columns, and there was no reason why it shouldn't come off. It was a tactic he'd employed successfully before – as indeed had other men before him. He wanted the oiler or the passenger ship. From the point of view of doing maximum damage to the convoy the oiler would take priority as a target, since you'd be depriving the escorts of their fuel supply; but the liner had a strong appeal for him, too. For one thing, it was the biggest ship in the whole assembly, and for another – well, there'd be value in destroying such a target.

'Steady as you go . . .'

One freighter to port, one to starboard. U 702 making only a couple of knots more than they were. This lively sea was ideal cover, but he was still being careful to make himself as inconspicuous as possible.

'All right as you see it, Oelricher?'

'Looks very good so far, sir . . .'

They'd both kept their voices low. As if thinking they might be heard in those dark, plunging hulks across a few hundred yards of wild sea. Feeling like wolves slinking into a sheep-run.

Then – torpedo-hit . . .

Ahead, and somewhere to starboard. And a second. Looff's brain registered that it would be Otto Meusel's work. *Drachen* Nine: one of the pair from the Brest flotilla. Also – although in the first seconds it wasn't obvious that this was going to wreck his own plans completely – that it couldn't have been worse timed, from his own point of view. White rockets scorched skyward, curving on the wind, away to starboard. Then Oelricher yelled, flinging an arm out to point that way, 'This one's turning!'

Snowflakes burst overhead, light-streams showering, another pair of rockets hissing up through the silver radiance. Night becoming day, and the freighter to starboard turning, its high, gaunt foc'sl looming against firework-bright cloud as it bore round. Looff had to act fast, or be trapped or run-down; certainly at any minute spotted. He shouted – whispering-time was over now – 'Full ahead! Port fifteen!' U 702 crashing and hammering through the waves, smothered in her own blanket of foam. The one that was bearing down from starboard was turning to stay clear of her next-ahead, he realised, that one being Meusel's victim. U 702 clear for anyone to see now, as brightly illuminated as all the ships hemming her in. There was no room or time to dive: a glance was enough to tell him he'd be rammed in the attempt. He shouted, '*Hard* a-port!'

Increasing wheel to turn her between the ship that was now abaft his beam – he'd cross this one's bow, in fact – and the one ahead of her. He didn't know it, but they were the *Cimba* and the *Archie Dukes*. The torpedoed ship had swung to port as well, broaching to the wind as she slowed, slumping in the sea, others crowding on around her and this side of the convoy already well disrupted. U 702 boring through the waves: trimmed down like this she was *in* them, with only her bridge any higher than their flying tops. Speed now about fifteen knots and mounting. As she battered her way round through sea already churned by others Looff saw a flash from the stern of the freighter ahead, then heard the *crack* of it and the rush of a shell passing close: he saw what looked like dancing cut-out figures cavorting around that gun on the stern platform, under the snowflakes' glare. U 702 was driving clear, thank God, of the *Cimba*'s threatening stem . . . He called, 'Midships!', and another shell scrunched over – the third, and close enough to hear it: but with his stern pointing that way he was presenting those Merchant Navy gunners with an exceptionally small target: if they hit him it would be sheer luck – sheer *foul* luck . . . And his stern pointing that way, into the centre of the crowd of ships, meant something else as well – he had a stern tube with a torpedo in it. He shouted, 'Stand by number five tube!'

Steadying her on about 210 degrees. Flat-out, sea drenching over solidly. No time to bother about a point-of-aim, a browning shot into the middle would hit *some* damn thing, and with luck and the help of Providence might, just *might*, hit one of the marks he'd been after anyway . . . Checking points rapidly in his mind: such as the depth setting on that fish being for sixteen feet – adequate for any of these middling sized ships or the tanker or the passenger-ship – who'd both be in line for it, all right, would at least have a ticket in the sweepstake so to speak . . . Another snowflake burst, showering white brilliance outside the tent-like cocoon of foam; Heusinger screamed from inside the tower, 'Number five tube ready!'

Glancing astern: seeing the orange-yellow flash of that gun taking another swipe at him. Ships widely scattered as they drew away, leaving two behind them, one still struggling to keep going but the other half over on her side, boats dangling and one up-ended, spotlighted, people falling out of it. A shell spout rose like a marble pillar in the snowflakes' glare: it must have come from some new assailant, because the one who'd been shooting before had been blanked off by others. He ordered, 'Fire five!', then pushed Oelricher towards the hatch. 'Dive, dive . . .'

As he got off the ladder in the control room she was already at forty metres and going on down steeply. Faces of men at their jobs around the compartment showed alarm and a lot of questions. Half a minute passed before at any rate *one* of the questions was answered – by the crash of that torpedo finding a target. *Some* target . . . Around Looff, his crewmen cheered. In his memory like a blurred photograph was a pile of foam out to starboard, a gun's flash miniaturised by distance and flying spray, and a starshell bursting overhead. It was the last thing he'd seen as he'd thrown himself into the hatch, part of a blurr of movement, noise, the desperate importance of getting under *fast*: and it could only have been that trawler pounding back eastward at its flat-out speed of next-to-nothing . . . The torpedo-hit was a dying echo in his brain: it melted into the sound of his own voice telling Franz Walther, 'One hundred metres.'

Willi Heusinger suggested, smirking at him, 'Your liner, sir, perhaps?'

Grins all round, as they waited for his answer. A minute

ago, they'd been scared enough to wet themselves. Looff, seeing clearly through the façades because he'd lived behind his own for a long time now, was contemptuous of them all, except for Walther. He and that evil-smelling, tramp-like object were the adults here, in a crowd of kids. He told the helmsman, 'Port twenty. Come round to oh-three-oh.' The night's action didn't have to be over yet.

In the middle of that mess of action Nick had been on the point of telling *Paeony* to discontinue her persecution of the noisy U-boat and rejoin, when Guyatt had piped up and reported, *Target believed destroyed. Resuming station.* So that at least was satisfactory: that *alone*, rather. He'd left *Stella* to organise rescue operations astern; he and Tony Graves had their hands full with the dual tasks of screening the convoy against further attacks while also bullying surviving ships back into columns and urging those in column to close up into newly-created gaps. Some had strayed outwards, and had to be shepherded back into the herd: and all the time, every minute, you were clenching your mind against the shock of the next explosion.

It felt very much like disaster. Four U-boats only – in fact three – creating this much havoc, with another five about to join the pack?

The last casualty had been the commodore's ship, the *Chauncy Maples*. She'd been holed right aft, and had her rudder and screw blown off at the same time. Her number six hold was filling and her engine room was flooding through the shaft tunnel. She'd dropped a long way astern by this time, immobilised and doomed even though she might float for an hour or two yet. Her crew were abandoning her, and the *Mount Trembling* was standing by to receive them, having already embarked the *Primrose Bank*'s. She and the *Asswan* had been hit in that salvo fired from the convoy's starboard side. The *Asswan* had been in column six, the *Primrose Bank* in number five; there'd been another U-boat inside the columns at that time, according to ships who'd seen it and particularly the *Archie Dukes* who'd loosed-off half a dozen rounds of four-inch at it, and the *Cimba* who'd been hit on the foc'sl by one of them when she'd been close to the line of fire.

Commodore Sandover was all right; he was on board the trawler. The vice-commodore, the master of the *Dongola*, had taken over the running of the convoy, and had moved over to the centre, ahead of the *Burbridge*. The *Asswan*, hit at the same time as the *Primrose Bank*, had kept going and tried to maintain her station, but she was falling back now and had just signalled that the bulkhead between numbers one and two holds was in danger of collapsing.

Guyatt had amplified his report on the destruction of that U-boat. It had been damaged by his first few patterns, which had slowed it and also produced sounds of pumping and blowing tanks. He'd had no difficulty maintaining contact with it, because of its high level of underwater noise, but after his final attack all sounds had increased abruptly. His asdic operator was certain the last pattern had put paid to it.

So you could reckon there'd be eight of them, by this evening.

At down, as the remnants of SL 320 forged northeastward with an orange glow flushing the sky on the bow, *Harbinger* was out on the port wing, *Astilbe* three miles to starboard of her, both zigzagging and searching with asdics and 271s, while astern *Paeony* and *Stella* escorted the *Mount Trembling* and her load of survivors up the convoy's wake, overhauling at a rate of about three knots. The *Chauncy Maples* had sunk and the *Asswan*, who'd been taking her time about it, had been sent on her way with a few shots into the waterline from *Paeony*'s four-inch. It would be mid-forenoon before the group astern could rejoin and then distribute survivors into ships that had room for them. The sea had gone down quite a lot during the night: wind was now about force four, stars were visible through patchy cloud and Mike Scarr was standing ready with his sextant, gazing up while he decided which stars he'd use and waiting for the horizon to harden.

Nick had sent *Paeony* to do the job astern because with her defective RDF she was less use than either *Harbinger* or *Astilbe* in the van.

Warrimer said, 'Be out of the air gap by this time, I'd guess.' He yawned, and asked Scarr, 'Aren't we?'

Scarr was still sorting out heavenly bodies. 'Just about.' He corrected: 'Yes – *well* out.'

Chubb observed, with surprising percipience and without lowering his binoculars, 'An air gap is where there are no patrolling aircraft. *If* we get some air cover today, we're out of it; if we don't, I'd say we bloody aren't.'

'We have a sage among us.' Scarr lifted his sextant. 'Rough-hewn though he may be.'

Nick thinking that Chubb had hit the nail right on the head, despite his ignorance of the circumstances. He was hunched on his high seat, with his glasses up – as always – part-hearing some of the sporadic mutters of conversation behind him. Another half-dozen pairs of glasses were searching the white-streaked seascape just as intently, and the 271 was circling, asdics singing their dismally monotonous note into the depths of green ocean. *Harbinger* zigzagging irregularly – at action stations, her guns manned and loaded while the light of a new day, Friday 6 November, spread its streaks of brilliance from the east.

All the assault convoys would have crossed astern by now. The Casablanca force, direct from US ports, would have swung eastwards around Madeira during the night just passed. Other sections of the great armada would have been progressing in silence and darkness into the Mediterranean: the last of them would be filing through the Straits tonight.

Scarr, behind him in the bridge, called down to his timekeeper in the plot to stand by. Carlish ordered starboard wheel, keeping her under almost constant helm, which was about the best way to be safe. Carlish had grown up a lot during this trip: you could consider him a watchkeeper now. Nick decided that when it was daylight and they fell out from dawn action stations he'd take *Harbinger* back for a chat with the vice-commodore, in the *Dongola*.

The seventeen surviving ships would have to be re-formed now, with the *Burbridge* and the *Redgulf Star* enfolded in a reduced rectangle. When that had been accomplished, *Harbinger* and *Astilbe* could top up their fuel tanks: and *Paeony* later, when she rejoined. Also, *Harbinger*'s RDF mechanic, who was still on board *Astilbe*, might usefully be transferred to *Paeony*.

He jerked forward on his seat, jarring the binoculars against his eyes. Torpedo hit – astern . . .

'It's the *Tolworth Tide*, sir!'

Chubb's raucous yell . . .

Leader of column one. Chubb must have had his glasses on her at that moment and seen it. Unless you'd had glasses on her, in this half-light you couldn't have. But he took Chubb's word for it: 'Hard a-port, full ahead together!' Displacing Carlish at the binnacle, getting close-up impressions as he moved there of shocked expressions in tired, stubbled faces in the greying light. Distress rockets soaring now – from the *Tolworth Tide* as she swung outwards from her column. The shock was worse for the fact they'd begun to ease off, believe the hours of respite were coming now as they routinely did with daylight . . . Warrimer was passing orders to the sightsetters at the guns, waking them all up in case they needed it, and Chubb was talking to Mr Timberlake back aft. Scarr, forgetting stars, had disappeared down to his plot. *Harbinger* heeling to her rudder, engine-room telegraphs clanging through the voice-pipe and CPO Elphick droning in that flat tone of his, 'Twenty-five of port wheel on, sir . . .'

Sixteen ships left, now.

She'd left him one half-slice of bread.

Jack stood in the kitchen, staring down at it. She was out, as was usual at this time of day, and the child had gone off to school earlier. Jack had just hobbled downstairs, deciding on his way that an idea he'd had of moving on today wasn't so hot, that the ankle hadn't yet recovered to the extent he'd hoped. He'd wanted to get away, though, because of yesterday's strange events – the food she'd left, and her peal of laughter when she'd come back and seen how much – or how little – he'd taken. The next thing might be the arrival of that Wehrmacht circus, or police. But he couldn't leave, not yet. There was some reassurance, also, in the fact that last evening at her egg-collecting time he'd seen her checking the outside of the house, each window in turn. He'd only seen her at two of the front ones, but she'd obviously been going all round, window to window, checking on whether or not they'd been opened and also examining the ground below them – for spoor, of course. She must have thought an intruder had been getting in that way to steal her food: so if she did report it to the authorities they'd be looking for someone hiding in the woods, not up here.

The half-slice of bread was the same size as the piece he'd taken yesterday. As if she was teasing him, saying, *If this is as much as you can manage – here . . .*

Damn her!

She had a dirty face, anyway. Either dirty or sunburnt – which seemed hardly likely in Germany at this time of year. He'd noticed it yesterday when she'd been at the window right below him.

He could have wolfed up all that sausage, and the bread-slice with it, in about two gulps. He could feel his own thinness as well as hunger. In recent days the secret had been not to think about it, to turn the mind to other things – like the Swiss border, London, Fiona, poor old Frank Trolley. He'd have to see Trolley's people, when he got back . . . Anyway – he was on his way to get eggs now, with a call as usual at the outside heads, and then he'd come back in here and boil them, same as yesterday. He had two hard-boiled ones left from yesterday, which he'd eat when he got back upstairs, and some of today's would be kept for tomorrow. If one always provided for one day ahead, a Sunday when it came wouldn't be quite as agonising.

He wasn't going to touch that slice of bread. The hell with her little jokes . . . Some sausage, though – why not? She might not notice, if he only took a little . . . Thinking about it while he was outside made his mouth water; he found he was actually dribbling while he scrabbled around for eggs. He got four, and came back inside – through the window of her room and making sure of leaving no traces inside or out. He was also careful to bolt the shutters again on the inside. He'd put the saucepan on, like yesterday, so the water was already heating.

You fell into a routine, he thought. However bizarre the circumstances, you adapted to them and the days soon acquired a pattern. In this case, of course, it was a matter of fitting in with *her* routine . . . Waiting for the water to boil, he cut off some sausage and ate it, afterwards dipping the knife-blade in the hot water and wiping it dry before replacing it in exactly its former position. Feeling strangely and annoyingly like a trained ape, a creature imitating human ways . . . The water was steaming by this time, but not yet boiling. He looked at the sausage, wondering whether he could safely take another slice. And since it amused her and she thought the thief was outside there somewhere . . . why *not* eat the bread?

Because – anger stirred in him as he thought about it – it would feel like being made to jump through hoops.

He was staring into the saucepan, willing it to start bubbling, when he heard the clink of her keys on the other side of the back door.

He ran – limping, and dizzy with the shock of it – to the stairs and over the stack of junk, then up to the landing and to his room. As he shut its door – too noisily – he heard the downstairs one slam.

Then silence.

He'd left four eggs in her saucepan. By now the water would be starting to boil. He thought – panting, still shaken by the sudden fright and the rush upstairs, leaning back against the closed door and feeling the hard banging of his heart – that if he'd had any sense he'd have left those shutters unfastened. Then she could have imagined he'd dived out, got away . . . But he'd never considered the possibility of her creeping back early and trying to catch him. Which she must have done. If he hadn't heard those keys . . .

She might be scared to follow up now, on her own. If she went for the police, it might give him time to scarper. Ankle or no ankle . . . He'd drawn a breath in so hard it had squeaked: he'd heard her coming, up the stairs. Clambering over that clutter now. He tiptoed to his mattress, lay down on it and pulled the strip of carpet right over him.

Not that there could be a hope in hell . . .

She'd gone the other way. But there were only two rooms on that side, and two on this, so the inspection couldn't take very long. He heard doors being pulled open and pushed shut again.

Rush out while she's on that side? Bolt for it down the stairs?

She was crossing the landing. Now, if he made any such move he'd come face to face with her. She might try to stop him, and then anything could happen. He didn't want that: for a number of reasons, one of them being that he'd never used violence against any female, and the idea of having to do so was extremely unattractive to him. This was strange – he hadn't thought about it before, but now he had to – it might have seemed peculiar to some people, in view of the fact that he was really quite a violent character, certainly had been at times . . .

He heard the door open.

She'd be standing there, staring at the mattress with its humped covering. He lay still, on his back, trying not to breathe hard or noisily. Although she could not, possibly, just look at it and not *know*—

She came over, in three quick steps, and jerked the carpet off him. He was staring up into a roundish, swarthy face. Not dirty: just dark-skinned. She had fair hair tied back in the German fashion, but with that dark skin she didn't look German at all. Portuguese, possibly, or—

Dark, slightly slanted eyes.

She looked shocked. He remembered how startled *he'd* been, at first sight of himself in the mirror . . . She'd stepped back, still with her eyes fixed on him. He saw her take a deep breath. Then her hand rose, pointing at him, and she asked a question in German. The raised hand was shaking.

The question might have been something like *Who are you?* Or *What are you?* When he didn't answer, just shook his head, it was followed by a quick, panicky stream of other questions. He guessed at *What are you doing in my house?* or *How did you get in?* and *What do you want here?* Then again, after a pause, the shorter one she'd started with.

He sat up. Moving slowly so as not to frighten her. He put his hands up, token of surrender.

'English.' He lowered his hands, and pointed at himself. 'English prisoner of war. Escaped.' He made a mime of running, with his fingers, then pointed south: 'Switzerland. *Suisse. Schweitzer*, whatever you call it . . . But—' he displayed his ankle, and indicated pain. Then he asked her, *'Politzei?'* He put his wrists together as if in handcuffs, and pointed to her, suggesting her going off to get them. 'Finish. Kaput.' Pointing to himself again. Then 'OK?'

She just stood there, staring at him. He thought she might have got the gist of it, more or less. She seemed less tense now, anyway. Probably getting used to his somewhat outlandish appearance, he thought. He'd be a terrifying thing to find, in one's own house, but after that rather hysterical flood of questions she seemed to have been in good control of herself. He'd been at pains to talk gently, to make her realise he was no danger to her, but it would take a strong nerve, for a girl on her own. He guessed most would have screamed and run for it . . . If she did go now, for the police, he'd leave the house behind her, try to get to where he'd hidden the bike, and hide himself near it ready for a dash southward when it got dark. These ideas were forming in his brain while he waited to see what she was going to do: he was to remember those plans later, and realise he would never have made it. They'd have had road-blocks everywhere, thousands of men between him and the border.

She beckoned to him.

'Kom.'

He stayed where he was, watching her. She made gestures – miming the use of a knife and fork, eating. Then she pointed at him and began a different act – washing, he thought. Shaving? She was chattering in German too – in a low, persuasive tone, as if *she* was trying to convince *him* of something now.

He got to his feet. Leaning with one hand on the shutters, and keeping that foot off the floor. She turned away and walked out of the room, to the head of the stairs, where she stopped and turned to see if he was coming. Seeing that he was, she nodded approvingly and repeated, '*Kommenzie*.' That was what it sounded like. He limped down the stairs behind her, and followed her into the kitchen. She pulled out one of the two chairs at the table, and made him sit down on it. It looked as if she really was about to give him a meal! He felt dizzy. *Being kind*, he thought, *before she turns me in*. He wondered if she'd have been this kind if she'd realised he was quite capable of breaking her neck one-handed. She'd put some large pots of water on the back of the stove. Glancing at him occasionally, bustling round . . . Now she was slicing sausage and also a new loaf of bread: she'd taken it out of the basket. Then she was mushing up the partly cooked eggs which he'd left in the saucepan – she'd have taken it off the boil when she first came in. But all four eggs, with bread and several slivers of the sausage . . . His hunger was so intense that the prospect of a full meal was making him feel weaker than he had before: also he was self-conscious about dribbling and had to keep licking his lips. He mumbled, while she bent over her work at the stove, '*Zehr gut*. Incredible. I mean, you're – *wundebar!*'

It was a word he'd heard. It sounded like a cross between a Mars and a Milky Way, but she seemed to get the message – she glanced round with a half-smile on her face, showing embarrassment and also amusement combined with that secretly-pleased look they always got when you hit the right note with them. But she might still have been scared of him, he suspected: she'd looked round again, as if wondering whether she'd been right about him . . . Her back was to him now. She was widehipped, heavy-thighed: it was the first impression he'd had of her, he remembered, when he'd seen her from that shed. It was odd that he hadn't noticed the dark complexion. A trick of the light, perhaps . . . She turned around, and dumped a loaded plate in front of him.

'Bitte.'

A kind of triumph. Standing back, looking at him expectantly. He smiled, half bowed: she laughed, pointing at the food. He found the word he'd been struggling to think of: *'Dankeschön!'*

He ate ravenously, while she watched. She didn't eat at all, but drank milk, and poured some for him. He toasted her: *'Prosit!'* She giggled. He asked her with his mouth full, *'Deutsch?'* Asking her, was she German? She shrugged – it wasn't exactly a denial but it wasn't affirmation either – and answered with a sentence which he construed as 'My man is German'. But it might have been 'was German'. He asked her, waving an arm around, 'Man here?'

'Nein.' Her face became heavier, older. She was about twenty-eight, he guessed, but for that moment or two she could have been forty. He thought she was going to cry. He would have liked to have asked whether the man was away in the Army, or in prison, or dead, or what . . . That empty photograph frame?

When he'd finished eating she directed him into the room with the washbasin and tub in it, then went back and began bringing the hot water from the stove. He helped with it, although she pointed at his foot and tried to stop him. She emptied most of it into the tub: he was anticipating luxury now of a kind he hadn't dared even to think about. She'd gone off again, in the direction of her bedroom, and eventually returned with a pair of scissors, a cut-throat razor and leather strop, a shaving brush and a bar of yellow kitchen soap. He guessed the implements might be her man's . . . She'd disappeared again, and came back with a bundle of clothes. Trousers, shirt, sweater with holes in it, felt slippers. The trousers were black and shiny from age, and the grey shirt was long enough to be a night-shirt. In fact it could have been . . . She pointed at his own clothes and at the washtub, then made motions of washing and wringing-out, indicating that she meant she'd do it for him: she asked him, 'OK?'

He nodded, staring into her eyes. She was close enough to touch, and if he hadn't known he stank he'd have kissed her. How this was happening, who she was or rather what her story was, *why* she was doing this . . .

She left him, and shut the door.

He thought – stripping, bathing, then trimming his beard but not shaving – that she could only be acting out of sheer kindness, perhaps the heightened degree of kindness of one who has some great sadness, suffering or anxiety of her own. And one should not expect too much: he had to accept, he knew, that afterwards she'd have no option, she'd have to turn him in. He'd make no problems for her: he liked her, and saw courage as well as kindness in what she was doing for him. He was in a state, he also realised – making use of this time to assess his position and hers and the way to handle it – a state of physical and mental imbalance – vulnerability might be a better word for it – and all emotions had to be closer than usual to the surface. When she'd been close to tears, back there in the kitchen, he'd felt like putting his arms round her, weeping with her – for her, for himself, for the sheer helplessness of the entire human race. And then the sudden urge to kiss her . . .

Well. She could go and fetch the military, if she wanted. He'd wait, be here when she came back with them. At least, he *thought* he would . . . Except they could hardly blame her if he took off: and having come this far, had this much luck – in contrast to the lousy deal poor old Frank had had – wouldn't it be *mad* to give up now, if there was still a chance?

He found her in the kitchen, at the table, slicing carrots into a casserole. She looked him up and down: said something in German with a laugh in it, something that might not have been far from, 'That's a hell of a lot better!'

He wasn't smelly any more, and his beard was trimmed. He stooped, and kissed her cheek.

'Danke schön. I don't know how to thank you. You're marvellous.' She sat still, with her dark eyes on his, knife in one hand and carrot in the other. He asked her, 'Now—' pointing – *'Polizei? Soldaten?'*

Chapter 14

6 November 1942: General Alexander to Prime Minister:
Ring out the bells! Prisoners now estimated 20,000, tanks 350, guns 400, MT several thousand. Our advanced mobile forces are south of Mersa Matruh. Eighth Army is advancing.

It was about an hour short of dusk. HF/DF had been eavesdropping on the chatter of six or seven U-boats ahead of the convoy and one back on the quarter, all of them identifiable by PO Telegraphist Archie Gritten as 'old customers'. The enemy ranges and bearings plotted by Mike Scarr showed that the Germans were spread in a shallow arc right across the convoy's front, at ranges varying between twelve and fifteen miles but remaining constant in that bracket. The enemy was keeping his distance and waiting for the night.

As a night, it didn't promise well. *Harbinger*'s condenser leak had worsened, for one thing, and two merchantmen – the *Orangeman* and the *Omeo* – had reported machinery trouble and doubts whether they'd be able to maintain the present speed. Then an hour ago Mr Timberlake had visited the bridge to moan about how few depthcharges he had left. For once the gunner's complaint was justified – even if it hadn't been strictly necessary, since Nick was well aware of the number they'd been using. The battle to defend SL 320 had lasted a lot longer than anyone had foreseen – thanks to speed reductions and diversions – and in their daily-state signals *Paeony* and *Astilbe* had also shown stocks as running very low.

It wouldn't be surprising if tonight all three did run out.

It wouldn't be the first time convoy escorts had been left toothless, either; but with so few escorts to look after sixteen merchantmen – all of them crammed with survivors from the other twenty-one – against a pack of eight U-boats who'd be doing their utmost to finish the job off tonight . . .

Nothing was getting any better.

Except *Paeony*'s 271 was operational again: *one* small mercy, attributable to *Harbinger*'s RDF mechanic, who'd been transferred from *Astilbe*.

In his noon signal Nick had repeated his request for reinforcements. He didn't for a moment believe anything would come of it, particularly at the crucial time for 'Torch'. But you had to try: *and* have that repeated distress call on the record. Sixteen ships left out of the original thirty-six – plus the *Burbridge*, thirty-seven . . . Who'd stand up for an escort commander who'd suffered losses of that size, or admit he'd been given a purposefully inadequate escort force? And ordered – verbally only, no evidence of it – to keep the U-boats with him? Who'd acknowledge – *ever* – that a whole convoy had been laid out as bait?

Not that he'd have sixteen ships tomorrow, anyway. Even though an evasive turn or two would be permissible now – now that all the assault forces would have passed astern, with no U-boats to bother them. The last of them would be inside the Mediterranean by dawn; and tonight the huge American outfit, UGF 1, would be splitting into its separate components aimed at points north and south of Casablanca.

Carlish was OOW, zigzagging *Harbinger* to and fro across the convoy's rear. The trawler, *Stella*, was closer in, and the two corvettes were as usual up ahead. The merchantmen were in four columns of four, and Commodore Sandover was back in the saddle, on board the *Dongola* at the head of column two. The *Burbridge* was astern of him, in position twenty-two, with the *Redgulf Star* abeam of her as always, and the two rescue ships, the *Mount Trembling* and the *Archie Dukes*, at the rear of the two centre columns.

Nick didn't much like this formation. It had been Sandover's decision, of course, and sixteen divided naturally into four columns of four; but he'd have opted for a wider front and less depth.

There'd be no moon tonight, and the weather would make things easier for the U-boats in some ways. Asdics might get more of a look-in, he supposed, but sub-surface conditions would still be unpredictable, after the long period of rough weather.

Warrimer had moved up to stand beside him.

'Splendid news from the desert, sir.'

Nick grunted agreement, continued searching with his glasses.

Rommel was on the run. At least, his German troops were. They'd taken what transport remained, and left six Italian divisions stranded without much food or water or the means to move, just waiting to be rounded up. Rommel's right-hand man, General von Thoma, had put on his best uniform before personally surrendering, and no less than nine Italian generals had turned themselves in.

Carlish was ordering starboard wheel. Nick added, to make up for the grunt, 'Best news for a long time.'

But in a way it made one feel more than ever out on a limb. Here, the main task had been accomplished, but the enemy's had not. Achievement of the convoy's purpose had been paid for very highly, and the U-boats would be exacting further exorbitant fees tonight. Ashore, meanwhile, they'd be thinking of the victory in the east and the imminence of the 'Torch' landings, not of SL 320 . . . He'd swung round, looking for a sight of the *Burbridge* among her lumbering companions. Grey hulls, white wakes, masts swaying against green sea, grey sky . . . He thought perhaps he *could* improve on that formation – if the commodore would consent to it. Also that if those two ships were likely to straggle, it would be better to reduce speed by a knot or two and hold the whole bunch together.

With the *Burbridge* in their centre.

There'd be time – just – to propose it to the commodore and make the changes, if he concurred, before the end of daylight made such manoeuvring too hazardous for the close-packed merchantmen. Glancing round towards Carlish, Nick happened to see Mackenzie, the doctor, coming off the ladder at the rear end of the bridge, coming forward with a sheet of pink signal-pad flapping in one hand. Looking *pleased* about something or other . . . Nick told Carlish, 'Three-six-oh revs, Sub. And come round to—' he pointed – 'there, up between the second and third columns.'

Mackenzie now: and this signal. Pink signal-pads were for cyphers, the secret signals in their various classifications.

'Just decoded this one, sir. It's to us, from—'

'Let me see.'

It was to *Harbinger*, repeated to Admiralty and half a dozen other authorities from C-in-C Western Approaches. The message ran: *Destroyers 'Wesley' and 'Vicious' detached from convoy HGS* 114 will join you at first light tomorrow 7 November in position . . .

He looked up: *Harbinger* heeling to her rudder as Carlish brought her round. Mackenzie looked as pleased with himself as if *he'd* arranged for these reinforcements. Warrimer murmured – to the doctor, as Nick looked down to re-read the signal more carefully after that first quick glance at it – 'Good news, is it?'

'I'd say it's a life-saver.'

Nick was thinking that if those two ships had been joining *now*, there might have been some lives saved. But – dawn tomorrow . . . He handed the flimsy sheet to Warrimer. It was astonishing, completely unexpected, but it was also a day too late. In fact several days too late. But even if he'd had those destroyers with him *now* . . .

Well, he hadn't. Effectively therefore, this didn't change anything that mattered.

'Give it to Scarr. Tell him I want to know how that position matches our dawn DR.' He called over his shoulder, 'Come up to four hundred revs, Sub.'

The plan he was intending to put to the commodore was to dispose the ships in five columns instead of four, but as there were sixteen, not fifteen, to pack six into the rear rank. Thus in ranks one and two there'd be five ships at one thousand yard intervals, and in the third there'd be six, with gaps between them of only eight hundred yards. It would make station-keeping more difficult for those six masters; but it would make infiltration from astern more difficult for the U boats, too. And having only three ships in each column instead of four meant fewer ships on the convoy's sides, which was where casualties tended to be most frequent. The *Burbridge* would be number two in column three, right in the centre, and effectively she'd have two ships astern of her – on her quarters – instead of one.

The house had gone silent, and Jack knew she must have put the child to bed. It was the routine here: the wireless was switched off at this juncture, but he knew she herself didn't turn in right away because on previous nights there'd been an interval of an hour or so before the back door opened and shut – twice, with a space of a few minutes between her exit and re-entry. Each night the last sounds he'd heard had been that door shutting for the second time and then her movement through the kitchen and – he assumed – to her own bedroom.

She hadn't been out yet. He pictured her sewing, or reading. Or washing the clothes he'd discarded. He wanted her to go on out, get the night's outing done with; then he'd know another day was over and it was time to sleep. If you went to sleep too soon, you woke too early. It was extremely boring, just lying here in the silence.

He wondered whether she'd give him a meal again tomorrow. If it wasn't Sunday. He wished he'd thought of asking her: he could have, since he knew that word, *Sonntag*. She'd surely have a calendar or a diary somewhere, and she could show him. Another thing he'd ask her, if she did invite him downstairs tomorrow, was to allow him to listen to her wireless, tune it to the BBC. It would be marvellous to hear what was going on – and in particular, whether anything had come of the offensive in the desert. Barmy Morrison had given them that item of news, having heard it over Hut Four's clandestine set, in the Offlag. Barmy, typically of the idiot he was, had insisted on jabbering about it just when they'd been marching towards the sentry at the camp gate.

That could have happened a year ago, the way it felt now.

He heard the door open: then pulled shut again. He murmured into the dark, 'Late Night Final . . .'

Today, as soon as he'd finished sprucing himself up, she'd made him go back upstairs. He'd wanted to hang around, even take a stroll outside; but she'd insisted, and it was as well she had because the boy had returned soon after. He wondered whether she'd tell the child about him, even send him straight out again with a message to the police. He wouldn't have held it against her if she had: she'd been kind enough already, she was *some* sort of German, and she'd be in grave danger for harbouring him. If he'd seen the boy go out again – it would have been a complete break with their routine – he'd have assumed the worst and tried to make a break for it . . . But nothing had happened. And if she wasn't letting on even to her own child, it could only be that she didn't want the secret to get out – which would suggest she might be prepared to shelter him until he was fit to leave. He'd come to these conclusions, and then her behaviour later had seemed to confirm them – at the end of the afternoon, when she'd gone out for the evening egg-collection, she'd paused near the corner of the chicken house, stared straight at this window and fluttered one hand in a wave.

The back door opened again, and banged shut. He heard the bolt slide over. Then as usual her rather heavy footfalls through the kitchen and into the corridor on that side of the house. A moment later, and quite clear in the surrounding silence, her bedroom door clicked shut.

Beddiebyes . . .

I am out of humanity's reach,
I must finish my journey alone,
Never hear the sweet music of speech;
I start at the sound of my own.

He said aloud, 'And balls to you, Cowper.'

Nodding, thinking, *There's* sweet music for you . . .

He hated those verses. The triteness of the little jingling stanzas had annoyed him even at Dartmouth. He'd only picked on the wretched thing, he guessed, because with its short lines it had been an easy one to commit to memory.

He thought she *would* make him a meal tomorrow. She wasn't likely to leave him to go hungry, having fed him once and provided the other comforts. Unless it did turn out to be a Sunday, and the kid stayed at home . . . Even then, she might sneak up with something: or send the little bastard out on some errand, so he could go down for a little while. He wasn't too keen on the child: perhaps because of that shrilled *'Heil Hitler!'* Its mother was something else entirely: the way she'd waved to him had impressed him as much as anything she'd done for him earlier – suggesting complicity, mutual involvement.

A sound. From the stairs?

Lying quiet and tense, on his back, straining his ears into the dark void of the house . . .

It had its own sounds, but he knew them. That one had been different. Unless he'd imagined . . .

A board creaking on the landing.

The child. Prospecting. Suspecting: and having waited until its mother was asleep . . .

He heard the door-handle turn. Then the faint creak of the door opening, and a soft, slithering noise. The door shut again, very slowly and quietly.

He smelt woman. Powder, eau-de-Cologne, and – *woman*. He was up on his elbows when her hand came groping, touching his head and then his face, the fringe of beard. She whispered something that was totally incomprehensible to him: then she was getting down beside him on the mattress, under the smelly carpet. His hands encountered some kind of woollen garment, but it came loose in folds then flew away: an arm's softness, a shoulder, a heavy breast . . . He'd turned in dressed for warmth, and his astonishment was mingled with embarrassment at having clothes on; but she was helping, while at the same time her mouth was on his and for a moment, still stunned, he had an impression that she was trying to inflate him. But it was a shushing, an instruction to be quiet. Hardly essential: even in the first seconds of alarm he hadn't considered shouting for help, and although in one spasm of it he'd wondered whether he'd have the strength, after days of privation, something was telling him now very plainly indeed that he undoubtedly *did* have – although he was finding it difficult to breathe and thinking that if this was all she'd had in mind she might have obtained it much less dangerously from the soldiery who'd come visiting. But his mind was steadying, and evolving two much less offensive and probably truer theories: first, that this was in such secrecy and privacy that knowledge of it would be only her own and his, the outside world as shut out of it as if it had been a dream; second, that perhaps she, like him, was in some kind of danger – she was certainly lonely and lived in peculiar isolation – and empathy in their matching predicaments might in her woman's heart foster a kind of love?

U 702 lay trimmed down so low that the Brits' RDF would have a target not much bigger than a bathtub to pick up. Looff was using his motors, not the diesels, with revs for about two knots, only about enough to give her steerageway. He was letting the convoy come to him, sitting waiting for it, but if by ill-chance an escort stumbled on him he could dive her so fast they wouldn't believe he'd been here. Down – then up again – and *whumpf* . . .

Drachens Three, Eight, Nine and Ten had attacked an hour ago – with some successes, of which Looff had no detail yet – and at the height of it, soon after he'd heard several hits, the convoy had made an emergency turn to port. Looff had been eight miles from it then, with *Drachens* Two, Eleven and Twelve in company, and he'd shifted at high speed to get into position for stage two of the assault. Just as, at this moment, those first four – Messrs Becker, Greissler, Meusel and Ziegner – would be surfaced and travelling north, reloading tubes as necessary *en route,* at full revs and ignoring any temptations to take further nibbles at the convoy. Their object would be to gain bearing on it, putting themselves into an optimum position for stage three, which Looff hoped might be a full pack attack, still well before sunrise. It was a fairly loose plan of action: it had to be, to allow for emergency course alterations by the convoy – this was the main reason for splitting the pack, to cover all eventualities as far as was possible. But if it came off more or less on these lines, he'd be taking advantage of the whole period of darkness and of the weakness of the opposition, making maximum use of his own resources and stretching their very limited ones to breaking point – if they hadn't reached such a point already. It would certainly keep them on the hop all night.

Ulrich Weddigen, *Drachen* Eleven, would be close by, perhaps no more than two thousand metres west of *Drachen* One, using this same tactic, lying doggo. The other two, three or four miles southwest, would be attacking more conventionally on the convoy's flank – and with luck they might draw all the escorts' attention.

Which would be lovely . . .

'Destroyer, sir!'

Looff glanced quickly at the quartermaster, to see what bearing he had his glasses trained on. About twenty on the bow . . . Then he saw it, too, and it was the destroyer all right . . . You could see her length – from the white splash at her forefoot and the upward slope by way of a gundeck to the bridge superstructure . . . You caught it in a single glance, though, like recognising a familiar face. She was steering from left to right: and she'd be passing close to Weddigen.

He was tempted to take a shot at her. Spread a salvo of four across her. But it would leave his tubes empty, and it was the convoy he'd been ordered to destroy. *Ordered* . . . Also, he'd have to move fast, really snap those fish off, and as one couldn't count on the destroyer holding a steady course there'd have been a chance of missing. Which in the circumstances one could not have afforded.

The convoy would be – well, say five thousand metres behind that escort?

'Come ten degrees to starboard.'

He'd reminded the others: their torpedoes were to be *used* not wasted. And if he was robbed of a good chance in this phase, he'd save them for the next.

One might assume, also, that the destroyer, as escort commander's ship, would be somewhere near the centre – where he, Looff, also wanted to be. So if he crept in there now, inserted himself between that Brit and the convoy . . .

One of the beauties of this kind of attack was it gave you time to think and observe. When you were charging in at full tilt there was always too much going on for anything but snap judgements . . . He guessed Weddigen would have dived by now. He'd have spotted the destroyer coming directly towards him and he'd have just quietly slid under. Then he'd surface again when it had gone over him; and that would put both U-boats in a very favourable situation. Ideally they'd attack from the convoy's front as soon as they heard action from the flank.

Kernéval – Flag Officer U-boats – had repeated an earlier demand for complete elimination of this convoy. The signal had been unequivocal: *Your confirmation that not one ship remains afloat is to be received here for onward transmission to the Führer within the next 24 hours.* Looff had passed the telegraphist's scrawl across the table to Franz Walther. Keeping his own expression blank, watching the engineer's reaction. Walther's lips had moved: soundlessly forming one short, lavatorial word.

The destroyer was just visible now, and at that only by the flicker of white from the mound of foam under her counter. The weather was much easier tonight, and with less broken water on the surface ships travelling at speed were easier to spot. A good reason for trying this 'sleeping dog' trick . . . But that signal from U-boat headquarters had put Looff in a straitjacket. Mention of the all-highest, even: you could sneer at it, but you couldn't ignore it. Incidentally, it suggested that Dönitz too might be under pressure. The

Führer doing a bit of his celebrated carpet-eating act, frothing at the mouth for *good* news? In contrast to the announcement last night that he'd authorised Field Marshal Rommel's strategic withdrawal for purposes of regrouping?

What *that* meant was a bloody rout. The Afrika Korps with its tail right up its arse. Hence everyone else getting the heat turned on *them*.

'There, now . . .'

The convoy. One – two ships – then a gap and a third and fourth . . . Puzzling formation though: you might say more jumble than 'formation' . . . Well – he saw that – in their emergency turn, all ships would have turned simultaneously, so that the rectangle became a sort of lopsided diamond. And there'd have been some holes blown in the pattern when the other four had taken their stab at it.

Before the night was over, given reasonable good fortune, whatever ships remained would be scattered, in no kind of formation at all, so that the final mopping-up would be of individual ships here and there. An easy and enjoyable finale, and its culmination would be his own signal to FO U-boats: *Convoy destroyed . . .*

'Destroyer's turned towards us!'

'Where?'

Oelricher's glasses were trained on the beam: one arm extended, pointing. Looff swung his own glasses that way, caught one brief sight of the destroyer coming bow-on at high speed . . .

'Dive, dive!'

A spark – like one from a cigarette-lighter with no fuel in it – somewhere behind those merchantmen: then the sound, torpedo . . . Vents crashing open, a ripple of thuds down her length, spray in a cold, salt rain, and Oelricher in the hatch, his leather-wrapped bulk blocking out the faint glow of light from the tower's interior. Looff heard a second hit as he dropped into the hatch himself, reaching to drag the lid down over his head, shouting as he fumbled with the clips 'Fifty metres! Hard a-starboard!' A penetrating, knocking crash: that would be hit number three. He rattled down the ladder. Frustration at not being up there at precisely this moment to add his torpedoes to that slaughter tightened his brain and nerves: he told himself, as if addressing some other creature inside his own skin and skull, that *Drachen* One's fish would get their share, before much longer . . . He'd get up there soon: with luck the attack on the convoy's flank would divert this destroyer, but meanwhile his aim was to pass under it while it was still only about half way to where its captain would imagine *him* to be: the Brit would be aiming-off to starboard, imagining he'd have held on towards the convoy . . . When he was reasonably well clear he'd come up – surface if possible, otherwise attack from periscope depth by sound, spread a salvo across the convoy's mass.

Or, save it for later. Transfer eastward for phase three. It depended very much on the convoy's own movements, how it reacted to the attack that was in progress now.

'Fifty metres, sir.'

'Destroyer passing over – port side . . .'

Looff told Walther, 'He may not have seen us. Could have been on that course by chance.'

Depthcharges blasted, close on the port quarter. Lights flickered, went out, came on again, and the gyro alarm bell broke into its strident racket. Heusinger had seemed stunned, Looff noticed, but Walther had got to the panel almost before it had started, and shut it off. An electrician was going to the gyro itself, which presumably had toppled.

Get rid of Heusinger, before the next patrol . . .

'Two hundred metres.'

Playing safe – although there'd only been two charges dropped, and he guessed they were economising. Walther was busy with the trim as the needles swung round the gauges. Within seconds U 702 would be below the reach of any more charges that might be coming: but he'd only stay deep for a little while. Just long enough to shake the bloody destroyer off . . .

'Slow both.'

'Slow both motors, sir!'

One of the corvettes had dropped quite a tonnage of depth bombs on poor old *Drachen* Six last night. Not for the first time, Ernst Pöhl had been very lucky to get away with it – if indeed he had, in the longer run . . . The vibration from his screws transmitted by the damaged casing had been making that frightful noise: he'd been in the dilemma of having to use his screws to get away, yet not being able to throw the corvette off his trail as long as he did use them. He'd already suffered damage from the depthcharging, had leaks here and there and a cracked battery and other defects. What he'd done – he'd wirelessed a full report of it this morning – was he'd brought his boat up to about thirty metres, then stopped everything, held her in a stop-trim as long as possible and then in a slow descent with no machinery at all running, even his gyro stopped: he'd let her glide down as far as 160 metres, which was 60 below his tested depth and must have taken an iron self-control to stick at, with his boat already badly hurt, liable to split open at any time, and depth charges still bursting round him. But the corvette captain had evidently decided he'd sunk him – which was what Pöhl had wanted him to think – and pushed off . . . So Ernst was now on surface passage to St Nazaire. He wasn't in a state to dive again – not without staying down for evermore – so he had no option but to take a longshot chance on the Biscay air patrols. Maybe his luck would hold; if no-one heard of him again, you'd know it hadn't.

Looff asked his hydrophone operator, 'Where is it now?'

'Red one-five-oh, sir, moving left to right, about – two hundred revs . . . Not in contact.'

'Two hundred metres, sir.'

He looked round at Walther. 'Right. But let's get back up there, now. Fifty metres.'

The *Lossiemouth*, the *Archie Dukes* and the *Coriolanus* had been hit in the first assault. The *Lossiemouth* was still holding on, down by the bows but maintaining station. The other two had sunk. Now *Paeony* had just been through on TBS to say the *Omeo* had been torpedoed, and – Guyatt thought – the *Cimba* too.

Slaughter. Snowflakes showering a distant brilliance as if to celebrate it. And quite a few hours to get through yet. So far they'd only nibbled at the edges of the convoy; but once they'd chewed *those* away . . .

'No contact, sir!'

'Keep trying.'

The deep-diver? There might be more than one of them in this crowd, of course. From the beam as *Harbinger* slowed – he'd cut the revs to give asdics a chance – Nick heard the commodore's siren ordering an emergency turn to starboard. Asdics pinging mournfully, Chubb leaning into the cabinet behind leading Seaman Garment: but there were no echoes coming back. The emergency turn might have been more useful ten minutes ago, Nick realised; if he'd thought of it when the 271 had picked up the first contact, and signalled to the commodore . . .

Well, he hadn't. So now he had a convoy of – what, twelve ships . . . And you couldn't make an emergency turn every time RDF got something on the screen. He couldn't paddle around here much longer either, probing for a German who most likely *had* gone down to some fantastic depth.

'Port twenty. Three hundred revolutions.'

'Port twenty, sir . . .'

You couldn't afford to potter along at a speed suitable for asdic work either, when you had so few escorts and so much territory to cover. He was taking her along the line of the convoy's van now. There were two of the bastards here somewhere: he'd had one on the screen and it had dived before he'd got near enough to see it, and then a second – this one he thought had gone deep. They'd both been coming in towards the convoy: the fact they'd dived didn't mean they'd have changed their plans.

Eagle – this is Gannet . . . Omeo has sunk, the Cimba's straggling. Making about three knots. Stella's standing by her.

Siren again. Sandover had swung his ships to the mean course, and now he was turning them another forty degrees to starboard of it. It was a good move: experience had shown that the only emergency turns that helped when enemies were close or in contact were the drastic kind.

Starshell: over what was now the convoy's quarter, and either from *Paeony* or *Stella*. He called down, 'Midships.'

In that first attack a lot more torpedoes had been fired than had hit. And in the last ten days some of the U-boats might have used most of what they had. Just as *Harbinger* and the others had done with depth charges. And in the recent foul weather there couldn't have been any re-stocking from 'milch cow' U-boats.

A small hope: but any hope was better than none. Elphick had acknowledged the helm order: Nick told him now, 'Steer two-four-oh.' To close in towards the convoy. What had been its front was now its port side, and the two who'd been put down out here would be pressing in again, he guessed. They'd aim to surface at close quarters to their targets, having got inside the sparse defence. They'd surface, because there wouldn't be enough light for a dived attack. With luck, though, he'd stop them simply by being there, close to the huddle of ships as they ran eastward. If you could call five knots 'running' . . . He hoped to God they'd be keeping close together, ships moving up into gaps left by casualties. Because if they straggled, if the formation opened up—

Gunfire, astern.

'Plot – where's *Astilbe*?'

'Course two-four-oh, sir.'

'*Astilbe* bears oh-eight-oh, five thousand eight hundred yards, sir, crossing left to right!'

So that gunfire – starshell, he could see it now – would be *Paeony*'s. Whom he wanted here, up on the convoy's port bow, just as *Astilbe* – and thank God Graves didn't have to be told what to do – was moving over to the starboard bow.

'Steer two-six-oh.'

Harbinger lurching, shouldering through the troughs. The convoy was a dark scattering on the beam: he didn't need to be any closer to it than he was now. And if *Paeony* had a target down there now it would be silly to blame Guyatt for not being somewhere else: systems of defence were no good unless they found and stopped attackers, which presumably was what he was doing.

That had sounded like a torpedo hit. Some way off – beyond the convoy. And now more gunfire. It gave him another thought: if those two Germans were trying to close in to attack on this flank, some starshell might discourage them – as long as it didn't conveniently illuminate the convoy for them.

TBS: and it was *Paeony: I think the Cimba's been attacked again. If not her, then Stella . . . I've just put down a U-boat, sir – on the convoy's port quarter steering oh-six-oh at about seventeen knots. Should I stay with it, or look after Stella, or resume station?*

'Tell him, "Rejoin, passing one mile to port of convoy."' It might help to ward off those two, the deep-diver and its pal. He told Bearcroft before he'd started calling *Paeony* with that answer, 'Then by W/T to *Stella*, plain language, "What is your situation?"' He bent to the pipe: 'Port twenty.' To bring her around, turning inwards towards the convoy; then he'd steer the convoy course, zigzagging . . . He called to Warrimer, 'Load A, B and X guns with starshell.'

'Twenty of port wheel on, sir!'

When he'd got her round and steadied on that easterly course he'd fire starshell at maximum range on, say, 020, due north, and 340 – to put a band of light behind any U-boats that might be encroaching. As long as the shells burst on the far side of them, it couldn't do any harm. Better warn Guyatt . . . But U-boats might be there and not attacking yet: Guyatt's information that the one he'd put down had been hurrying eastward suggested they might be trying to gain bearing on the convoy on this eastward course: joining the bunch who'd attacked earlier?

Gritten's report a few minutes later seemed to confirm it: while the first three starshell were still hanging, yellowing the undulating northern seascape as they drifted down . . . Gritten had been listening to several U-boats conferring with each other, on bearings that varied between northwest and due east.

'Starshell, stand by!'

It might keep them at a distance: or slow them down, while he slanted *Harbinger* northeastward, taking her out between the convoy and what seemed likely to become the area of their next concentration. Also *Paeony* would be coming up this way now, and by turning outward he was leaving room for her.

'Starshell ready, sir!'

The 271, in the last ten minutes or so, had had three or four surface contacts none of which had remained on the screen for more than a few minutes. There were some doubts down there whether the set might be playing up.

'Course, oh-five-oh . . .'

A perfect time, he thought, for the RDF to pack up. Right in the middle of this particularly fateful night, and when the mechanic was away on board *Paeony*. He cursed himself for not having brought him back: he could have done so, and he'd thought of it . . . *Harbinger* rolling hard as she turned her quarter to the convoy and her beam to the weather: and a call from the W/T office presaged the reply from *Stella*, at last. The *Cimba* had been torpedoed for a second time, and had sunk. Broad had been busy picking up all the survivors he could find, and he was now plugging eastward, about six miles astern. If the convoy held this course and speed he'd be back with it in less than an hour . . . But twenty minutes after that message had come in, there was an explosion somewhere astern. The crashes of the three four-inch, as Warrimer maintained the starshell barrage, came closer and infinitely louder on its heels: as the ringing echoes died, Garment reported from asdics that there'd been a torpedo-hit somewhere astern of the convoy. A few miles astern, he guessed.

Stella. The last of the three . . .

Starshells bursting out to port. Like street lamps, while they lasted, over black, empty-looking ocean. And TBS calling: *Eagle, this is Gannet* . . . He was sure it was going to be a report of *Stella* having gone; then he heard Guyatt's report that it was a straggler two or three miles astern. Guyatt had

Stella on his 271 screen, and he said she was in a good position to look after it. White distress rockets streaked up at that moment: and Guyatt too was turning to investigate.

'Tell him no, resume station, leave it to *Stella*!'

Nobody had said anything about any ship straggling, until now. And *Paeony* must have had her on his RDF screen – whoever she was . . . The northern horizon had three separate pools of yellow over it as the starshell flares sank lower and the illuminated areas under them contracted. The W/T office bell rang: Wolstenholm almost flew to the voice-pipe, as the ship rolled that way to help him; he called, having cracked his face hard on the pipe's rim, 'From the *Orangeman*, sir – struck by torpedo starboard side number four hold!'

The *Orangeman* was one of the two who'd had engine trouble earlier in the day. Sandover had slowed the whole convoy for her and for the *Omeo*, who'd been sunk in tonight's first attack. But TBS was calling again, and it was *Astilbe*, who hadn't been heard from for some while: *Eagle, this is Fox: I have three U-boats on the screen, ranges four, five and seven miles, oh-four-five to oh-eight-oh . . .*

'Chief – by W/T to the commodore – U-boats are concentrating about five miles ahead on present course. Suggest emergency port.'

Crack on at full speed, get up there with *Astilbe?*

But there were some on the beam as well . . .

'U-boat on the surface red six-oh, sir!'

Warrimer had it in his glasses, by the last glimmer of starshell light: he lost it again before he could direct the guns to it and without anyone else having seen it. There'd be no point in chasing out there: it would probably have dived, and all you'd be doing would be leaving this sector unguarded. He called into the pipe, 'Starboard ten. Steer oh-seven-oh.' He told Warrimer to stand by with more starshell. 'What was it doing when you saw it?'

'Parallel course, sir, going like a bat out of hell.'

It made sense. Shifting eastward, getting up ahead again for a third bite at the cherry . . . 'Chief. Make to *Paeony* on TBS, "Convoy is about to make emergency turn port. Give

Stella amended course to rejoin thereafter".' Because *Paeony* would have *Stella* on her screen . . .

The minutes passed. Fifteen, and no acknowledgement from Sandover. Then – at last – siren . . . Like a wail out of the night, a cry for help. And *Astilbe* calling again: the U-boats she'd had on her screen had vanished from it but had now reappeared and were closing rapidly: Graves was turning out to meet them head-on, firing starshell . . .

The convoy was turning now. On its new course, the attack in *Astilbe*'s sector would be coming in on its starboard bow. Nick told Bearcroft, 'W/T to commodore: "Request second emergency turn port immediately."' He wished to God he could have been up there now with *Astilbe*, and had *Paeony* here to look after this sector. *Harbinger*'s starshells were bursting out to port again, and distantly he could hear a popping of gunfire from *Astilbe*: he'd swung round for a quick check on the position of the convoy during its turn, to see whether any of its nearer part was visible from here – because the turn would bring it closer, he'd be on its port bow as it steadied and before Sandover turned it again: he had his glasses up, searching for it, when the *Burbridge*, the *Cressida* and the *Redgulf Star* were hit, in four explosions fast as drumbeats, and a pause with the first leap of flame – like a knife in his gut as he saw it and knew it would be the oiler – then a fifth . . .

It was the cavalry charge this time. It had to be, to get in there fast enough to synchronise with the others, the four attacking from the convoy's front. Looff, with *Drachens* Two and Eleven to Starboard of him, was pounding southeastward on his diesels, under the impression that he was on the convoy's quarter, at least abaft its beam. He didn't know the convoy had made one forty-degree turn and was about to make another.

Starshell broke again, back on *his* quarter. There'd been plenty, in the last hour, hour and a half. He'd last surfaced, for the umpteenth time, five minutes ago, after yet another quick dip to avoid detection, and still intent on gaining bearing on the convoy but not with any thought of attacking this soon. He'd surfaced – having got himself clear of the destroyer, earlier on – and started eastward at high speed, signalling to Köning and Weddigen to follow and telling Waldo Speyer, *Drachen* Twelve, to shadow the enemy from astern. For roughly ninety minutes, chasing eastward on a course parallel to the convoy's, he'd dived and surfaced a dozen or more times under the intermittent light of starshells. He'd surface, run hell for leather for ten minutes, dive, surface again . . . *Cursing* the starshells. He'd seen one of the others – or it could have been both of them, a different one each time – twice at close quarters in the brief, high-speed surfaced periods. Dodging up and down like ducks: but they'd managed to transfer themselves eastward at more than twice the convoy's rate of progress overall. He'd been worried about the enemy's RDF, but not so very greatly, seeing that the escorts were so hugely outnumbered, so hampered and restricted as a result of it.

Waldo Speyer, trailing the convoy, had knocked off a straggler only minutes ago, and it could have been the sound of Speyer's single torpedo hitting that had prompted Becker in *Drachen* Three to signal *Attacking*! and start moving his four boats in towards the convoy's front. Becker's initiative had been premature, to say the least: but he must have thought he was about to be left out of the action, that others were starting without him. So Looff in turn had had little option but to attack as well, else *he'd* have been left out of it.

'See either of 'em?'

Yelling at Oelricher. The quartermaster poked a gloved hand to starboard. 'One sir, half a minute ago, but—' His voice was drowned in the roar of the sea as it burst over, thumping against the forefront of the tower and geysering upward. The wind and sea was in fact astern, but she'd been bow-down, driving into that one. One other U-boat, Oelricher had meant, in that shouted reply. If a third was with them – Looff couldn't be absolutely sure of it – it ought to be close on the other side of – well, Weddigen's. He guessed Weddigen *would* be with him. Speyer, having polished off the straggler, would be pushing up to attack the convoy's rear.

Starshell – on the bow, to starboard.

An escort on the convoy's near quarter? He thought they'd be all up around the merchantmen. Except for the trawler . . .

Gunfire: again to starboard . . . Oelricher yelled, pointing again as the boat whipped over in a savage roll, 'Convoy in sight port bow, sir!'

Naked eyes were more use than binoculars, in these conditions. Looff suspected that either Köning or Weddigen had run into trouble out there. Not that he had time to concern himself with it . . . He'd dried the glasses and he had them focused on the vagueness which could only be the nearer part of the convoy. A grey smear in black surround with a hint of white here and there: it shifted confusingly if you stared straight at it, as opposed to moving the glasses to and fro across it. But still, becoming clearer . . .

He wasn't on the quarter, he was on the bow!

'Ship's head?'

Oelricher checked it: 'One-three-seven, sir!'

'Bring her to one-five-oh. Stand by tubes one to four. Open bowcaps.' He was stooped over the master sight, lining his binoculars up with it. Oelricher passing figures to Heusinger in the tower: enemy speed five, course oh-three-oh, own position thirty on the bow, range—

'Tubes one to four ready!'

Starshell right overhead: yellowish light flushed the rolling, heaving surface and she was lifting to a big one, foam streaming and her afterpart drowned, when he heard the crashes of torpedo-hits: four, he counted – then a fifth . . . Fire – a gush of bright flame rising, starshell-glow dimmed by an expanding fireball shooting skyward, more flame spreading under it to silhouette Looff's target for him. He had two freighters in line, overlapping . . .

'Fire one!'

* * *

Siren: for the second forty-degree swing to port. White rockets fizzing up from the centre of the convoy. Ulrich Weddigen's quartermaster in *Drachen* Eleven screamed, 'Destroyer!'

Pointing wildly, as the boat rolled and nearly threw him off his feet. Weddigen, jammed into the fore-corner at the master sight, saw a flash of gunfire before he saw the ship itself. He was narrowly on the destroyer's port bow: it was bow-up, ascending a rolling hump of black, white-fringed Atlantic, ship and seascape behind it lit by the glow radiating from a burning merchantman a mile away.

'Hard a-starboard! *Dive, dive!*'

There was time. Since his boat was moving fast, she'd turn fast. If he'd tried to hold on, the Brit would have had him cold.

'He's diving, sir!'

God alone knew where A and B guns' shots had gone . . . Carlish shouted, 'U-boat green one-five, sir!'

And that was *another* one! Within a couple of cables' lengths of the first!

'Starboard ten. Depth charges with shallow settings, stand by . . .'

The image of the blazing oiler filled his mind: and she'd been abeam of the *Burbridge*. There'd been five hits . . . Warrimer intoning over his telephone into the ears of the sightsetters at the three four-inch mountings and the multiple point-fives amidships, 'Shift target: second U-boat green one-five, range twelve hundred yards . . .'

The third torpedo of Looff's salvo of four had just left its tube when Oelricher saw the destroyer bearing down on them at high speed and close. As he yelled the warning, U 702 was plunging into a trough – forecasing buried, tail up, the sea from astern swamping over, boiling through the 'conservatory' and around the raised sill of the hatch. He'd have kicked the lid shut if he'd seen that one coming and had time to care about a bit of wetness down below. But for those few seconds the destroyer had been out of sight: Looff at the master sight shouting with impatience and waiting for her to rise.

At last . . . 'Fire four!'

Then he had time to see how close the Brit was. The shock flattened his mind into a two-dimensional black-and-white still photograph: with himself in it, looking on, and the end he'd always dreaded – *one of them* – staring back at him out of his own eyes before the blaze of colour from burning sky ahead, in the next fifth of a second, jerked him back into reality . . . He screamed, *'Starboard twenty!'*

She was taking an age to answer her helm. But he'd get by – just – and then reverse the rudder . . . One of the destroyer's for'ard guns fired again, but it was too close to depress enough. Once he was astern of the Brit he'd pull the plug, be well on the way to safety before a destroyer with her comparatively large turning circle could drag itself around . . . Machine-guns flamed and blared from a mounting between funnels looming tall as houses: Oelricher flung back against the for'ard standard and collapsed. And she was *swinging in* – Looff had been distracted in those two vital seconds, looking round at him: he yelled into the tower, 'Hard a-port!' And just that much too late: she was still swinging, and the two ships struck, beam to beam, the destroyer leaning over as huge-seeming as a battleship as they smacked together with a crash and the sound of steel ripping as if it was cloth: it was the top edge of U 702's bridge that had gone, and that side of the 20mm gun-platform and all its railing . . . Careering on, port rudder taking effect now to turn her close under the destroyer's stern: she'd been flung on her beam by the impact, a whole mountain of foam avalanching over: a four-inch crashed and flamed from the destroyer's stern as it swung too and the machine-guns opened up again, bullets in a torrent with ricochets from the after bridge and the periscope standards. Heusinger and his fire-control petty officer were dragging Oelricher down into the tower, clumsy in their haste: Looff had ordered the wheel amidships but had to delay his shout of 'Dive, dive!' by perhaps ten seconds – which felt like ten minutes . . . He yelled it as he fell into the hatch – he'd been crouched for shelter against the machine-gun fire – and as the vents banged open to flood her tanks a shell struck glancingly overhead, *whirred* away without exploding . . . Dragging the hatch shut and clipping it, yelling down to Walther to take her to two hundred metres, he was mewing in his mind *Please God, please* . . . Hedging his bet on the pressure-hull having suffered no damage . . . He was stepping off the ladder in the control room when *Harbinger*'s depth charges went off: close, shatteringly loud explosions, the worst he'd ever heard or felt. U 702 shifted bodily in the sea: men were flung off their feet, all lights went out and the gyro alarm began to shriek again: some high-power circuit blew, an arc of crackling blue flame . . . Looff heard a shout of 'Bad leak over the port engine, sir!' There'd been other yelling too. He was opening his mouth to stop the dive, shut main vents and blow her to the surface, when Franz Walther forestalled him with a bellow of, 'No bother, lads, we'll soon have this lot to rights!'

The gyro alarm shut off, and emergency lights came on. as if responding to that shout from the engineer. Looff felt personally removed, dazed, staring round at the half-lit shambles. Men sprawling everywhere, broken glass and other gear, and Oelricher's bloodstained, blood-leaking body. Walther reached down to grab an arm belonging to Kurt Hopper, the second engineer, and haul him to his feet. He pointed at the depth gauge needle which was swinging past the fifty-five metre mark, and at the trimming order instrument switched to 'pump from forward': 'Look after this for me, laddy. She's heavy, you'll need to take plenty out. Depth ordered two hundred metres. I'm going aft to see what this rubbish is about a leak.'

Daylight, poking over from the direction of Spain, found seven merchantmen in convoy, steering northeastward at three knots. They were in three columns, the columns only six hundred yards apart to give a tighter and more easily defensible block of ships. In the centre the *Dongola* led the *Burbridge* and the *St Eliza* between two shorter outer columns – the *Sweetcastle* and the *Mount Trembling* to port, the *Sukow Trader* and the *Lossiemouth* to starboard. Seven plodding hulls, not all of them whole; half an hour ago they'd looked grey but they were jet-black now as the sea around them turned silver with the dawn.

The *Burbridge* was listing heavily to starboard, and the *Lossiemouth* was so much down by the bows that she had only about eighteen inches of freeboard at her for'ard welldeck. Waves broke right over her at that point, foamed around the cargo hatches. The *Burbridge*'s damage had been well below the waterline, flooding a refrigerated store and some other compartments on that side; she'd had no casualties among passengers or crew.

The *Mount Trembling*'s more sheltered upper deck spaces were crowded with survivors for whom she'd had no room below. *Stella*'s load – from the *Cimba* – had already been transferred to the *Sukow Trader*. The *Sweetcastle* had most of the men who'd come alive out of the *Redgulf Star*, and Mackenzie, *Harbinger*'s surgeon-lieutenant, had transferred to her by seaboat to look after them. In that last assault the *Burbridge* and the oiler had each been hit by one torpedo, and the *Cressida* by two – which had sent her straight to the bottom. Then a minute later a single hit from another salvo had sunk the *Baltimore Cross*. The torpedoes that caused so much havoc must have passed closely ahead and astern of the *Sukow Trader*: all the casualties had been in that corner of the formation, only with the *Burbridge* deeper inside than the others; and as the convoy had been turning, her beam had been exposed just at that moment.

The *Redgulf Star* had blown herself apart. She'd left a couple of acres of sea on fire, and many of her crew must have been in it.

Not long after that sudden flood of casualties the

Colombia, who'd shifted earlier to take the place of the *Coriolanus* at the head of column two, had been hit by two torpedoes, dropped astern and sunk in about twenty minutes. It was fairly certain those torpedoes had come from one or other of the two U-boats that *Harbinger* had attacked, out on that bow as the convoy made its turn. *Harbinger*'s collision with the second one had torn away some plating and guardrails on the port side amidships, and left deep score-marks down her side, the full length of the iron-deck section. Some curved railing that had never belonged to her had been found wrapped round the port-side depth-charge thrower: it hadn't done the thrower any harm, but it had very much annoyed Mr Timberlake, for some reason. There was no way of telling whether the U-boat had survived or not.

Nick had signalled to the destroyers who were supposed to be joining him, giving them an amended position, course and speed, also giving Scarr's estimated positions of some of the sinkings where boatloads of survivors might be found. The *Orangeman* was a case in point, but there'd been other stages when it hadn't been possible to hang around for more than a perfunctory search. So now *Wesley* and *Vicious* would cover swiftly the route over which the convoy had dragged itself so painfully during the night, and join the escort force by dusk at the latest.

In another signal he'd reported – amongst other things – the loss of the *Redgulf Star*, requesting a rendezvous with some other oiler within the next forty-eight hours. Presumably there'd be follow-up 'Torch' convoys from which one could be borrowed.

Harbinger pitched regularly to a long, westerly swell. This was a gentler, softer dawn. Wind force not much more than two, sea still white-streaked but tamer, lazier.

Well fed? Even gorged?

'Sir—'

Wragge – bridge messenger – pointing, gulping, too excited to get words out . . . Chubb, at the binnacle, beat him to it, whooping 'Aircraft, sir!'

He swung his glasses, focused them on the Sunderland as it came droning out of the rising dawn. What was this – Christmas, suddenly? Two destroyers, *and* air patrols?

What am I supposed to do? Be grateful? Give thanks?

In time, perhaps, he would. Not yet, though. Not for a long time yet.

Chapter 15

Telephone conversation between Marshalls Goering and Kesselring, quoted in the diary of Marshal Cavallero, Chief of the Italian General Staff:
Kesselring: 'Herr Reichsmarschall – supposing a convoy attempts a landing in Africa—'
Goering: 'To my mind a landing will be attempted in Corsica, in Sardinia, or at Derna or Tripoli.'
Kesselring: 'It is more probable at a North African port.'
Goering: 'Yes, but not a French one.'

Outside her bedroom window, the rain drummed down. It had started before dawn this morning and there'd been no break in it. It drove slanting across the front of the house, rattling noisily on the shutters which she'd hooked slightly open. It had got warmer, with the rain.

Jack had always enjoyed matineés. With Fiona especially: weekend afternoons in her flat in Eaton Square. Destination – ultimate but also soonest possible – of Lieutenant Jack Everard, DSC, Royal Navy . . . He wondered – as he did quite often, when he had so much time on his hands – how much of his fascination with Fiona had been due to her being Nick's girl.

Probably quite a lot, initially. But *only* initially. Since then, he'd swallowed the hook.

'Heidi?'

She smiled in her half-sleep. Or it could be that she was really asleep and dreaming, reacting to the sound of her own name in his voice. Her dark-skinned face lost ten years, became small-girlish in this total relaxation. Nobody seeing her would have thought she could be the mother of a child of Otto's age.

Jack still knew nothing at all about her – except that her name was Heidi. But he did know this was Saturday 7 November, and also that the child wouldn't be home before tomorrow evening. Otto was going straight from school to spend the night elsewhere – at some schoolfriend's house, he guessed. This morning Heidi had seen him off as usual; the morning routine had been unchanged, up to that stage, but as soon as her son was out of sight she'd been in a tearing hurry with the hens, just about throwing the food at them, and she'd run back into the house, more than walked. Moments later he'd heard her rushing upstairs and she'd burst in, gabbling happily and incomprehensibly, still talking at him while they kissed and he tried to ease her down on the mattress with him: she'd resisted it, and brought him down here instead. To a proper bed, with sheets and blankets, pillows . . .

She'd brought lunch to the bed on a tray. Scrambled eggs and sausage, black bread spread with mutton-fat dripping, and apple tart. A feast. Naked, and in this half-light, she'd seemed really rather beautiful. She'd taken the plates away afterwards and washed up, then returned to bed and it had been as if they hadn't seen each other for a week.

His guess was it had been a long time for her, man-less for some reason, and for some other (or the same) reason estranged from the locals. Not from all of them, because she went *somewhere* with that basket of eggs, on weekdays. But estranged or frightened or under threat, vulnerable in some way. She hadn't referred to her man again, so far as he knew. The only questions you could get anywhere with were those that could be put in simple combinations of word and gesture – 'You – *Heidi*? Me, Jack . . .' And the calendar was useful; for instance, she'd told him about the child's weekend arrangements by indicating his height – holding a hand flat at that level and saying 'Otto . . . *Otto?*' Then pointing the way he'd gone, down to the lane, and to the calendar again, pointing it out – today, Saturday 7 November, to

Sunday 8, and towards the end of Sunday Otto walking back in again.

In fact he didn't *want* to question her, about her background. This was only a staging-post en route to the Swiss border, just as the border would be a stage on his way to Fiona. It was Fiona he thought about in bed, not Heidi.

The wireless was good for BBC programmes, if one could put up with a varying amount of static. He'd tuned in to an overseas programme of news earlier on, and heard that the Eighth Army was well past Mersa in its westward pursuit of Rommel; also that the German Sixth Army under von Paulus was still bogged down in front of Stalingrad. Heidi had begun to look scared while he'd been listening to it, and the bulletin hadn't finished when she'd reached over, throwing herself on top of him and switching it to German music. He hadn't minded: he'd heard enough and he'd been cheered by it even to the extent of suffering Wagner. She'd been genuinely scared, though: she'd gone to the window and peered out into the rain-sodden yard, as if she really imagined someone out there might have heard the booming English voice. Jack had teased her, made jokes about chickens with long ears, and hers being German-speaking hens, so what the hell . . . She'd spat a lot of German at him urgently, angrily: she meant it, she genuinely did feel some danger threatening them. Or threatening *her*. He'd been up on his elbows on the pillows, enjoying the picture she made standing there naked in the gloom with the sound of the rain drumming behind the shutters and the awful music droning: he'd drawn a finger slowly across his throat and told her 'Rommel kaput! *Deutsche* kaput!' Then thought immediately, as she still stared at him angrily out of those slanting eyes, a gleam of them in the dark face, that he might actually have hurt her. This could be an exclusively personal affair with her, and he had no evidence – other than her attitude to himself, which wasn't proof of anything at all – to suggest she might not be a German patriot. A situation like this one could arise, he guessed, in England: a lonely, unhappy young woman, and a German on the run?

Particularly a very good-looking, *charming* German? It wouldn't need to relate to patriotism or politics; in this area a female could be as detached, self-sufficient and solitary as a cat. And as unreasoning . . . The way she'd been looking at him at that moment – more feline than anything other than a real cat could be. The eyes, and the walk as she'd moved back towards him, and – closer – the gleam of her small, white teeth: at risk of being clawed he'd opened the bedclothes to let her in.

Wind force two, sky cloudy, visibility good. Seven merchantmen in convoy, and six escorts now to guard them.

During the afternoon watch two friendly aircraft had been sighted, and in the first dog the destroyers had arrived from astern. The survivors they'd picked up, mostly from the *Orangeman*'s boats, were immediately transferred to the *Burbridge* and the *Dongola*, who made a lee for the ships' boats to work in. With the sea as low as it was now you had to allow for the possibility of U-boats attacking in daylight, dived, periscope attacks, and he'd disposed his escorts to counter this. The two destroyers were four thousand yards ahead, with a corvette on each flank at half that distance, and *Stella* between the destroyers and the convoy's van. *Harbinger* wandered as she pleased, constantly on the move. At dusk action stations he'd send the destroyers farther ahead, move the corvettes to the convoy's bows, put *Stella* astern and retain his own roving commission. Up to now there'd been no reports of any transmitting, not since noon when Gritten had picked up a lot of chatter astern, fifteen to twenty miles south. It had lasted only a few minutes: the explanation he'd have liked to have believed in might have been a redeployment of the U-boats – that they'd been leaving, departing southward.

It was possible, but unsafe to count on. The only course for SL 320's escort to take was to continue to act as if the U-boats were still present in force. As they well might be. Or *some* might, if others had been withdrawn.

This afternoon he'd been through the convoy, and close

past the *Burbridge*, with the quarterdeck name-boards rigged. They were varnished boards with the ship's name in large, highly-polished brass letters; they secured to permanent fittings on each side of the after super-structure, but they were for show, not for use at sea. He'd been giving her a chance to see the name *Harbinger* – because a passenger might not necessarily have known it. He'd been half expecting a signal, then, a light to start winking from the *Burbridge*. It hadn't, and he'd thought, Well, that's that, she *can't* be . . .

Now, three hours later and about to drive up through the columns again, it struck him that nothing had been proved for certain. She might have been resting in her cabin, or doing a stint of nursing duty. Even if she'd been embarked only as a passenger, a lot of injured survivors from other ships had been put into the *Burbridge* and they'd have been glad of extra hands, particularly skilled ones like Kate's.

He wanted to know now. The ostrich was ready to pull its head out of the sand. Ostrich feeling safe: anyway, less desperate, for those passengers.

The *St Eliza*, third ship in the three-ship central column, was coming up to starboard. The *Mount Trembling* was farther ahead to port, and the *Burbridge* was next ahead of the *Eliza*.

He looked round at Carlish.

'Straight up the middle, Sub. Just watch out for the zigzag.'

'Aye aye, sir.'

Carlish looked pleased. This was the first time he'd been allowed to take her through the convoy on his own.

'Signalman.' Nick beckoned to McCurtin, signalman of the watch. 'By light to the *Burbridge* . . . "Do you have any passenger on board by name of Everard?"'

McCurtin repeated it: he looked interested as he reached for the Aldis. A few other heads turned too. The *St Eliza* was abeam to starboard now. McCurtin sighted the Aldis out over the bow, and began the calling-up procedure; the *Burbridge*'s bridge staff must have been watching the destroyer approach, because the answering flash came immediately. McCurtin rattled off the question: there was a pause, and then the signal *Wait, please.*

Harbinger and the passenger ship were abeam when the convoy began turning to a port leg of the zigzag. Nick saw it coming, but said nothing, leaving it to Carlish. At that moment HF/DF called, and McCurtin was right beside that voice-pipe. He stooped with the Aldis lamp in one hand and answered, 'Bridge?' Without hearing the operator's words Nick could tell from the intonation it wasn't Gritten on watch down there. Carlish was putting on ten degrees of port wheel . . . The signalman reported, 'U-boat transmissions on oh-two-seven, nineteen miles, sir!'

'Very good.'

For the moment, it wasn't U-boats he was primarily thinking of.

The light from the *Burbridge* began to call. All ships halfway through their turn. Nick read the first word of the answer to his enquiry: *Yes* . . .

He had to look away then – under the impression Carlish was holding the wheel on for longer than he should have. But in fact it was all right – or would be. He'd need to bring her back a few degrees to starboard in a minute, and in the process he'd have learnt something – in the best way there was to learn it . . . By this time the flashing light was on their quarter; looking back at it, he read the words, *who wants to know*.

And that had been the end of the message – without an interrogative sign, they'd just signed-off. McCurtin flashed a K, acknowledging.

'Reply from the *Burbridge*, sir – *Yes. Lance Corporal Horace Everard, RAF Regiment. He asks who wants to know.*'

Behind him, Carlish called down, 'Steady!'

'Steady, sir – three-five-eight . . .'

'Steer oh-oh-three degrees.'

Nick told McCurtin, 'Make to him, "Sorry, wrong Everard."'

The *Dongola* was on the starboard quarter now, and the

Sweetcastle was abeam to port: and nineteen miles ahead those U-boat transmissions would have been just about right on the convoy's mean course.

Heidi had produced a supper of vegetable soup which they'd eaten with hunks of black bread, dipping the bread into the hot liquid to soak it up. She'd had soup all over her chin. Then she'd gone outside, to the garden privy, and when she'd come back into the kitchen, leaning against the door to shut it, shut out the rain and darkness, Jack had been waiting there, needing to make the same trip himself and wanting to borrow her coat. It was a man's coat anyway, grey and heavy and with moth-holes in it, he guessed a private soldier's originally and at that quite possibly from the previous war. Catching her against the back door, unable to communicate his intention and therefore just starting to open it and pull it off her otherwise nude body, he realised she'd got the wrong idea of what he wanted; she was giggling and trying to keep the coat closed around her. He had to go along with this misunderstanding for a while, since otherwise he might have hurt her feelings . . . Then it wasn't a difficult act at all, because getting the heavy garment open and then easing it off her shoulders he found himself inclined the way she'd thought he was to start with. And thanks to the stove it was warm in the kitchen, much warmer than the bedroom. But finally he did have to go out – in the coat and holding a tin tray over his head as an umbrella – aware that Their Lordships of the Board of Admiralty might not have considered his bizarre appearance quite becoming to an officer and a gentleman. Except – wasn't there a paragraph in King's Regulations and Admiralty Instructions to the effect that an officer should dress in accordance with the sport in which he was engaged? It would be an interesting line of argument . . . He returned to find Heidi very nervous, scared by his having been outside the house: she'd bolted the door quickly, in a kind of panic again as if her garden was likely to be full of enemies. He wondered again about her obvious insecurity, the impression she gave of living precariously in a foreign and potentially hostile environment.

The only time she seemed really to relax was in bed. And between the intervals of love-making she had an enormous capacity for sleep. Perhaps on her own she slept badly, lay awake in fear of whatever troubled her so much, and found security now in a stranger's arms. He, of course, had had more than enough of sleeping in recent days. But it was easy to work up theories about her, and irritating that one would never know the truth. Not that he cared: it was curiosity, not any real sense of concern.

He'd decided he'd take off on Monday. He lay on his back now, hearing the rain first ease off and then stop, so that he was listening to a desultory dripping from trees and eaves – with her face on his shoulder, her breath fanning his ear, an arm and a leg across him; she was as softly and warmly relaxed as a sprawling puppy. But Monday – the day after the Sunday which would be dawning soon – after she left the house to go wherever she did go every weekday, he'd sneak off, hide himself somewhere near the bicycle until dark, then pedal south to find the frontier. The ankle was a lot better, and he still had all Sunday and Sunday night to rest it. To go suddenly, without goodbyes, would be far the easiest way. He'd tell her – using the calendar again – one more week. It would seem like a long time, and it might well seem long enough – her nervousness, fear of discovery, might even incline her to see him on his way before that.

A continuing tattoo of the rain's aftermath: soft drumming in the darkness, the wind's murmur in the trees. Her breathing was light and even in his ear: that, and the interminable dripping.

Drip, drip, drip . . .

No. It was 'break', not 'drip'. Sea, not rain.

Break, break, break,
On thy cold grey stones, O Sea!
And I would that my tongue could utter
The thoughts that arise in me.

Thoughts, for instance, of Fiona. Who'd be amused, when he described this interlude. Or disbelieving . . . He'd make her laugh, anyway . . . It would have been pretty frightful if Fiona had married Nick – as she'd fully intended. She'd been Nick's mistress for several years, on and off. Jack wondered how Nick, even married to his Australian, would react to the announcement of Fiona's marriage to his young half-brother. And where Nick might be now. Paul, one knew about – Paul would be in his submarine in the Malta flotilla, where survival chances were said to be about fifty: fifty – had been at the beginning of the year, anyway. And if Paul should happen to get his come-uppance then he, Jack, would be in line for the Everard baronetcy if anything similar happened to Nick. It was a thought one had entertained for quite a while now. A new element, however, was Nick's marriage to the Australian, because if they started a family any son would take precedence over a half-brother.

They'd better keep Nick at sea. And the Australian in Australia!

The shutter had moved.

Or – he *thought* it had.

He was straining his eyes towards the indistinct, slightly lighter rectangle that was the window. He could still hear that sound in his head, behind the continuing drip, drip, drip. Not exactly a creak, more a sound of sliding . . .

He moved sideways out of Heidi's embrace, and off the bed. She'd sighed, rolled the other way. He went to the window, seeing the shutters' slats like bars against a sky turning starry now. The cold breeze made him shiver as he felt for the rod with a hook on it which had held the shutters in this half-open position. But he couldn't find it. Then his hand pushed against one shutter, and it swung back. The hook – he found it now, hanging loose – had been disengaged.

For a minute, it had him worried. Then he realised – she most likely hadn't fixed it properly. So the wind had moved the shutters and dislodged it. The movement of the shutter would have been the sound he'd heard.

He hooked it firmly, this time, and went back to bed. Cold, glad of the bed's warmth and hers. He put his arms round her, and she turned back, snuggling against him. Kissing, then, while she was still more asleep than awake and he was still listening, for sounds other than the wind and the noise of the rain as it began again. She murmured sleepily with her mouth against his, while he assured himself that there couldn't possibly have been anyone out there.

'Three minutes to go, sir!'

Hugo Wykeham called it up the helmsman's voice-pipe. Ruck, who had Paul Everard in the bridge with him, answered, 'Depth under us now?'

'Still one hundred fathoms, sir.'

He'd just checked it. The hundred-fathom line at this point was six and three quarter miles from land. McClure, *Ultra*'s navigator, had just left the chart and gone to the ladder, was scuttling up it to the bridge where he'd stay and watch shore bearings – Cape Matifu to the east, Cape Caxine in the west, and some leading marks ashore as well. The bight of land inshore of them was Algiers Bay: *Ultra* was in position and on time, on the spot she'd been detailed to occupy while serving as a navigational beacon. She was slightly nearer the coast than the other submarines who were performing the same task in other sectors – *Unrivalled* was to the east of her, on the other side of Matifu, P 48 was off the town of Algiers itself, and *Shakespear* was lying as marker off the western sector beaches.'

Two minutes to zero hour.

McClure was at the gyro repeater, constantly watching the shore bearings. The diesels were growling through muffled exhausts, one charging the battery and the other driving one screw at low revs, holding the submarine in position by stemming the westerly set. If you made even a small mistake on this kind of job you'd be sending assault troops ashore in the wrong place; navigational accuracy equated to men's lives and the success of the invasion. Ruck and Paul both had their glasses up, sweeping all round but concentrating mostly on the seaward sector. A minute to go . . . Farther out to sea, at 6 pm – four and a half hours ago – convoy KMF(A)1, which had been at sea since leaving the Clyde on 26 October, had split into separate detachments for the various landing beaches in this sector, and one part of the landing force should be appearing here at any moment.

'Blue lamp on, Sub.'

Paul dropped his binoculars on their strap, and raised the lamp. He aimed it out to sea and pressed the trigger.

Ruck asked McClure, 'Bearings all right?'

'Spot on, sir.'

Quiet voices in the quiet, apparently empty night. But you knew it was far from empty. And this would be happening simultaneously at Oran, two hundred miles west. At Oran the beacon submarines were P 54 and *Ursula*.

'Twenty-two thirty-five, sir!'

Wykeham, from below . . . and the LSIS – Landing Ships Infantry – were now five minutes late. It didn't augur well – after so long a passage, so much preparation in the surrounding areas. Paul thought of the Count – who'd most likely be dead by this time – and of the Germans and Italians who'd be on the alert for invasions of Sicily and Sardinia, who'd have had reports today of very large convoys steaming east into the Mediterranean all through the daylight hours. They would *not* have known that under cover of darkness all the convoys had turned south. But they'd know the convoys had been covered by battleships and aircraft carriers as well as squadrons of cruisers and flotillas of destroyers, and a host of smaller support ships.

'Ah. Better late than bloody never.'

Ruck's tone was of relief, but not excitement. What had been expected was now happening, ten minutes late. The landing ships would stop at this point, lower their swarms of assault craft which would then form up and head in to the beach, returning to the LSIS for follow-up waves of troops. The ships would have moved in closer, by that time, to speed up the flow. A primary target from this sector would be the

Maison Blanche airfield, only a few miles inland from the landing place.

McClure warned Ruck, 'We're getting too far east, sir. If we could stop for about a minute, the set would—'

'Stop port!'

You could see the oncoming ships now. A silent, purposefully approaching column growing powerfully out of the night, spearhead of an army which, astonishingly, had been brought in secrecy across two thousand miles of sea and would be ashore before light came.

It was now Sunday 8 November, and for as much as was left of SL 320 it had been a quiet night, so far. *Wesley* had put down a U-boat six miles ahead of the convoy about an hour after dusk, and kept it in asdic contact for long enough to drop several patterns on it. Nick had been thinking of sending one of the others to join in, but he'd decided to wait in case it might turn out to be a concerted attack from other directions as well – as indeed it did, when torpedoes were fired at the convoy from somewhere ahead to starboard. Two tracks were seen, one passing close down the starboard side of the *Sukow Trader* and the other streaking right under *Astilbe*. Graves had said it was seen too late for any evasive action to have been effective: all he'd done was hold his breath.

Then *Paeony* had had a contact, about two hours after midnight, but she'd lost it while Nick had been on his way over to help. And that was all. By this convoy's standards, a very quiet night indeed.

Having those two destroyers would make a difference, of course. You could often relate the aggressiveness of U-boats directly to the weakness of a convoy's defence. As Cruance, among others, had well known.

Convoy speed was four knots. The *Burbridge* could have done better, but the *Lossiemouth*'s master had said he might not be able to maintain even this speed for long. His pumps were holding their own, but only just, against the extensive flooding in his foreport. *Harbinger*'s condenser leak was no worse, thank God.

Mike Scarr had the watch. Nick was relaxing, but not sleeping, in his deck chair. It was a rare and unexpected blessing to spend a night at only the second degree of readiness, guns' crews and depth-charge crew actually sleeping. Not that Mr Timberlake's teams could have won any battles to speak of, when they had only four Mark VIIs left. Fortunately this might not matter, since it did look as if the main battle might have ended. Obviously a large part of the U-boat force had been withdrawn – possibly into the Mediterranean, if the enemy had seen the 'Torch' convoys streaming east from Gibraltar all day – and they must have . . .

He had a pipe going. He smoked slowly, enjoying the quiet passage of the hours and the comparative quiet in his own mind – which he could have established right from the start, if he'd had the courage . . . Thinking about her – where she was and how soon he'd have her with him: thinking also about what he knew must be going on now, this very minute, on and off the Algerian and Moroccan beaches. And whether Paul might be involved – he probably would be . . . Then Kate again – in London, perhaps, already there, trying to find out where *he* was?

Looff had taken U 702 deep, after firing a salvo of three torpedoes from which there'd been no result at all. He attributed it to malfunction, failure of the warheads' pistols being the most likely. His hydrophone operator had heard the fish running, and on course, and then – nothing. Nothing except a destroyer coming straight at him at about thirty knots: and an insolent remark from Franz Walther, some comment muttered into his beard . . .

He'd fired from long range, certainly – because of those destroyers, and the corvettes a short way back on their quarters. He *could* have pressed in closer, to make sure of it, but he'd been on a firing track and he'd suddenly realised he could just as well loose off *now* – and be sure of getting his fish away. On a decision like this you couldn't hesitate: you either did it, or you didn't, and if he'd held on one of those bastards might have got in his way.

He didn't know what had happened to Waldo Speyer – formerly *Drachen* Twelve – either. There'd been a lot of depth-charging from that side, so obviously he'd been getting it in the neck. Their attacks had been reasonably well synchronised – not that it made all that much difference, with only two attackers in place of ten . . . Since firing that salvo he'd been busy with his own immediate problems, too busy to take Walther up on that muttered comment: Looff had let it go, and now he wished he hadn't; but it was too late, the engineer would have denied it, played the innocent . . . Anyway, the obvious thing had been to get those tubes reloaded as quickly as possible, and also to regain bearing. He'd stayed deep until he was able to surface on the convoy's quarter, well out: he'd stayed well out, too, out of the escorts' RDF range while steering a parallel course at high speed, getting himself back up into position for a new attack. He was dived now, deep again, nicely distanced ahead but with the propeller noise of the escorting destroyers loud and clear in the hydrophones, while up for'ard the torpedo-men hauled U 702's last three reload fish into her tubes. The convoy was only crawling, probably because some ships in it had been crippled in earlier attacks, and it was easy to stay ahead of it, even at a speed that took very little juice out of the batteries.

Having missed with that salvo, another attack did have to be made. Unfortunately he'd have to use the search periscope; daylight was coming very soon, and the attack 'scope was out of action. The damage had been done when that shell had bounced off, when he'd been diving her just after the collision. Walther had had his artificers up there working on it, on the surface yesterday forenoon at the same time as they'd buried Oelricher. The engineer had reported finally that effective repairs were impossible. So the attack would have to be conducted from down below in the control room, using the air and sea search periscope. Which was not so good.

The leak in the engine room hadn't amounted to anything.

The air-intake valve: they'd fixed it in a couple of minutes. Walther very pleased with himself at that time, for some reason. He'd acted in those few minutes as if he'd been taking over the command! Looff's memory of the precise sequence of events was hazy, but he did remember Walther throwing his weight about, giving orders to all and sundry. There was nothing to pin him down to now: *another* incident that had been let slip by default . . .

The two destroyers had arrived to join the escort this afternoon, so there were now six escorts to seven merchantmen. This meant stiffish opposition, and Looff had of course drawn attention to it, in one of his reports to Kernéval. It was a very significant change, coinciding as it had with the withdrawal – yesterday, Saturday – of most of the *Drachen* group. The group had in effect been disbanded. Ziegner – who'd been comparatively well off for fuel and torpedoes – had been sent into the Mediterranean, and the rest had been ordered south, back into the Azores air gap where they were to rendezvous with 'milch cows', supply U-boats, for replenishments. Looff and Speyer had been told to remain with this convoy and 'complete its destruction'.

It was an order that couldn't possibly be carried out. Particularly if Speyer had been lost now, or damaged. Even if he showed up again, it couldn't have been achieved even in terms of the number of torpedoes they had left. And with the odds changed so drastically, it virtually amounted to being told to commit suicide.

Punishment for failure?

Hardly . . . He bit his lip, thinking about it. This was a new, extremely valuable ship, with a crew of highly trained, irreplaceable men and a commander whose name had been blazoned in the national headlines. FO U-boats might be under pressure, but he couldn't have gone completely mad.

Except there wasn't always that much logic . . . Certainly not if the carpet-eater was frothing at the mouth. Admirals and generals ran for cover, then!

In any case, there was nothing to be ashamed of. Looff had personally sunk five merchantmen and one armed trawler, adding in his own estimate 30,000 tons to his bag. He'd have done better if on more than one occasion he hadn't had rotten luck, an escort right on top of him by sheer chance at just the crucial moment: it was all on record, in the ship's log and also in his personal notes, for inclusion later in the patrol report. But when you considered it from this point of view it was obvious that FO U-boats' order wasn't either a punishment or a reproof: Max Looff had commanded a group that had sunk thirty out of thirty-seven ships in one convoy – plus one of its escorts – and you didn't reprove a man for that, you gave him a hero's welcome!

Dawn wasn't far away. Maybe forty minutes . . .

Willi Heusinger asked him, in that ingratiating tone of his, 'Will you make a dived attack, sir? With the search periscope?'

Looff turned his head slowly, and stared at him. Letting him see his contempt. He had no intention of keeping Heusinger with him, after this trip. His lips twitched – some involuntary spasm which he controlled with difficulty – as he formed the words to answer cuttingly, 'Since it will now be daylight, and since my engineer has found himself unable to repair the attack periscope, I have very little option, have I . . . Instead of wasting time with stupid questions, go for'ard and find what's making them so slow!'

Heusinger looked as if he'd hit him in the face. He muttered, 'Aye aye, sir . . .'

Walther asked Looff in a murmur as he turned to enter the wardroom, 'All right, sir? I mean – you're feeling OK, are you?'

'Are you a doctor now?' Anger flared: anger he'd suppressed for hours. Glaring at his engineer . . . 'What the hell are you suggesting?'

'I – beg the captain's pardon . . .' Staring, as if he thought his captain might be sick, or crazy. Oil on his face, crumbs in his scraggy beard, gazing at his commanding officer like some laboratory worker studying a microbe . . . Looff suddenly saw clear through the bastard: 'You think you saved the ship – is that it?'

'I'm sorry, I don't understand at all!'

'D'you imagine I'd hesitate to deal with you, Walther? Because you've served with me for a long time d'you think you can get away with impertinence?'

'Sir, if I've said or done *anything*—'

'One more sample of your insubordination, Walther, and Leutnant Hopper will take over your job! D'you understand *that*?'

'Why, yes, sir – but – but . . .'

He'd got him stammering, got him off-balance. That was *good*. He leant closer – eyes blazing, expression triumphant – 'I'm *Max Looff* – remember?'

'Guns' crews closed up, sir, circuits tested.'

He nodded to Warrimer.

'Depthcharge crew closed up, sir.' Chubb went back to the telephone, to swap early-morning insults with Mr Timberlake. Early morning of Sunday, 8 November.

It would already be light, Nick realised, over the Algerian beaches. There was an hour's time-lag, near enough, between here and Algiers. Light would have come to the Moroccan coast perhaps twenty minutes ago. Daylight like a curtain rising on a completely new stage in the war.

Please God. A turning of the tide. From Africa, into southern Europe. And the Mediterranean open . . .

'*Wesley* and *Vicious* have both acknowledged, sir.'

'Thank you, Chief.'

He'd just told them to drop back, closing the defensive screen around the convoy. Its front was a width of only twelve hundred yards now, and with *Harbinger* moving up into the centre, those two falling back to take station on each side of her and the two corvettes as wing-ships to the resulting broad-arrow formation, any U-boat would have a very tight screen to get through.

Stella was on the move across the convoy's stern. At such slow speed a dived attack from the quarter or the rear was not impossible. If there were any U-boats in attendance now, they could run round these tortoises like hares. But in fact, since the attacks last night, which hadn't amounted to anything, there'd been no sight or sound of any enemy.

The rising flush of dawn colour was too pale to be called orange, or even tangerine. Gold might be the best way to describe it. A widening, brightening, fire-like glow under roofing cloud.

Asdics pinging, 271 aerial steadily revolving; half a dozen pairs of binoculars carefully examining the surroundings. Wind was down to force one, but it was from the north and very cold. *Harbinger*'s motion was rhythmic, leisurely, as she rocked over the long, low swell.

The new day's brightness had spread half round the horizon when TBS crackled into life . . .

Eagle – Gannet – periscope in sight – attacking!

'Port twenty. Three-eight-oh revolutions. All quarters alert!'

He'd decided – any contact that was obtained, he'd go for with two or even three ships. He had the resources now and he didn't believe there'd be more than one or two U-boats to contend with. Certainly once the news of the invasion was out, there'd be no U-boats left hanging around a piddling little convoy such as this one had become.

Harbinger was heeling to the turn, and speeding.

'Twenty of port wheel on, sir!'

'Steer three-one-oh.' He straightened. 'TBS to Gannet, Chief, "I am joining you."'

Chubb murmured, 'With my four depthcharges.' But that message would also warn the others that they had to share the convoy's frontal defence between them, in *Harbinger*'s absence from the centre.

Depthcharges exploded, out on the bow. *Paeony* had enough Mark VIIs left for a couple of full patterns. If they both ran out and still held the contact he'd turn it over to the newly-arrived destroyers. Astern, the *Dongola*'s siren was ordering emergency turn to starboard. *Harbinger* stretching herself across the swell, taking it head-on while she was turning, but paying-off again now, leaving the rising light of day back on her quarter. Guyatt should have been regaining contact now, as the disturbance from his charges faded.

TBS . . . *Eagle – Gannet . . . Unable to regain contact, as yet. Could be the deepdive merchant. Out.*

'Course three-one-oh, sir!'

'Chief – call Fox, tell him, "Join me. We may have use for your heavies."' He leant down to the voice-pipe: 'Two hundred revolutions.' He was slowing her to give the asdics a chance: and guessing that the U-boat would have turned away to something like a northerly course – away from trouble, but in a direction that might allow him to get in an attack later.

'Steer three-two-oh.'

He looked round, saw Chubb leaning into the asdic cabinet, communing with Leading Seaman Garment. TBS was calling again as soon as Bearcroft signed-off after his call to *Astilbe*. It was Gannet, reporting, *Contact regained, confirmed sub contact bearing three-two-four range fifteen hundred yards!*

Joy in that tone . . . And an amplifying report now, *Target steering north speed six knots . . .*

'Tell him, "Hold the contact at present range. Do not, repeat do not, try to attack."'

Just about full daylight now. Against the brightest part of it *Astilbe* had the golden glow behind her as she came ploughing across the convoy's van. All the merchantmen were swinging away to starboard.

Nick had time to talk to Guyatt now, over the radiotelephone. 'Have you ever taken part in a creeping attack, or exercised it?'

Guyatt obviously didn't know what he was talking about: he said he didn't *think* he had . . . The creeping attack was one of the anti-submarine ploys devised by the famous Captain Johnnie Walker, most successful and best-known of all the escort-group commanders. Tony Graves knew all about it, anyway – and *Astilbe* had some 'heavies', deep-firing depth charges on board, too. Nick told Guyatt, 'I'll try to take over your contact, and then direct *Astilbe* on to it. Graves knows this technique.'

Ten minutes later, *Harbinger*'s asdics found the U-boat, guided to it by *Paeony*. Garment reported, 'Confirmed sub contact, range fourteen hundred, right ahead, closing!'

'One two-oh revolutions.' He told Bearcroft, 'To Gannet, "Many thanks. Resume station."' *Astilbe* was waiting a few cables' lengths on *Harbinger*'s quarter. The convoy was drawing away eastward, almost into the rising sun. He saw *Paeony* turning, and her bow-wave rising as Guyatt increased speed.

'Range twelve hundred yards, sir!'

That was all right. He'd already cut *Harbinger*'s revs, to give about six knots, same speed as the target. Ideally he wanted one thousand yards between them – that was the Walker prescription. The object was to stay out at this distance, simply hold the contact at arm's length. You could hear the asdic impulses bouncing back loud and clear: it was unmistakably a submarine down there. Like having a big fish on your line, and deep. You had to play it exactly right, or lose it.

'Eleven hundred yards, sir, still right ahead!'

He ducked to the pipe. 'One hundred revolutions.' Then – 'TBS to *Astilbe*, "Target is right ahead of me on course three-six-oh, range one thousand yards, speed six or just under six. Start your approach now."'

Graves would have switched off his asdics. He'd be as quiet as he could, just paddling up towards the target while Nick stayed clear and directed him. The German would be listening to *Harbinger*'s pings bouncing off his hull; he wouldn't be enjoying it, but he wouldn't see any menace in it either. He'd be feeling cosy, unreachable, down there. The quiet approach of a second hunter from right astern would be masked from his hydrophones by his own propeller noise.

Astilbe slid by, very slowly overhauling, and passing within a stone's throw. A stock figure in the front of her bridge came briefly to the side and saluted, was already disappearing as Nick gave him a wave. He said, still watching the corvette pass – on a converging course, coming in to put herself immediately ahead of *Harbinger* – 'Navigating officer on the bridge, with the distance meter.' Scarr came up at a rush; Nick told him, 'Creeping attack. I'll want ranges on *Astilbe*.' He accepted the TBS microphone from Bearcroft.

'Fox – Eagle – Captain to captain only now. Nothing except emergencies from anyone else, please. Are you there, Tony?'

Yes, sir. All set.

'How many heavies?'

Only twenty-six, sir, I'm afraid.

'Use them all in one solid stream, starting at the order "fire".'

Aye aye, sir.

Mike Scarr moved up behind him. He'd set the Stuart Distance Meter to the masthead height of a Flower-class corvette: if he didn't have the figure in his head he'd have looked it up. The distance meter was a little hand-held rangefinder: you put it to your eye and turned a milled knob; you saw two images of the ship ahead, and adjusted until one's masthead was at the waterline of the other. Then you read off the range from the distance-scale. It was used mostly when flotillas and squadrons were steaming in formation, for maintaining distances apart.

'Bearing has drawn one degree right, sir. Oh-oh-one.'

That came from Garment, on asdics. Pings were singing out, reverberating loud and sharp, echoes coming back exceptionally clearly. Asdic conditions were, conveniently for once, very good today. Nick said into the microphone, 'Target bears oh-oh-one from me. Probably just bad steering, I don't think he's altering. Come two degrees to starboard.' He was sighting on *Astilbe* with the gyro bearing-ring; when she was back on the same bearing as the target he'd correct again as necessary. Scarr told him, 'Range now a hundred and seventy-five yards, sir.'

Chubb pulled his head out of the asdic cabinet. 'Target speed five point three knots, sir.'

'Fox – speed by rev count is five point three. You could come down a little.'

Aye aye, sir.

Except for a slight buzz in the speaker, Tony Graves might have been standing here beside him. As he had so often. He'd be reducing speed by up to half a knot now. The slower the better. If you tried to rush it, you'd muff it.

'A hundred and eighty yards, sir.'

Chubb called, 'Target bearing is three-six-oh, sir!'

Squinting over the bearing-ring, crouching to put his eye to it, he saw *Astilbe* right in line. He said into the mike, 'Fox – resume course three-six-oh.'

'Asdic range one thousand yards, sir!'

Scarr said, 'A hundred and eighty-five, sir.'

Softly, softly . . .

You could visualise the Germans down there – quiet and comfortable, probably guessing this British escort was only aiming to keep them down and out of the way while the convoy passed. As the merchantmen were only making four knots, the U-boat captain would anticipate no difficulty in overhauling it again when this nuisance ended.

'Time now?'

Warrimer told him, 'Just on oh-seven-double-oh, sir.'

'Range one-ninety yards, sir . . .'

Here is the first news for today, Sunday, the eighth of November, and this is Stuart Hibberd reading it.

United States troops have landed at several points in French North Africa.

General Montgomery has issued an Order of the Day to the Eighth Army calling on them for a supreme effort to remove the Germans from Italian North Africa.

Home-based bombers of the Royal Air Force were over Italy again last night.

In the Far East, Allied Forces – including troops recently flown from Australia – now control all of New Guinea except for the coastal area near Buna.

In Russia, the Germans are still barred on all sectors.

Stuart Hibberd paused, then read on . . .

Shortly after two o'clock this morning the news came in that United States troops had landed on the Atlantic and Mediterranean shores of French North Africa. The first announcement was in what was headed Communiqué Number One issued by the Commander-in-Chief of the United States Expeditionary Force. It said: 'United States Army, Navy and Air Forces started landing operations during the hours of darkness this morning at numerous points on the shores of French North Africa. The operation was made necessary by the increasing Axis menace to this territory. Steps have been taken to give the French people, by radio and leaflets, early information of the landings. These combined operations of United States Forces were supported by units of the Royal Navy and Royal Air Force. Lieutenant-General Dwight D Eisenhower of the United States is Commander-in-Chief of the Allied force . . .

In *Harbinger*'s wireless office, a telegraphist was scrawling it down in longhand. The ship was at action stations, so the bulletin was not being broadcast over her loudspeakers.

Paul Everard heard it, though, in *Ultra*. She was heading northeastward on the surface; a dived passage would have been dangerous, on account of the heavy concentration of Royal Navy ships close off-shore, and as the RAF and Fleet Air Arm had complete command of the air over all the Mediterranean beachhead areas there was no overhead threat anticipated – except from the RAF, which was a danger submariners were well used to.

Ultra's crew were all listening to the broadcast. They knew already, from plain-language signals intercepted, that at 6.40am the Maison Blanche airfield had been captured by American troops. They did not know, yet, that at about this moment the other airfield, near Blida, was being taken by Fleet Air Arm fighters from the *Victorious* whose pilots would hold it until commandos arrived. But from other signals they'd learnt that only a few miles away HM Destroyers *Broke* and *Malcolm*, attempting to penetrate Algiers harbour to prevent the scuttling of French warships, had run into fierce opposition. *Malcolm*, semi-wrecked, had been forced to withdraw, and *Broke*, who'd charged the boom and smashed her way in and landed her assault troops at about 0530, was now under heavy artillery fire.

Jack Everard heard the broadcast in bed – sliding an arm round Heidi to calm her and keep her quiet while he listened. She had the jitters again: that nonsensical fear of the English voice being overheard . . .

Next, a message from the United States and British Governments addressed to the people of France itself: The landing of the American Expeditionary Force in French North Africa is the first step towards the liberation of France. The object of the present operation is to destroy the German and Italian forces in North Africa. Our forces arrive in French North Africa as friends. The day when the German and Italian threat no longer weighs on French territories, they will leave. The sovereignty of France over French territories remains unaffected. We enter today into the offensive phase of the War of Liberation. This is the beginning . . .

Outside, rain deluged. The wireless had to be turned well up in volume to be audible over the incessant drumming. It wasn't all *that* loud, but there was a lot of static in it and Heidi was panicking – it was silly, and beginning to annoy him: he wanted to hear this news, and she was acting like a restless, fractious child.

Here is the rest of the news:

An overnight despatch from Godfrey Talbot in Cairo says that as the men of the Eighth Army proceed with the job of capturing and killing Germans, they have received another Order of the Day from their commander, General Montgomery, stressing afresh that the battle just won is only the beginning of their task. 'There is much to be done yet,' General Montgomery told them, 'and it will call for a supreme effort and great hardship on the part of every officer and man.' The message goes on, 'Forward, then, to our task of removing the Germans from North Africa. The Germans began this trouble, and they must now take the consequences. They asked for it, and they'll . . .

Heidi's scream was ear-splitting . . .

Then he heard it too – the back door slamming back: a pounding of heavy boots on the kitchen's board floor . . . He was half off the bed when Heidi's door burst open: throwing himself across it, towards the intruders, while she went the other way . . . He saw a black uniform, a long pale face under a peaked cap, and a Luger pistol in a gloved hand. Another, different uniform behind that one – civil police he thought, and then saw the boy – the policeman's hand grasping Otto's shoulder. It was a confused, kaleidoscopic impression, a montage of stills and movement and faces in the crowded doorway. The mouth under the peaked cap was open, shouting in German over the noise of the wireless and Heidi's screaming which was now continuous, like some alarm signal that couldn't be shut off, drowning the loud British tones still emerging blandly from that fretwork facia. The Luger lifted, aimed: its three successive crashes stopped the screaming, left the newscaster droning on, a foreigner in the corner talking blithely to himself. Heidi's mouth was open but no sound was coming out of it. She was crouched, naked, frozen in shock, terror, shame, hiding from bullets and from her son's frank stare. The Englishman was dead. He'd fallen and rolled sideways and was on his back with blood gathering all over him, dead eyes open to the ceiling. The announcer's voice continued: *. . . communiqué from Australia reports that Allied forces now control all of New Guinea except the Buna-Gona area on the north coast. Strong forces of American ground troops have been transported by air from Australia during the past month . . . Near Oivi, on the trail from Buna to Kokoda, Australian forces are keeping up constant pressure and carrying out local encircling movements to dislodge the defence.*

Finally, here is one item of home news. The Ministry of Food announces that owing to reduced supplies of liquid milk available it's been found necessary to restrict allowances to catering establishments which haven't priority claims to one third of the quantity they're receiving now. Catering sections and canteens—

The Luger had tilted, fired twice. The English voice cut off in flying splinters of three-ply and a tinkle of the valves' thin glass. Heidi was on her knees, face wet and slack, staring at Otto across the tumbled bedclothes. The man with the gun holstered it on his way to the dressing-table. He picked up the empty frame, looked at it as if it amused him, glanced at the girl with the same wry expression as he put it down again – flat, on its face.

Astilbe wallowed, half a mile ahead. Mike Scarr read figures from the distance meter, 'Nine-seven-five yards, sir.'

'Asdic range one thousand, sir!'

Dead on track. Target course still north. *Astilbe* had seventy-five yards still to gain: she'd have to get to a point fifty yards ahead of her target in order to allow for the time it would take for the charges to sink to target depth.

Nick was stooped at the binnacle, sighting on her with the bearing-ring, microphone in his other hand . . .

'Thousand yards, sir.'

'Asdic range still one thousand, sir!'

Binoculars levelled: breaths almost held . . . He'd got the revs exactly right, matching the U-boat's speed. He thumbed the switch again and told Graves, 'Twenty-five yards to go. Stand by.'

Standing by, sir . . .

This was the crisis point. If the U-boat heard *Astilbe* passing over it might turn and speed away from the deathtrap. But with any luck the Germans' ears would be filled by *Harbinger*'s remorselessly pinging asdics.

Way off on the quarter, SL 320's remnants pitched northeastward across the long Atlantic swell. The *Dongola*'s siren had bleated again, about twenty minutes ago, turning them back to port. The two destroyers, and *Paeony* with them now, were across the convoy's van, *Stella* doggedly plugging to and fro astern.

'About ten yards to go, sir.'

Scarr's hands were shaking. He put the range-finder back to his eye. Nick said into the radio-telephone, 'Ten yards to go.'

'Asdic range one thousand!'

Seconds ticking out. Down there in the black water the Germans would still be thinking they were safe. Slightly irritated by now, perhaps . . .

Scarr said sharply, 'Thousand and fifty!'

'Fire!'

He straightened, lifting his binoculars in time to see the first 'heavy' splash down from *Astilbe*'s stern. A second followed it, and a third. Then the throwers: from each quarter a drum-like projectile lobbing out. Another splash under that broad counter, and number seven dropped from the chute just as the pair from the throwers hit the water simultaneously on each side.

Then the first explosion. It felt as if *Harbinger* had hit a sandbank. Warrimer muttered, 'Glad *I'm* not down there.' Explosions continued, breaking the ocean apart, the throwers firing again and charges still rolling from the chute. *Astilbe*'s stern wasn't visible all the time as the sea behind her swelled up in round-topped swirling geysers, mounds that lifted, turning white as they broke like boiling milk and the noise rolled on like deep sub-surface drumbeats, *Harbinger*'s steel hull shuddering . . .

Graves's voice came over TBS, *Twenty-six heavies fired, sir*.

The last of them were still exploding, concussing.

'Starboard ten.' He was turning her so all her guns would bear – if that thing came up, now. Warrimer warning the guns' crews, 'Stand by. Set range oh-one-oh. Fire when your sights come on.'

The surface was settling, the pattern of the swells beginning to reassert itself. *Astilbe* swinging to port: Graves turning her so *her* guns would bear.

'Midships.'

Chubb muttered, with his glasses on the place where at any moment the thing might show itself, 'Come on, duckies, don't be shy . . .' A lot of binoculars were focused on the smoothing surface: breaths probably *were* being held. Gunners' fingers on their triggers.

Spirits faltering, as nothing happened. Thrum of ships' engines at slow revs, sea slapping against steel and swirling by.

'Deep explosion, sir!'

Leading Seaman Garment's face, framed in earphones, had a delighted grin on it as he rose from the little cabinet. 'Sir—'

Eagle – Fox – we got him, sir. I heard it myself – explosion, long way down, deepest I ever heard.

The charges must have sent the German down, out of control, to a depth where sea pressure had crushed him. Like an egg in a closing fist. And that had been the blooding of skipper Graves.

Nick thumbed the switch. 'Well done, Tony. I'll circle you while you wait and see what comes up. Out . . .'

There was time, and lack of pressure from any other quarter, to hang around for evidence to take home: woodwork, clothing, even papers that might be of interest to Intelligence. If there were any bodies, for instance, blown out of that crushed hull, there could be papers in their pockets. From such a depth there'd be no live ones.

Congratulations came by TBS from the others. Including from *Paeony*. Nick pointed out to Guyatt that he had a share in the kill. He moved away from the binnacle: 'Take over here, pilot. Keep her circling.'

'Oil on the surface, sir, port side!'

TBS from *Astilbe, I'm passing through oil, sir. Floating up thick, all over the place. Out . . .*

'Body on the surface red four-oh, sir!'

Bodies came up in pockets of air or from the buoyancy of air trapped in their clothes. They sank after they'd become waterlogged, rose again later when the gas in them expanded.

Astilbe was stopping, lowering her whaler.

'Captain, sir?'

He looked round. A lot of stuff was appearing on the surface . . . But this was Goodacre, CPO Telegraphist, with a sheaf of signal-pad in his hand.

'BBC news bulletin, sir. If you've a moment? Thought you'd want to know – Yanks've landed in French North Africa!'

'Have they, indeed.' A glance showed him what a thick wad of transcript Goodacre had brought up. He raised his glasses again. 'Read me the main points, Chief, will you?' He was focusing on something white: it was an officer's cap, and only the captains of U-boats were allowed to wear white ones. It wouldn't stay white for long, if the boat didn't get to it quickly . . . A souvenir for Mrs Graves, perhaps, to hang in the hallway of her little house in Liverpool? For Graves to show his children, years hence and after he'd gone back to making cornflakes? Goodacre was reading, 'United States Army, Navy and Air Forces started landing operations during the hours of darkness this morning at numerous points on the shores of French North Africa . . . These combined operations of the United States Forces were supported by units of the Royal Navy and Royal Air Force . . .'

He paused, turning pages, picking what to read next. Nick seeing the whaler's grey clinker strakes – and *Astilbe*'s side too – already foul with oil. He called to Scarr, 'Keep us clear of that muck, pilot!' Goodacre had begun again, but through it Nick heard Jack's voice in his ear, as sharp and clear as if he'd been standing in the bridge beside him, Jack complaining, *You should have told me* . . . He thought – startled, even glancing round at empty air as if he *might* have been there – Christ, I must be nearer the edge than I knew! He shook his head – to clear it, and astonished at himself: he was dirty, unshaven, tired, he knew all that, but since yesterday when things had got easier he hadn't been conscious of it, whereas two days ago he'd felt like a walking corpse. In any case there'd be time for sleep now – fortunately . . . Goodacre telling him after another pause, 'There's a lot of guff 'ere from President Roosevelt to the frogs, and from this General

Eisenhower—' he'd pronounced it *Aysen'ower* – 'an' from the government, and – well . . .' Nick still appalled: hallucinations, for God's sake! In any case it had never been *his* secret: it had been and still was Sarah's, Jack's mother's, and it would have killed her for Jack to know it . . . They were dragging a body over the whaler's transom, holding it there while they turned out its pockets. There were only three others floating that he could see, so the job shouldn't take much longer . . . Then with the convoy on its way again, there *would* be a chance to catch up on sleep, get somewhere near sane again; it should be easy from here on, because any U-boats would surely have been redeployed by now against the forces massed off the beachheads. SL 320's surviving fragment would still need nursing, but you could reckon to get it home, all right. Partial and *un*timely arrival: and nothing at all to do with the armies pouring ashore at Algiers, Oran and Casablanca. Just a very small convoy crawling home, on the turning of the tide.

POSTSCRIPT

There was a convoy, SL 125, homebound from Freetown at the end of October 1942. It was weakly defended – by escorts who had not worked together before – and having passed through the centre of a patrol line formed by eight U-boats (later reinforced to ten) of the *Streitaxt* ('Battle-axe') Group, was badly mauled in a running battle which lasted a week. The approaches to Gibraltar were thus cleared of U-boats a few days before the arrival of the 'Torch' assault convoys. But this has only served as the idea for a novel: there is no other similarity between it and the fictional convoy SL 320. I should add that in researching the facts of the convoy operation and 'Torch' itself, I came across no evidence of SL 125's timely passage through those waters being anything but fortuitous.

AF